DAVID STOREY

as it happened

JONATHAN CAPE
LONDON

Published by Jonathan Cape 2002

2 4 6 8 10 9 7 5 3 1

First published in Great Britain in 2002 by
Jonathan Cape
Random House, 20 Vauxhall Bridge Road,
London SW1V 2SA

Random House Australia (Pty) Limited
20 Alfred Street, Milsons Point, Sydney,
New South Wales 2061, Australia

Random House New Zealand Limited
18 Poland Road, Glenfield,
Auckland 10, New Zealand

Random House (Pty) Limited
Endulini, 5A Jubilee Road, Parktown 2193, South Africa

The Random House Group Limited Reg. No. 954009
www.randomhouse.co.uk

A CIP catalogue record for this book
is available from the British Library

ISBN 0-224-06274-3

Papers used by Random House are natural,
recyclable products made from wood grown in sustainable forests;
the manufacturing processes conform to the environmental
regulations of the country of origin

Typeset by Deltatype Ltd, Birkenhead, Merseyside
Printed and bound in Great Britain by
Mackays of Chatham PLC

to: E. A. S.
without whom . . .

as it happened

1

GRIM DAY, Maddox was thinking. If I've gone over the edge that's quite all right by me, this place as good as any.

In a space scarcely sufficient to accommodate twelve with their donkeys and easels there were, by his calculation, twenty-one. Although, unlike the previous week, the model had turned up, the instructor's insistence on teaching, rather than an aid to concentration, was proving a distraction: no doubt, being paid, he'd felt obliged to do something, periodically shifting the model so that no pose was held for longer than fifteen minutes, the day, as a consequence, devoted to little more than sketching, a procedure intended, evidently, to prevent the class from getting bored.

Following the line of the breast, he indicated the nipple, adjusted its alignment and pursued the shape of the hip to the thigh; etching in the Venusian slit, his mind drifted on to thoughts of Simone.

How often and how deeply he had buried there – at his age, approaching seventy, less achievement than intention – moving his pencil to the knee, the calf, the model an effulgence, seemingly, of the room itself: the hall of a former primary school, the structure given over to adult classes in calligraphy as well as carpentry, motor-engineering as well as art, evidence, mainly, of the burgeoning of Third Age talents, much of which was displayed, periodically, in the entrance hall below.

Stooped, head bowed, glasses perched close to the tip of his nose, sighting the object over the top of the frame, he pursued his thoughts in counterpoint to the movement of his pencil. To his left, Rachel (Mrs Herzog), widow of a jeweller, posed, legs astride, before her paint-smeared easel, the model's shape achieved by an indecorous use of crayon. A film of coloured dust drifted down her pinned-up sheet of paper and settled on her blue, white-stitched overall: an elderly, short, attractive creature, her breast agitated engagingly by the vigorous movement of her arm.

To kalon.

The Greek came to him.

To prepon.

Thought and feeling so rarely combined – eradicating blankness, supervising space, more dream, he felt, than image . . .

In a glass partition, blanked out by paper on the other side, at the end of the hall, dividing it from the landing beyond, he glimpsed his figure astride its donkey, short, stocky, white-haired (cut short), the baldness at the crown invisible from this distance, recalling the suggestion made by Simone – eight years his junior, mercurial, slight of build – that he was about to undergo a 'change' (a 'chance', as she described it).

Mrs Loewenstein (Ailsa) becalmed in widowhood, too, a fragile (sensitised) creature, also standing at an easel: the steady drift downwards of charcoal dust. What had these women and he in common? age, death; a final refinement, introspection – engagement, in his case, with what, after a lifetime, he might, if not instinctively, consistently have avoided (primal: carnal: tethered in a cage): instead of inspection, assessment – retribution – a scoring-out from the blackness of forms – shapes (not unlike the one before him) a perspective on his life narrowed to a focus – this specific focus of appreciation. After a lifetime of exposition he was trying 'it' himself.

Mrs Sutor (Mary), a robust, pugnacious figure astride a donkey, its structure creaking beneath her weight, reducing to miniscule yet frantic proportions the figure before her, a bullet-shaped brow focused on the space ahead: wealth, age . . . Simone: his mind distracted, feeling, at that moment (he'd meant to tell her), he had learnt – was learning – a great deal

2

from his sons: something unforeseeable, the distance their minds had come, a perspective from their childhood, he looking through papers the previous night, after she had rung, coming across a photograph of Joseph (Joe!) sitting on his knee, aged three or four, in his arms, Steven, not much more than one, and had to acknowledge that that impertinent, self-conscious look had matured into the circumspection which now characterised the man.

Similarly Charlie (what plain names Charlotte and he had given them) last night on the phone, conjuring commitment out of the air on the strength only of a dream: his view of his chosen profession as 'clerc', as Maddox described it – television presenter and high-liver – questioning him on what he felt and what he thought, particularly re Taylor, now Taylor had made a request to see him, as if it were specifically of interest to him what his father thought and felt, Maddox recalling his son's final question, 'Were you called Mad Ox at school?'

Simone would be back from Vienna by the time he'd told her this: the rumour – from Taylor's lawyer – that Taylor had tried to hang himself (again) in Brixton, had been transferred and was once again the subject of a twenty-four-hour suicide watch.

Poor sod.

Love for ever.

Yours sincerely,

Matthew Maddox.

Hannah (Mrs Steiner) astride a donkey like a horse (her husband, reportedly, in terminal decline) moving vigorously in his direction: the piercing, animalistic, snarling expression with which she perused the model from across the room (drawing him, he assumed, in the background).

Mrs Herzog standing beside him, a tower of strength (the similarity of their ages). All he was conscious of was her crayon torturing the pinned-up sheet before her. How she stormed, alarmed, excited: the spontaneity, the transposition, the generosity of feeling bereft of thought (calculation: doubt) eschewing what, on other occasions, in different circumstances, bereft of such agitation, he might easily have alluded to as common sense.

The longer the course went on – all day Thursday, every week – the more he was aware that it wasn't the model he was observing so much as the women, selecting his position, for instance, with Rachel in mind, a lascivious intent; in reality, an appreciation of an alertness of an uncommon kind – as implicit in her looks as much as the way she held her crayon, consumed by a forcefulness he not only admired but found inspiring, a forcefulness characterised, paradoxically, by probity, sensibility, commitment, he long of the opinion it would have been more fruitful for her to draw in pencil, refinement in her style, her eyes, her manner ... watching her hand, left-handed, the crayon darkening her fingers, aware of the objects – the items, the flesh – she must have held there in the past: the activities of such a hand, the pregnant space between thumb and forefinger, the nakedness which her hand, her cheek, her ear – half hidden beneath her hair (tinted auburn, the grey showing through in flashes) suggested (insinuated, confirmed, evoked).

When they talked – he, Rachel, Mary and Hannah – over coffee in the canteen – the mid-morning and mid-afternoon breaks, lunch in the pub next door – the same discoloured hand, like Ailsa's, was laid before him (unusable, untouchable: a longing to plunge it beneath the kitchen tap, exposing the delicacy and pinkness of the nail), the configuration beneath her smock of a still dynamic figure, carelessly presented ...

He had been so taken up with Ailsa (Mrs Loewenstein), Rachel (Mrs Herzog) and Mary (Mrs Sutor) that he had long neglected Ruth, the most youthful of the women in the room – thirty-five or thirty-six – youthful, apart from the dysfunctional and irregularly attending Sheba: the week, for instance, when the latter's social worker had stormed into the room and called her fiercely, dramatically, sensationally outside: shouts (screams) associated with 'cash', 'missed opportunities', and the plight of her unfortunate baby dumped in the crèche below.

He had – as had most of the women – heard of Ruth's three children, ensconced in private schools, her husband a 'trader' in

4

the City, her car invariably parked across two spaces in the former playground below: her photographs of Martinique, her yacht, her chums (her husband: lithe, close-cropped: expansive, unwavering eyes) passed around the table at coffee time: all the vitality appropriate to her age, a tall, lean figure, despite her three children, a wholesome, innocent, unknowing face, an engaging, infectious gaiety, vividity evident in her ingenuous glances at the model: spontaneous, alert, unperceiving, confirming what she knew already, had seen, registered and digested from inspection of her own remarkable body: the alacrity she brought to what she described as her 'measly efforts', an unexpected sobriety intervening, a moment of hesitation, *doubt*, which appealed to him immensely, her long, tapered fingers braced to her pencil, the arc of her neck as, standing, half leaning at her easel, she peered round her board at the model: the delicate moulding of her ear in contrast to the stringency, the alertness, the synchronicity of her features, her hips braced inside her jeans, a figure full of potency, fun, irreplaceable, unapproachable, a sombreness rather than a calmness evident in her nature which relied – belying her vivacity – on something durable, solid, unassailable, as if the world, her world, were arrested from time to time and more than carelessly examined.

All of them middle class, except for Mrs Angenou (Maria), ninety-one years of age, seated astride her donkey oblivious, or so it seemed, of the shortness of her skirt: fists like hams, a jowled face, eyes sheathed in horizontal folds of flesh: back stooped, shoulders heavy, a Cypriot background, reducing everything in her sketch-book to matchstick proportions, Neil, their instructor, tall and lanky, standing bemusedly beside her, wondering on the relevance, at this belated stage

of saying anything at all

stooping, close-focused, denim-jeaned (red sweatshirt: gold chain around his neck, suspended, a tiny filament, from his narrow throat), suggesting the alignment of her figures might be adjusted: the one memorable occasion when 'Harold', their gay Lothario, had fallen asleep in his recumbent (model's) pose and they had watched, with stifled amazement, humour, finally

5

embarrassment, an erection of the most colossal proportions taking place before (specifically Maria Angenou's and) their astonished eyes.

Arthur the only other man in the room, apart from Duncan, the actor who had told them on more than one occasion he was asexual ('a sexual what?' Ruth had enquired), looking, he, Arthur, for a companionship which couldn't be shared in any way other than the one he and Maddox shared with the women – 'artists', as Neil inappropriately (democratically) described them, he, Maddox, finding the intensity of Arthur's application, as well as the evidence littered around his feet, intimidating to a degree. 'Do you think you could draw less and concentrate more?' he had asked him, Arthur's grizzled, bearded head, with its long, white hair and balding brow, his massive, excessively muscled figure dominating the room ('not an ounce of fat on him': Duncan) as might Moses' on his descent from the mountain, the tablets, like Arthur's, tucked conspicuously beneath his arm: his boots, his robust legs, his shorts, his 'tropical' top, reeking of sun and sweat: was it essential to get down to art as if it were an expedition, swathes of charcoal-ingrained paper strewn around his feet, his easel, those adjoining . . . ?

He had attributed 'Genius' to Arthur's performance – a nickname picked up and adopted by the women – but how oppressive, putting his and their own work in the shade: seventy-five, he'd told Maddox, and never been ill, apart from when he had been shot at Arnhem, the evidence vividly revealed whenever, frustrated by his output, he opened the front of his shirt, mortality, at his age, a frightening thought: the blistering of the flesh in the crematorium flame – likened to his description of a German tank with its cindered crew intact inside.

So how did his insistence on 'reality' help someone who had come, as they say, to the end of the line? Arthur's size, domination of the room: how could something so enhancing be embracing 'art', as he was inclined to call it, as 'a final answer', a 'last, redeeming feature', particularly when he, Maddox, had embraced it as a theoretician all his previous working life, not least before he knew anything about it, those intoxicating teenage years alive with Fra Filippo Lippi, Signorelli, Uccello, Cimabue? Genius's wife, Genius had reported, having died the previous year ('if only she could see me now'), he not inclined to look for another, potency, he had suggested at his age, out of the question, 'mind' all that mattered – imagination, he'd described it, stretched beyond its resources (fear, its inevitable corollary, Maddox reflected).

Mrs Samuels (Susannah) a plain, high-breasted woman with the arms and the shoulders of a pugilist, jeans too tight, arthritic feet, positioning her easel beside the wall on which she leant from time to time, a tree-trunk of a woman with a decorous intent: leaf-like extrusions on her paper, a scarcely discernible figure shaded in as if in defiance of her stoical if occasionally groaning nature, Maddox reflecting on himself, the morning light already fading, weariness evident before the coffee break, stretching his legs on either side of his donkey . . .

Glancing down at his effort, Rachel returned her gaze to her own as if, in him, she had found a marker, a comparison which enlightened as well as, going by her expression, dismayed. So much, Maddox thought, for being here, amidst an activity which, only a short while before, he would have had no time for: the women, too, children and husbands (mostly) gone, succeeded by a generation where these things counted less, if anything at all – Mrs Angenou excepted, time an element to ignore . . .

his gaze moving to the ceiling, spattered here and there with paint . . .

eschewing the past, resistant to it absorbing the present, reducing it to what could only be described, distorting it by what could only be imagined

senses tuned to what might have been recalled

as to what might have been discarded . . .

scrutinising something which he would never touch, the obscurity of its source, its subtlety, its light

its nakedness, its charm, its

vulnerability and, in posing there at all, its thoughtfulness –
above all, its vulnerability, ashes to ashes in another form.

His gaze turned not to his drawing – the detritus left on the
paper by his moving arm, the carbon held between his thumb
and finger – but to the skin on the back of his hand, blotched,
the veins conspicuous.

Genius, as always, was hauling them along, his booted feet,
the toe-caps glistening, laces tight, the bulbous, wool-stockinged
calves overlooked by the robust, sunburnt knees, the lower
extremities of his sunburnt thighs . . .

Maddox's mind slipping into abbreviation (parentheses
included), the light angular from the former schoolroom
windows: Jeanette, the diminutive Scotswoman, a pale sliver of
a face – a past written there as libertine or slave – a school-
marm with a lifetime's dedication forfeited to rooms no doubt as
resonant as this, an angular figure astride a stool, heel sportively
tucked into a strut beneath, half sitting, half standing, a
remarkable conjunction between eye and hand, as if not
drawing but writing, a fiction inscribed, in its casualness, for all
to see, a riposte to something omnivorous in the other women:
cvc's, so named, by Genius: 'cultural vacuum cleaners' sucking
up all sorts of rubbish, 'mine, not theirs, I mean'.

That endowment of flesh, good humour, grace, the unconsidered, post-menopausal flourish
    leaving carbon in lieu of child
    here to think, not draw
Maddox surprising himself, once absorbed, by humming
hymn tunes, a rhythmic exhalation, stanzas learnt fifty or so
years before.

Why now? Why here? he living along the street (or two) from
the institution, Genius and Duncan the only other men in the
queue on enrolment day, following the latter's account of his
acting career in The Dreaded Beacon at the corner a few hours
later (all morning queueing to sign on), from a 'vagabond on the
road at twelve' when he allegedly ran away from home, joining
a circus 'with no questions asked', his benefactor-cum-patron-
cum-inductive-lover paying for him through acting school at the

8

age of nineteen, 'seventeen years in rep' before parts in television, in film and finally, 'on the West End stage', progressing to a life he described as 'a suitable occasion for indiscretion' . . .

more seen by inadvertence than direct glance
what they, at the centre, could only infer
portentousness his style

a misjudged, misplaced, misperceived phenomenon, dispensed with in the life-room more easily, he suggested, than anywhere else, Maddox watching him from across the room as the actor struggled with his drawing ('more difficult than learning a part: at least, with that, there's an end to it'), a lean, ascetic face, and figure, wearing a beret, diagonally, across his brow: aquiline nose, thin-lipped mouth, protuberant cheekbones, pale blue eyes: a weathered flange of flesh above his smock's blue canvas collar: 'How I resist doing *anything!*'

'In which case,' said Genius, 'why do it here?' his own expanse of flesh, Arnhem-flawed, dominating not only them but the room, Duncan, a discontented expression, demoralised by what he mistakenly recognised as the facility inherent in every other drawing but his own, including Maria Angenou's stick-like scratches ('mice could do better!' Genius exclaimed), the reality being he had come here for distraction: 'Every word has meaning,' Duncan had complained, 'while all I make are indecipherable sounds, though not,' he pleaded, 'from want of trying,'

sitting, standing, crouching, Maddox observing the observers not the model, she, the latter, Alexis, a twenty-six-year-old refugee, her child and husband, at home-time, coming to the life-room door, occasionally stepping in to observe the wife and mother: the dark-eyed, masculine, gracious face smouldering with recollection and, presumably, disaffection (did he want his wife to be posing in the nude, even if to a room largely comprised of women?), the infant's incredulous, unmoving, tiny face cradled in his arm, its dark eyes fixed on its unsmiling mother: privacy enclosed in their departing figures as, the mother dressed, they descended to the street.

9

In Kosova she might not have reckoned with this, stripped of dignity in one place to be stripped of it again in another – Maddox, in his solitariness, calling less to a maker, less to her, less to her silent, solemn, sultry husband – dark-faced, dark-eyed, expressionless – than to a reciprocal stillness within himself, a stillness, in this instance, emanating from the room, a place of exclusion which, in his mind, paradoxically, included everything.

The mores of a life-room which no one, not rightfully there, could enter without Neil calling, 'Would you wait outside,' less question than injunction.

'Rest,' he said, the observers sighing, Alexis stretching, Genius, groaning, watching the novel movements of that head and body, motionless for the past quarter of an hour, his features arrested in revisionist thought, charcoaled sheets around his booted feet, bellowing from his outstretched throat, his arms flung up above his head: the room as view of something other than a studio – Maddox standing, too, reflectiveness abandoned, the majority of the women drifting out, Genius remaining, examining the floor, finally glancing up at Maddox, he, having stretched, re-seating himself sideways on his donkey.

'Coffee?' a sheet in one hand, Genius, his hair pulled back by the other.

'It keeps me awake at night.'

'Long time between then and now.'

'Nevertheless,' Maddox said, 'enough.'

'Too many changes.' Genius gestured round. 'Keeps shifting the model. Doesn't want any of us to *draw*. Talks all the time of *essence*,' adding, 'No sooner get going with one than you have to start another,' glancing down at Maddox's final effort. 'Isn't he a t'ai chi enthusiast?' his head turning upwards, blue eyes examining the ceiling, a look, Maddox surmised, which had gazed over oceans, deserts: 'The specious end-game we're all playing,' the weathered skin (reptilian past). 'Odd, at our age,' returning to his drawings. 'Get anything out of coming here?'

'A lot.' Surmise, or lying, he couldn't tell.

'Really?' The reptilian eyes looked up. 'Seems a terrible waste of time to me.'

'Why?'

'Museums full of the stuff. Too much to exhibit, yet here we are, producing more. Might call it affectation,' gesturing round.

'Where the t'ai chi comes in,' he said. 'Not what, but how.'

'Say?' One studded boot placed firmly on his drawings, pushing them away as if a mat. 'Public school prole, I call him,' gesturing to the landing, the stairs, the canteen, adding, 'Our instructor. Affectation to do as much with life as art. What I'm looking for, on the other hand,' head lowered, 'is engagement. If I die this minute I would die involved,' scrubbing his boot over the drawings again. 'Not drawing *on*, drawing *in*. Get it?' his hand, his heavy, muscular hand, the forearm visible beneath his tropical sleeve, pushing at the air as if at a solid object. 'Out of the particular into . . . not the divine. Nor hell. Something amoral. Aseitic,' he concluded, 'as the philosopher might have it.'

'Which means?' Maddox said. ('Ascetic', he was reckoning.)

'Independent. Self-supporting. Not to be glimpsed in this place. The ladies, on the other hand,' he paused, 'are nice. Aseitic, if you like. We labour,' he suddenly expanded, '*they* exist,' moments later, without adding anything further, moving to the door, his boots, seconds after that, pounding on the stairs.

Sobriety, verging on unease, the object of Maddox's morning, so much having preceded him until this moment – a moment (glancing at Rachel's drawing above his head) when it felt as if he were about to reinvent himself.

2

RETURNING FROM the Centre exhausted: adulthood in doubt: wife re-married, children gone: after the day's distraction, nemesis avoided, drying the pots in the sink in the kitchen at the back of the house, glad, at least, of a further distraction, waiting for Simone to ring: due home from Vienna (one conference too many), her voice with its light (infectious) interrogative tone: one of nature's enquirers: why and how and when – the where excluded – a further perspective suddenly revealed, the ghost of his successor, prospectively, always on his mind: somewhere, anywhere, everywhere: to be announced when least expected, the model (that day) a catalyst, he thought, in that respect, less object than subject for reflection, recently matured, her body, no signs of pregnancy visible upon it; evidence, rather, of bounty, richness – 'essence', which Genius and the t'ai chi Neil so much went on about; that strange divergence from their own physique, mysterious, elusive, a resonance which transfigured, rounded, contained – plausible: different from that attachment between his legs, speaking of loss, dismemberment, being wrenched apart, anxious for reconnection, no wholeness associated with it. Old enough to be her father, his thankfulness for what she serenely expressed: a seraphic expression, guilelessness not that of an equivalent man, or her husband.

Conscious of pieces of paper lying around the house, on table, chairs, cupboards, shelves, the floor, on which inscribed
  unconsciousness ⌒ disharmony: *sing for a living*
  ask Simone the meaning of intent

are anxiety attacks due to missing letters in the DNA; if so, where learnt experience?

are the accretions (epigenetics) recently discovered on genes the beginning of a causal theory of behaviour?

is space matter; if so, to whom?

still in the foothills: *make everything plain*

transitoriness a permanence of its own

which was why he looked at her more than at his drawing, to the delight of Neil, the jeaned instructor (slow motion: quick awareness) who conceived the perfect drawing: eight hours of concentration with nothing at the end to show for it, beholder and beholden one

brutum fulmen

her Balkan mind crossing a frontier few had known was there, extant in ways no amount of drawing, even less, photography or filming, could record, a rapture commemorated by her body, its disregard for what they, on sheets of paper, were actively pursuing

carbonating her

standing at the kitchen table (a narrow projection, the kitchen, from the back of the house), adding 'a resonance which is shared by the stillness of your husband and your child, waiting for this mundanity to come to an end,' his house, he had to face it, almost a wreck, subsidence evident in its outer as well as inner walls, an alarming or, in any other circumstances, would-be-alarming tilt to the windows, the building held together by those on either side. 'Good job it's in the middle of the terrace and not,' he had told Simone, 'at the end, otherwise,' he'd gone on, 'it would have fallen off,' the 'falling off' a condition he recognised as his own – away, from, down – propped up by circumstance, chance – the 'charge' (the 'chance') Simone had mentioned, the residue of a life which, but for her, he had abandoned (left intriguingly at the side of the road to be picked up by anyone who happened to be passing: she as it turned out)

beyond his reach, these speculations, other than as something embodied in Alexis's untroubled gaze, the trance she went into before their eyes, a spiritual residuum.

13

A sidestreet, in his own case, off the Chalk Farm Road: terraces one hundred and fifty years old, once strawberry fields approached, from the east, by a footpath crossing the River Fleet at Kentish Town, subsequently encroached upon, the river covered, by Victorian dwellings, associations unknown to him until recently, which absorbed him more and more, not least the tube line which ran through the London Clay directly beneath his feet.

Above the narrow rear extension, the bathroom, the main body of the house comprised of a single through-room on the ground floor, opening directly on to the kitchen, and two bedrooms on the floor above, a double one at the front, a single one at the rear, the furniture sparse, a post-marital requirement minimally expressed: drawers, a wardrobe, in the upper rooms and, in the loft, entered through a trap-door on the landing, the bric-à-brac he had stored there in a number of cardboard boxes.

Somewhere, in one of the boxes, were the photographs of his children, three infants (mainly) whom in most instances he was no longer able to differentiate, one from the other: the maternally expressive mother, the paternally apprehensive father, a source of fascination, the former, to her (second) husband Gerry, a peripatetic entrepreneur moving from company to company as executive bagman: good old G! (Brady: publicist and mesmeric raconteur).

A photograph of his children in their maturity he had by the bed: three men of strangely variable build, Charlie, like his mother, tall and slim, the eldest; Steven, the youngest, slightly built, neither like Charlotte nor himself, and Joseph, a broad, expansive figure who represented something of Maddox in nature and build, a formalised aloofness characterising their expressions, misleadingly, in this one photograph, creatures of Maddox's own inventory: he had taken the picture, the occasion the announcement of his and Charlotte's separation, paternity, however, despite their parents' negative example, common to them all, offspring, he'd been delighted to see, eschewing

14

complexity and self-division, beholden to their mother for composure, fair-mindedness, familial restraint (bearers of grace).

Charlotte, with some misgivings, had left him: he was getting old; so was she, it adding to her attractions. His expectations of anything better had been judiciously withdrawn, hers focused on excitation (companionability, curiosity, warmth), he, as it turned out, travelling in the opposite direction, a reductive if not, on reflection, annihilating process, she a volitional creature, he, he'd concluded – they'd both concluded – not: Ariadne winding up her string, leaving him deeper in than ever

a sinner: his disgrace

grateful, nevertheless, to Gerry, the avuncular MD, for providing her – providing all of them – with a life which otherwise they couldn't afford.

The white walls (of his residence) were now a uniform grey, embellished with darker patches: the marks of his grandchildren's hands on the stairs, a reminder, the infrequency of the visits, he was reluctant to remove: less house than alcove, quartered into use – distracted, at that moment, by voices, the crashing of a door, the sliding up and down of a window, audible through the party-wall: Berenice, known familiarly as Berry to her numerous callers, a voice as penetrative as a rock-drill, its harshness interspersed at intervals with the interrogative, '*Right?*', a punctuative exhalation as potent as a shell expelled from the barrel of a gun – his neighbours on the other side, the Connollys, he a minister at the local Presbyterian church, relatively silent (hymn-singing, occasionally – with which, through the party-wall, he often joined in – on Mrs Connolly's Wednesday evenings), Sundays a popular day for addicts at Berenice's front door, marshalled in and out by Isaiah, her definitively non-Christian Afro-Caribbean minder, the poker-work wood panel beside the front door, below a snarling Dobermann head, inscribed 'I can get to the gate in five seconds. Can you?' putting no one off, as far as he was aware: the nightly recital of benefit and credit card fraud, fencing, the itinerary of Berenice's more sporadic (now she was

15

ageing) intimate engagements often accompanying Maddox's reflections as he fell asleep.

He was missing Simone, night closing in: slim, high-bosomed, past her prime (in reality, coming into it): the high forehead, the dark hair, the fangs of grey on either side drawn back from carefully – erotically, magnetically – mascaraed and pencilled-in brown eyes (great care in preparing and laying on her make-up): an inquisitive, searching nature – given over, in maturity, to declamation: no children, despite three marriages. Having gone to her as a 'client' – recommended, ironically, by Charlotte, on the recommendation, in turn, of Gerry, several of whose employees had allegedly benefited from her 'work' – he'd come away, after several months, as something else entirely, she announcing an involvement at 'something other than a clinical level', a curious innocence, amounting to naïvety, having, in his view, characterised their encounters, one which, he imagined, rendered her immune to the potential depravity, despair, cynicism not only of him but of all her clients: something he'd belatedly, perhaps confusingly, recognised as 'faith', though in what, and to what purpose, even now, he had no idea, associating this with the 'grace' he thought he'd recognised that day in the Kosovan model.

Re-tracking his career in the dark: the prodigal essayist, one year out of the Courtauld (there as postgraduate, via Wadham), a junior curator at twenty-six (at a highly competitive time), a senior one at thirty, the Raybourne Professor of Art History at the Drayburgh School of Fine Art, succeeding Viklund who'd moved over to a similar but more remunerative post at the Royal College, inertia (and hack-work, ironically) at this point, coming in: lassitude, or indifference, or a liking for the atmosphere of the Drayburgh (its activities confined exclusively to fine, as opposed to applied art), together with the character of Pemberton, the unprecedentedly long-term, avuncular Principal, the college off the Euston Road, in any case, more accessible to his north London address than, should he have followed Viklund on the older man's retirement, as many had imagined he would, South Kensington and the Cromwell Road? Tendentiousness, speciousness: a vocabulary he was inclined to favour retrospectively in assessing his career, having focused his attention, at that time, on his sons, the 'familial triptych' he'd assembled with Charlotte: their beauty, their grace (again): their divinity, even, drawn on, once more, to what he thought he'd recognised that day in the Kosovan model.

Night, on the single bed in the back room, where he slept when not in the front room with Simone: away from the sound of Berenice's activities through the party-wall, the window open to the tiny backyard below, alive with birdsong, the evening light still strong. Aircraft lumbered up from Heathrow. Hers would have landed, he assumed, he disinclined to go and meet her amidst her colleagues, convinced, for one thing, his successor was amongst them, his insecurities in this area so entrenched that, exhausted by a day of speculation (observation: self-expression) he couldn't rest. She would ring him once home: even, on one occasion, had rung him on arrival, anxious to reassure him that 'nothing had changed', her interest, at such moments of return, directed normally to her faxes, her e-mail, her answering machine, her collected calls on her mobile (no similar machinery, he reflected, at his end of the line): the slim, upright, recalcitrant figure, addicted to clothes, high heels, the paraphernalia, it invariably seemed to him, of an earlier existence: a charmed and constantly changing nature, com-mandeering his weaknesses, his strengths – his hopes (his remaining aspirations). Why so enamoured? he plaintively enquired: the fervour of his – and her – 'conversion', as she described it, he, one moment, sitting in her consulting-room on the ground floor of her house, the next, scarcely three months later, ascending the stairs to her living-quarters overhead: a further ascent to her roof garden: the plants, the air, the insects, the flowers (winter turning into spring), the view over the surrounding roofs to the West End, the smear, like a trail of smoke, of the North Downs in the distance: in the opposite direction, above the intervening roofs, the sky above the St Albans hills. It had – the word came spontaneously to mind –

felt like home: the intimacy of the wood-panelled sitting-room below and, not long after that, the greater intimacy of her wood-panelled bedroom, occupied almost exclusively by the double bed: the fragrance of the sheets, the covers, the pillows.

Amidst her machines – her telephone rarely stopped ringing – her cellular containment amongst the skylights, gardens and chimneys, he identified a solitariness to match his own, he disengaged from her as a client, an echo (a facsimile) of those figures who came up the eroded stone steps to her door, attracted less to a favoured-by-nature mentalist than explicitly to a healer, he, from such speculation, evoking an image of someone alarmingly beyond his reach.

What, conversely, in him, appealed to her: to the extent of diverting her, uniquely, from a lifetime's practice? An emeritus professor, to boot, with, currently, a singularly discredited background. Previously, the discursiveness as well as the dynamic of his life had been focused on a process which turned animal, vegetable and mineral matter into something, at the least, elusive, at the best, transcendent. He had, to this degree, set his signature on the past, a challenge to be superseded, if not by his own interpretations, by those of others. Atrophied by the process, he had reached the point where, in arresting history, he had arrested himself: writing in the notebook beside his bed, his head bowed, his body arced to the light still coming from the window . . .

'What is her attraction?' Charlotte had enquired – on the phone, having heard of the outcome of their encounters (engineered by her, he had begun to suspect, a prank, conceivably, on both their parts, he tossed helplessly between them). On the whole it had been too early, too unexpected, too sudden, too unlikely, to warrant hers or Gerry's (or their sons') intrusion: he and Simone had behaved like children, a regression to hitherto undiscovered, certainly unconsidered parts of their previous lives, a regression of which they were instantly aware, fear, of an inexplicable nature, having, ironic-ally, in him, in the first instance, brought them together. 'Like all men,' he might have said by way of explanation of his

18

attraction to a woman whose attractiveness, to him, was both alarming and profound. 'My only regret,' he'd told all of them, 'is it's too late for us to have children.'

The darkening sky outside, the lights appearing in the windows: rarely did anyone draw a curtain, the intimacy of the yards proscribing it. On the floor, by the bed, was one of the drawings he'd been preoccupied with throughout the day, the fragmentary outcome of several hours of observation: whatever had been achieved had been absorbed, the model an embodiment of something he had unknowingly been preoccupied by throughout his life

death around the corner: *an aversion to signalling left or right*
the language of an earlier discipline had found a muse
long after he might have expected it . . .

The phone rang, the window still open, the room dark. He must have fallen asleep, lighted transparencies, the other windows along the backs.

Obliged to get out of bed, the phone in the other room where, on her rare visits, they slept, he picked it up.

'How are you?'

He was well.

'We didn't say much on our previous call.'

'Nevertheless, I'm relieved you're back. I take it the weekend and your paper went well,' imitating, he noticed, her interrogative tone.

'I was thinking much of you.'

'I of you,' he said. 'When you're away, a tabula rasa on each occasion,' a baby crying from across the street, Berenice mercifully silent through the party-wall.

A light went on behind a curtain: the crying stopped.

'I'll see you tomorrow,' arranging the time. She might have suggested his coming-up now, or her coming-down, her e-mail read, faxes examined, messages listened to, he concurring, however, tonight was too late, unease at her absence brought to an end.

'Much love!' the sound of her voice.

'Much,' he confirmed.

The sound of her laughter.

'Much,' he repeated (a bottomless well).

How far, reflecting, back in bed, having curtained his window, the top ajar, should speculation go? Two miles away – less than that, a mile-and-a-half – two tube station stops beyond Chalk Farm, the pilgrim route to St Albans, over the crest of Holly Bush Hill, she, he imagined, would be pottering around her flat, the lamplight on the panelling, the cretonned furniture she went in for, rugs with extravagant Iberian designs ('murillos', she called them), intimacy in her domestic life as in her work, something of a whore in this situation, too, a lending not of her body but of her mind, her acuity, her spirit, a reinforcing of a persona not her own.

Dreams, when they came, had involved, over recent nights, a house he had left forty-seven or more years before, reinhabiting its rooms – deserted, in some dreams, in others cluttered with the furniture which, unseen for all that time, was more familiar than his own: a fireguard he'd forgotten, bought when his younger brother was born; a cot, a Victorian creation, with embellishments, carved animals in relief at either end, its woodwork glowing in the light from the nursery fire: their biblical names, Matthew, Paul, Sarah, his elder sister, his imagination fired, finally, into wakefulness by Simone's call: his brother's jobs, his high-pitched, almost hysterical apprehension, as a child, peculiar in the context into which he was born, youthful, in appearance, even at sixty, 'engaged and engaging' in his description of Paul to Simone who, he had discovered belatedly, had a liking for sensitive, high-minded men (something of the same which, if extinguished, she'd located in him): had 'gone into the Church' in his early twenties, a process phrased at the time as if into a building (St Albans Cathedral and Abbey remains at the end of the road), 'coming out' at the age of thirty-one, God 'a misplaced endeavour, sought but not found (knocked, but not opened)' his (credible) reasons, rather than excuses, relief, Maddox recalled, to both of them, at this confession ('I gave it a try'), apprehension, so conspicuously evident in his youth, disappearing, never to return, Paul passing,

20

as if by means of a natural process, an evolutionary procedure ('the ethic's much the same') into 'banking': discretion, sobriety, fidelity to a system, much play made at the time with the parable of the talents: 'praise by employment', a 'secularised religion', 'work as prayer', water into wine displaced by rock dust, clay and ore into concrete, brick and steel: the pointed, inquisitive, curiously trusting Maddox face tuned to application, tuned, too, specifically, to belief – in what, in Maddox's own case, however, he no longer had any idea, vocation, initially, in his brother's case, as also in his . . .

his thoughts, at that instant, turning to their sister Sarah, vocational solely in maternity (heavy on her now), a biblical source of their names in common – but something else, he, a man as well as a brother, incensed on her behalf, she forging ahead throughout her life, a forager on her own as well as their behalf: strength, fortitude, dispassion, he privy to her nature, all things seen by him, in his youth, as if by her. How could Bully have walked away from her? the nickname, given affectionately, initially, by her, licensed by his surname Bulford, christened Charles.

Three Charleses in the family, as Sarah had pointed out, if Charlotte's equally affectionately ascribed 'Charley' counted.

Was this – she the most religious of the Maddox family – the triumvirate she was always seeking (Father, Son and Holy Ghost), Paul's apostasy, at the time, decried (bitterly) by her, while 'lost to the Church' their father's ambivalent cry had greeted both Paul's ordination as well as his subsequent recantation – his 'reconversion to mundanity' as Sarah had described it: 'Wasn't there room for another saint in St Albans?' 'Paul' possessing, Maddox had assumed, at least for his sister, a canonical ring.

Plus: why was she so much stouter – taller, broader – than Paul and himself? femininity, giving her grace as a child, now endowing her with bulk, mass, scale: the inscrutability with which she looked over her children's lives displaced by a familiar Maddox moral fervour, sensitive not so much to the proverbial 'catch' in life as its explicit moral resolution, as if, pro

21

Maddox, their ends were not relative or personal but universal: 'materialising death', as she had once described it, distinguishing artfully between body and soul: a prescient sister, predicating Bully's departure long before he had even thought of it, a passion for renewal, a reinvigoration, post-children, post-grandchildren, living subsequently, contentedly, enliveningly, engagingly, on her own.

Placed by their father in the seats of his cars, lined in an intoxicatingly scented row behind his showroom windows, the light reflecting off their bonnets – mudguards, roofs – the 'massage', as he called the paintwork, the odour of metal, oil, leather, polish sensationally, entrancingly, erotically combined, the garage and showroom fronting the old Roman road leading in from the south, '*straight as an arrow*' his father's claim on his own behalf printed in lower-case gold letters across his principal showroom window: an allusion to probity, speed, openness (honesty, reliability, directness, common sense), proven Maddox-ian traits. From this, Paul had, Maddox had always assumed, acquired his early religious and later secular conviction.

From this, too, had Maddox acquired his appetite for art: the nebulae of his early Albanian life.

And school: sent away, with Paul, by his parents because of the bombs, Sarah alone remaining, a familial retainer, it had seemed, at the time: the ancient brick building enclosed by others of a more recent, formal design, facing eastwards, on a hill in Yorkshire, the coat-of-arms and inscription on the gates those of the manor's original owner

nosce teipsum

taken over, the injunction, by the nineteenth-century 'propri-etary school for boys', set, the inscription, on a scroll beneath the design of a lion rampant either side of an open book, 'Fierce in Faith' the title of the school anthem:

> . . . and strong in duty,
> keenly tuned to nature's beauty:
> trust in justice, truth and learning,
> faith for which our hearts are yearning,

22

moving on, his thoughts, from those of his sister – vocational, too, in later life, in teaching – his sons, his former wife: generational, too, the dissolution of disbelief, prompting Charlotte, a post-marital gift, to send him to Simone, a woman who, in treating several of Gerry's colleagues, after he had finished with them, had 'impressed' her – the 'mystic woman' on Holly Bush Hill, singularly not prone, he'd discovered for himself, to disbelief, or doubt, or hesitation.

Far from him to complain: altruism's roots not to be examined: the image of the labyrinth with something terrible happening at either end.

As usual, in the early hours of the morning, he woke, got up, sat in the kitchen, then, drinking tea, walked through to the other room, Berenice active through the wall. On many (most) evenings he fell asleep to the sound of her voice – waking, finally, scarcely rested, to find her still talking: from the moment she woke until the (dubious) occasions she fell asleep, the staccatic, bass-based, pneumatic crescendo, heightened by coke, amphetamines, what else, the suffix *'Right?'* finalising each sentence, self-exculpation the dominant tone:

non utile dulce

how did he say rock-drill in Latin?

Charley had visited him once, to reassure herself about the house: scented, radiant – 'effulgent' the word that came to his mind, bringing a message of reassurance from their sons, she sitting where he was sitting now, facing the non-functional fireplace and, at the sudden incursion of Berenice's voice, had risen, spontaneously, as if hoisted by invisible hands, gazing incredulously to the door and then the window.

'Berenice has the ability to shift you,' he had said, 'when not even in the room,' anxious to reassure her about the virtues of his living in an otherwise characterless house.

Now he listened without complaint, the content of her speech muffled by the wall, the gravel-crunching, visceral, gravitational bass transposed to something of an abstract sound, 'fuck', in its

23

various declensions, resonating through the brickwork, and the final, interrogative, affirmative, '*Right?*'

Reverie at three a.m. gave way, an habitual visitation, to preparing himself for execution, waiting, numbered, the beckoning call.

Clinging mentally, meanwhile, to Simone.

Tomorrow was his 'group'.

With this recollection he went back to bed. Was it in a dream or had he in reality gone recently to Berenice's door and, despite the canine five-second warning, rung the bell, Isaiah putting his head out of the upstairs window to announce, behind his back, that someone, below, was ringing the bell, to hear Berenice enquire from the rear of the building, 'Is it that cunt from next door?' he merely requesting, on this occasion, that she lower the volume of her radio?

preferring the sound of her voice

living, increasingly, a synthetic exercise, mandatory, on the one hand, volitional, on the other

the past reduced to a tunnel, the future an ever-widening plain

recalling, as he did each night – each day, each morning – the incident on the Camden Town tube station platform, waiting, with others, for a northbound train, when, as the train drew in, he had been seized by what he could only describe – had insistently described – as a giant hand, one finger of which was the width of his chest, and flung at the line, striking the corner of the driver's cab to be thrown back across the platform. Screams, he recalled, from someone watching. Cries of a more personal nature from himself

nolens volens

sectioning: confusion and distress of an unprecedented nature

followed, months later, by Charley's suggestion (insistence) he visit 'a woman in Hampstead' recommended by Gerry ('naturally he's concerned'): people he had employed had gone to her with 'beneficial' results (more amenable, in reality, to Gerry's cost-cutting knife). 'It won't jeopardise your National

24

Health treatment,' his wife had advised, the woman's address, he'd noticed, on the pilgrim route to St Albans, its one establishing credential: the abbey-turned-cathedral which, even as a child, he had likened to an upturned boat, he, Paul and Sarah, their mother and father, trapped inside, a reductive, alarming, sinking sensation he associated with a sense of extinction, a degalvanising experience scarcely – its impersonality, its vastness – to be identified with something as directly appealing as the notion – *a* notion – of a personal God, creativity, in that instant, replaced, obscurely, by an appetite for comment.

And now, equally obscurely, a lightening of the heart at the association with something he had always mentally avoided.

She, at the first meeting, he had, initially, scarcely noticed: she had, he observed, a liking for prints: Dürer: a harsh, unsensuous, graphic presence: the hare (victim), the praying hands (supplication), the unyielding, anachronistically sensually-lipped self-portrait (her?) – and melancholia: a dreamlike, abstracted, oppressive gaze, the latter positioned immediately behind her head: a condition, he assumed, she identified with most if not all of her patients (clients, analysands) – and noticed, too – could scarcely fail to – the wood-panelling which gave the room a feeling of confinement, the room itself adjacent to the front door of the house, a sensuous woman in an ambivalent setting, they sitting not knee to knee as, at one time, he might have imagined, but facing each other beside, not on either side of a desk.

There was a table for writing – a Victorian cabinet and desk adjacent to the window – and a fireplace, conceivably the original one, black, cast-iron, an odd, idiosyncratic, domestic touch; and, more startlingly, a cat, he only aware of its presence as it stirred, rising from an upholstered chair, itself covered by a travelling rug, its eyes, almost luminescent, turned in his direction before, having risen, it turned once more and settled.

The light on him, he had faced the window, a skein of muslin shading the view to the narrow street outside – scarcely more than an alley, cobbled, with a long flight of stone steps leading up to it from Heath Street below. Directly opposite was visible the lower half of a large, through-floor window, evidently of a studio, with smaller, street-level windows either side of a metal-studded door.

Here he was, confronted, unexpectedly, by 'art', talking of things he had never considered, or even been drawn to before: an imperative – coming out of where? as a result of what? – to fling himself, almost abstractly (directed by forces which, seemingly, at the time, had nothing to do with him) in front of a train, forces – *a* force – which, at her request, he described as 'elemental', then, persuaded into allegory by the Dürer prints, he suggested, colourfully, he could more graphically describe as 'synonymous with the Demon King himself'.

'What Demon King?' she had enquired, scepticism in her repetition of the phrase.

'The one I assume tempted Christ to leap from the mountain,' the analogy coming to him as he spoke. How odd, the promptness of his response, he'd reflected, in the silence that followed, avoiding her look, his attention, once more, drawn to the studio window opposite: the inside of the single, massive pane was cluttered with plants.

Finally, glancing back at her, he had noticed her make-up, the dark colouring above the even darker eyes: a penetrative, yet almost disingenuous gaze, abstracted (melancholic?) self-contained. And had noticed, too, the lace frill of her blouse which, high-necked, showed within the opening of her formal, sharply cut dark jacket.

On greeting him – shown in by a receptionist occupying a room across the hall – his attention had been drawn to the length of her skirt, cut halfway across her calf, and the square-heeled shoes which extended the slimness of her ankles: so much was contained, so much was revealed, a composed, self-pos-sessed, self-referential figure, her appearance a signal that 'psychology', or even 'science', had an unavoidable personal edge. Like God, he reflected, as he (as we, he mentally amended) were taught: something he associated with sacrament, if not with sainthood: a few yards down the hill, immediately below the house, shielded from it by equally ancient domestic buildings, was the original lane which led northwards to the St Albans hills: a choirboy collar, dark skirt: a spiritual rather than psychic mentor, he a supplicant (the praying hands), a potential devotee, turning, reluctantly, towards an awareness of 'higher things' (the piercing, astringent directness of the Dürer portrait). The phrase came to him as unexpectedly as his earlier reference to the Demon King, turning his look once more in her direction, taking in another feature of her appearance: a ring on the third finger of her left hand, on her right hand another ring (a bracelet, gold, thin, on her delicate left wrist).

A second swift glance to confirm the first: her mouth, thin-lipped, tinted with a near-natural colour: broad, receptive, braced, seemingly, to an appetite not yet acknowledged, let alone fulfilled.

Perhaps, he'd reflected, they had something in common, she, too, a supplicant; all these years prescribing to others: refine-ment, repetition, exclusivity (associated with the house and its location); art for God's sake, at one time, in his case, obeisance to nature, conceivably, in hers: the slender, rather suffered hands, held lightly, one within the other. So much of what he said she had, he assumed, in one form or another, heard before: the externalising of an energy (the Demon King) which came exclusively from within – he aware of her examining stare, the supposedly 'objective' look which took him in, he scrutinised, disconcertingly, in the direct light from the window, her own face and figure silhouetted against it. Only as he rose to leave did the face, once more, present itself as something companion-able, informal, reassuring, the inquisitive, or seemingly inquisi-tive nose, the nostrils small, dilated, the indentations on either side, like thumb prints, suggesting playfulness, a remnant of childhood which the clarity of her other features assertively disowned, a suggestion, in effect, of 'another nature', lightly contained, elusive, self-amused.

Intrigued, he had set his scepticism aside; he couldn't afford – in a sense, didn't even 'believe' in the visits, yet decided he should: he could borrow the money from Gerry, or one of his sons; from Paul, or Sarah – dismissing the idea, surprised,

27

however, by the urgency – the recklessness, almost: he had never borrowed from any of them, or even thought of it (half his pension still going to Charlotte, even though, he suspected, she didn't need it): a further encounter the following week, a third a few days later, several on alternate days, finally, absurdly, daily visits: a fish, he reproached himself, being deftly wound in.

'You are in control,' she told him. 'You are in charge. You can always change it. It's up to you how frequently we meet. I can only suggest it. I'm not inclined,' she'd concluded, strangely, 'to make conditions.'

It was the familiar interrogative tone that had warned him – warned her, too, he suspected – that they were crossing or had already crossed a line. Perhaps, too, he reflected, it had been the cat at that first visit, not merely its presence but its unconscious regard; she, he thought, like him, unaware of the animal until it stirred, turning, instinctively, to remove it, he discouraging her. 'It's no bother,' he'd told her. 'I rather like it there,' reassured by its presence, the animal, a dark, ochreish creature, circling once more in the chair before settling down.

'It's normally upstairs,' she'd said, 'or out in the street. Mrs Beaumont,' she'd added, naming the receptionist who had shown him in, 'should keep an eye on it.'

'It's really all right,' he'd insisted.

'It comes in when I'm not looking.' The sudden informality had lightened her mood.

Perhaps the high collar of the blouse, with its chorister's lace frill, hid the evidence of ageing, the sharply cut jacket, similarly, with its unwinged collar, curtailing speculation. The crossing of her legs, beneath the skirt, both attracted and bemused him, a form of defiance, he'd reflected, but in the face of what?

'Is she a tease?' he had asked Charley on the phone, having first had to give a résumé of his encounter to Gerry, the overseer of the event, whose seemingly guileless nature had so much attracted his wife to him in the first place. 'Sounds a good lay. How about it, Matt?' he'd concluded, to be reproached by Charlotte when she immediately took over: 'The instincts and

28

intellect and morality of a mouse,' she'd affectionately complained. 'Like all women in these situations, she has to draw a line between selflessness and presence.'

'What the fuck does that mean?' Gerry enquired in the background.

'Matthew,' Charley said, 'will know what I mean.'

'I'm not sure I do,' he said, anxious, as he had always been since the break-up of their marriage, to discover what, in his wife's reasoning, might have led to their divorce: why so free with Gerry and never similarly with him? Children, he'd concluded, the inhibiting factor. 'Find, I suppose,' he said, 'a middle line.'

'Precisely.'

An exhalation (self-justification) came familiarly from the other end.

'Identity,' she'd added.

'Oh, identity!' he heard Gerry calling. 'Obtained at any broker. Cheap at any price.'

'Simone's no magician,' Charley had gone on, a door closing, the sound of Gerry's commentary suddenly cut off. 'The change, if it is to come, has to come from you,' she'd concluded.

'I'm not expecting magic,' Maddox said. 'Though there was a cat in the room.'

'Are you suggesting she's a witch?'

His wife's – his former wife's beleaguered cry rang out in a familiar warning.

'I hadn't thought of it,' he said. 'It's purely,' how should he describe it? 'empirical at present.'

The odd thing was, though married for over thirty years, whenever he spoke to, or even thought of Charlotte, no image of her, familiar or otherwise, came to him: the vivacious, blooming, expansive – and, let's face it, extravagant creature he had first picked up at the Courtauld and subsequently seen maturing, step by visible step, over the following decades, had disappeared from his memory as well as his imagination, replaced by a cipher, a voice familiar only at the end of a telephone. They rarely met (the last occasion she had come was

29

to confirm his referral to the psychiatric department of the North London Royal, his sectioning, at that time, at an end: 'we can't have you living on your own without knowing how you are,' a mixture of guilt and attachment with which he had become increasingly familiar). Should he encounter her in the street he was convinced he would pass her by without any sign of recognition, she increasing in size in her post-menopausal years, her innate good humour subdued, he had assumed, by her stewardship over their sons – to be subsequently re-ignited by Gerry's tasteless, animalistic presence. After all, it was in her interests – and Gerry's – he should come to no harm as a result of her defection ('we don't want *that*,' she'd told him, 'hanging over our heads').

'Simone knows what she's doing,' she'd finally told him. 'The woman is no fool.'

Foolishness, however, was what he was presently absorbed by. To support, in the past, a wife and three children on what, at the best, might have been described as a vocational disposition, was foolishness enough (how many times had he thought of giving it up?). Greater foolishness was to see his wife depart for what, at the time, she had described as 'a livelier camp': the jolly, peripatetic (vocational in his way, too) MD, in Maddox's view, epitomised juvenility itself.

In their last meeting in her consulting-room, Simone had merely said, as if to confirm the room's domestic atmosphere, 'I shall have to bring these appointments to an end,' he unsure, for a moment, what she meant. Had he said something to offend her? Was he too recalcitrant a client (patient, analysand)? Was what he had revealed too boring? Was he '*cured*'?

Most of the time, despite her prompting, he had talked little about his past, convinced he had little, if anything, to complain about: his younger brother, his older sister, his automobile-focused father, his mother – a secretary when her three children had left home, not in his father's showrooms – too familiar and domestic – but in a local school. He had, on the other hand, felt obliged to talk about cars, the Wolseley in particular: its name

30

had, like the thought of his younger brother's potential sainthood, a canonical ring.

Its odour, too, he had been significantly attracted to, an intoxicating smell, the appeal of which had only increased with time – as had the potency of his recollection of watching the movement of its bonnet, and specifically its radiator cap, against the contour of the road ahead: an aesthetic sensation, visceral and overwhelming, which had scarcely lost its power. What else? Away to school in the north because of the bombing, with his younger brother Paul: an unnecessary precaution he'd thought at the time (not many bombs on St Albans) but, since everyone with 'sense' had done it, he'd felt obliged to go along with it. It hadn't 'transformed' him in any way; he had even felt an odd reluctance, at the end of each term, to remove himself from what, later, he had been inclined, portentously, to describe as the 'provenance' of the place – its unique situation at the brow of a hill overlooking the enigmatic municipal buildings of the nearby town, identifying himself unobtrusively and, for the most part, undemonstratively with what, in his maturer letters home, he had referred to as the 'industrial conflagration' in the valley below: the mill and factory chimneys, the triangulated slag heaps and the headgears of the collieries, several of which were visible on or around the surrounding hills, the polluted streams, the dams serving the mills, the even more polluted river: a dour and unavoidable presence which, in an indiscernible way, had thrilled him, the evidence of a dynamism which he rarely, if ever, associated with the south, least of all with St Albans.

Yet, when she had said, 'I shall have to bring these appointments to an end' (not 'terminate' them, he had noticed), the formality of the declaration had been sufficient, first, to alarm him and then, triggered by his alarm, to lead him to suspect a challenge, he blurting out, 'You mean we're getting nowhere?' about to add, 'I'm too defensive?' as startled by this enquiry as he had been by the attempt of 'another' presence to hurl him in front of a train, continuing, however, 'I know what you mean,' she waiting in a by now familiar manner for anything further he might add, he finally announcing, 'I see you less as a therapist than as a woman. It's been the problem all along, as if I'm here to entertain, distract, rather than examine or explain,' waiting as if – a curious sensation – he'd been suspended from the ceiling, or thrust up from the floor, his gaze fixed not on her face but on her hands – hands which, he realised, he'd long felt a desire to hold.

'It happens occasionally,' she'd said, adding, 'but not previously with me,' her hand, her left hand, the one with the ring and the bracelet, waved helplessly in the air.

'I shouldn't see you again?' he'd suggested.

'Under different conditions,' she said, 'I suppose you could.'

'What conditions?'

It was as if these conditions, these precise conditions, had been anticipated, rehearsed.

'Not today. Another day.' Again, the wave of the hand. 'At a café, perhaps. Away from here.'

'Somewhere neutral.'

'Yes.'

A decision already taken: no longer suggestion, fact.

'Okay.' Equally crude and direct.

She'd moved in her chair: the same long skirt, the same jacket, a similar high-necked blouse: formal, anonymous, contained.

'You think I ought to continue.' He gestured round as if to suggest a venue different to this. 'With someone else.'

'That's up to you. There are people I could suggest. I wouldn't wish to dissuade you. There are clearly things waiting to be discovered.'

'But not with you.'

'Not in this context.' She waved her hand again. A moment later, she added, 'It's a significant event to feel an urge to kill yourself, particularly,' she went on, 'if you identify it with a force coming from somewhere else.'

His gaze, as it frequently did, returned to the window, specifically – he hadn't realised it until now – to the view of the artist's studio, with its vast through-floor window – unused, he'd assumed, because of the density of plants strewn on the inside of the pane: *that* was its significance, he reflected: it had reminded him of something.

'I don't feel it's likely to happen again,' he said.

'*That* you may have felt before the first occasion.' She was looking at him directly, as if, having got so far, predictably, she no longer knew which way to go.

Already he was standing. 'Maybe we should just shake hands,' he said. 'See how we feel after we've had time to think.'

'Fine.' Expectation and disappointment encapsulated in a single sound.

Having risen herself, she extended her hand.

For the first time he took it in something other than a formal manner, delaying releasing it until he felt hers withdraw.

They were stepping back, she into the room, he into the hall.

'Shall I call you?' he said. 'Or you call me?'

'Either,' she said.

'Fine.'

No Mrs Beaumont: she only came in two days a week, Simone herself opening the door on other occasions. Conceivably, she'd chosen a day when her receptionist wouldn't be there: nor the cat, fastened in, presumably, upstairs.

'Until we hear from one another.' He smiled, suddenly alert: it was like the conclusion to a quarrel. Having opened the front door himself, he paused on the steps outside. 'It's been coming for some time,' he added, continuing with a smile, 'It won't mean you're unfrocked, or whatever they do on these occasions?'

'I doubt it. Unless,' she paused, 'you've a cause for complaint.'

'None at all,' he said. Having followed him to the door she'd stepped back inside, he turning, descending the steps, glancing back moments later, not having heard the door close, to see her emerge, he waving, she waving too before, stepping back once more, closing the door behind her.

Walking to the tube that morning: the bizarre fibreglass shop

33

fronts: an aeroplane – a Dakota – in vertical descent, a gigantic pair of ill-shaped boots, a simulated pine-wood rocking-chair sufficient to accommodate a giant, gargantuan android human figures, dissimilitude, seemingly, the theme – changing his mind, turning back on his tracks and setting off, past Chalk Farm, up Haverstock Hill, the dome of St Paul's, at one point, visible behind, emerging, from the steepest ascent, into cleaner air, as if from a lake of pollution: the demarcation line, he always felt, between his place and hers. Up Rosslyn Hill into Hampstead High Street: boutiques, cafeterias. Up the final steps to the summit of Holly Bush Hill, the prospect below, briefly visible, extending to the Thames and the familiar smear of hill-land at Crystal Palace, the view still fresh, brilliant, sparkling (his state of mind), Mrs Beaumont just arrived, in the hall, as he let himself in (a key of his own): 'How are you, Matt?' a conspiratorial smile (a medical as well as social enquiry), the door to her room already open, the phone ringing, the constrained voice of a caller, male, on the answering machine, the message, continuing, indecipherable, following him up the stairs – Simone already up (the cat he'd seen in the street, sitting on an adjacent window-ledge, stretching itself, as it recognised him, yawning, turning away), she dressed, coming through from the sitting-room to the kitchen, post in her hand, the interior's narrow window looking out to the backs of the encroaching houses: the formalised embrace as she prepared herself for the day: some clients, he knew, she had seen already, her earliest, one day a week, scheduled at five-thirty: dark-suited, long-skirted, he an envious glance – her activity, her absorption – turning on the kettle, putting a tea-bag in a mug (already prepared: showing she had thought of him), she sitting companionably at the kitchen table, examining her correspondence (voluminous), laying it aside, aware of his gaze, if not his inspection, she somewhere to go, something to do, he, he reflected, nothing.

ex nihilo nihil fit

little (he) to communicate this time of day, nevertheless, she

34

sitting there, braced, he, sitting, too, the tea once made, full of admiration.

Amare!

'I'll walk with you,' she said. 'I've delayed my next appointment,' adding (when he protested – 'I'll be all right') – 'I need to get out before I start again. I ought to do it every morning,' so that, not much later, his tea drunk, she fetching a coffee through from the sitting-room, they were descending the south-westerly slope of the hill to the clinic off Fitzjohn's Avenue, above the Finchley Road, a recently constructed building of red brick and matching tile, domestic in its proportions of walls to windows to roof to door, pausing on the brick wall fronting the forecourt, where they sat, knee to knee, he holding her hand, at her prompting, before, seeing others entering – signalling or averted looks – he decided it was time to go in; on this occasion, unlike previous ones, they having scarcely spoken: observations on the weather (mild), and the buildings, domestic, they had passed – Edwardian, villa-like constructions – something, he conjectured, on her mind, the conference in Vienna – Vienna itself – her lecture scarcely mentioned: the journey back, a colleague sick in the aircraft: 'Some of us are getting too old for these outings.' 'Not so,' he told her, alarmed: should she go again? an imponderable presented as if to conceal another.

'I'm glad you're back,' he finally declared. Perhaps, he reflected, she'd been waiting for this, he waiting for – and receiving – something in return: her offer to accompany him to the clinic – imagining, then, her walking back up the hill (halfway down the slope to the Tavistock Clinic, her one-time home), wondering why their conversation had lagged, both the previous night and this morning, as if, solemn, silent, each had identified an interlocutor in the other that neither of them could recognise.

'We seem two different people since you went away,' he suggested, the brightness of her face of earlier that morning fading (she had spent much time on her make-up); even her

35

coat, a casual affair, she'd slipped on without her usual enquiry as to her appearance.

'I'm not much company today. I rarely sleep well after a trip,' she said, adding, 'which is why I didn't ask you to stay last night.'

Such freedom, he reflected, yet it was as if a principle, undefined, unmentioned, had suddenly divided them, she waiting for him to go before she turned away, calling, 'You'll come up afterwards?' waving.

He waved too, nodding, the sliding doors opening before he reached them, focusing, as best he could, on the ordeal before him, his one-day-a-week submission, as he saw it, to the self-defined day clinic 'for the older person', a self-inflicted form of retribution which, at present, he saw no way of bringing to an end.

Such tact! Beth already there, and Alex, his thoughts, at that instant, turned, curiously, to Rachel, the benevolently featured life-drawing widow, her sensibility, her sensitivity, her perplexity – her suffering: what else? – evident in her harried features as well as her drawing, qualities which he identified, prospectively, as his own: a vitality, too, he identified exclusively with women, the pain of separation on him now, as if, at any moment, he might rush back up the hill, overtake her, move ahead of her, be at the house when she returned: that tentative first meeting in a High Street café, sitting in 'civvies', as she'd described it, though not much different, in appearance, from before, their previous clinical encounters disassembled, two respondents to a formal invitation: stillness as opposed to agitation: a post-engagé misalliance

noli me tangere

yet he had, taking her hand between his own, talking of the past, she knowing much more of his: three marriages, in her case, each, in her view, less a failure than a 'moving-on', 'stages' to where she was at present, brought out, her husbands, as credentials: a catalogue of virtues, a modicum of vices, this woman Charley (and Gerry) had landed him with, more than he could handle, an unnatural division, he suspected, between

36

thought and feeling – and action – between the formality of their previous encounters and the formalised informality of this.

Beth the first person he saw as he entered the reception room: the wary 'good-morning' as they milled around the table by the window – looking out to a garden at the back – its surface set out with cups and saucers, a tin of biscuits, the apparatus for making tea and coffee. In the centre of the room a circle of half-upholstered chairs with wooden arms, his thoughts engaged still with Simone: the glimpse of her departing figure, wrapped in thought (her inelegant coat), head bowed, shoulders stooped, age – their relationship, too – maturing into reflectiveness: his impression as she walked away from him.

Beth had taken her seat across the room: the one she sat in every week: tall, thin, dark, bowed by an unspoken physical affliction, legs sheathed in a track-suit bottom, a cardigan, her arms not in the sleeves, around her shoulders, beneath, a jersey the same dark colour as the trousers, inclined to move with difficulty whether standing or sitting, the *Guardian* one of two newspapers available on the coffee table before her, opened on her lap, a cup of tea in one hand, its saucer on the arm of her chair, Maddox noticing the way the daylight came into the room, lighting up the circle of chairs, not unlike the life-class without the model, a totemic, druidic, congregatory event, five women, he and Alex – a sixth woman entering the room, poling herself along with a stick, easing with a sigh, a stiff articulation, into a chair, accepting an offer of tea from across the room, Richard, the charge nurse, a tall, cadaverous figure, holding up a cup in greeting, celebrants, each, of a new, unspoken, unclaimable religion – a new, unspoken, unclaimable routine, sobriety, excision; its characteristics, death – its environs – its provenance

ist dies etwa der Tod?

Two had died since his joining the group, Alex, seemingly, about to join them – a gaunt, lean, angular figure, with a sharply featured, fleshless face, dilated cheeks, brow furrowed laterally and vertically above pale, almost colourless eyes, a soldier, traumatised by Dunkirk: preponderance of women, two statutory men, the day beginning with a solicitous, enquiring, cautious conversation, prompted and sustained by Richard: sandals on his feet, a sporting, genial, enterprising man, hair sprouting in confusion above and below his head, features quizzical, suspended, furrowed: 'How are you this morning, Anna?' a slight, crepuscular, apprehensive figure, bulbous eyes protruding from a tiny face, her posture in her chair erect: evacuated, as a child, from Breslau, her origins finally a cipher: 'Judith?'

'Very well, Richard,' beneath her breath, a slim, white-haired, full-breasted woman, in her youth (a photograph previously passed around) a celebrated beauty: a sensuous, appealing, enquiring face: had shot, in her youth, a British soldier, had never left Jerusalem until her marriage (resentment that the camps not part of her legacy: pain – distress – of a diurnal nature), she, like the majority of the others, like Maddox, living alone.

'Sally?' a sprightly, bird-like presence, inquisitive, close-set eyes, companionable, contentious: 'Not too good. I had a bad night.'

'Bad nights are normal,' Beth, twisting in her chair. 'Don't you take pills?'

'Too many.'

'I get up and read.'

'I listen to the radio,' insomnia a common thread, Maddox dismayed to be included, his geriatric group pre-dating his first visit to Simone: a thoughtful collation, abandoned if not by relatives, friends, their own cohesiveness.

'How are you, Matthew?'

'Pretty good.' Never inclined to say less, courtship, in his case, unlike with the others, starting anew.

Déraciné: off the shelf, back in use.

When the tea, the coffee and exchanges had been completed they filed, separately and with difficulty, for the most part, into an adjoining room: a narrow, light-filled interior with windows looking onto a central lawn surrounded by and interspersed with beds of flowers. Tables, chairs, cupboards and easels were formally arranged in a classroom fashion; paints, already mixed in cake tins, stood on the tables, brushes, pastels, pencils, charcoal and crayons set out, too. The previous week's exercises had been pinned to the door, a half-circle of chairs confronting them. Melissa, a stout, broadly featured, middle-aged woman, vivaciously dressed in a patchwork skirt and a maroon blouse, was seated on the central chair, indicating to each of them as they came in that they might care to take their places beside her.

Maddox, far gone in thought, took in the images before him: a bird, its beak bigger than its body, a boat, appearing about to sink, a horse with, seemingly, five legs, a baby, lying in a crib, the edges of which were engulfed by flames, several figures being fired upon by others, a garden comprised entirely of flowers: last week's instruction (differentiated strictly, by Melissa, from suggestion) had been to draw the first thing that had entered their heads.

'What do you think was in your mind when you painted your animal, Ida?'

'I've always liked animals,' a swarthy, muscular, working-class woman, pre-empted from an overdose by the unexpected arrival of a son-in-law: paint, fortitude, resourcefulness: pills, heights: the apartment, in Beth's case, in Vienna, the jackboots on the stairs, the humiliation of her father, her mother, her sisters, none of whom she saw again (grief interminable at their departure): Anna, he reflected, scarcely alive, three attempts at suicide; pale, thin – skeletal – holding a brush, when she painted, in a tremoring hand, transferring colours from cake tin to paper, watery washes indicating a flower-bed (an unvarying image), the proportions of a grave.

Nor could he accustom himself to Alex's soldierly horrors, resuming in old age (he was eighty-seven): his picture of a figure sheltering in a cave, its features, like its limbs, distorted, a figure, in a previous week's drawing, falling down a cliff, another crushed beneath a rock, a face, its eyes bolting from its head, graphically, linearly, weekly depicted.

Criticisms by others, a criticism of himself.

Meanwhile, at the top of the hill, Simone analysing her

analysands – her engagés, her therapees – a line of exclusivity marked by the space between their two confronting chairs, while he, fulfilling his National Health role 'for the older patient', submitted himself to a routine which he admired – to the point of idealisation – but the efficacy of which, he suspected, he hadn't entirely grasped. At intervals – invariably at lunchtimes – he would be called in to see Kavanagh, the presiding consultant, a genial, companionable, youthful figure, in shirtsleeves and jeans – not unlike, in his informality, the charge-nurse Richard: discussion of his medication – dothiepin, thioridazine – he unsure if his behaviour were merely consistent with that of the world around, an irresistible urge to destroy himself a not unreasonable proposition, his curiosity, in this respect, vividly ignited: what was it like? was that – is this – the limit of endurance, he, otherwise, a chemical aberration?

His days, as he'd known for some time, were numbered.

He was, on the other hand, discovering his past, reminded by Plutarch of the significance of depression in the lives of Socrates, Plato, Heracles and Lysander: anxiety, terror (Carlyle, Tolstoy, Michelangelo), an integral part of any excelling view of human nature, dismay – despair – as an equitable rejoinder to the perversity of nature cyclically destroying itself, as healthy a sign, he concluded, as any.

Without dread, nothing is real
without psychosis, sanity unconvincing
absit invidia
absento reo

Of what, after all, was reality comprised? an awareness, subliminally as well as otherwise, of what was going on at present, as well as what had preceded it, and the invisible and unknowable extension of the same that not only went on for ever but, a moral proposition, went on for good. Pain, otherwise, of a, so far, exclusively mental sort, had produced little if any further illumination. How could he absorb himself in a reclamatory process which eluded his understanding? How, in short, could he believe in something that possibly didn't exist?

All his relationships, he could safely assume, were based on a perception of himself which provided little if any insight into anything other than *what had been arranged*: that system of beliefs (paternity, loyalty, dedication) which had sustained him to the point where, consistency alone the dominant feature, he had cracked – in a fashion: *his* fashion (come to that, in Ida's and Anna's fashion, too). He was, he had been, overcome by a sense of fear – alarm, dread – which emanated, or appeared to do so, from all inanimate as well as animate matter, a fear that broached the bounds not only of all he had previously known (a lot) but all that previously he might have imagined.

He was, on the other hand, intact; as a consequence, his awareness of the past amounted to little more than a sense of separation: there *it* lay, here *he* was, between the two a gulf which no amount of speculation would allow him to cross, pain an intermediary between one thought and the next, one feeling and another. He was, as he'd come to regard it, not only within but the instrument of a process which had, in its exclusivity, little to do with what previously he had considered – he *might* have considered, however tentatively – to be himself.

Or, as he was coming to propound it, his self: there 'it' lay (all he had been, and was – unwittingly, for the most part); here *he* was, divorced from 'it' completely.

Somewhere there was an image, not necessarily of himself, but of a gnarled and suffering creature which, having ventured outwards all its life, in its final days had returned to its past: a forgotten, an unconsidered, at least unconsidered until now to be relevant past, one which came back to it in 'snatches' – bouts, spasms – paroxysmal, unsolicited, uncalled-for, a reassertion of something which, in his own particular experience, had attempted to hurl him in front of a train (to 'execute' him, he had no doubt), the equivalent, he had imagined, of that force which had tempted Christ to hurl himself from the peak of a mountain (no suggestion of salvation in his own case whatsoever).

He was, he recalled, into reverie, persuasion, reflection, opposed to dispersal, dissemblance, obtuseness, doubt: singularity, in his case, governed all, his achievements – struggles,

41

confrontations (failures, even: he might have learnt from those) – had come to nothing. Thoughts of ending it – since his tube train encounter – had absorbed him completely, interspersed as they were with a longing – a sceptical, rear-guarded, almost posthumous longing – for Simone – all the while composing requests, reports, pronouncements, the 'what-if?' at the beginning of every line. He was, he'd discovered, in the process of making amends: a life unlived, or, in his more recent speculations, lives unlived. Where was he now? where had he been? a reasonable expression, his enquiries, of his variegated gifts: no peaceful expiration in a bed, more the albatross brought down at the apogee of its flight, or, in his case, in the midst of its final, fluttering descent.

This was how it happened – an event with a name but without a prescription – he had been a success, art a synonym for life: known as as known by: where he had been others were inclined – were persuaded, were cajoled, were encouraged – were challenged (were finally obliged) – to follow.

There was, after all, a code he'd always lived by (he had always unwittingly subscribed to): it had something to do with a forgotten time: not consciously forgotten, merely set aside, initially, he suspected, for examination, analysis, reflection – relevances, records, evidence of some sort, an elusive configuration (it had the potential to acquire a shape), elements within as well as without, he the agent if not the organ of destruction – recalling, at that instant, crouching with his mother in a cupboard beneath the stairs: a sense of upheaval, finally of terror, expectation, the oscillating moan of aircraft overhead. And then, out of this excitation, the screeching, he assumed, of an object, increasingly louder, in its invisible descent: the vibration of the ground: the same vibration inside his head: something indisposed to his isolation, specific, spectacular, all-powerful, conclusive – his mother, in his recollection, wearing a nightdress underneath a coat, her ankles bare above the wool lining of her slippers: the whiteness of the skin, the blueness of the veins: her silent face, her silent stare, an abstracted, brooding, melancholic look which, years later, he recognised as

42

something of his own, flesh, blood and bone, in his imagination, spattering their enclosure: whereat, whereas, wherefore, where born? what circumstance? what formative agenda? body tuned to a new awareness, he prospecting a way ahead, disarmingly engaged by the one behind, shaped not by events but speculation.

Alex had drawn a figure astride a bomb, descending at an angle; similarly, Beth had drawn a child being stoned on its way to school, the stoners anonymous, stick-like figures, the child, female, vividly in colour. Anna had drawn a garden, as ever: muted, pallid, pastel, mild. He who had recently lectured on della Francesca, Brunelleschi, Masaccio, Uccello, Signorelli (Fra Filippo Lippi, Fra Angelico, Cimabue), who had stood for hours – days, in his youth – in front of the San Francesca, Arezzo frescoes, currently obliged to comment on his own affliction, was reminded that art, aesthetics (he had produced another abstract) were not required: references to Klein, Winnicott, Bowlby by Melissa, Alex's misfortune, on the other hand, not hard to guess, nor Beth's Semitic exercise, Anna a wraith, the frailest of creatures, likening her three flower-beds, when invited by Melissa, to a tapestry or curtain, then, prompted more vigorously ('realistically') by the therapist – 'You have attempted to kill yourself three times, Anna' – responding, kindly, gently, discreetly, 'I don't see that at all.'

Dothiepin, in his case, plus thioridazine for otherwise unmanageable moments, fear purporting to be terror acquiring the upper hand. Meanwhile, in St Albans, the first Anglicised Roman martyr, he, eighteen or so centuries later, sent away with Paul, by mother, father – Uncle Joseph alone demurring ('they'll both be safe enough with us'): rugby, cricket, athletics: idiosyncratic buildings which, five decades later, still littered his dreams: collieries with their triangulated heaps, the concertinaed roofs of factories, the rectangular silhouette of mills, the single stems of industrial chimneys, the effulgence of smoke, steam, the lowering clouds swept by and away by the prevailing westerly winds, the gentler, eastern incline of the Pennine escarpment: *nosce teipsum*: the inference of self-division, 'thy' in one place, 'self' in another – leading to an impulse to bring the two together, a process, in this instant, conducted by Melissa: 'we are not here to hide' (what we know is there), an interval of painting followed by another of analysis, Alex, on this occasion, summoned to account ('What are you drawing there, Alex?'), 'A feeling of falling without stop,' his Scottish accent still lyrically engaged. 'Plus the certainty of extinction.'

'Is there no escape?'

'None.'

Not Melissa but the rest dumbfounded: no exit, implied, the other end? the unspoken, communal enquiry, Alex's pictorial suicide note pinned, oppressively, before them to the inside of the door.

'I've had enough of suffering. I want to rest,' Anna's gentle eyes turned courteously in their direction.

'We are here for support through awareness,' Melissa said.

'You could say Alex's only recourse is to blow his brains out,' Beth responded.

'Or, his having expressed it, to feel free of it,' Melissa said.

'I've had enough of suffering,' Anna's continued rejoinder.

While he, Maddox, as on previous occasions, with no specific image in mind, had painted, in bright colours – pink, red, blue, juxtaposed against grey – another abstract.

'I see lumps of meat, hanging in a butcher's shop,' Melissa said, Maddox not inclined to disagree.

'Having identified a subject it becomes something you can deal with,' Melissa insisted. 'Assessing its relevance, or otherwise, puts you in control,' her attention reverting to the figure astride the descending bomb. 'Is that your final statement, Alex?' the tortured eyes, the tortured smile, the tortured nose and ears and brow, the tortured, supplicating, bereft expression which, refracted through an overlying look of deprecation, characterised them all

malum in se

all these women, two statutory men, Simone's endorsement of the same, her sole reservation 'cerebral awareness not your line', a lifetime, however, of the same, 'visceral engagement' (presumably with her) 'your only way out', something he, for his part, endorsed in her

reductio ad absurdum

glancing at her watch, Melissa standing. 'We'll return to these next week. Judith's contribution,' a dormitory of figures lying comatose: dead? asleep? 'I'm particularly keen to get to,' adding, 'Put out the lights, the last one to leave,' neon strips supplementing the light from the windows, her audience, eyes turning from the paintings on the back of the door to the gap left by the therapist's departure, their feelings, reactions, thoughts, reflections – aspirations, even – terminally suspended, they returning, a bedraggled line, to the reception room, the room itself prepared for lunch.

Standing in a queue: the assiduity of the staff, the assiduity of the patients. After eating, they retired to the chairs – newspapers, magazines – and, as the clock on the wall struck two, rose, with varying degrees of alacrity, and returned along the corridor, past the art room, to a smaller room at the opposite end, the charge-nurse, Richard, already there, alert, straight-backed (formalised, his posture, despite the informality of his appearance), his hands cupped upwards – a meditative gesture – in his lap, Stephanie, middle-aged, grey hair cropped short, dark eyes inclined enquiringly towards each entering figure: dark skirt, a high-necked jersey, a fleshless, harrowed, haunted face enlivened only by the light reflected from her glasses, she facing Richard across a by now familiar circle of, in this instance, metal-framed chairs. 'The silent hour,' Beth had said, having, on previous occasions, declined to speak, 'specifically to this character here,' indicating Stephanie, beside whom, nevertheless, she always sat, their elbows almost touching. 'Who is using,' she'd expand each week, 'everything we say for her PhD.'

'A bit late for her PhD,' Maddox (invariably) responded, gallantly inclined, *pace* Simone, towards the austere, dispassionate presence of the psychotherapist, her benignity warily concealed beneath the remoteness of her gaze.

45

'She's not having my insights for nothing,' Beth said.

'In which case, what's the point in coming?' Alex enquired.

'I don't want to talk about personal matters,' Anna said, a distraught expression, subdued over lunch, reignited.

'What are personal matters?' Ida, the working-class virago, enquired.

'Family matters,' Anna said, her walking-stick beside her, seated uncomfortably in the metal-framed chair.

'We all have family matters,' Judith said. 'We wouldn't be here if we hadn't,' she went on. 'So what's the problem?'

'I'm not talking,' Anna said, smiling, a courteous expression of withdrawal, bowing her head.

'So what's the point in coming?' Alex enquired again, face furrowed, starkly, his hairline descending towards his brows: doubt, perturbation, confusion: the nakedness they each unwittingly revealed.

'The rest of us can talk, in that case,' Maddox said, Richard and Stephanie significantly silent.

Formality and intimacy inextricably combined. Had he earned, was he earning, the right to ignore what anyone else might think? enough time gone to make concealment irrelevant, he concluded, the 'I' he was engaged with here at last, the responsibility – examining the other faces – devolved to him, this, in reality, the end of the line, not a way forward or back, merely – specifically – a circle of chairs, he examining his reflection alongside Stephanie's in the window: the severity of the therapist's expression, the bulbous projection of her nose, a bracing of her lips suggesting an underlying tension: the vista of the garden beyond, he, bowed on his chair, white-haired, framing his reflection against the flower-beds outside, his final glance at Anna, cowed, since her admission, rather than sitting: everything relevant, revealing, connected, as Melissa, earlier, had been keen to point out, once-lived-a-life accounts seeking a refuge, an explanation, requesting a purpose – he returning his stare across the room, Judith, finally, driven into speech, a slow reddening, conspicuous, of brow and cheek – accentuated by the whiteness of her hair: belligerence stored up from her past, her having missed out on Beth's, Ida's, Anna's Holocaustian accreditation, familial insults from half a century before, less than casually intended, obsessively recalled, venomously expanded, the intolerable isolation incurred by subsequent widowhood, the distance of her children: the horror of everything, '*everything!*', coming to an end.

The fissures in Alex's face, the shadows beneath Beth's eyes, the declivities in Anna's cheeks, the ascending scale of self-deprecation, animadversion, the oppressiveness of houses, streets (sky: stars: the immutability of nature, the variety of custom no longer a distraction), an account, a summation, he concluded, not drawing them together, driving them, rather, further and further apart.

From his earliest days a sense of exclusion: something suggested by his father's cars, their elegant bonnets, mudguards, wheels – pain, in this context, a prerequisite of pleasure: what he had been searching for all his life, his occupation recognised from the start as 'observer': the scent of cars, the intoxicating, quaintly animal, certainly exclusive odour of woodwork and leather, metal and oil, petrol and rubber, the infiltrating smell of the engine exhaust: his earliest memory of sitting beside his uncle Joseph, his father's exotic, macaronic brother, to be driven along an unpaved lane at the back of the house – circling his father's premises, the dipping and turning of the bonnet against the rutted surface: a sensation of fluidity, motion, lucidity, light, the constant realignment of shape against shape, a frame – the windscreen – transposed, in the end, to art, to line and colour, to Cimabue's iconographic glow.

As with Melissa, once the hour was up, Richard and Stephanie rose, the group – startlingly – abandoned, they, left to their own devices, finding their way back to the reception room: tea, biscuits, a desultory conversation – anomalous after the comparative silence, the resistance, the waywardness of the previous hour. Obtuseness: a sea-change in those for whom the ocean never rolled.

Taxi-cabs for the infirm, the drivers' bulky figures silhouetted against the outer door.

3

It was his habit, on these occasions, returning up the hill to Simone's, to buy supper in the village, preparing it for when, exhilarated or exhausted, she came up from her room: a pause on the way to check the e-mail, the faxes, the answering machine. Sometimes, however, if she were 'charged' (a successful encounter with her final client, customer, patient, analysand) she'd come up directly and embrace him: the fragrance of her hair – even after hours in the room below (smoking in the building not allowed).

Today he could hear her talking in the hall, evidently to Mrs Beaumont, who hadn't been in her room when he'd arrived – to realise, in fact, she was speaking on the phone, her voice peremptory, focused, sharp.

'Who was that?' he enquired when she finally appeared, flushed, offering him her mouth, a brief cessation, or so it seemed, of breathing. 'An assessment I've been waiting for,' she already in the other room, picking up the phone, having recognised the voice on the answering machine.

Finally, free, they sat at the table he'd prepared in the sitting-room, by one of the two windows, looking onto the alley-like street, the upper part of the window of the artist's studio directly opposite. Occasionally, when the weather was fine, they ate on the roof, enclosed by plants and overlooked by attic windows, 'What sort of day?' a mutual enquiry, she disinclined to talk about her clients unless and until persuaded, a reluctance which, in recent weeks, had been decreasing, provoked invariably, over this interval, by questions recalling their past: Dennis, a theatre

48

director ('schizoid, like many of his profession'), Ruebeck (Claire), an actress only 'fulfilled' in front of a camera and, more fragmentally, on stage ('what do I do with the rest of my time?') 'entertaining reality', for her, diminishing all the while. And Maddox: what did he come up with? familiar, his account of Semitic grief, Celtic nightmare ('Alex reducing himself to the obscurity of a Scotch mist'). In this instance, however, face to face, he was aware of her fatigue: the ringing of the phone below, the varying voices on the answering machine: male, female, predominantly male, she finally turning the volume down. Popularity, accessibility, put her under stress as well as, paradoxically, reassuring her, her relative silence on this occasion indicating a subject she was disinclined to talk about.

Much in both their lives was hypothetical, his principal thesis which, like she with much of her work, in regard to him, he kept from her, focused on his self-named, long-standing and much abused 'New Philistinism' agenda – he suspended in a curious position for an academic, as a polemicist, a hack (an agitator, at extremes) when, in reality, at this stage, all he had wanted was a quiet life: articles for the *Critical Review*, the *Atlantic Quarterly* (he not admired in the United States), the arts pages of the broadsheets, the arts pages of the weekly magazines: propositions, aversions, a preternatural disinclination to take anything for granted, an inability not to provoke, qualities of character, of native disposition extended in correspondence columns over several weeks, art subsumed by mechanical procedures his unvarying line – 'The Mercantile Aesthetic' another of his themes – that which had dominated the visual arts in the second half of the century, specifically, in the Anglo-Saxon 'mind'.

He was provocative, contentious, challenging: he was also, by any as well as recent reckoning, nuts: if only his enemies could see him – life-class, on the one hand, psychiatric day clinic, on the other: art and lunacy ineffably combined.

He'd credited himself, as he'd grown older, with a sensibility enhanced by common sense; almost, conceivably, by a common touch, a quality he'd associated with his experience – his earliest experience – of cars: a particular car: its shape, its colour, its sheen, an aphrodisiacal, or so it had seemed, aroma – a cultural aroma, he'd finally decided, of a highly exclusive kind.

Machines, however, were one thing, aesthetics another, he having crossed the gap between ('Product and Sensibility', another of his projects), an elderly creature, his skin, like his hair, his bones, his muscle – his sexuality – in terminal decline (impotence, the threat of, waiting in the wings). And then, of course, his mind: something elusive there, a presence urging him on, at one time, to good things – now, the same, to something significantly not: on the one hand, suspicion, on the other, humiliation, his weapon against complacency, subdued by as well as subject to something even worse, women in extremis his numerically superior companions, a few male eccentrics, not unlike himself, thrown in, each alternately galvanised and denatured by a need, an appetite, a hunger, a stimulus they could scarcely understand: he no longer called the shots (made legitimate demands), an image memorably re-occurring in many of his dreams that of a ship, unaware of its destination but convinced it had one, slowly going down.

They transferred from their chairs at the table to the couch facing the television, his arm around her shoulder: war, starvation, ruin, the retrieval, from a sewer, of an endearingly stranded dog: obsolescence, inferred, of everything, not exclud-ing themselves, movement requiring continuity, continuity requiring engagement, engagement presupposing if not synony-mous with death (make sure you're not caught out).

'More cells than stars in the universe,' he said, for no reason he could think of referring to the brain.

'All stars in the universe, by definition, haven't been and never will be accounted for,' she said.

The set turned off, she stretched out on the couch, her feet propped across his thighs, evening light, at the windows, shadowing the woodwork, the grid-like configuration of the fireplace, its flames, amongst the simulated coal, fed, he reflected, from a subterranean duct beneath the North Sea.

Hypothetical: her interest in himself, someone whom she knew little if anything about, he, she'd nevertheless insisted, an

50

indispensable presence, one from within which he was gazing (rapturously) at her now, at the fireplace, at the cat which, roused from the hearthrug, was now settling in her lap. His estimation (in her view, his imagining) of himself – this objectively realised presence – was practically nil, below a certain perceivable level a token effort to remain afloat alone attracting his attention. That, he concluded, he could see and recognise (the view of himself measured exclusively by displacement): recognition, too, amongst his peers, something, also, to take into account – dominant amongst them, of course, Simone: arbiter, agent, co-respondent – responding to what, for the most part, he offered as himself, someone going if not already crazy, 'him' and 'self' divided in a way which, clearly, 'her' and 'self' were not, his estimation (of how much he could see and recognise of all this) all he had to go on: 'Stigma and Aesthetics', a seminal essay (*Art Monthly*), 'Post-Victorianism in Anglo-Saxon Art' a more laboured repetition.

Into this confabulation he had introduced Simone: a conflagration (up a sidestreet) she knew little if anything about, he having decided long ago man not manner seductively her style, 'Form as Content' another of his less mind- than career-bending contributions, 'Plasticity as Style: Lundquist to Auerbach' another.

How much, or, conversely, what did he know of her (she peripheral to his vision at this point)? Did he imagine, had he imagined, was he about to imagine there was another dimension to her waiting to be exposed – unravelled, examined: yielded to, absorbed? 'Style as Content', plus, 'The Demon of Novelty in the Arts', updating Wyndham Lewis, the upper half of the first page taken up with tabloidesque pronouncements: 'The Gratuitous Imperative: Twentieth-Century American Painting' another of his 'stingers' as Devonshire, the broadsheet's arts editor he worked most closely with, invariably described them: 'Philistinism and Commodity: the present seen'.

He was coming, had come, to the point of making amends, a will to set things right – if only to discover what the right, in his case – his unique and much troubled case – might be: the vivacity which, even now, with Simone, showed through after a day in the room below: not words, in her case, but people, insights, perceptions, suspicions, speculations, entrancingly described. Once her reluctance had been overcome he cherished listening to her accounts of lives endured, confiscated, submitted to at a point where, not unlike his own, facility and meaning, expression and accountability had come to an end: the chimera that, in his case, sensation had become: her face, her brushed-back hair, the luminosity of her eyes as she re-lived in her descriptions these inward encounters: the inquisitive and acquisitive nose, the childlike candour.

'Redeemed': the word came to him – at an angle, he half turned to gaze at the fire, she a child of grace (of light), he listening to her voice, its interrogative tone, elevating – liberating – statement into query: her self-possession, autonomy, belief. Where should she begin but with the news they had been watching? so many of her therapees rocking to a momentum begun before their time: out-of-the-world encounters, end-of-the-world decline – he glancing sideways: the receding light, the silhouette of her face against the window, the corners of her mouth turned down, still visible, in a gentle, wry, self-deprecating smile: the presence within of an otherwise invisible observer, dispassionate, suspended, deftly owned, he liking, above all, her self-sufficiency, even as it alarmed him. What he was clinging to might, at any moment, move away, yet here she was, her ankles in his lap, her feet twisting and turning as she described her day's encounters, tied in, as he was, to the dexterity, the clarity, the alacrity, finally the elusiveness (the transcendence) of her thoughts.

Everything in a moment might be removed; her authority undermined his own, he on his knees, if not prostrated, praying for compliance, acceptance, recognition, something other than defeat, requesting understanding by and of something other than himself – identifying, listening to her voice, a collateral built up from other people's lives, a collateral extending, validating her own (he, crouched beneath the table, grateful for the crumbs).

the subtleties of his situation allowed him to complain.

Later, in the cabin-like room beneath the roof, they went to bed: intimacy, containment (security, style), the window, its sill level with the bed, looking onto the roofs of the houses lower down the slope. Invariably, enclosed like this, he slept deeply, contentedly, the cat between them, in contrast to the broken sleep when he slept on his own, even her snores a reassurance, the cat, at an early hour, vacating the bed, leaving a space into which either of them might roll: the sound of her breathing, her sighs, her groans, the helplessness, the candour, the intimacy of a life attached to his own, his dreams on these occasions invariably occurring in the room in which they were lying, he struggling, as he was, to find a line, something he might cling to (Ariadne, inevitably, came to mind), he wondering if she didn't pity him, something less than oddity in his appeal; or whether she had glimpsed, identified, even, something unlike anything she had glimpsed before: three husbands an immediate line, he'd imagined, to disenchantment – sudden, unequivocal (remorseless, he suspected, too), she subject to sudden urges, like the cessation of their appointments, pursuing a divergent course to his own, one which took her, had taken her, amicably, for the most part, from one husband to another, each male sensibility absorbed by its successor, an ascending scale of enhancement reaching, conclusively – or so he hoped – himself: art as polemic, involvement, even prank, she having stayed clear, previously, in her own work of practitioners, those clients with paint-stained fingers, cluttered rooms, messy quarters, studios dirtier than a factory floor, preferring, as in his case, combatants of another sort, belligerents more akin in appearance, manners, thought and purpose, to herself: she was 'for' observation, taking apart, examination, then reassembly.

He, him, it, he was blind to: could no longer see the shape, the outline – the content, even – she had made for (and had taken into bed), he, for his part, prepared at a moment's notice to bring what couldn't be recorded to an end: the trauma of the tube train driver, the not dissimilar of the watching crowd, seconds only, as far as he was aware, between sentencing and execution: intuition, instinct, something equally spontaneous and as seemingly unknown, had drawn him back – thrown him back: that intervening second of hesitation precipitating him too late at the edge of the track: could such intervention, for instance, be relied on, the Demon King a subliminal, ever-watchful, seditious, equally spontaneous presence?

On the other hand, only by touch could he sense the delicacy of Simone's approach, what she was encountering foreign to himself, a liability, for one thing, not to be relied on, a composition of effects, defects – presences of varying and often contradictory natures, evidenced by his expression, specifically his eyes, the only part of his 'self' that reached the surface, he in the hands of a creator he had, at one time, mistakenly, assumed to be precisely that same self. No such authority existed: he clung to images of his mother, his father, his uncle, his brother, his sister; to recollections of the past – and not always of his own – to memories of his school, the games he'd played, the texts he'd learnt – more vivid than anything between – and, most potently, and strangely, weirdly, even, to the image of a car, a vehicle invariably in motion, the movement of the road ahead, object and subject ineluctably one: 'this is my construct in which I am well pleased', a direct line, or so it had seemed, to his creator, an emanation from outside as well as, more profoundly, from within himself, machinery and art aesthetically combined.

In the morning he left, she dealing with her post, her figure bowed over the desk in the room used by Mrs Beaumont, reading, as she did all her messages, from a standing position, her first appointment mounting the stone steps to her street – a figure – tall, cadaverous, a briefcase in one hand, a portable telephone in the other – he'd nicknamed 'Doctor Death'. 'Aids?' he'd enquired, coldly, on a previous occasion, she responding, equally coldly, 'Far from it,' refusing to further explain, despite his curiosity (masking his dislike: a subliminal suspicion of all her male patients, if, more conspicuously, of this one). Now, habitually, whenever he encountered this figure in the street, he acknowledged it with a querying nod, the same response, more minimally expressed, effortlessly returned, the figure moving on.

Earlier – no appointments to interrupt her breakfast – he had asked her again, 'Is anything the matter? Is anything troubling you you'd like me to know?' she responding, 'Not a thing,' an immediacy of reply which, rather than dissipating, confirmed his suspicion, a shadow of some sort, almost visible, passing between them. Was it him? he reflected as he walked away, or her? braced by the morning traffic descending the hill at little more than walking pace, an unusual feeling absorbing him that things, despite his previous unease, were moving his way – disappointed only when, beyond Chalk Farm, approaching Camden Town, he reached his home and was suddenly reminded he was returning to confinement (isolation, if not worse), no life-class or peer group to distract him, the process of renewal, of revival, if such it was, to be continued on his own.

Maybe it was too late to change more than his appearance (Simone's occasional, if regular insistence he smarten up), his principal energies, like his principal interests, now curtailed. The introductory, formal examination (a professional exercise) – Simone's – had been abandoned in favour of something more intrinsic; replaced, in that sense, by something more dramatic – reprehensible, professionally, he assumed – Simone herself, however, sharing no similar unease, if anything approving his 'egalitarian' line: the democracy of the National Health Service: no more private sessions with anyone; the one-day-a-week clinic, supervised by Kavanagh. It was as if she had recognised (and responded to, against her current practice) the virtues of a system, the perversities, anomalies, inconsistencies and incompetence of which, characterising her earlier career (her first husband had been a GP), she had derided when they'd first 'got together'.

She had seen and acknowledged, that is, the virtues of 'nature' taking its course, the facilities available to him for guidance (recovery, illumination) and supervision no different from those available to anyone else. Here he was slotted into what, she concurring, he had described as a 'universal' system (over-burdened, under-funded) while the optimal agent of recovery was, some nights – she liked 'slumming' in Chalk Farm – in his home: she, her it. Initially, he'd thought himself sufficiently advanced – adept, proficient, self-aware, intelligent, perceptive – to examine and explore what was, after all, a not uncommon medical condition, focusing, in the process, on what, presumably, had eluded him in the past – largely, he suspected, because of the pace of his earlier life: too busy, too constant, too inclined, desirably so, it had seemed at the time, to look forward rather than in.

Even now, what was there to recognise and examine in him that hadn't been recognised in so many before – Judith, Beth, Alex, Anna, to name but a few? a realisation that, in any final summation, life was scarcely worth the living (Giotto, Ghiberti, Donatello notwithstanding), the preponderance of pain – in this instance a mental phenomenon, hard to describe as well as to grasp – over what might have been described as the benignity, even the grace and resourcefulness of human nature, too (painfully) apparent. The unpremeditated leap at the line: the sum, otherwise, scarcely added up: he was there, here was it, the answer still in his head, a head over which he'd had little control, an inconclusive, mutatory device focused primarily on pleasure, hunger once appeased, pleasure an impulse as exhaustible as any other. Apart from that he was – had been – obliged to subscribe to a reality in which he no longer believed (he an indissoluble element of it: no meaning, as no end), fortuity, he'd concluded – even with Simone – governing all, 'significance' as gratuitous as everything else.

What did Simone mean by abandoning him to a regime she had previously, if not despised, dismissed as hostile, at best complementary to much of what she did herself? Abandoning him, in effect, to a course of treatment which would set them even further apart. Retirement (redundancy) had played a part in, if not been the start of his decline; previous to that his life, by any normal measure, had been both sustainable and pleasant. Succeeding Viklund at the Drayburgh had provided a base from which his censuring of the art of the last half of the previous century had been, in his view, a legitimate and inevitable advance, a Ruskinesque brief he'd been delighted to take up – and (if no longer a judge in the matter) vigorously to extend.

He visited Viklund from time to time, invariably at the great man's invitation, a summons he rarely if ever declined, and which, occasionally, he even prompted with a card or a letter: a familiar and, to Maddox, reassuring figure, small, slight, with a disproportionately prominent head, blue eyes gazing out – at least, in his direction – with an invariably benevolent expression, the hair, silvery, dense, thrust backwards and upwards to create – reassuringly to Maddox – the impression of someone moving at speed, the shoulders supporting this unusually dominant head alarmingly thin, the arms similarly fragile and ending, disappointingly, Maddox always thought, in curiously blunt, short-fingered hands, reminiscent of a child's, a perverse denial, or so he felt, of the eminently practical nature not only of Viklund's commentaries on the manner and content of trecento and quattrocento Florentine art but – inevitably linked with the same – life: Viklund's legendary post-war achievements from which Maddox had had great difficulty in disinterring – disentangling – his own pronouncements.

A post-war regenerator of pre- and early Renaissance art – a written-out period at the time – Viklund's texts, originating, many of them, from his earlier life in Rome, had blocked the way, initially, to Maddox's own advancement. Only recently had many of them been set aside (abused, disregarded) to be replaced by his own – a continuing process as his successors, in turn, set about his, empiricism ('social expressiveness') replacing aestheticism, grandeur, style.

Brought up in Vienna, Stockholm, Berlin, Rome and Paris, his father a Swedish diplomat (and humorously alleged 'spy') at the 'heart of darkness' throughout the Second World War, Viklund's own accounts of this period in Rome and later in Paris, which had witnessed the beginning of his 'Renaissance' career, were uncharacteristically fragmentary, perversely obscure. Unlike Berenson, he had acquired little wealth from his scholarship, largely, Maddox concluded, because he hadn't needed to, his grandparents Swedish industrialists whose legacy, even now, stretched across Western Europe and the United States, Viklund, as far as Maddox understood, a significant, if reluctant beneficiary. An indifference to personal wealth was characterised by an indifference to carrying cash, something which, in the past, had cost Maddox dear: 'a scholar millionaire, if of an unusual kind', he invariably described him to anyone requiring a synoptic description of his friend, someone whose character, like his reputation, he had long ago abandoned more thoroughly explaining. His house, overlooking Regent's Park, was exclusively his wife's creation. 'A lease, not a freehold,' he would explain, dismissing the building with a wave of his hand, its size, its scale, its (seemingly) superfluous rooms ('I was brought up in anonymous interiors and don't really know anything better: certainly don't feel at ease with anything else'), on one occasion only, in Maddox's experience, revealing any concern about his situation, looking onto the eastern flank of the park, and, referring to the recent removal of several diseased elms, remarking disconsolately, 'It looks more like Clapham Common, don't you think?' turning Maddox aside to show him a recently purchased Matthew Smith ('Ilse likes it: I had no choice,' referring to his wife. 'I couldn't afford a Matisse, of course. We have to make do with this'), a curious insensitivity to pre- and post-Second World War art ('I leave it up to you') conspicuous in his, or Ilse's – Maddox was never sure which – choice of pictures to hang around the house, a choice, if it were exclusively Ilse's, he was too proud and too protective, other than on this one occasion, to own up to. Of several William Nicholsons, no hint of the son Ben's, he would remark, 'A touch of Velázquez, don't you think, certainly Ribero, or would you say Murillo?' quickly passing him by the landscapes with the same mischievous expression – Norfolk, the South Downs, the south coast – the still-lifes and occasional portraits ('fortunately, no one we know'), Nicholson numerically the most prominent of the artists scattered about the house, his not infrequent remark whenever he opened the door to Maddox, 'Welcome to the home of a very poor collector,' his stress on the word 'poor' never satisfactorily defined.

Now, returning from Simone's, he examined his mail (bills only) and, reminded by a note he'd left purposely lying on the floor in the hall, set off again, in the same southerly direction.

Turning west, to his right, at Camden Town, at the top of Parkway he turned south again along the eastern façade of Nash houses overlooking the park, approaching the door of one which, with another, stood isolated from the terrace. The ringing of the bell aroused the barking of Ilse's dog, the animal evidently ushered into a room, a door closing, before the outer door was pulled back by Viklund himself.

Dressed, as usual, in a formal grey suit, white shirt and diagonally striped tie – his only affectation, his membership of a club – a formality from which he rarely departed ('life, in every sense, is a business, don't you think?'), he opened the door wider as if to facilitate the entry of not one but several figures, calling, seemingly, into the road behind, 'Come in, my dear friend!' his accent, part Nordic, part Mediterranean, melodious, half lilting, pitched between enquiry and exposition. 'How are you today? Looking better. Much. Much improved since the last time,' gazing directly into his face before, disarmingly, turning aside to indicate the way down the hall, the door closing behind Maddox's back. Passing between several Nicholsons – Sussex Downs, the south coast: Lulworth Cove – he entered the principal room at the front of the house, its three tall windows looking not onto the park but onto the approach road which gave access to the terrace.

Somewhere in the house a female voice was singing and moments later a young woman in a white overall entered, carrying a tray of coffee and biscuits. 'Loreen, meet Matthew,' informally, from Viklund, 'our latest acquisition from Hong Kong,' the girl laughing, and adding, 'Tel Aviv!'

'And how many young women in Tel Aviv are called Loreen, I wonder?' Viklund enquired.

'My *grandmother* is called Loreen,' the young woman

responded, her laughter, after she'd closed the door, coming from the hall outside.

'And how are you, in fact?' Viklund asked, offering Maddox the coffee, the biscuits – waiting for him to sit down, taking his own seat by the marble-fasciaed fireplace with a sigh.

'I'm well,' Maddox said, seated, formally, some distance across the room, its furniture spaciously divided. 'I'm relying exclusively on pills, psychotherapy abandoned.'

'Oh, pills,' Viklund said. He held up his hand, the curiously gnarled stump, or so it seemed, protruding from the sleeve of his jacket. 'I've any amount of those,' the vividly, companionably animated face turned in his direction. 'Swap you some, if you like. Mine are red and green. How about yours?' adding, 'Most of them, otherwise I'll throw them away. Don't tell Ilse,' shading his eyes to examine Maddox once again, amused by the formality of the furniture that obliged them to sit so far apart. 'You're right,' he concluded, 'you're looking *much* better. Suicide no longer, I assume, in mind.'

'It never was,' he said.

'Exactly!' the telephone ringing in another room. 'Not long to go, in any case. Nevertheless,' he raised his hand again, 'the trip's been worth it. We can talk candidly? No need for circumlocution?' Lowering his hand, he went on, 'I can leave the rest, of course, to you. Something of which we never wished to take advantage, namely,' smiling, 'how to deconstruct my past and – how should I describe it? – bring it into the present.'

'Biography,' Maddox said, 'is not my line,' a suggestion of Viklund's made on several occasions, the older man anxious that Maddox, a favoured pupil and his successor, might take up the challenge of, as the older man invariably put it, 'renegotiating my work'.

'I get so many requests for autobiography and reassessment, even after so many years refusing. You, on the other hand, have your ear closer to the ground. Not, for instance, like living here,' gesturing round, 'where I hear nothing of relevance, close to the Drayburgh though we be. Halfway to paradise, I call it. *Not* a good place to write from. The other half, I trust, of course, to be

60

travelled rather faster. It's ages, Matt, since I wrote anything at all. What say?' urgency, for the first time, in his manner. 'You write so well. My subjects, which I've always been glad, relieved, to be precise, to leave to you. Francesca, Masaccio, I almost see as my children. I *do* see as my children, if in the hands of others. Yours, I hardly need to say, the safest of all. Not much space, perhaps, to manoeuvre. Here, however,' he stretched out his arms, 'all the space you require. Viklund in remiss, Viklund as error.'

It was, unmistakably, Maddox thought, a mark of senility – of self-preoccupation, a reversal, in many respects, of his previous nature – he was witnessing in his old friend now, a process not dissimilar to that which recently he recognised as proceeding, if at an earlier stage, and at a slower pace, within himself.

'Historicism, after all, is fiction, and what could be more fictional,' Viklund went on, 'than living like this?' a quizzical, blue-eyed expression, courteously presented, the lips framing to a smile, anticipating Maddox's response. 'If I wasn't so badgered,' he added, 'I wouldn't ask,' raising his hand to indicate a revision of that thought. 'I wouldn't suggest,' he amended. 'Others, I'm only too aware, are anxious to get their hands on it. My work. The moment I have gone.'

'Attendance at a psychiatric day-hospital, for the older person – older than whom, or what? I fruitlessly enquire – is hardly a recommendation, even for fiction, if it is to be that,' Maddox said.

Having, earlier, taken a seat which favoured Viklund's left ear, he virtually deaf on the other side, he was sitting not only some distance from his friend – a 'psychological' explanation for that, too, he reflected – but diagonally facing him. Friendship between them, however, had never been closer, even if it still required, as in the past, discretion – a wilful suspension of obscurer desires – on both their parts: they were – always had been, after all – sparring for the same position – one from which Viklund, it appeared, was now formally withdrawing: a new stage in their relationship

'To me it's common sense,' his friend responded. 'It's the

61

ones who aren't attending, like myself, I'm most worried about. You've stolen a march on all of us. As usual, Matt. Even your psychoanalytical friend recognised that. She responded to the man not the patient. A degree of common sense in her as well. I envy her, someone who didn't know you, coming so swiftly to that conclusion.' He clapped his hands. 'Let's face it, Matt, between the two of us there's a great deal of *interpretation* still at stake. We say a great deal about ourselves and, hopefully, our times, messages we assume we've fathomed, one way or another, and which neither of us, retrospectively, would like to see disowned, abused or, even worse, ignored. All this,' he gestured round, 'passes so quickly. Here today and much, if not all of it, gone tomorrow. What say either of us will have another chance? Posterity, as far as I can see it, is the only thing that counts. At this stage. I'd even say for both of us.'

Maddox was examining the frail figure of his friend as he turned away, too grieved, or perplexed, or perhaps simply confused to carry on. Viklund's alertness was unusual for this time of the day, he notoriously a 'night person', known often to go to bed at dawn and sleep all day, embroiled on these occasions in his earliest and never abandoned passions, a dedication which Maddox had, in the past, imitated to his cost, resorting, finally, to a daytime routine which, to this degree, measured the difference in commitment, concentration, *penetration* between the two of them.

A tenacious, at times predatory nature, Viklund's, the eyes curiously lightless on these occasions of obsessive preoccupation – or, as now, unusual self-preoccupation – indicating the intensity, almost dreamlike, of his inward reflection. It was as if, in these bouts of concentration, Viklund took his subjects into a cave – re-emerging, blinking in the light, to disseminate his conclusions as to their nature to an invariably receptive and, in this instance, certainly appreciative guest.

'The exchange now, of course,' his friend went on, 'is more relevant. More *sexual*, for one thing. Between you and your therapist. It is, to that extent, I'd say, a step forward. One both she and you, I assume, felt obliged to make. To do what? Move

62

forward in the only way you recognised.' Smiling, he added, 'A situation as intimate as that could, in any case, scarcely be expressed otherwise. Isn't the nature of it sexual to start with? No new theories, I take it, on the evolution of the motor-car?' a calculated provocation, preceded by flattery, intended, Maddox reflected, to soften him up. They were back, he concluded, on common ground.

At one time he'd been considered not merely Viklund's successor at the Drayburgh but his supplanter, his victor, Viklund's reputation, at the time of Maddox taking up the vacated post, then at its height, *The Roots of the Renaissance* (a title disclaiming exclusivity), a nevertheless far-reaching search through Greek as well as Italian art, an unprecedented post-war success, paralleled, as it was – a subsequently realised necessary ingredient – by a serialised television commentary, a medium for which, until then, Viklund had had outspoken contempt. 'Sup with the devil at least once in your life, don't you think?' exposition and enquiry blended, as usual, into one, adding, slyly, 'Though not the first time,' Maddox concluding, on this occasion, his friend had sensed his eventual, if not imminent decline – responding, as a result, in the only way he'd thought available: popularisation (before it's too late), encapsulation (just in time). 'Life, after all, is a business, wouldn't you say?'

Maddox's own position at the Drayburgh had been one of little strategic significance, other than – though not to be despised – as a platform from which to extend his influence, less as interpreter than critic. 'Ease of access to the next generation not something to be sneezed at,' Viklund had told him on his own departure. 'It's amazing how quickly juvenilia comes to the fore, first to be recognised and then accepted. Increasingly quickly,' he'd gone on, 'to the point where, if you don't keep abreast, it becomes too late to turn round.'

Much of Viklund's time, after moving to the Royal College, he had spent abroad, a prerequisite he'd negotiated before his appointment: visiting professorships in the United States, lecture tours in the Far East ('Ilse's very fond of Japan,' wryly. 'Have I mentioned her *buddhist* inclination? – Much enthusiasm in places

63

where you'd least expect it, though I'm not entirely convinced the Japanese are focusing their interests elsewhere').

In the years previous to his appointment to the Royal College, he had been generously licensed by Pemberton to pursue his interests overseas. 'After all, the first two or three decades of my life were spent in a diplomatic corral: not only in the blood, I'd say, but the central nervous system. It advertises the Drayburgh as much as our Professor. Or, rather, it advertises our Professor as much as the Drayburgh: not much to choose between the two, as far as Felix is concerned. I'm convinced he believes the college will disappear into the ground the moment he retires,' Pemberton offering Maddox, on his succession, a not dissimilar facility: 'The terms are barely eight weeks long: half the year to pursue your own enthusiasms, as long as our *name* comes to the fore,' Pemberton dismayed by the parochialism, at that time, of British art, anxious for 'influences' from overseas (many foreign students on the register), particularly American (an alarming progressive in this respect). 'France, Italy, Spain, Germany, where you might reasonably have looked for a guide, I despair of. The war, in that respect, too, has a great deal to answer for,' directing Maddox's attention to appropriate figures at the British as well as the Arts Council. 'Get in with the *government*. They never know what to do until you tell them. And often, of course, not even then. Can't do any harm. Look at Daniel. He milks them by the hour. He's milked them white for years. He has – he won't mind me mentioning this – more connections than a fireman's hose. His father was allegedly an agent for the CIA,' Maddox's own reflections, at this point, returning to Viklund's sepulchral figure seated before him, focused on his friend's curious Christian name, recalling that recently his attention had been drawn to the presence of the Danish Church – Den Danske Kirke, announced outside – along the road which, he'd been startled to discover, Viklund and Ilse attended each Sunday: 'a devotional couple', Donaldson, his co-critic on his Sunday broadsheet, had facetiously described them.

64

'You haven't, I take it, got yourself a computer?' Viklund enquired.

He shook his head. 'I haven't.'

'I have one in the study.' He pointed overhead, a room, devoted to his interests, at the top of the house. 'You can have that, if you like. I can't get it to work. When it did, as the result of a visit from a technician from the College, I managed to disable it in a matter of seconds. Without it, I'm afraid, you – we – haven't a chance. Pen and ink are less than Third World stratagems now,' smiling at Maddox, small, irregular, yellowish teeth suggesting, within the narrow configuration of his lips, a degree of impishness which the eyes themselves denied: a 'divided' face, Maddox had always thought, mischievousness, in Viklund, carelessly obscured, charm, of an equally casual nature, to the fore in appearance as well as expression.

What was it that Viklund had identified in those pre- and early Renaissance figures which had rarely been remarked upon before? A graphic distinction (a graphic vitality) as if, in Viklund's phrase, they had 'gone behind the back of God', reality displacing iconography, a mutatory phenomenon (yet another) identified and singularly promoted: an event – as spontaneous and as seemingly miraculous as the summary arrival of a saviour – around which Maddox had focused much of his own endeavours, 'liberating consciousness from nature', his own ambivalent phrase, 'like fruit from trees', technology another of his wonders: 'the propagation of the species by other means': a 'false fruit', in his estimation, requiring 'separation, distinction, alienation, the sublimation of the ends by the means', a process to be 'arrested' and, as a result of his own (momentous) intrusion, reversed.

'Writing letters, I'm afraid, is all I'm fit for. And those I dictate,' Viklund went on. 'Ideally they should be sent by e-mail. Occasionally I do it. Not from here. The College. They still look with favour on a poor old man. Resources minimal. Message delivered, but I'm not deceived. Which is where you come in, do you think?'

65

'Perhaps there's much to be said for redirecting communication away from machinery, even if it is to a bottle of ink and a pen,' Maddox said, wondering, as he spoke, what might be the purpose of his visit, other than to receive the by now familiar invitation to 'renegotiate' what Viklund was inclined to call his 'misspent' life: to readdress (to 'revisit') it in terms that a present generation, 'far removed from mine', might understand. 'I can no longer make any sense of it, or them.'

Something of the grandeur of the room was affecting his senses, a not uncommon experience when visiting the house: a feeling of being airily suspended, some distance from the floor, taken up into a space immediately below the cavernous ceiling with its stuccoed surrounds depicting birds, animals, foliage – exclusivity (again) involved, something which his own accommodation, and thereby his life, he assumed, could neither suggest nor, if suggest, sustain: a sensation indistinguishable from the aura of Viklund himself, so much an element of the place, inseparable from it (he had lived here for over thirty years), as if, confusingly, he had produced it, or it had produced him.

'Maybe the incident at the tube station, Matt – a place, incidentally, I've avoided since your experience there: I'm quite prepared to believe, I must tell you, in "other" forces – was less a prospective than a retrospective event. Drawing a line *beneath*, literally and metaphorically, before moving on. In a sense, in that respect, an artistic decision. "If I do this what will it mean?" Or don't you agree? Am I being presumptuous?'

'A fresh start promoted,' Maddox said, 'by a threatened end.'

The incident, after all, had been a defeat, a grievous defeat – almost a lifetime's defeat and submission – for both of them, so embedded was Viklund's life in his, and his in his friend's.

'The spontaneity with which you drew back shows you had no intention of completing the exercise. The one, in other words, could not be had without the other. Debit here, credit there. Sum added up, in an instant, in favour of the latter. I take it,' he waved his hand again, 'we can talk about these things. It's not off limits?'

He waited while Maddox shook his head.

'I'm much interested in the subject, as you're aware,' he went on. 'Not in your death, of course, nor mine, but in death as a cessation of sensory perception, of a totality of experience as we've come to know it. The knowing, too, part of the same. In front of a tube train, for instance, an almost popular form of execution, though a selfish one since it vicariously involves other people. Disregarding the effect on the driver.'

He was forcing these sentences home, Maddox observed, watching, though not waiting for his reaction.

'But conducted, let's say, in the privacy of one's room. In bed, for instance, if medication is involved, or in the bathroom if something messier. The latter, too, of course, involves someone else. Nevertheless, the cessation of sensation is what I'm constantly drawn to. The peculiar *counter*-imperative which nature insists on, glorifying the senses, on the one hand, on the other, discarding them completely. What, I wonder, does that reversal mean? What, for instance, does your therapist *mean* by abandoning her discipline, and thereby, presumably, though offering an alternative, in the form of a colleague, returning you to the situation from which you were hoping to progress?'

'She's conducting what, I presume, is her therapy by other means. Something more tangible,' he said, 'more certain, conceivably,' he added, facetiously, 'more productive.'

'So we're still in a therapeutic situation?' Viklund said, turning in his chair to regard him directly.

'To that degree, I assume I am,' he said. 'But, then, no more than you and I are, sitting here,' he went on, 'discussing this.'

'She can see in it something for her, but how do you perceive it. Is everything a therapeutic exercise?' He placed his hands – his strange, stubby, impractical hands – beneath his chin, lowering his mouth towards them. 'Do you *want* to go on living?'

'I do,' Maddox said, wondering if this was the purpose of his visit: to decide, once and for all. 'By doing nothing,' he went on, 'we simply hang around. The only choice we have is to pre-empt what, at our age, is increasingly apparent, or simply to let matters take their course. Having confronted the former, I've settled for the latter, with, in this instance, a witness in tow. Whether she'd like to be described in those terms I'm not sure,' he concluded.

'I suspect she wouldn't.' He smiled: the small, neat, mischievous teeth again. 'She, of all people, must be aware of the degree of perversity in *everything*, self-interest not excluded. After all,' releasing his hands to spread them out on either side, 'what are we here for if not to be stimulated by *something*? We have art, of a certain kind, she, presumably, has people. And you. Her latest, how should we put it, post-doctorial exercise?' He laughed, looking to Maddox to join in. 'Another biscuit? More coffee?'

Maddox got up and crossed to the table beside Viklund's chair: a convivial, mercurial, confrontational nature, ironic – derisive – self-amused: he wondered how much of his own was reflected in the other man, or – not for the first time – whether it was the absence of any similarities which drew them together. After all, Viklund had the habit – had always had the habit – of expressing aloud what he, Maddox, at any moment might be thinking, an engaging and at times startling facility which, while warming him to the man, had also had the effect of thrusting them apart.

He poured more coffee into their respective cups, took another biscuit, and returned across the room.

A formalised informality (again): one which had characterised their relationship from the start when, after the interview with Pemberton, Viklund and the Registrar of the Drayburgh, together with several anonymous figures who rarely spoke, Viklund had rung to tell him, 'unofficially', he'd been appointed to his own soon-to-be-vacated chair, something, he'd said, which he'd like to 'nail down: the post not the object' (laughing at the reference), the Registrar, he'd confided, not altogether sure. 'He was for someone older, and less contentious, but Felix, of course, was on our side. Registrars are obliged to be nothing else but prudent. The only ones at the Drayburgh who are,' laughing again, a light, derisory sound. 'If they don't confirm it in the next few days let me know,' less, at that time, a spiritual

68

than a paternal presence, one which subsequently he was quick to outgrow, the preoccupation with death a recent speculation. To someone so attached to sensibility, to the formulation and re-formulation of what he invariably described as 'primary vision' – that prospective expedition behind what he had imagined to be the 'nature' of God – it was of final importance to understand the experience of all that ending. 'Call me Daniel, this is Felix,' Viklund had said, familiarly, since they all knew one another, at the beginning of the interview, adding, 'And this is Johnny,' indicating the small, bespectacled figure of the Registrar, 'whom you also know,' regarding him with the impish smile which accompanied most, if not all, of his more contentious statements. 'Trouble-makers I like,' he'd said on another occasion. 'Which is why we hired you. This man, I thought, will be nothing but that. So here you are, toeing the line, living up to expectations.'

When describing – 'confessing' – to Viklund his experience on the tube station platform, his friend had responded, 'That is a behind your God experience, wouldn't you say? seeing how far you might push it. And seeing how far,' he'd added, 'you might be pushed back. A terminologist's gamble, wouldn't you say? "Means without ends" your castigation of your times, if not of mine. What a field-day the mechanics you despise would have had if your Demon King, as you call him, or it, had succeeded. I hope you'll go to church on the strength of that and say *something*, however mild, "Where do we go from here?" for example.'

'Apart from what you describe as your peer support, and the orthodoxy of taking pills, you're on your own, I take it?' Viklund went on.

His personal injury: his personal grief: he had no such injury to show: everything was perfect, commendable – yet here he was, disabled by something he knew nothing about: his father, his mother, his uncle, his brother, his sister – himself: innocent. All of them.

'There's Simone, my principal collateral where well-being, or even survival, is concerned,' he said.

69

He waited for Viklund to respond: perhaps he'd brought this problem specifically to his friend to resolve, not merely to articulate what he suspected might be in his, Maddox's, mind, but to persuade him – to convince him of the need, the inevitability, even, of moving ahead, of moving behind him, 'to see what I can't see,' he reflected, 'even while I speak.'

'No doubt she thought you'd had enough of exposition. After all, half a lifetime is quite enough. I take it you did *have* a life before you came across Cimabue?'

Another reference to one of Maddox's celebrated tracts: art as containment, the stricture of the medium, the tyranny of form: whereas all the while, he, it, they were responsive – should have been responsive – to content, form dictated by style, style by convention, convention by dictat: dictat determined by apprehension, fear of God preceding love of man.

Viklund, while he waited for an answer, glanced away, his head turning in the direction of the nude suspended over the large, caryatid-decorated marble fireplace (the latter 'an idea of the previous lease-holder, I'm afraid,' Viklund had explained its presence): a diagonal of cream-coloured paint crossed a green and alizarin background: his compromised Matthew Smith. 'Mediterranean eye, or would you say a calciferous Nordic one?' Viklund had enquired at the time: the strange antinomies in Viklund's nature: somewhere upstairs a Clausen, in addition to further Nicholsons, a Tissot (loaned for exhibitions: 'another Franconian source'), paintings which, even if his wife's taste, suggested something obscure, self-contradictory, if not consistently perverse in Viklund's nature.

His friend and former colleague had had no children, professing earlier in life he had had no time for them: 'And then, of course, it got too late,' a succession of dogs, some of bizarre appearance, taking what might otherwise have been their place, largely, Maddox assumed, as with the paintings, at the suggestion of his wife. The same indifference, regarding children, he'd shown to Maddox's excursions into reviewing, the revisionist 'The Demon of Novelty in the Arts' attracting the enquiry, 'Can indifference increase in intensity, do you think, or

70

am I merely confirming my worst suspicions?' adding, on another occasion, 'I have no eye for contemporary detail. It *is* detail, I take it?' expanding into, with regard to this particular publication, 'Anglo-Saxon art without an Anglo or a Saxon in sight. The best painters in Britain appear to be foreign. What would you Anglicans produce if you *were* to try?' division of taste and absence of children not alone in separating them. Viklund's wartime activities, occasionally hinted at but never revealed, a separate source of obfuscation: the peculiar trips from Rome to Stockholm during the Second World War, from Stockholm to Berlin, then back to Rome, mentioned in the context of matters other than war ('family business: we had so much of it' a familiar line); further trips from Rome to Lisbon, to London, and back again, Viklund's parents' house in the via Campagna a meeting-place for Axis, neutral and Vatican 'celebrities' ('even the Pope'), 'les ingénus' who had 'nowhere else to go', the 'civilising arena we managed to sustain' where paintings and drawings and sculptures were allegedly exchanged ('in the interests of preservation – including self-preservation: every-thing, and everyone, was black market in those days. What else might you expect?'), the 'market' Viklund père controlled ('someone had to do it: who better?').

Matthew Smith, Nicholson, Tissot, Clausen, Sargent (a late addition in the bedroom), plus several looming, patrician Chinese screens, Matisse-like configurations in black, red and gold, he was openly possessive of ('a touch of Simone – not *your* Simone – Martini, do you think?') attested to a peculiar parochialism which he was content to live with, a disguise, a testimony to his devotion to Ilse, or to a 'blankness', as he had once described it, 'in the centre of the eye: I see so much, and more strongly, at the *edges*. That's why the history as opposed to the practice. I see a long way sideways, but never very much, I'm afraid, ahead,' a testimony to a taste that had been Anglicised: rumoured purchases, earlier, of Matisses and Picassos, Legers and Vuillards, quickly sold on. Once, briefly, a Braque had appeared on his wall – in his dining-room – but had quickly disappeared: 'I was hanging it for a friend. He brought

71

his client here and sold it. An appropriate setting, the baroque? I refused his offer of commission,' a taste which, Maddox suspected, was intended to mislead, as if, in a corner of his life, not least his domestic one, he had wished to escape from the grandeur, the austerity, the mathematics, even – the monumentality – of his trecento and quattrocento idols – escape, that is, into something inconsequential, consciously evasive, taking on 'native cover'. 'A philistine at heart,' he had protested when Maddox first enquired about the paintings which, at regular intervals, began to appear on his walls, he not sure he had heard the aspirate preceding the final word. 'Art, after all, is commerce first, and commerce last – who owns what – and commerce, as we know, is invariably unfair in that value is vagariously determined. That's where you and I come in, the two of us, wouldn't you say, ingenious fellows?' a remark, or aside – presumably the latter – intended, Maddox suspected, to put him and others off the scent.

'Daniel is a very secretive fellow, for all his charm,' he had said when first describing him to Charlotte. 'No wonder the suggestion he and his father were dealers and agents during and immediately after the Second World War. There's much there to be written up,' providing room, this process of dissimulation, for Viklund to manoeuvre, deploy and despatch his more radical ideas – his early discrediting of the authenticity of the Giotto St Francis Assisi frescoes, the turbulence from which had never subsided throughout his professional ('I wouldn't call it vocational') life, Rome not Florence the source, if not co-agent of naturalism's demystifying drive.

Attempts to pin down his friend to his wartime past, a source of fascination to Maddox, invariably prompted the same discursive reaction: how old had he been at the time of the German occupation of Paris, similarly of Rome, he professing to have known Eluard, Sartre, Queneau, Camus, and both the underground and the collaborationist press, carrying messages (for whom?) on several occasions: texts of declarations as well as warnings (to whom?). He had had a friend ('a fellow enthusiast') and acquaintances in the SS; as a neutral he had relative

72

freedom to travel: he was watched (by whom?): 'Whereas you, old fellow, were an evacuee of an entirely different sort. Where was this industrial town of yours? And wasn't your brother too *young* to be leaving home?'

He saw, too, in Viklund, reflections not only of his father – the subscription to an (obscure) ideal, to a 'notion' of 'experience' (a phenomenological event) – but of his uncle Joseph, a man who, in Maddox's youth, had dominated his life more than his father (or mother): a 'macaroni' – a name he lived up to, an habitual performer, given to Homburgs, in a town of bowlers and trilbys and flat caps – cigars, silk cravats, suits made by 'a tailor in town': flared trousers, unusually so, waistcoats of variegated colours (almost luminous in the dark), an uncle who sold cars, cigar in hand, while his father merely serviced and admired. 'Your dad's the craftsman, I the connoisseur,' his uncle had announced on the memorable first occasion he had driven Maddox into town and taken him to the theatre, introducing him – 'My genius nephew, Matthew. Watch his progress': a world of bars, lights, declamatory people, a curious parody, he discovered later, of something substantial – subtler, intenser – which Viklund had been the first to bring to his notice, a celebratory flourish which deepened into a final, agonised, silent gaze: man in nature as well as isolated from it, 'consciousness' a gift which both elevated and maimed, illumined and injured: Donatello, Ghiberti, Masaccio, and particularly Giotto, despite the Assisi reservation, the 'move behind God', expulsion into reality, the irreversible decline, the irrepressible defeat: the flinging (of something) at the tube station line frozen – suspended – in a permanent image – 'Mad Ox' trailing in his mentor's wake, the man who, he'd lately discovered, weekly attended with his wife the nearby Danish Church, Maddox responding to something undeclared in all his pronouncements: something Viklund had witnessed and clarified exclusively himself.

'Psychology, I take it, in that case, is out?' Viklund had said, returning his attention to the room. 'Has she, I wonder, any interest in art?' He gestured to the nude above the mantelpiece:

art as parody, the gesture said: 'A bit like opening a Woolworths in Buckingham Palace,' he'd observed, once, to several guests admiring it, subterfuge, disguise, very much to his taste.

'Not even that.' Maddox gestured back.

'What on earth do you talk about?'

'Everything,' he said, 'other than that.'

'Probably,' Viklund said, 'a good sign. It's time you turned a new corner.' Pausing, he added, 'Younger or older?'

'Younger.'

'By how much?'

'Eight years.'

'A lot at my age, but scarcely anything at yours. You are, after all,' with a smile, the mischievous teeth on display, 'still a handsome fellow. I imagine the women at your art class scramble to get their easels – or is it their donkeys? – next to yours.'

'Three times married,' Maddox said, anxious to provoke him.

'There you have me. Once, as you are aware, was always, and, I assume, will continue to be enough for me. Unless Ilse has other ideas. As it is,' he waved his arm again, 'both of us are out of fashion. Everyone, these days, gets in on the act: intellectuals, students, social workers, *policemen*, "art-like" the sole criterion now. Appearance, not substance, facetiousness in lieu of wit, "Anyone can do it". *Donaldson*, your colleague, in place of you.' Turning in his chair, once more, to face him, he added, 'I'm still looking to you to reverse the decline. When you're better, not now,' continuing, as if this were part of the process, 'Bring her along. I'd like to meet her. She can explain her science. I've always thought it adjacent to ours. If either is a science. It might also illuminate what she sees in you. I don't want her to place you on a lower level of appreciation than, let's say, the one, long ago, I placed you on myself. Would you say,' he smiled, 'there's something paternalistic in her choice of men?'

'As far as I'm aware they were all, roughly, the same age as herself.'

'Did she leave them? Or they her?'

74

'She them. She'll leave me, too, I assume, when the appropriate moment comes.'

'On the other hand,' Viklund said, turning to look at the foliage outside the window, a lack of animation showing for the first time, 'she may have found what was lacking in the others,' glancing back at Maddox to add, 'Bring her,' Maddox's attention distracted by the barking of the dog, the scampering of its claws on a wooden floor followed by the closing of a door.

A doorbell rang: voices came from the hall, then, as a further door was closed, faded. 'I won't be able to make much of her, of course. Not sight, so much as judgement failing. I find myself, as no doubt you've observed, coming out with things I would never have considered mentioning before. She, on the other hand, might make something of me. It might help you,' he went on, smiling, 'in your research.' His look wavered in Maddox's direction. 'It's all,' he continued, 'a question of *procedure*. Something we've omitted to consider until now,' his look shifting to the window, abstracted.

More guardian than parent, Maddox reflected, seeing his former mentor in terms of a past which obscured more than it revealed, a past, in effect, he could scarcely imagine, invoking the presence of someone who had moved through so many stages of development that what was, or might have been, there at the beginning was no longer apparent: transcendence rather than transformation, someone continuously travelling beyond – obscurity prefacing obscurity, a process he'd long thought of as being involved in himself: an enigma, a mountebank, conceivably, even a criminal: those wartime packages associated with a process Viklund had described as 'saving art', objects rather than pronouncements.

No wonder he had counted on trecento and quattrocento speculations, and what he had uncovered there, to 'save' him from the 'mercantile aspirations of my background': a salvationary process achieving its fulfilment, legitimately, it must now have seemed, in his weekly attendance at the church along the road. 'A time of truth, a time of renewal,' his one-time observation on his immediate, post-war career – 'an apostle of

75

an even higher truth than that' had been, at the time, Maddox's own reaction: a servant to higher things placed fortuitously in a position to which no one else could respond: an exclusivity of means to achieve an equally exclusive end: he 'who went before to prepare a way' leading, as it had happened, from the camps, from aerial bombing, from nuclear fusion to a world removed from all these things when 'time' – the time prefacing these disasters – began.

What, on the other hand, Maddox reflected, lay behind his own exterior? the face that ran up from the pugnacious chin: the muscular throat, the rudimentary, naïve, expectant eyes – eyes which, whenever he caught a glimpse of them, 'betrayed everything' (Simone's phrase), he not at all sure what, in this context, she was suggesting, a preoccupation, he'd concluded, with extremes, flaws, a perception of things no longer sound, no longer reliable, dominating his life.

The privilege, he reflected, of sitting here, the identification with, the empathy he felt for this elusive, older man, something he had felt from the beginning, someone with whom he had little if anything, materially, in common, both of them seeing one another, engagingly, as opposites, by temperament, by nature, yet focused, reassuringly, on a similar if not identical goal.

Or, perhaps, it was that Viklund was feeling his isolation more intensely: saw it vividly confirmed in his friend and former colleague, seizing on Maddox as someone whom he might 'charge', or change, servant to his servant, if, at first, deferential, a justifier of his ways.

Less isolated, in some respects, the older man, than facing a situation in which art, and everything associated with it, could play little if any part, at least, in which the 'ethic' identified with it – impersonal, extreme, inclusive – took him beyond what, in the past, he would have described as his 'reckoning', life *as* art becoming merely life as something (anything) else, two contrary distinctions which, though divided, represented a single faith: a fidelity to 'space', instinct and reason mellifluously combined, an effulgence of the spirit cohesively aroused.

What Maddox – what Viklund, he imagined – had considered as most relevant to their relationship were those companionable silences which had characterised their first meetings – initially in the corridors of the Drayburgh but subsequently more often in Pemberton's office, Pemberton absent, they alone, he and Viklund, theoreticians in a place of practitioners, and set, as a result, conspiratorially apart.

It was, notoriously, from Pemberton's own disciplines as a painter – observation of the object, rigorously adhered to – that Viklund had extrapolated much in his study of della Francesca (*Mathematics and Muse*). Over the previous few months, on his walks to and from Simone's house, he had, on several occasions, met the retired Principal of the Drayburgh, Pemberton, singularly unaged, using a studio in a friend's house off the High Street and living in a flat around the corner: a tall, avuncular, bearded figure, cast more in a Romany role than an academician's, the genial source of many seemingly irreconcilable pronouncements (following Viklund's amply misunderstood example): 'measurement as feeling', 'mathematics as intuition', a cornucopia of contradictions which sought and occasionally achieved their resolution in his meticulously constructed figures, landscapes and still-lifes, a man who, with his devotion to Courbet and his dislike of Cézanne ('the source of all our problems'), represented to Maddox a past which, for all but Pemberton and, to some extent, Viklund, had ceased to exist: a retrospective sentiment which, despite his vulnerability to it (certainty, of a sort), despite being, at this moment, seated in Viklund's house, he was hoping to discard (intending to disown).

It was the hands, he thought, which gave Viklund away: impractical, small, he often allowing them to retreat into the sleeves of his jacket, a habit which, on standing, gave him a misleading air of helplessness (how many, in the past, had fallen for that) and which the frailty of his body inevitably confirmed: something, too, which turned him away from life to its representation, as if translation were the only thing to count. 'The gap in the fence' was how, previously, he had referred to this late illumination in his life, 'an appetite for faith', another

77

designation, occasionally accompanied by, 'which may possibly be replaced'.

And where – and what – was Maddox in relation to all this? 'Maddy', to his friends, 'Mad Ox' at school, 'Maddox Major', alternately 'Maddox Primus' to his teachers, 'Oxey', at the Courtauld, he something of an enthusiast in all things, an 'idealism' he thought he had acquired from his father, an entrepreneurial zeal (quickly discomfited), recklessness associated with it, responding to Viklund's art as something other than chance with something of a zealot's passion. Only later had 'philosophy' taken over, a rancour which, belatedly, he'd come to recognise, had been creeping up on him throughout his life: a premonition, at first, then something not unlike a seizure, a Demon-designated lurch, a vividly resisted near disaster, an 'exercise in execution', so described to Simone in one of their first exchanges, she, curiously, never querying, 'Why?'

Perhaps – he'd long suspected it to be the case – he was neither sufficiently mature nor advanced to reflect on what might have happened; or even, he concluded, on what might be happening now, exclusion rather than inclusion his principal, late-life passion, a fevered process of subtraction, effect attended to, rather than cause, something he could associate with 'time' (what little left of it, 'space' another factor) and which precluded something as abstruse, or as precise, as 'recognition' (of himself, to start with) – anxious, however, in this instance, to define something in the presence of the other man: a cathartic thrust towards the line, a soundless interjection, self-violation of one sort or another, an unexamined life, in this sense, not worth living, an examined one leading him, however, to the same conclusion.

On the other hand (again), what did he know of Viklund, a man he cherished and admired, and involuntarily looked up to? a slight, cadaverous figure (he in, he estimated, his eighty-seventh year), a residue of something once substantial, the curiously insensitive 'normal' hands, the inquisitive features (not unlike Simone's), the protruding cheekbones, the galvanic eyes, self-amused – corrosive, too – as if, beyond his achievements, he had glimpsed something which reduced his best endeavours – his resourcefulness, his playfulness (his insights, his pronouncements – his suggestion, at one time outrageous, that Cavallini ('the unknown') was the author of the Assisi St Francis frescoes) – to 'inadvertencies' (his description).

'A certain pleasure in disowning what others see as your achievements.' He suddenly intruded into Maddox's thoughts, a not infrequent feature of their conversations, as if their minds, in these exchanges, were mesmerically one. 'Arrogance to do so, yet . . .' a hand held in the air. 'Bent, as we are, on a similar, if not identical venture. What does it matter if we leave nothing behind? As if faith in something unimaginable has replaced a faith in something we thought we had perceived,' glancing across at Maddox to add, smiling, 'Bent on a mission which doesn't amount to what your American adversaries – mine, too, at one time: I should never have mentioned Cavallini, and Santa Cecilia, Trastevere, left Giotto and Assisi quite alone – would have called, in reference to your own reflections on postwar American painting, a hill of beans.'

Himself, set, in silhouette, he imagined, against the profile of the other man: appearances, he concluded, no longer mattered, that evocation of himself – the boldness of the head not quite outmatching that of Viklund's – the whiteness of the thinning hair, the sombre sense of introspection, the eyes, capable (still) of lightening in the presence of Simone, his sons. Who else? His brother, his sister – Viklund: his friend's less a rake's or a pilgrim's than a mere itinerant's progress: not to perdition, but something more elusive, as if Viklund were prompting him to a recognition of something intrinsic in his nature which he himself had yet to identify, let alone respond to.

Raising his head, Viklund looked up at the stuccoed ceiling, the plasterwork birds, leaves, flowers, animals, the whirls and volutes, a forested menagerie suspended in friezes, reliefs, and the ornate central 'rose' surrounding a chandelier. 'The unspoken question of earlier conviction brought into the open.

All we – I – can do is stare, unable to describe, analyse, decipher. What does it all add up to?'

Maddox, too, was gazing up, his attention distracted: the corpse he was carrying – which Viklund, for all his graciousness, his mischievousness, his charm, was carrying too, if not had almost become: the vehicle, the harness in place, which would carry him on to where the event would finally occur, this material burden his sole credential (his spiritual signature hopefully in place: to be evaluated by whom? Evaluated by Maddox, if he could find the time, the inclination, the reason).

Pemberton, too, on those aimless encounters in Rosslyn Hill, in the High Street, in Heath Street, the avuncularity of the taller, bearded man, away from the Drayburgh, his lifetime's domain (the longest-serving incumbent of the professorial post), seemingly an affectation: the rumour of breakdown following his deferred retirement (echo of his own predicament): the first occasion in the former Principal's life when he had had the opportunity to paint without disturbance, to catch up with Courbet, overtake Degas, the weighty tonality of his carefully constructed, relatively colourless pictures: Pemberton, too, had felt the lurch towards the line, a resolution, involuntarily extracted, viciously expressed – inexcusable, unwarranted, undesired – the signature on yet another failed attempt, an irretrievable commitment to something other than himself.

Love!

His heart, or something approximating to it, vibrating in his chest: echoes, he reflected, of wartime bombing: the accelerating screech of a metal object descending a metal chute: a fear-ridden allegiance to something other than himself, a systematic reappraisal, Simone, in this sudden recollection, convener and subject in one: a marker to where he was at present.

Love!

Viklund's voice across the room was suggesting he sit closer. Removing his teacup from the arm of the chair, Maddox drew forward, the pile of the carpet resisting. 'I have difficulty hearing, even on my good side. So much have I missed. Not that it's any matter. We know each other too well,' adding,

'Don't you think?' Regent's Park, the Nash terraces, Hampstead, Maddox's modest refuge in the declivity between. Beneath him, too, at home, the rumble of the tube.

There was his purpose, too, in ringing up Viklund several days before to make the appointment to see him, Viklund out at the time, Maddox speaking to Ilse, the dainty, bird-like creature Viklund had married over fifty years before ('another souvenir from Stockholm'), attempting to decipher from her still Nordic-inflected accent how enthusiastically or otherwise he might be welcomed, surprised by the warmth (she, since his 'incident', apprehensive of his influence on Viklund), by the vivacity, the flirtatiousness on this occasion: 'Dan will be so disappointed to have missed you. He sees you as someone of increasing significance in his life,' adding, 'Well, we both do,' with something of a laugh. 'You see what it's like, my dear, to be not merely old but very.'

'Scarcely,' he'd told her, thrilled, nevertheless, by the flighty voice, the frail, delicately featured, elfin figure who had remained, seemingly contented, certainly unobtrusive, in the background of Viklund's extravagant, at times turbulent if not mysterious life.

Now she came to the door, knocking, Maddox standing to embrace her, to kiss her cheek, first one side then the other, then the first side once again – a formality he invariably resisted – to feel his hand taken between hers, squeezed, retained, while she exclaimed, 'It's so good to see you, Matt!' he adding, mentally, in parenthesis, 'alive'. 'Don't let me interrupt you. Any more coffee? Cakes, perhaps, instead of biscuits. I never realised Loreen had brought up those. And you've scarcely eaten any,' turning to indicate the girl who had followed her in.

'One each, or was it two, Matt?' Viklund said, standing, meticulously attentive to domestic detail whenever his wife was present. 'The coffee's cold, otherwise I believe we're both all right,' the girl collecting the cups and saucers, stacking them on the tray, returning with it to the door, Ilse turning, too. 'Don't let him leave, Dan, without saying goodbye. So rarely do we see you, Matt,' she added before the door was closed – Maddox, by this remark alone, recalling those occasions when he had almost haunted their home, at that time off the Cromwell Road, having been offered a room there, Viklund, on that occasion unwell, exhausted, listless, inert, seemingly about to expire, 'Hiatus Drayburghia,' he'd suggested to Maddox, whom he'd called in to help. 'Mind you don't catch it. I'm fed up with the place. But for Felix. So many regressive students. All they're interested in are introductions to Cork Street.'

Re-seating himself, he said, as if prompted by his wife's appearance, 'What of Taylor? Any more news of him?'

'I've received a visitor's pass,' Maddox said.

'Good Lord.' Viklund put his hands together, a prayerful gesture, the fingers pointing up, the thumbs, indicating, misleadingly, someone of a practical nature, curled back: the knuckles he pressed against his lips, tapping them slightly as he breathed out.

Maddox looked up at the plasterwork again: the frieze of animals, birds, vegetation: even there, in the fortuitous circumstances of a leased house, something of Viklund's nature was oppressively defined.

'Tomorrow,' Maddox said.

'In prison?'

'They'd hardly allow him out.'

'I'm not familiar with the procedures.' Viklund glanced away. 'In wartime, of course, it was different. I visited a number of prisons then,' a sudden leniency apparent in his manner, as if a digression, if not canvassed for, were a necessity at present. 'I was once invited to visit an acquaintance – no stronger than that – in Paris, after his arrest, convinced, once there, I'd be arrested myself. Only,' he released one hand from its prayerful gesture and waved it in the air, 'he'd agreed to co-operate, his captors wondering what the effect would be on his former colleagues if he were suddenly to reappear. I couldn't tell them. Nor could I tell them if the news of his arrest had got around. It was done discreetly at his girlfriend's, who was also taken in.'

'What happened next?' Maddox asked: it was unusual of Viklund to talk of his past in such detail.

82

'I had the impression his arrest had been what, in peacetime, would have been described as an administrative error, one department not knowing what another was doing. That he'd been turned, as the saying went, already. As it was, having been reassured by me it would be best if he were released, they shot him. I assumed, at the time, they were fingering me, wondering how far my influence went. Not a few of the resistance at that time were informers, their only means of staying alive. The Germans, with their familiar thoroughness, affected, even in that peculiar world of loyalties and self-interest, to keep a system of checks and balances: so much coming from one side, so much going to another. As the son of a neutral diplomat, it was the closest I came to being arrested myself. As it was ...' He paused, abstracted, almost to the point, Maddox reflected, of confessing he was a collaborator: so many drawings, so many paintings, so many sculptures, to stay alive. 'Close shaves,' he added, 'were something of a norm, rather than, as with Taylor, being the exception.' Looking across, his head at an angle, he smiled: something of a more intimidating nature crossed his mind, crossed and re-crossed, as if he were struggling to restrain it.

'How well do you remember Taylor?' Maddox asked.

'An inanimate character. Droll. Recessive. Or have I confused him with someone else?'

'Distant. Recessive. Bright. But very,' Maddox said.

Viklund looked up once more at the painting above the fireplace.

'Something visceral,' he added, following Viklund's gaze.

Something visceral, too, he reflected, in Viklund's response to the garish, lavishly painted nude.

'His essays were outstanding. More cinquecento than quat- tro-,' he added, as if building on something Viklund already knew. 'Also,' he paused, Viklund's gaze returning to his, 'his religious identification was very strong. Wrote as a believer, one instant, as a sceptic the next. His paintings were not dissimilar. More application than intuition. He followed Felix in that. But without the talent.'

83

'Norfolk?'

'That's right.'

Viklund's enquiry had been direct, his eyes fixed fiercely on him: blue, intense, suddenly, characteristically, viciously alert. 'For how long are you allowed to see him?'

'I've no idea.'

'Strange his inviting you.'

'I was his tutor. Perhaps no one else is inclined to go.'

'No relatives.'

'I assume there were.'

'Not inclined, I imagine, to get involved.' He paused. 'According to the papers and the televison at the time, his neighbours found him pleasant. His family, too. In which case . . .' He paused again, inviting Maddox to continue. 'Have you any experience of murder?'

'The only person I've been close to killing,' Maddox said, 'is myself.'

'Of course.' Viklund's look was turned away. 'How does your psychologist friend explain it? His case, I mean,' he added.

'She doesn't.'

'Have you discussed it?'

'A little.'

'Depression, whatever that means, was suggested at the time.'

Maddox didn't respond.

'Though, since most of us get depressed without, apparently, killing anyone . . .' Again he waited. 'Particularly one's wife.'

'Yes.'

'And children.'

'Three.'

'Two.'

Maddox paused. He'd been reluctant to ask Simone for an explanation, afraid, he suspected, she might provide one; afraid, too, of coming to a conclusion about something which eluded analysis as well as definition: it wasn't 'explanations', he concluded, he was looking for, or anticipated, either.

'And himself,' Viklund said. 'He failing, in that respect, like you.'

84

'I think he was more intent,' he said. 'He's attempted to do the same in prison, and is evidently under close supervision.'

'I hope he appreciates you going. After all, in one sense,' Viklund said, 'some might see it as an endorsement of what he's done, if not a gratuitous involvement in something in which they have little to lose, if anything at all. I, on the other hand,' he smiled, testing Maddox's reaction in a by now familiar manner, 'know neither is the case.' His smile fading, his tiny teeth concealed. 'Does he know you were prompted to do something not dissimilar?'

'I don't see how he could. In reality,' he added, 'there's no comparison.'

'Of course.'

'None at all.'

'His first name, I believe, was Derek.'

'Eric.'

'Not very grand.'

'No.'

'Domestic, rather than archetypal.'

'Yes.'

'Though an interesting subject. If one is capable of looking at these things. Suicide, or, as I would call it, self-election.'

'Non-election,' Maddox said.

'Precisely.' His look had intensified, his eyes shadowed, the receding hair-line drawn down to his brows, a deep, vertical declivity between.

'When it first appeared in the news I couldn't remember his name. His first name,' Maddox said. 'I thought that very odd. He was my student for almost four years. Apart from his first name,' he went on, 'I remembered him so clearly.'

Reality was imposed upon something, he reflected, but what? the configurations of his own life, for instance, reaching beyond feeling, beyond thought: merely a blankness: nothing – the nothing that something was imposed upon but which was included in reality itself: his examining, for instance, via Taylor, his own capacity for self-destruction, if not the destruction of

85

others – the war, everything, by inference, as well as direct experience, he had envisaged.

Examining, too, the furthest reaches of compassion, his motive, if only one of them, in going to see Taylor at all: this rage, in his own case, though not in Taylor's, to stay alive – a rage which had subsided, again, in his case, to quiet perturbation, finally to a compulsive gesture of dissent; subsequently, that failing, a return to the 'flow', the submission, biological in origin and expression, which took him casually, haphazardly, along with everything else: this room, their two figures, those trees outside the window (decades of growth and pruning) – everything directed towards the light – awareness creeping into hands and feet, limbs, head, body, events, a slow, inexorable dissolution; awareness arrested by distraction.

It was as if, he concluded, the event involving Taylor paralleled, or echoed, something not only in his own but in Viklund's life.

'Are you in a fit state to get involved?' Viklund said. 'Won't this add unduly to what troubles you at present?'

'It might distract it,' Maddox said.

'Distraction won't last long.' The response came quickly, Viklund leaning forward.

'It might clear something up for both of us,' he said.

'Wasn't his wife a student as well?'

It was this Viklund had been intending to ask all along.

Maddox looked away, avoiding his friend's expression.

The previous evening he and Simone, watching the news, had witnessed an interview with the distraught parents of a seven-year-old child who was missing: a girl – the tear-streaked faces, the mask-like confrontation with something beyond the imagination, an involvement with prurience indistinguishable from the prurience of the daughter's possible fate, an involvement with something which only gratuitously involved themselves, murder, the possibility of, a specious form of entertainment.

'She was.'

'Did you know her?'

'Yes.'

His response came out without any stress.

'Were you her tutor?'

'No.'

'She was in the years you lectured to?'

'That's right.' Glancing back at Viklund, he added, 'Rebecca.'

'One never knows where these strands from earlier in one's life might lead. The significance of attachments which you thought you'd long ago abandoned. Suddenly, out of nowhere ...' he waved his hand.

The girl had knocked at the door and re-entered with the tray, setting it down once more beside Viklund. 'Shall I pour?' she said.

'Matthew will do it,' Viklund said.

It was as if a dividing line had been drawn and, recognised, lightly stepped across.

'What was she like?' Viklund said as, with an acknowledging gesture to Maddox, the girl went out.

'Attractive.'

'Talented?'

'Yes.'

'Were she and Taylor connected at the time?'

'Shortly after.'

'Of course, relationships between students and staff were prohibited,' Viklund said as Maddox got up. Crossing to Viklund's chair he poured the coffee, the tray set on a low table beside him. 'It was included in the contract at the Drayburgh when I first arrived. So delicately phrased I asked Saunders, the then Registrar, what it meant. "You may not fuck the students," he replied, adding, thoughtfully, "Either sex applies." ' He paused. 'Deleted, of course, in your time.'

'Yes.'

'Though left implicit.'

'It was.'

'And at the Courtauld.'

'The Courtauld, too.'

87

'In my time it was written in.'

'Not in mine.'

'But left implicit.'

'Of course. Charlotte, for my part, never complained.'

Viklund smiled: a tendentiousness, familiar to Maddox, lightly played.

'What was Rebecca's background?'

'East End.' He waited. 'Her father was a tailor. Ironical, her surname, when she married. Robust. Good-humoured. An oddly contrasted couple. He with very little humour. She, I thought, a lot.'

He paused again: so much of this had come out without preparation, a summary, he concluded, he'd been assembling, if only for himself, for some time. Having filled one cup and placed it beside Viklund, he filled a second, added milk, and returned to his chair. Despite having moved it closer, something of the formality of their encounter still remained: a discourse, rather than a conversation, he suspected, had been intended, Viklund inclined to tell him something to which, he had already decided, there would be no adequate response.

'And all we have by way of explanation was that Taylor was depressed?'

'As far as I'm aware.'

'So have you been, recently,' he said. 'At least, diagnosed as such,' he added.

'Yes.'

'No similar inclination, I take it?'

'No.'

'Taylor, of course, is younger.'

'In the midst of life.'

'Almost.'

Something dream-like about the proportions of the room, as if, a not uncommon occurrence, he was suddenly aware of this conversation having happened before, in precisely the same location, and in precisely the same form, absorbed Maddox completely; as if, in effect, his life had been lived not once but several times, if not, conceivably, simultaneously, touching at certain points where the congruity between the several versions had suddenly, without warning, overlapped.

'Look here!' Viklund was getting up, alertly, as if having contemplated the action for some time. 'Let's take a stroll. The air is stifling. I'll fall asleep if I sit any longer. Nothing to do with you, of course. Far from it. I realise the importance of staying awake. I ought to walk, though rarely have anyone to walk with, other than Ilse, and she's quite bored with me after all this time. The chauffeur, sometimes. And the girl. No, really,' he went on, 'I need someone fit and young, like yourself,' laughing as he turned to the door.

In the hall Ilse reappeared, the dog, sensing a change in the atmosphere, scampering behind her, a small, tousle-haired animal which, at its impetuous approach, Viklund pushed away with his foot. 'I'll take him,' he said. 'I'll take him,' in response to a silent enquiry from his wife. 'Give me the lead. No need for him to mope in here,' a coat lifted from the rack by the door into which, with Ilse's and the girl's assistance, he thrust his arms, a hat, a trilby, set at a rakish angle on his head. 'Just the job for Matthew and me. No telling how long we'll be. Don't wait up!' laughing once again.

Moments later they were crossing the road at the front of the house to a gate set in the park hedge the other side. 'As you can see, they've made up for the elms. Like missing teeth in a familiar mouth, but finally I've got used to them,' indicating a footpath leading to a further gate which, in turn, via a road, gave access to the centre of the park.

'Something we were saying back there in the house,' he added, releasing the dog, 'reminded me I saw a man shot dead in the street, in Paris, at the end of the war. There one minute, gone the next.' He waved his arm, as if anticipating a similar event taking place on the path before them. 'A collaborator, I was told. What I'm getting at,' he waved his arm again, a man much given, Maddox recalled, to involuntary physical move-ment, before leaving the house refusing a walking-stick held out to him by Ilse – presumably, like releasing the dog, to leave himself free of impediments, 'is the barrier between something like myself and *that*,' stabbing at the air before him. 'A restlessness I could never trust, or even accept, and which, as a result, I filled with pictures. Well, *principally* pictures,' with a laugh. 'Anything, in other words, which proved, if in one sense only, to be static. A religious convocation, don't you think? Looking for steadfastness, certainty, and so on. Pictures, of course,' he went on, 'invariably of a reflective nature. None of your Nicholsons. Ilse's idea. The Tissot I like. More painter than illustrator, the damned English disease. As for the rest,' waving his arm before him. 'A space between being here and being *there*,' adjusting his trilby to a more rakish angle, a sudden alacrity evident in his movements ever since he had risen from his chair in the house, 'which, a religious aspiration, you'll think, I'll be glad to be rid of. The same goes, I assume, for you. Weren't you foreclosing on that space when you leapt at the line? Or, rather, in your text, the leap was provided for you. In the *thrust* at the line. As it turned out, a premature expectation. This allegiance, Matt, to a space that doesn't exist. *That* indifference I'll be glad to be rid of. A nightmare, don't you think? You, of course,' he glanced across, 'have your wonderful children. And *their* children. I've only got the dog,' calling, 'Jefferson! Jefferson!' bringing it to heel, the animal, for a moment, followed by a bigger dog, trotting behind. 'Your journalism, too. We mustn't forget that. A determination, in your case, to tear the space apart and fill it with something, anything, irrespective of the cost.'

He held up his arm to arrest anything Maddox might have said in response.

'The quality of your selection I have rarely been disappointed by. I, on the other hand, have had the curse of the diplomat to contend with. Bred into me, from the earliest age, and impossible, at least, until now, to relinquish. Formalised activity requiring you, at all times, to leave the space intact. Into it may enter anything the diplomat is obliged to consider. Obliged to receive,' he went on, 'and courteously acknowledge. Alienation, on the one hand, exclusivity, of a sort, on the other, "the man who is nowhere", my father once called it, referring to his job. A

90

rarefied combination, the two. Distance from everything at the same time as identification with the same. No such reserve, however, with me any longer.' Calling the dog once more, 'Jefferson! Jefferson!' he concluded, characteristically, 'What do you think?'

'That kind of exclusivity,' Maddox said, 'I never had,' adding, 'not exclusively,' waiting for Viklund to laugh: a sound, 'Hah!' came out briefly, his own thoughts, evidently, moving on.

'There aren't such barriers or spaces any longer,' Viklund said. 'If nothing else, technology has removed them. Messages,' he went on, '*expel* themselves, no longer simply arrive, the pertinence of what's transmitted no longer of account. Transmission,' he paused, 'has entered everything. We're assailed, not, as only in the recent past, informed.'

Maddox's own thoughts, too, had moved on: something formalised in his response to Taylor which had scarcely if ever been there before, a reversion to their earlier relationship as tutor and student: a proximity to evil, of a clearly definable sort, left him bemused – suspended, atrophied, even – disinclined to consider it – what it was comprised of, what it entailed: something abstract, at this distance, overwhelming, which took – had taken – a specific physical form. The definitive nature of what he was confronting had never been more apparent, driving him back, mentally, to resources he suspected he'd never had: the shadow Taylor represented was the corollary of light – *his* light: forgiveness, toleration, the overriding of that which, uniquely, in his case, could scarcely be imagined, recalling the news feature the previous evening: entertainment, the fanfared introduction. Cynicism, regarding his motives, was, he reflected, creeping in on every side: a vicarious indulgence in feelings he could otherwise disown. Was it for this reason he'd visited Viklund? Was it for this reason he was walking with him now, anxious for a 'line' which might complement if not, more hopefully, displace his own?

The park was where, recently, he'd been much inclined to walk himself, approaching it along the canal footpath from Camden Lock, a colourful route following the curve of the waterway, passing beneath low road and rail bridges and alongside a variety of converted barges, the smoke from their coke stoves reminding him of similar walks in the north of England, away at school, a recollection of industry and commerce, mixed inextricably with domesticity.

The inner park, which they'd crossed into, Viklund finally resetting the dog on its lead, with its rose garden, artificial waterfall and lake, was where he was inclined to sit and reflect – invariably in a corner shaded by climbing roses strung along overhead rope structures, the formalised flower-beds, richly variant in colour, contrasting vividly with the asymmetrical contour of the lake, its surface laden with water fowl, fluttering and splashing, ducking and diving, the elegance of the swans, both black and white, vivifying the restlessness of the smaller birds.

His thoughts were moving in the same contrasted fashion, perturbation of one sort in conflict with the staidness of the rest; that is, a feeling that the whole of his formalised existence was about to be overwhelmed, if not discarded – to the point where everything he had previously recognised, however tenuously, as 'himself' was to be dispensed with, as clinically, as involuntarily, as decisively as that plunge towards the line – impelled, this event, he reminded himself, by forces, or a force, not only beyond his control but foreign to his nature, something possessed of its own dynamic, indifferent to who or what or why or where or how he was.

A final evaluation had been set determinedly in place.

It was that final matter towards which his thoughts were now directed: something cool and hard, unplaceable, unapproachable: a figure, in one sense, emerging from a mist, in another, shrouded by a curtain, to be contained before unleashed, a creature, as yet, only to be imagined, there to be confronted, the precursor of worse, much worse, to come.

His suggestion to Viklund they might sit was rejected by the older man, the dog straining backwards, leashed, dragging behind: a curt, 'Jefferson!' and it ran ahead, tugging rather than dragging. 'Let's walk. Keep moving. Imprudent thoughts, in that way, are inclined to go away. I often walk in this place,' gesturing to the more open spaces confronting them, the path leading, to their right, towards the open-air theatre, a barricade of trees and shrubs concealing it from view. 'You were saying you knew his wife as a student. I recall her. An anachronism at the Drayburgh, a healthy-looking figure. Felix had hopes for her as a painter. That I do recall. Much better, in that respect, than Taylor, I believe you said.'

'That's why she fascinated him, and why Taylor, bound up in theory, fascinated her.'

'And still the conundrum. Why did he kill her? And their children.' Glancing aside, he added, 'And the nature of your involvement. Evidently with both of them, at separate times. On the other hand,' his steps faltering as he decided, from several paths, which one they'd follow, 'there was an extraordinary range of students, year on year, Felix's theory being, with an annual intake of eighty, he could only reasonably expect six or seven to have any talent, selecting the rest on the basis of diversity, age, sex and background. "The in-filling", he once described them. How many would that be? Seventy-three or -four. Always likeable, always fascinating, at least, at first sight. Army officers, graduates from other disciplines, misfits of almost every description. Out and out delinquents. Do you remember the Irish peer with his open-top Bentley? Artisans, clerks, schoolchildren. A unique collection, quite unlike any other institution. Rebecca, did you say? fitted in like a fist in a glove. Taylor, too. Very many said, later, it was the best period of their lives.'

They were moving towards the exit from the inner park which, across a secluded road, led to a gate giving access to the larger lake and the vaster spaces beyond.

To their right, from the distance, came the trumpeting of elephants at the zoo: late morning, midweek, there were few people about, Viklund releasing the dog from its leash once they'd crossed the road.

Listening to the older man Maddox's reflections had refocused: images of Taylor and Rebecca came to mind, walking, arms around each other's waist, out of the Drayburgh, across the yard opening onto Gower Street; or, conversely, walking in, separately, on a morning, the taciturn expression of the Norfolk youth, a sturdy, square-shouldered figure, the open-faced expression of the girl, receptive, vulnerable, expectant, lips parted, she invariably wearing a smock or – the garment he remembered most clearly, endearingly, even – a large, loose-fitting, ex-army greatcoat.

He was reminded, too, recalling his own solitary walks in the park, that he was finding it increasingly difficult to retain, for any significant length of time, his thoughts or feelings. Here he was, accompanied by someone he knew, respected, had long looked up to, someone whose deliberate obtuseness, arrogance, even, brought out reciprocal qualities in himself – his introducing, for instance, the nature – the content – of his relationship with Taylor, and particularly with his former student's dead wife. The prospect of something immovable, impersonal – terrifying in its indifference – preoccupied him intensely, this the subject of many of his solitary walks along the path they were following – something to which he and Viklund were, in varying ways, irretrievably connected, something, he reflected, devoid of intimacy, tenderness, anything likeable, let alone lovable – anything, in short, that might be adhered to – something, in his own case, caught up with, defying, even, the illness for which the nightly dose of dothiepin was intended to be a palliative, if not a partial cure.

'What do you think?' He gestured aimlessly at the scene below: the curve of the path to their left, bordered on one side by recently planted flower-beds and, on the other, by an expanse of smoothly mown grass running down, past the bandstand, to the lake. A solitary rowing-boat left a jagged wake between the edge of the lake and the heron-nested island opposite.

The vagueness of his enquiry had caused Viklund to smile: for the first time since entering the park he glanced at him directly.

'I was thinking,' he said, still smiling, 'of how Masaccio said

94

goodbye to God. Let's keep, he might have said, to something that we know. Listen!' He held up his hand to the sound of the elephants trumpeting in the distance. *'No more metaphysics!'*

'Speculation doesn't die,' Maddox said.

'Arrogance in promoting it gives way to irrelevance.' Viklund waved his hand at the view. 'We have too much to contend with. Let's be satisfied with that.'

'Consciousness, nevertheless, relates even to this.' Maddox gestured at the bridge crossing the easterly extension of the lake, they turning towards it.

'Ignore it.'

'I can't.'

'No point in doing otherwise, old fellow.'

'It doesn't ignore us,' Maddox said. 'Something overwhelming. Something, for instance, overwhelming me. Overwhelming Taylor. Overwhelming his wife. His children.'

Viklund quickened his pace, as if the boat landing-stage at the far end of the lake was now his destination. His attention to the dog had faded and, as if sensing this, the animal desisted from roaming on either side and trotted at their heels.

Unaccountably, Maddox was reminded of how Simone, after reducing the intervals between their appointments to a daily pattern, had suddenly extended them before finally declaring they were at an end, he suddenly aware, for the first time, that, unlike his supposition at the time that he was either on the mend or boring her, she was struggling against his attraction, a thought which, rather than amusing or pleasing him, disturbed him, a curious reaction, and a curious reflection in relation to the trees beneath which they were walking – a place where he had never walked with her, only alone – plane and chestnut for the most part. In the distance, beyond the lake, was the relatively treeless space stretching to the concrete structures of the bear enclosure at the zoo.

How his 'engagements', as she called them, darted around, one moment caught up with Taylor, the next with her – the next with the ruffled surface of the lake, the movement of birds across it: the recollection of Rebecca crouched on a stool, drawing, in the mixed life-room at the Drayburgh, looking up, her gaze abstracted, as he signalled her from the door.

A sense of sadness transposed to a feeling of dread, as if the ground were about to disappear beneath their feet: a naïve presentiment, yet something other than a naïve response, a transposition of an otherwise incommunicable activity within himself, a draining away, a removal, of every mental and physical resource, a degenerative force which he couldn't otherwise describe, as if, in walking at a brisker pace, the older, slighter, almost childlike figure were walking him through, conducting him through, a mandatory exercise the inevitable consequences of which he knew in advance: adverse, painful, destructive.

'I knew Rebecca well,' he said, startled by the suddenness of his confession. 'We were together for a while. Some months, in fact. Before she took up with Taylor. I'd visit her in her student hostel and, when she moved out, the visits becoming too conspicuous, in a room we rented.'

Viklund said nothing, the dog still at his heels, concentrating, or so it seemed, on the goal ahead.

'I withdrew, in the end, because of Charlotte. Because of Rebecca, too, of course. In addition to which, I was putting my job at risk. She had an abortion. Though I wasn't altogether sure it was mine. We went to some trouble not to conceive.'

'Did Felix know?'

'I imagined he did. Though it could well be he didn't. Other students must have known.'

'How did you feel when it ended?'

'Saddened. Grieved. Quite ill. She, too. It was shortly after that she took up with Taylor.'

'On the rebound.' An odd term, Maddox reflected, coming from him, sophistry, semantics more his style.

'Possibly.'

'Did he know about you?'

'I imagined he did. But then, I was inclined to imagine everybody did. A form of endorsement. "If everyone knows and is doing nothing, what on earth am I worrying about?"

Inevitably, of course, I felt like a shit. I still do. Even worse, now, of course. It may be why Taylor asked to see me. I was always surprised – astonished, even – it never came out at the trial. That he had a grudge against her.'

'Other things, I assume, were more pressing.'

'Yes.'

They walked in silence for a while, the western façade of the Nash terraces to their left, the bridge crossing the head of the lake taking them past the boat landing-stage, in the direction of Viklund's house on the eastern fringe of the park. 'She was, at the time, new to the place, my own life bogged down in domesticity. I felt renewed. Spurious, of course. Mad, even, if it were known.'

'And have felt guilty ever since.'

'Oh, yes.' He was glad to admit it, but surprised by how much. 'You never disengage from these things, however unrelated to real events they might have been. And still are. Because they're dismissed they become more real. On top of which,' he paused, 'she was a virgin.'

'So Taylor must have known. Something, I mean.'

'I always knew he did but resisted acknowledging it. *After* their relationship began I was still his tutor. He didn't ask to change, which he could have done, and I didn't suggest it because I didn't wish to acknowledge what had happened. The inevitable consequence, of course, was, although I was the tutor, I always took the lead from him. Deferred to him,' he concluded.

'It should be quite a meeting,' Viklund said. 'I can well imagine neither of you actually saying anything.'

Maddox paused, Viklund's pace decreasing: it was as if – he couldn't dispel the feeling – he were being manoeuvred through the conversation. 'On the other hand,' he said, 'she got something of significance out of it. Not least a dramatic introduction to the Drayburgh. She quite relished the hold she had over me, and even threatened to go to Charlotte and complain.'

'But didn't.'

'No.' His own pace slowed further. 'As for Taylor, he showed

97

exceptional interest in art history. Something unusual for a non-academic, particularly at the Drayburgh where it took second place to everything. I'd even say he was exceptional. We spent sometimes an hour discussing his essays, once or twice a whole afternoon. That's after he took up with Rebecca. No sign of resentment or lack of interest. He was totally absorbed, too much so, I thought, at times. It was me,' he suddenly went on, 'who recommended he apply to the Courtauld. Unfortunately, in his case, he thought theory took second place to painting. If he'd gone to Reading, or the Courtauld, things might well have turned out quite differently.'

The path ahead ran straight for a considerable distance, the flat, open space of mown grass stretching away on either side, to their right to the tree-enclosed eastern extension of the lake, to their left to the zoo on the park's furthest northern limit, the dog, sensing the homeward stretch, hanging back, running to and fro, as if anxious to delay their progress.

'In which case we mustn't expect too much from your connection with his wife.'

'I suppose not.'

'We *hope* not!' Viklund laughed, the short, sharp, 'Hah!', more exclamation than evidence of amusement. 'If all the women we had affairs with were subsequently killed by their husbands there wouldn't be many of the sex around. The place,' he waved his arm, 'would be littered with corpses.'

'Nevertheless,' Maddox said, but added nothing further.

'Liaisons with students,' Viklund said suddenly, 'were almost part of the job.'

'Did you take part?' Maddox said, surprised again by Viklund's coarseness.

'I could see the temptation.' He laughed again, the sound not unlike an attenuated cough, glancing back at the dog, not calling it, however, turning to the path again as if he, too, were reluctant to return to the house. 'With a younger man, of course, all the greater. Plus the Drayburgh, where exercising your temperament was mandatory, wouldn't you say?'

Glancing at Maddox, who had fallen silent, he added, 'What distinguished his essays?'

'Their subjectivity.' He paused. 'Their *air* of objectivity. Their enterprise. Sensibility. Enthusiasm. Vasari, as it were, all over again, including the misstatements. Yet, engagingly, writing, or seemingly so, about people he knew, almost, even, about pictures he had painted. Giotto he was extraordinary about. As if he had known him all his life, the artist illuminating the paintings, not, as in our case, the other way around. Fascinating stuff for someone from the Courtauld.' He pointed at his chest. 'Not history, of course. But absorbing. It felt a privilege at the time to have him as a student. He lit up for me much that had previously been obscure. Another window, illumination coming from a previously unconsidered source. In addition to which,' he paused again, wondering how he might express it, 'it was as if who he was writing about was more relevant than anything else in his life. In a way, of course, had he known it, his painting was theoretical, his theory unconscionably real. To that extent he'd already sacrificed himself to his art, when his salvation, had he known it, lay elsewhere.'

'Poor fellow.' Viklund shrugged, glancing away.

'Naturally, later, I set all this aside for fear of Charlotte getting to hear of it. Finally, however, I told her. It, and much else, much later, part of the reason for our break-up. *Her* break-up. I think I'd have gone on with the marriage if it had been left to me. A pretty damn silly thing to say. What I mean,' he faltered again, 'it was she who left though it was I who left the house.'

'She's happily remarried, however,' Viklund said, dismissingly, this subject, for several years, having rarely come up. At the time, to Viklund, he had reported the divorce as little more than a formality.

'She feels she's done the right thing. Is that happiness? I wonder. As for Taylor, he was a very involving student. I recognised some of my own aspirations, not in him, but in his facility. To some degree I rather envied him, yet, at the same time, out of guilt as much as admiration, wished the best for

99

him. I certainly *did* my best by him. He talked of painting, particularly Florentine painting, as if he were engaged in it himself, not reporting or interpreting it. Yet, despite that, perhaps even because of it, he lacked any kind of distinction in his own work. Rather like Pemberton, but without the flair. Looking back, rather than forward. Unlike his wife. Her touch of originality unmistakable. Only a touch, however. Nothing substantial.'

'Even then,' Viklund said, 'enough to turn him against her.'

'Evidently she gave up because of him. Seeing how her work undermined him. That, of course,' he went on, 'and the children. Most of the talented Drayburgh women gave up once they had children.'

'Probably applies no longer,' Viklund said, his tone still dismissive. 'Though it must have made it all the worse, in their case, a husband endeavouring unsuccessfully to do what his wife did with ease. And which, the worst rub of all, she abandons in his favour.'

They'd left the principal path and, aimlessly, it seemed, crossed the area of grass to the left, following the dog, which had run off in that direction. Walking on, they came to the top of the embankment looking on to the zoo, pausing to gaze over at the concrete terraces of the bear enclosure and, directly in front of them, the more recent structure of the elephant house. Two of the animals were being sprayed by an attendant with a hose, the view partly obscured by trees. Viklund, abstracted, seemingly distant, had paused to watch, the dog running to and fro at the foot of the embankment, searching the base of the zoo's railing.

'What Taylor was doing instinctively,' Maddox said, inclined, after some hesitation, to pursue the subject, 'I was doing by application, a curious image, if inverted, of his future relationship with his wife. Even then, at that stage, it warned me off. I'd rather modelled myself on your detachment. How did you describe it? *Hauteur*. All the while I was looking for signals that he knew me in ways more intimate than I knew him. That she'd told him, negatively, a great deal about me. She certainly *knew* a great deal about me. At different moments I must have told her everything. And then my final humiliation, of course, in running off. I think, even at that stage, she'd had visions of setting up as a professor's wife.'

'You're quite preoccupied by it,' Viklund said, again dismissively. He had taken Maddox's arm and turned him away from the zoo and once more along the top of the embankment in the direction of his house. 'Whereas I,' he suddenly added, 'am pointed a different way entirely.' He laughed, his arm more firmly in Maddox's. 'Get rid of the past. I've no inclination to recall it. I have no wish to remember. Only,' he went on, stressing the phrase, 'to *get rid*. Nothing,' he waved his free arm, 'that can be remembered can be retained. Yet, at the same time, the notion of cessation is unacceptable. I'd like to *be* remembered even if I have a wish *not* to remember. The same, I suspect, is true for you. The decline, amounting to the disappearance, of what we know as sensibility. The capacity to reflect, assimilate, conclude. A childish perception, for sure, but one which gives me no rest. I *resent* the cessation of awareness. Put it as simply as that. As if we've been put in a packet which, after a certain amount of time, has to be disposed of, contents and all. Why the contents? Surely they could, and should be preserved. Otherwise we're reduced to assuming that everything we've judged estimable in life has little or no validity at all. Childish, as I say, to wish to retain, but compulsive. If we are meant to die it's gratuitous to be sustained by a desire to live!'

So Viklund, Maddox reflected, had achieved neither resignation nor acceptance: his identification with the finest elements in his own life had rendered him incapable of letting them go. It was as if his friend and former mentor envied him the involuntary nature of his experience on the tube station platform – an event which, outside the family, had been reported (to Devonshire, Donaldson and others) as an 'accident', a misrepresentation he wasn't sure he'd got away with. Surely everyone, by now, knew precisely what had happened, suspicion emboldened into fact. Reminded of the incident – principally by the direction of Viklund's thoughts – he recalled, vividly, how compulsion to do one thing had been met by an

101

equally, if not more powerful inhibiting force: caught between two such conflicting elements, it was as if he were frozen – had been frozen – in mid-flight, flung forward and back at precisely the same moment, self-restraint, self-resistance, a death-in-life posture insecurely secured.

'All this, I assume, is old-fashioned.' Viklund was indicating the zoo – the chatter, the cries and screeches of animals and birds in the hidden enclosures – they passing its outer limits on their left. 'Fastening up animals a reflection, I assume, of what we do with ourselves, playing safe with something that shouldn't be confined. This appetite to contain and define amounts, does it not? to a recognition, unacknowledged, for the most part, that everything comes to an end, as plain an observation as remarking it must therefore have a beginning. From what, however? To what effect?'

It was the zoo, Maddox reflected, which absorbed both of them, the cries and screeches, the occasional movement of figures between the enclosures, even the smell, coming to them on the southerly breeze. Was it this spot to which Viklund had intended to proceed since their entering the park? Even the dog, he noticed, was subdued, its scurrying to and fro at an end, and was walking beside Viklund, its tail lowered, occasionally glancing up as if questioning, silently, the direction in which they were going. Was it this Viklund was intending to point out, the confinement of both their lives, his, Maddox's especially, in something of a self-constructed prison, the 'envelope' of the body one thing, the 'cage' of the mind another, the construct of circumstance a third? 'Beware where you go after your near death,' he might have been saying. 'Beware, too, where you go with Taylor. If art is to be – has been – abandoned take care what you put in its place: promiscuity, distraction, self-enquiry. None of these will be enough.' In which case, he reflected, what was Viklund suggesting? The animal and bird cries, which had appeared to bemuse his friend, were beginning to alarm Maddox himself. He was glad to respond to Viklund's suggestion they move on: the paroxysmal screeches paralleled, in a curious way, the wave-like consistency of his anxiety attacks (a recent feature of his illness). Here they were, reneging, to some extent, on Viklund's work, and, by inference, on his own – as casually, as rakishly, even, as his friend had set his trilby on his head, as if to defy his age and, even, his appeal to women: a dandy, a macaroon, not all that different from his uncle Joseph.

'Things we appreciate are, by definition, there to be discarded,' Viklund said, breaking into his thoughts. 'Discounting everything seemingly an irresistible urge at this age, not necessarily, of course, at yours. Getting rid of it *all*,' he swung his free arm again, his hand clutching the dog's leash, 'has a positive attraction, not least because everything that has gone before has deceived us as to its significance. There's something *intractable* in nature, it appears at first, only for us to discover there isn't. Extinction alone guaranteed. Everything in the process of dissolution. Quite right we don't acknowledge it at the time. Recognition at such a moment would require a response and, inevitably, should recognition have occurred, it would not be positive.'

'Or provoke us,' Maddox said, 'to appreciate the moment more.'

'Persuading us to cling on tightly!' Viklund laughed – a barking sound – the dog looking up, startled, as if it had suddenly been called. 'Take our house on Crown lease. I've assigned that to Ilse. Yesterday I realised my last will and testament was thirty years old, and the one before that I made at the end of the war. On my father's advice, he not, at the time, having long to live and I, I assumed, as one should at that age, destined to live for ever. Well, that episode, as you can see, is at an end. Which brings me back to yesterday. In a wholly nominal way, I'm broke, having handed over everything to her. If she wishes she could push me into the street. All I'd have left is Jefferson. And I can't be sure of him. He responds to me more than he does to her, though she's the original owner. It was her idea to get him,' glancing down at the dog, still reluctant, it seemed, to go in the direction they were proceeding, trotting by his side as if waiting a contrary instruction. 'I've had no corresponding desire to yours, to bring my life to an end, but, inevitably, at this stage, I foresee the possibility of doing so. Is inertia sufficient to hold one back? Should we exercise our option to pre-empt? Are we little, if nothing more than a neurological function, triggered and controlled by chemicals which, fortuitously or otherwise, may or may not be there? Are we merely a mutation which, by repetition, has acquired a "spetial" authenticity? An authenticity which, because of its novelty, we go on so much about? A difficult thing to let go. You'll know from your earlier interest in cars,' the barking sound a vibration passing now into Maddox's arm. 'It's the pre-emption I'm inclined to go on about. Its voluntary or involuntary nature. Is freewill another neurological function, aimless, artless, misleading, imprecise? These questions! You see why I had to get out of the house. To sit in there and think at all is becoming, for me, impossible. The room, particularly *that* room, and those paintings, with their inference – arrogance, even, in light of their quality – they'll live on even if, or when, we don't, are an imposition. After a certain age. *My* age, for instance. I've been, I've concluded, in that respect, imposed upon too long. Either they go or I do! Do you get that feeling? At a certain stage you start to say goodbye. No sooner introduced to life than we endeavour to secure it. No sooner secure than we're obliged to let go. It lives *us*. After that point I'm not at all sure what *we* are supposed to do.'

'A welcome challenge, in that case,' Maddox said, angling his arm to facilitate Viklund retaining his grip on it. 'After all, everything we do now we can be pretty damn sure is something we won't do again. I'm glad I came to see you. It's loosened everything up. Perhaps we have more in common than we thought.'

Perhaps, he reflected, Viklund was knowingly 'loosening' him up (characteristically, if obscurely, another favour). Alternately, too, came the thought that his friend might have wanted him, Maddox, to do his dying for him: to stand between him and death as art had stood in before – an art which no longer provided a defence, that short cut to life which, ironically, meant more than life itself: an ignominious entity known as

'Maddox', a representative – an active and (presently) ongoing representative of a process known as 'dying', life, the absence of, in motion: someone known to him, if not affectionately attached: someone he could count on, someone he could trust (someone who had had a foretaste of the very thing) – no longer, death, an advance into 'nothing', but into 'something' (associated profoundly with his friend): would Maddox do the trick, perform the exercise, before he, Viklund, was obliged to do it himself, life, with all its accoutrements (children included, in Maddox's case) voluntarily thrown aside?

All he was confronted with, so far, however, was a figure pitched irresolutely towards a tube train line, waiting – involuntarily or otherwise – to be saved, salvation as procurable, at that instant, as freedom would be for the animals and the birds should the walls of their enclosures fall down. He, Maddox, had stepped out (had been hurled) from his enclosure – into what? A misalliance with someone whose nature, whose motives, even, were growing increasingly elusive: the longer he observed them the more perplexing they became: life was there to be lived as opposed to a life that was there to be lost.

'Let's sit down.' They had come to a fountain marking the convergence of several footpaths, the paths themselves laid out, at their conjunction, in a curvilinear pattern, benches arranged asymmetrically on either side. The sun was out, the air, despite the southerly breeze, warm, if not warmer than when they had set out.

Viklund undid the buttons of his overcoat, freeing his figure, freeing his legs, the dog, reassured by the sudden lack of movement, taking its place beneath the bench. Some distance away, beyond the irregularly sited trees, the spires of the Danish Church were visible: conceivably, because of their proximity and visibility, Viklund had chosen this place to sit, a feeling, in the ease with which he reclined, that he had sat here on not innumerable occasions before. He had closed his eyes, his head, the remarkable boulder-like protrusion above the now loosened collar of his overcoat, thrown back, an aspiration, a specific

105

desire, Maddox suspected, passing through his companion's mind: the furrowing of the brows, the tightening of his mouth.

Conversely, he might have been in pain, their walking, previously, a distraction from it. Reluctant to disturb him, Maddox merely moved his position on the bench.

'I like it here,' Viklund added suddenly and, reverting to their previous conversation, went on, 'Like being requested, on pain of death, to solve a problem when the significant integers have been deliberately, we can only assume, withheld. Commissioned, on the one hand, prevented, on the other. The problem in a nut shell.' Opening his eyes, examining the scene before them down the length of his nose, he suddenly announced, 'To come to the point, after all this prevarication, I have two pills.' He paused. 'Of an anonymous colour. In a box where they have been for a very long time. If, for instance, my medical condition were to become irreversible, I could, within three or four minutes, taking either one, be gone from the scene. Similarly, Ilse, who doesn't presently know of their existence, if we took one each. I used, occasionally, when younger and their use appeared hypothetical, to take them out of the box and examine them. They even came with a putty-like substance, with which, in order to secrete them, you could attach them to the inside of the mouth. I got them during the war. From a fellow who had several. I assume they haven't lost their potency. The trouble is, I could only find out by using them. Not a good idea if they didn't work. On the other hand, assuming they do, they provide what, paradoxically, might be called a life-line. A lift from this life into something which, by inference, might be better. The older one gets, curiously, the less reason I feel I have had to use them. A comfort knowing they are there. But also a threat, even a challenge. Such tiny little things, and yet such power. A world of mystery, both what they do and how they do it. The proximity to something definitive and small, a convenience almost, promotes a peculiar feeling. Abstract, in one sense. And yet not quite.'

Having lowered his head, he glanced at Maddox who, half angled towards him while he spoke, had been examining his expression. 'Less messy than your method. At least, I assume so. The fellow who gave them to me said he had witnessed their use – he was in the Resistance – and they had been, without exception, effective. I recall him saying that, curiously, those who were most reluctant to use them were the ones who kept them on their person. Spontaneity, not knowing, less than seconds before, what will happen. Something similar, I discovered, in my case. Now, of course . . .' He glanced towards the church. 'Odd thing to talk about. Taylor, I suppose. Would you have imagined, as little as ten years ago, for instance, we'd be sitting here, discussing this? Decline for men, I'm told, as opposed to women, comes with a rush. Fair, one moment, something else the next. What do you think? Do you find all this intrusive?'

'Helpful,' Maddox said, yet didn't know why. Viklund, for some reason, was laying himself open to being examined, probed, a feeling that he no longer had anything to lose dominating his manner. On the other hand, he was also conscious of his friend looking to him to provide a suitable response to a question neither of them, as yet, had raised, as if each of them were circling the unmentioned subject, casting glances at it, at one another, but referring exclusively to other things, death, as a subject, a mere distraction.

'Art, taste, determined by a neural condition, the differences between us,' Viklund went on, 'so slight that, increasingly, as our resilience runs out, they become indistinguishable. The dilution of the species by repetition, to the point of irrelevance, if not excrescence.' He smiled. 'Is that,' he concluded, 'authoritarian?'

He was, however, no longer looking at Maddox: it was as if a fresh dimension to his life had been revealed, something concealed, previously, by erudition, by sophistry – by insight, even, one perception distracting another; as if, greedily, he were holding on to something which much in his nature, to his surprise, disinclined him to release, he, Maddox, something of a challenge, one which, at this point, at least, he was anxious to acknowledge. 'Even this, even this,' he appeared to be saying, art an exercise synonymous with confinement, reduction, removal; synonymous, that is, with displacement, even the highest, even the best: the superlative, the exemplary, the revelatory: all this, he appeared to be saying, had misled him (to its true intent), an entropic misadventure, an entropic exercise, decay – disintegration – displaced by something worse.

Maddox was tempted to shout: to get to his feet, to cup his hands to his mouth, to scream, as if a spirit of immeasurable proportions, having seized him, was about to be released. Yet, sitting there, all he was governed by, exclusively, was fear; an exclamatory impulse to ask for reassurance – wondering, in that instant, if he were indeed regressing; that, rather than moving on – the sensation of release – his medication, his treatment as a whole, even Simone, were progressing his decline.

Wondering, too, if Viklund's presence, his responses, weren't doing the same, a curious, vascular sensation, located in the upper half of his body yet governed by his brain, his sense, his sensibility, as if, once again, he were feeling the vibration of the descending then exploding bomb, the indifference of its flight, the indifference of its damage, reducing his sense of exclusivity to nothing, at the centre of everything (in the region of his heart) an otherwise indiscernible and inexpressible fear of which the waves of anxiety he was feeling were merely the slightest reflection.

And yet, he didn't wish to leave: he no longer knew what he wanted from Viklund, nor what Viklund, any longer, wanted from him, other than attendance (in itself, no mean demand), each exposing a wound to the other, a vulnerability neither knew, even at this late stage, how to cope with, either within themselves or in relation to each other.

Maybe, vis-à-vis the Danish Church, Viklund was moving back to an evaluation of himself (a continuing reference) which might well have come to him first in the Capella Scrovegni in Padua, the levering open of a door to something so serene, so implacable, so delicate, so robust and complete, that no other feeling, spiritual or otherwise, not even love for his wife, had ever surpassed it. It was, after all, the 'anoetic indifference' of death, as he had once described it, in reference to Giotto, that preoccupied him now – preoccupied him now to the exclusion of everything else, a soullessness which neither love nor constancy, nor faith, nor belief, could arrest or distract: nothing to note but disappearance, excision, darkness. Blank.

'Shall we walk?' After sitting for some time in silence, Viklund rose. As if waiting precisely for this signal, its own thought processes having arrived at the same conclusion, the dog rose, too, and Viklund, stooping, reminded of its presence, stroked its head, the first gesture of affection he had shown the animal since setting out.

'Back to the ranch,' he added, thrusting his arm in Maddox's again: whatever he had hoped to achieve by their walk had either been realised or abandoned.

'Indifference a difficult thing to grasp when difference, seemingly, is what it's all about. How to discard everything we might have saved. All we certainly treasured. Not greedily. Dispassionately. Lovingly. Much of which has been thrust on us. Urged on us, even, as a gesture of faith, constantly on the lookout for what has justified that faith in the first place,' Maddox, as Viklund spoke in this curious manner, awkwardly matching his stride to that of the other man, so that they walked at a pace scarcely brisker than a shuffle. 'Taking on board the injunction to live then obliged to pitch it back again. What do you think? A post-mortem on your case would suggest you had everything to live for. "No excision necessary", the verdict of the court.'

He thrust his arm deeper into the crook of Maddox's, squeezing his lower arm against his side, Maddox reminded again how thin and frail he was. It wasn't, he reflected, sympathy or understanding he wanted from Viklund but clarity of mind – from someone, he realised, whose own condition gave him cause for alarm: Viklund was grappling with something he, Maddox, had only glimpsed, a fear not so much of dying as of a closing-down of sensibility, of consciousness itself.

'Since everything is appropriate to its circumstances, if not, it ceases to exist, what is this appropriate to, I wonder?' Viklund

109

added, his gaze moving along the façade of the Nash terraces towards his house, its presence, at the moment, obscured by trees. 'Misery, confusion – confusion, certainly – terror, in your case, appear to be the appropriate reactions. To what? Everything round here? Is there something we've *missed* which drives us to these conclusions? If not, where does the incongruity lie? In Taylor? In the circumstances in which we live? Are both of you, to that extent, neural aberrations? Am I?'

Was this, then, what Viklund was requesting? Was he, at this stage, 'consistent with his circumstances'? Or was something significant missing? Maybe it was Taylor he had wished to talk about, pre-empting any reaction in Maddox which might have resulted from their meeting. Had they both, he and Viklund, gone beyond the 'appropriate': were they now on a descending scale – into the inappropriate – having previously convinced themselves – been assured by others, even – they were safely on a scale ascending? Were they being, in one of Simone's phrases, describing his current state of mind, 'plucked down' (the corollary, presumably, of being fucked up)? 'Nothing lasts for ever,' another of her paradigms, 'eternity, in that case,' she had concluded, 'out of the question.' Nothing, similarly, went on for good, 'Time,' in that case, too,' she'd further concluded, 'a moral attribute,' life appropriate to circumstance an ambivalence: the impulse to leap at the line united him with what was everlasting. Was he, in short, living his own conversion?

'Facing up to death amounts to facing down life, don't you think?' Viklund went on. 'Eradication of life, wouldn't you say, was our overall business? Only at this point does it become apparent,' gesturing at the park ahead, as if, oddly, to indicate himself. 'Consistency, now the veil is down, with what *in reality* is all around. Quite a conclusion. How are we to separate, now we've established this link between us, this supernormal connection?'

Was this the last he was to see of Viklund, his mentor, friend and colleague? Was this the preamble to his taking out his box and testing the efficacy of one of the pills (conceivably offering the other, to be taken then or later, to Ilse)? Or, like his absurd lunge at the line, would he only discover he was back in the circumstances, if not worse, in which he had started? Were the circumstances appropriate to his action, his action to its circumstances? Was affluence, of the sort Viklund enjoyed, not the antithesis but the progenitor of morbidity – poverty, ill-health, insecurity, like art, merely distractions (death visiting, in short, less destructively)? Was Viklund, like himself, locked into a logic which, once introduced, sustained its own momentum, one initiated, in their case, by their introduction to art – anterior time anteriorly extended: a momentum governed by a dynamic which, they were alarmed to discover, having been persuaded otherwise, came, in this instance, exclusively from themselves?

Detaching his arm from Maddox's as they reached the gate leading, across the road, to his house, Viklund called the dog and re-attached the leash to its collar, the animal seemingly reconciled to their return. It, too, Maddox reflected, might have been thinking: its bright eyes, its wagging tail, its demonstrations of affection, loyalty, gratitude, Viklund, too, suddenly energised, in a not dissimilar manner, his face flushed, looking up at the windows of the house with a startled, enquiring, engaged expression, as if seeing it for the first time: the tall windows at the side, fronting a strip of garden, the windows higher up – coming finally to those of his study, overlooking the park, on the top floor, a look of surprise which faded to one of disaffection: this I have acquired, this I dispose of.

Replacing his arm in Maddox's, as if whatever had passed between them was now permanently secured, the dog's leash in the other, they crossed the road.

'We must do this more often, weather permitting,' he said. 'Now we are both *free*. A companionable experience, much passing between us, even if, particularly when, we say nothing at all!' the barking, 'Hah!' then 'Hah!' again. 'I don't recall our having that before. I appreciate it. Immensely. Expediency on top of us, so to speak, decline, if not extinction, inextricably bound up, let us hope, with renewal. In decline, shall we say, we renew? Nature's law!'

He was smiling, the dog, associating a return to the house

111

perhaps with food, now tugging at the leash. 'A really jolly walk,' he said to Ilse who met them in the hall. 'Jefferson would have preferred it to have been more active. But then, we can't all have what we want, and even he is getting old. Another day, another walk,' he added, indicating the girl who had appeared from the kitchen below. 'Loreen can take him on the next one.'

'I should be getting back,' Maddox said to Ilse's invitation to stay to lunch. 'I've enjoyed the morning as much as Jefferson,' he added, with a laugh.

'But you must stay to lunch,' she said. 'Dan will be so disappointed at you leaving.'

'Don't pester him,' Viklund said. 'He'll come another day, I haven't a doubt,' returning with Maddox to the door where, shaking his hand, he added, 'Come any time. I'm almost invariably in. Give me a ring before you leave. Make sure I'm still alive,' winking, Ilse, her hands clenched together, smiling behind.

As he walked back along the front of the Nash terraces he endured the curious sensation that Viklund was walking beside him, even to the extent of feeling the pressure of his arm inside his own, the next moment talking aloud, 'Nothing is arrested, nothing is still, another of Simone's aphorisms,' adding, formally, a figure ahead turning at the sound of his voice, 'I await my execution with equanimity,' recalling Simone's enquiry when hearing this phrase, facetiously presented, 'Why do you call it execution?', he describing the image of a crowded room, inclined to recur not infrequently in his dreams, at the door of which, at irregular intervals, a figure appeared, beckoned, and led one of the occupants out, the numbers declining, one by one, until, finally, having been distracted by the antics around him, as, indeed, had everyone else, there was only himself, the empty door, the imminently expected figure, a feeling of helplessness conjoined with apprehension, heightening the terror which he associated with the imagined physical sensation of being consumed by fire.

This was the illness which brought him awake each morning, an anxiety, the source of which he identified in everything around – he, however, he reminded himself, descending Parkway at the time, the vehicles in the road going in the same direction, the houses converted on the ground floor into shops, their contents a scarcely acknowledged distraction, as if the accessibility of so much – restaurants, cafés, travel and house agents: sportswear, toys, pets, paintings, books – were a reminder of all he had to lose: an implacable extension of that repertoire of fear which appeared, misleadingly, to emanate from everything which passed across his field of vision.

A reminder, too, of all from which he was now detached, as if everything, even himself, all he had considered, tortuously, to be himself, were no longer his to dispose of; as if everything were being presented in order to be removed, the scale and intensity of this removal, an ever-quickening enterprise, the sole purpose of his senses to record, animate, quantify, respond to: recognise. 'Everything moves,' he reported once again, noting the sunlight now as a filtering beam flecked with dust flung up by the traffic, the deadening, indissoluble conjunction of scent and sound, 'a part and yet apart', he further noted, 'a singular subtraction', as if, having passed from the vicinity of the stuccoed royal terrace, he were once more back with that fragment of himself to which the 'him', divergent from the 'self', insensibly belonged.

4

THE TELEPHONE woke him: a rattle, first, inside his head, the sound bursting outwards, enveloping the room, the bed, the detritus of books and papers, the files and folders, even the dust, he noticed, floating upwards in the light from the window, he crossing to the landing and into the other room, the phone by the double bed. He must have simply got back from Viklund's, lain down and, peculiarly exhausted, fallen asleep.

'I wondered if our morning's conversation had disconcerted you,' Viklund said after his initial introduction.

'Not at all,' he said. 'It clarified any number of things.'

'Good.'

'Has it,' Maddox enquired, 'disconcerted you?'

'Not at all.' A cheery note at the repetition of the phrase, 'I felt heartened by it, as a matter of fact. *Heartened*,' he repeated. 'I was hoping that you might have had a similar reaction.'

'I have.'

'Good luck, of course, tomorrow. We might have spoken more of that,' Maddox confused, scarcely awake, before recalling Taylor.

'I'll let you know,' he said.

'I'll look forward to hearing, Matt. Ilse sends her love. She omitted to mention it on your leaving, she was so concerned you stayed to lunch.'

'Next time,' Maddox said.

Replacing the phone, he was about to leave the room, rising from the double bed on the edge of which he had been sitting, when it rang again. Assuming it to be Viklund he lifted it directly and enquired, 'Was that too abrupt? What did we forget?'

'Nothing,' Simone said. 'What a curious thing to ask.'

Confused for a second time, he said, 'I've been talking to Dan. I thought he was calling back. He's concerned, talking of death, his, he might have had what he'd describe as a negative effect.'

'Has he?'

'Not at all.'

'I, too, was ringing to see how you are.'

'I'm well,' he said, remaining standing. 'How did your day go?'

'My day is still going,' she said. 'I've just been talking to a client who has no one in the world, she says, to love. My immediate response might have been to say, "How about yourself? As good a place to start as any." Instead, my dear, I thought of you. I have someone to love so why do I suggest she take a grip on herself? Continually,' she added, 'I'm overstepping the mark. Ever since,' pausing for a response and getting none, 'I've taken up with you. I was hoping I'd find you at home. Merely to hear your voice. And here I am, making protestations which are singularly ill-received.'

'Not at all,' he said. 'You can ring me any time you like.'

'I shall.'

'I shall be waiting.' He sat down, once more, on the edge of the bed.

'How is your friend Viklund?'

'Braced,' he said. 'Preoccupied with dying. He was looking to me, I thought, for reassurance. Not that I provided any. He usually comes up with Lucretius, who allegedly committed suicide, when he talks of nature *and* dying. Today not a word. Nor of Plato's admonition against such speculation. Nor of Aurelius, who spent the whole of his life thinking of little else. Nor of Seneca, another of his favourites, who also killed himself.'

Why was he telling her this: was this his reaction to Viklund, buried beneath the rest?

115

'Why waste one's life prospecting its end?' he added, 'is usually his bottom line. Plato invariably his chosen text. Socrates' death . . .'

He waited, puzzled by his conversation.

'It sounds as if it's cheered you,' she said.

'On reflection,' he said, 'it has.'

'It's odd when, for no conceivable reason, I find I'm missing you. We were only together a few hours ago.'

'I'm in my recovery phase,' he said. 'Things, on the whole,' he went on, 'are looking up,' yet all he could think of at that moment was her. *She* was looking up. He was looking up to her, carried along by what he, too, was beginning to call her 'charge': that force which carried her – carried him, whenever he was with her – from one bountiful moment to the next: he was, he concluded, relying on it entirely.

'Doctor Death, as you call him, is my next client. I wonder if he'll turn up. Last week he didn't, but rang Mrs Beaumont to apologise and make an appointment for today. He's in a manic state. At least,' she paused. 'I think he is.'

Uncertainty was, he reflected, something new in her, specifically where her work was concerned: perhaps, he further reflected, it was why she was ringing.

'I always think I should be in the house whenever he's there,' he said.

'Oh, I'm perfectly safe,' she said. 'He's harmless. I haven't a doubt. That's been his problem. Though I shouldn't talk about it. At least, not now.'

'Why aren't you sure he's manic?' he said, his unease increasing.

'I have the curious feeling he's rehearsing his symptoms. Nothing unusual, of course, in that. On the other hand,' she paused, 'he's very convincing. It could be real. Yet at times I feel he's playing a game. I usually have Mrs Beaumont in when he's here. Today she wasn't available.'

'I'd better come up,' he said.

'Not at all.' She was instantly dismissive. 'I can handle these situations, Matt. After all, my dear, I've been doing it for years. I'd feel *defeated* if you should even think of it.'

'In that case,' he said, 'I think I shall.'

'Not at all,' she said again, fiercely. 'I'm quite capable of dealing with it on my own. I shouldn't have mentioned it. You know the prohibition I put on talking about my clients. Not always kept to, I know. But on this occasion I have to insist. You must allow me to make my own judgement.'

'Okay.' The bed creaked as he shifted his weight.

'Was it all death and dying with Viklund?' she said.

'We talked about Taylor. I haven't seen him for fifteen years, possibly more, and suddenly, out of the blue, I see him tomorrow. It was useful talking to Viklund. He used to come in and give lectures after his retirement, whenever I invited him, and Taylor made himself conspicuous by asking the most pertinent questions. And invariably querying the answers. Viklund was much taken up with him at the time. Whenever I invited him in, he'd say, "Will *genius* be there, who knows all the answers?" He became quite focused on him, and on the student who subsequently became Taylor's wife. He gave her a prize on one occasion when he came in to judge a Sketch Club. He was quite taken by her flair.'

'What's his view of Taylor now?' she said.

'Like mine,' he said, 'but more faded. I knew them both much better, of course.'

'Do you want to come up this evening?' she said.

'I'd like to,' he said. 'I'm feeling pretty alone down here. At least you have clients and/or patients coming in.'

'We can talk about that, too,' she said. 'I'll be finished by seven. There's something in the fridge. If I'm not up already I shouldn't be long.'

Returning to the rear room he sat in the chair beside the bed and contemplated the houses opposite: still half asleep, he reflected on the morning's conversations, glancing at the diminutive clock on the desk to discover, surprisingly, it was mid-afternoon: he must have been asleep longer than he'd thought.

He was, he recalled, constructing an agenda – a structure of some sort – conceivably to his life, one comprising elements which had, other than his possession of them, and the use to which they had been put, little, if anything, in common – recollecting, too, at that instant, a bench in the overgrown, bush-shrouded garden at St Albans, a bench his father had constructed towards the end of his life, assembled from miscellaneous pieces of wood which, aimlessly, or so it had seemed, he'd been collecting for some time. 'Something,' his father declared, 'I'd like to sit on. Something,' he'd gone on, mysteriously, 'I've always wanted to do.'

'But you can buy one,' his mother had protested. 'Buy two, or even three, if you want.'

'I'd like to make it,' his father insisted, until then having shown no interest in woodwork. 'Living tissue,' he'd remarked to Maddox on the one occasion he'd watched him at work, his shirtsleeves rolled, his jacket off (itself an unusual sight), hammering and sawing, Maddox's sole contribution being the suggestion his father use screws rather than nails. 'Otherwise,' he told him, 'at some point it will come apart.'

'This will do well enough,' his father had responded, complacently almost, despite his application, hammering, if anything, even harder.

In the end an asymmetrical, lop-sided structure stood against a sunny section of the wall at the rear of the house, a bench which, having sat on it once, he rarely, if ever, sat on again. After his death, a few months later, it stood against the wall in a half-collapsed condition, a testimony of some sort – to transience, Maddox suspected – a singularly transient gesture – which was finally broken up by a refuse collector, on his mother's insistence, and taken away.

Much of what he was endeavouring to assemble from elements of his own life, he concluded, was of the same disparate nature, obscure, confusing, resistant to identification. He was, furthermore, acquiring the characteristics of a hermit, reluctant to go out unless he was obliged to and, once out, immediately aware of his anxiety to return. A life, he reflected, without dynamic, other than the one provided by Simone, she, even then, a partial element – one, however, without which he wondered if he'd survive. Without the promise of her house, her flat, her work, her, on the whole, imperturbable nature, he doubted there was sufficient left of his own resources to sustain him until, during, and after what, even now, he conceived as the next, inevitable attack.

By what? A presence, he knew from previous experience, could seize him without warning and precipitate an event over which he assumed he would have little or no control; a presence which had separated itself from, or been expelled by, a power he associated with a detached, disassociative creative force – less a term, or a description, than a sensation, a fluctuating awareness of which came and went similarly without warning; one he could scarcely conjure up or sustain by mental application, a welcome diversion, nevertheless, from the malignant and oppressive one he associated with the 'other' – or, alternatively (demystifying its source), with 'himself', in this evaluation a self-divided entity where observer and observed were inseparably combined – each confounded by the other, each clamouring for release (each clamouring for expression), each immobilised by a desire, or so it seemed, for a separate existence.

He had long ago abandoned 'organisation': that system of beliefs, assumptions (conclusions, even) which afforded grace and peace and understanding – in his view, of a specious nature (something his brother Paul was, or had been, addicted to, having, in his late teens, 'gone into' the Church), a metaphysical attribution to what, in Maddox's own case, he was convinced was a pathological condition, a neurological exclamation, a conflagration – an abomination, as he'd finally come to know it, the preliminary ingredient of a final stage of terror and the sudden, irrepressible impulse to bring it, and everything with it, to an end: a diurnal arrangement intended to preserve a mental equilibrium balanced between terror on waking and what he recognised as 'normality' (peace of some sort) before he went to sleep each night.

119

There was, on the one hand, feeling, on the other the thing that felt: the thing that felt was at the mercy, or so it seemed, of the feeling it sensated, if not engendered, a tortured mutuality which functioned without intrusion from 'himself', the 'nature', the 'presence' of this experience the embodiment of something which extended itself, helplessly, into everything around.

He was, he reflected, in an indeterminate state – life, of one sort, was coming to an end, another, more obscure, more indefinable, more unpredictable, about to begin – he thinking, in the first instance, of his marriage, his children, the end of his 'career', in the second of what he had started and was seeking to sustain with Simone. The chimera, if it had been one, of art had been superseded by something he recognised as 'nature', urgency, not reflection, in this interim period, preoccupying him more and more. Otherwise, a cumbersome, unauthenticating process in which thoughts succeeded one another without any conclusions being drawn, or decisions being arrived at. He was taking on board a cargo without designation, he and Viklund, he had assumed, earlier that day, fingering each other's load with a view, conceivably, to lightening it or lightening their own. 'Salvation' had never been further from his mind: the liberation celebrated and expounded by others had extended itself so far it had disappeared: a sense of longing, of attachment, had only been appeased by the appearance of Simone. How much might he rely on that; how long would it last? With it came the remembrance of an attachment even more profound, the severance of which had been the precursor to so much he was feeling now, 'limbo', he reflected, a portent of worse to come.

Simone, to this extent, was a recapitulation of his past; at least, in those first encounters when he was scarcely aware of her as a person, merely as an agent, a facilitator, something, even, of a voyeur, looking on, gratuitously, at what, misleadingly, he was encouraged to expose – she an attraction, after this introduction, promising fulfilment of a familiar kind, an extension of much of what had gone on before – the 'melting-pot', he had told her, in which the viscosity produced by the process provided the material, the foundation, even, of what he was to become, a suitable opponent of what he had determined was, and had described as, the Demon King, the metamorphosis of something, presumably, hidden in his nature.

So Simone represented something to sustain, to encourage, there to reinforce, there to endorse his otherwise recalcitrant and despairing nature, Viklund's presence still uppermost in his thoughts, the evocation of a more sensitised, creative, revelatory figure in conflict with or transcending what he had hitherto considered to be his own, behind it all and, to some degree, formulated from it, an indifference which, on the tube station platform, had almost overwhelmed him.

All that, he reflected, despite the security of a house, together with a pension and someone to clarify what lay ahead – and what might have lain behind – he as unsure of her, however, as he was of himself, she an arbiter and dispenser of common sense, he of something peculiar only to himself: he dismayed by the vulnerability of a woman who meticulously 'made up' her face each morning, who chose and assessed her dress each night for the following day – asking his view of her final decision but rarely, if ever, changing it: a woman who attended to her hair, her skin, her clothes as conscientiously as she did to her appointments, lectures and meetings with friends.

And the time, too, she spent on her e-mail and faxes, more of the former than the latter, her messages on her answering machine, the formal way she stood to receive these communications, distanced from the screen in the first instance as she might be from a stranger encountered at the door, examining her faxes with the same detachment, listening to her phone messages with her gaze abstracted, distant, remote, as if summoning a voice from the end of a passage, her eyes downcast, the pencil, moments later, busy in her hand as she listed the calls in order of importance.

And he himself: where did he fit in, a silent attendant, insight suspended, bemused, by her inclusion of himself in something whose complexity, at first sight, precluded his participation? Detached, fragmented, on one side, cohesive and articulate, on the other: her detachment, his fragmentation; her cohesiveness, their joint articulation, the endless flow of her imagination into areas represented by other people, not paintings, artefacts, but flesh and blood – Doctor Death prominent amongst them.

His mind flowed back to the skeletal figure and the wisdom of being there or not: the consanguinity of her engagements realised by a coherent – in his experience, novel – perception of where she stood, an experience, mesmerically, in his case, shared with others.

All this, he reflected, and therapy, too, 'we are our relationships' a dictum she considered to be almost true, the dividing line between this absorption in lives other than her own – something, in this sense, of a self-reflecting mirror – and what, in isolation, alone at night, for instance, she experienced (she 'almost' experienced) as herself – a division neither she nor he could clearly distinguish, perception and cognition bewilderingly apart. A societal compulsion, on the one hand, an inclination – on his part, for instance – towards self-enclosure, on the other, he almost seeing it as a confrontation, compulsion-v-absorption, with the suspicion they might, in reality, be the same thing, nature consistent with circumstance.

So, he concluded, he was of her as she was of him, a conjunction of dissimilar natures, ironically, drawing them together – divergent yet complementary elements, if only they could see it, of the same thing.

It was his 'knowing' of his perception that drew him on, almost, in effect, a consistency with much if not all that had gone on before set aside, the *sum* and the *cogito* vividly apart. Division was, he conceded, inseparable from his nature, an ironic coloration of who or what he was; or, he further reflected, an attribute of what otherwise could only be described as an aberration, a chemo-neurological function inside his skull which appeared, in many respects, to have little if anything to do with 'him' at all: everyone experienced 'themselves' in a similar way: what, paradoxically, couldn't be considered as peculiar to himself sublimated by an awareness of others (her).

He was 'into' a suspended part of himself, something which, he suspected, he had held in abeyance throughout his life, function determining everything, an aimless submission to whatever came to hand, not least within himself – to the extent that he perceived an interior necessarily different from the exterior which contained it.

The telephone, at this point, rang again and, no more composed than when he had lifted the receiver to hear Viklund's enquiring voice, he lifted it once more to hear Devonshire say, 'I'm worried,' the sound echoing inside his head: no mention of a name identifying the caller, the presumption that Maddox would be preoccupied by no one else.

'I rather liked it,' Maddox said, assuming assumption his best defence.

'I'm not sure like, or dislike, come into it,' Devonshire said: a blond, close-cropped creature, he recalled, with a predilection for wearing round-lensed, wire-framed glasses tucked in behind comically recessive, almost absent ears: a moon-like face which, without the glasses, suggested the persona of a twelve-year-old child: a kindergartenic effect which the glasses, presumably, were meant to disguise: shirtsleeves, no tie, open-necked: a convivial, domestic personality, the new demos in action.

Maddox cleared his throat; having returned from the back bedroom to pick up the phone, wondering, not for the first time, why he didn't have an additional extension by the bed, he was breathless (a lack of strenuous exercise): anxiety thickened his voice, and intensified further at the presumptuous nature of the sound in his ear, someone young enough, he reflected – almost – to be his grandson: Devonshire, less than half his age, hadn't been born when he, Maddox, had been at what, euphemistically, he might have referred to – retrospectively – as the height of his career.

' "Let's face it, it's not painting, it's illustration." The collegiate chumminess apart, Freud happens to be recognised as one of the most outstanding representational painters of our time.'

An expansion at the end of the line of Devonshire's lungs: he daily cycled to work and played football, or was it cricket? with a journalists' eleven. 'His Christian name is spelt with an "a" not an "e".'

'Surely you mean given name,' Maddox said, flinging out the bait.

'Another thing,' Devonshire said. 'Everything, or almost everything, comes in as an e-mail, if not a fax, if not,' he went on, 'directly to setting. A typewritten sheet sent by post is a method of communication we have, apart from writs and injunctions, largely abandoned. I don't understand why you have to be different. There's surely a fax machine in Camden High Street, or Chalk Farm, or you could even get on a bus, or a bicycle, or the tube, and bring it down without undue inconvenience to yourself. You have, I take it, heard of the internet?'

A helicopter – he assumed a police helicopter – was circling overhead, the oscillation of its blades vibrating the glass in the windows. The sound drifted away and returned, several times, while Devonshire was speaking, Maddox sensing this was the prelude to a more pertinent enquiry, if not a declaration, and not inclined, as a consequence, to ask him to repeat what he'd missed.

' "The paintings might well be likened to strips of wallpaper expensively framed and gratuitously isolated against a white wall in order to insinuate their relevance." Hodgkin happens to be one of, if not the most highly considered of our lyrical abstractionists. If I'm not mistaken he has, or is about to be given, a knighthood.'

'There you are,' Maddox said. 'The whole system is corrupt.'

' "A scene-painter given to portentous effects. The closer you observe them, the more they fall apart." Thank God he's dead. Normally, Bacon is considered the greatest British, if not European, if not global post-war artist, as close to, if not the equal of Moore, as makes no difference. He also you have a word for. "Fibreglass monstrosities, as close to form without content as anyone might reasonably manage." I'm only relieved you've been kind to the maquettes.'

'And carvings.'

124

'And carvings.'

'And bronzes.'

'And bronzes.' Devonshire inhaled, lustily, the other end. 'You do realise this "Millennial Exhibition of British Art" would be the envy of any major gallery in the civilised world? I stress "civilised" for obvious reasons. The Metropolitan would give its eye-teeth for the loan of it, as would the Musée d'Art Moderne.'

'Or the Louvre.'

'Not the Louvre.'

He inhaled again; perhaps, recently, he'd had a cold – conceivably, still had it: his voice gurgled, as if asphyxiated, the throat obstructed. ' "Wall-coverings". Do you know how grateful the Tate were to receive those paintings? "Vacuity eclipsed". Rothko could have given them to any gallery in the world. Do you realise how pissed off, for instance, were the Metropolitan when he chose the Tate, at virtually no cost to themselves? They'll form a central, if not the central part of the Bank Tate's collection.' Checking the copy before him, he paused, his voice a lowered murmur.

The police helicopter chuntered once more overhead.

'Your dismissal of the whole of post-war American painting, as, indeed, the whole of American painting as "literary" and, what is it?' he murmured again before adding, ' "sentimental", "sound without content". I choose the phrases at random. "Noise without form". So it goes on. "Sloppy", God help us. You realise our proprietor has a unique and much-admired collection of post-war American art and if he doesn't take this as an attempt to lower its value and villify his taste I've no idea what conclusion he, and a lot of other people, will come to.'

He paused.

'And another thing.'

He paused again.

' "Much of his painting is dreary. Uniform tones, uniform brush strokes, repetitive colours. The product," you describe it, "of stigmatic vision, a medical not an aesthetic imperative. The whole of twentieth-century art reduced to an aberrant eye condition." This is Cézanne you're talking about.'

125

He liked Devonshire: he was an enthusiast (something which, as with Taylor, earlier, he'd always relished), enthusiasm, in Devonshire's case, indistinguishable from ambition, ambition, similarly, from opportunism, opportunism from predictability. He liked him, he reflected, because he didn't trust him; if he didn't trust someone he knew precisely where he was – in a 'real' world as opposed to one of his imagining. With people he could trust, like Simone, like Viklund, each in their separate ways, like his former wife, whom, despite her loyalty, he'd betrayed on several occasions, like his sons, whom he loved and didn't understand, he invariably felt at ease, unable to decide, because of their veracity, what precisely they were up to. He wondered – had wondered – to what degree this reflected adversely on himself, or whether it was a sense of reality – *his* sense of reality, a valuable if elusive property – which was so finely, so astutely tuned that it gave him an inadvertent advantage over everyone else.

' "Conceptual art," to which you say the British cognoscenti are inevitably addicted, "is an oxymoron, 'moron' the operative word." Apparently, if it's conceptual it can't be art, if it's art it can't be conceptual. As for heading the article, which may well be my job, "Neo-Philistinism in British Fin de Siècle Art", likening it to the facile illustrative traits in Victorian painting, "the end of a century seems to bring out the worst in us", it gives the feature a wholly negative ring. What standards are you referring to? Sienese? Florentine? Quattrocento? Cinquecento? The overall tone is regressive. Singularly so. Overwhelmingly so. I wondered if you'd like to amend it? It will have to be faxed in by the end of the day.'

'I'll leave it as it is,' he said.

'You think so?'

The helicopter chuntered once again, an exhausted and exhausting sound. Something Devonshire said was drowned by the roar of the engine and the percussion of the rotor blades: the glass in the window vibrated more severely.

'I'll have to ask Donaldson to review "British Art",' Devonshire said. 'At least he'll give a more balanced picture.'

126

'Balanced with what?' he enquired, his own voice lost, he assumed, in the overhead sound, for next he heard Devonshire remarking, 'I'm inclined, in his case, to think he can.'

'He likes to screw women artists, of course, and to get pissed with the male ones. Or is it the other way around? He'll write whatever they tell him.'

'At least he writes well. By well,' he said, 'I mean convincingly. Your postscript, for instance, on the desultory nature of British public sculpture doesn't resonate well, either. "An ossified honeycomb". Montgomery, in Whitehall. Viscount Slim caricatured as "an incorrigible wanker". "Field Marshal His Royal Highness, George, Duke of Cambridge mounted less on a horse than something extruding from his bowels". Then music, God help us. This in a piece on art. I have someone to write on music, who certainly wouldn't agree with your gratuitous aside. Mahler "unique in twentieth-century music, every note a false one, unless borrowed from someone else". I think a rest from your fortnightly pieces would do us both some good.'

'You're not inclined to print it?'

'Definitely not.'

'Am I fired?'

He waited for Devonshire to make up his mind, or, having made it up, to decide how he might care to express himself.

'We're not a public school notice-board. I like to think,' he went on, 'that our arts pages carry more weight than those of any paper. In fact, I'm pretty damn well sure they do. I'm not inclined to allow them, even out of loyalty, to be fucked up.' He paused. The helicopter, meanwhile, had retreated, like an insect, he reflected, having had its fill. 'Let's give it a break. Until Donaldson's away in the summer. You could well have recovered your resilience by then.'

'Resilience is not a requirement at this stage,' he said.

'Perhaps it's ageing,' Devonshire said, safe in the limitations of his youth and apparent good health.

Replacing the receiver, he lay on the double bed: here he and Simone slept whenever she stayed over, both of them, however, if sleeping together, inclined to spend the time at her place, 'civilisation' of a sort involved, 'civility' suggested, not least by the age of the building (eighteenth-century) and its immediate environment close to the summit of the Hampstead hill. There he could be 'different': there was history to commemorate, associations of a definitive nature to take into account, a past resonating with the present: Johnson, Southey, Wordsworth, Keats, Dickens: Marx, Freud – Moore, Hepworth, Mondrian: the list went on, concluding, finally, close to the crest of the hill, with Simone Leiter (her maiden name), an inheritor of a legacy which he, Matthew Maddox, marooned in the detritus at the foot of the hill, could only partake of as a visitor.

But she: he was confused (seduced) by her completely – she who had known Bowlby, Winnicott, Ivan Illych (briefly), Laing, Esterson, Cooper, whose current friendships (he had met quite a few of those involved, immobilising himself in the process: why had she chosen *him*, not them?) included luminaries from the Tavistock, where she'd trained, the Analytical Forum, the prestigious Cenacle Foundation for Psychoanalysis, where she did most of her lecturing; whose entrée into equivalent American, Swiss, Austrian and Italian centres of analytical propaganda had been commented on in the press; she who, from amongst her clients, acquaintances (relatives, even), colleagues and friends, had chosen a burnt-out case, a luminary (at one time) whose luminosity had expired a little while before – not only burnt out, he reflected, but teetering (once more) on the edge – whose powers of recovery were very much in question, whose regression (to what?) was, if not imminent, certain.

She, on the other hand, someone whose approach to him, over a series of appointments, he had seriously misjudged; who had herself been the initiating party; who had had three husbands – what faith in marriage! the remnant of a passing age – having learnt 'a great deal from each'. What, in the process, was she learning from him; what, disregarding a tutorial role, had he in his possession, by way of appearance, intellect or reputation – by way of destiny, even, or potential, at his age, of any sort – which would draw her in his direction, someone as enigmatically self-possessed, self-sufficient as Simone?

Each occasion he approached her house, even though he had a key, something she'd handed to him, he his to her, at the beginning of their relationship, it was with the expectation, entering the wood-panelled hall (Mrs Beaumont in the room on one side – a judge's former wife, someone not needing the income, merely the twice- or occasionally thrice-weekly distraction – Simone in the room on the other), that he could, quite easily, peremptorily, without warning, his usefulness expired, be dismissed – a challenging note to this effect left on the table in the hall or even with Mrs Beaumont, suggesting she had, as expected, changed her mind, with an afterthought, only, he might leave his key, a saucer or a small receptacle provided (she much given, he recalled, to collecting miniature, artfully constructed, ingeniously decorated wooden boxes (along with her prints), a relevance here though of what, as with everything else, he couldn't be sure).

This was his regressive state, referred to, bluntly, by Devonshire, the one, along with other manifestations of arrested development, that he brought with him whenever he mounted the indented stone steps from Heath Street to his beloved's abode (loft, refuge, sanctuary). Women, as a species, eluded him – increasingly so whenever he reflected on what had happened to his wife, she a woman alone, at the time, as she'd frequently pointed out, in a house of men, not hesitating, once three of them had gone, to start thinking of and for herself, coming to the conclusion that, other than their children, there was, bearing Maddox's infidelities, if invariably of a trivial nature, in mind, little if anything any longer to bind them together: a menopausal conclusion which had finally taken her, by tortuous routes, into the arms of the peripatetic Gerry, who had borne her along, had carried her along, as lightly as a breeze. 'Why not?' had been her response, salvation, of a sort, for her, if of an incredulous nature, something of the reverse for Maddox, the Mad Ox epithet restored as, bereft suddenly of wife and children, and a shared home, he spun around not quite knowing

129

where or who or why he was, nor what it was he intended, or had intended to do.

She, Charlotte, had, in the process, grown opaque, having previously been nothing but transparent – transparency, in his mind, associated with domesticity, their mutual absorption in it. Had their lives really been reduced to a preoccupation with food, clothing, accommodation, holidays, finance? had they really not noticed one another on either side of the marital bed, meeting in the middle in occasional, mannered, repetitive embraces, getting up each morning like a pair of mechanics totally aborbed in the outrageous demands of the machine they managed? A sense of wonderment at her advancement – a postgraduate degree in her middle fifties – coincided with the unmistakable signs of his own decline, an abyss of obscurity opening before him, one into which, if he wasn't mistaken, he had now descended (been hurled – lowered, certainly, without his permission) – so dark, so deep, so sudden its first appearance, associated with fears, the intensity and scale of which he could only liken to his childhood experience of sitting under an audibly descending bomb (which could descend no further, seemingly, other than into him), imagining, as he did so, the totality of extinction; a feeling, then, that he was lost for ever, that everything was lost for ever, that there was, no longer, anywhere to go – a feeling which, less than sixty years later, diverted, in the interval, by art – belief, fidelity, *something* – had returned and, in returning, dramatically, sensationally increased.

While he was descending into his self-designated pit, Charlotte was climbing – higher and higher: effortlessly, with, so it seemed, invisible wings: a female precocity, a female facility, a female felicity: a return to academe (a study of Sanskrit, yet another seminal source), and then, further released, ascending higher, energised by her elevation, her abandonment of him in favour of the twice-married Gerry ('three times for luck, Matt, what d'you think?' he at the announcement of their intention as he genially took over), who had, on his own confession, 'never read a book' since taking his engineering degree – though secretly addicted, Maddox had subsequently discovered, to children's stories: Richmal Crompton, W. E. Johns, Romany, several volumes of which Charlotte had found beneath his bed (before their marriage), confiding the discovery to Maddox as a source, but one of many, of his endearing, irresistible charm.

In no time at all, after their marriage, she was working in his office; shortly after that she had a department of her own, 'handling people', according to Gerry, her principal if hitherto unrecognised talent, 'although,' he'd gone on, 'she handled you and the kids in a commendable fashion: if we'd looked more closely we might have known,' sharing Gerry's peripatetic course, no sooner installed in one IT company than head-hunted for another, his unstressed, juvenile appeal the source, seemingly, of his entrepreneurial skill, 'first a curiosity, then a need' his self-proclaimed approach to exploiting what he referred to, phonetically, as 'ticknology'.

Plus: a dulled, postdated attempt to acknowledge Maddox's presence in his current wife's former life ('most men my age pick a bird twenty years younger: I picked an eagle, Matt, in full flight') by mentioning, at intervals, whenever they met, the art gallery he'd visited in Tel Aviv, Houston or Hong Kong, 'good old Charley!' his invariable identification of the source of what he called his 'late development': 'she's taught me a lot of new habits, and not only in bed. Know what's the first place I ask for when I hit a new town? The picture gallery. Hell, I've even bought one or two. You must come round, Matt, and tell me, tell *us*, what you think,' Maddox, so far, no subsequent invitation having arrived, spared this final, horrific humiliation. 'We've got to take care of the mentally ill. No stigma to me, I can tell you, at all. Hell, I've seen executives go down like ninepins in this shit-arsed world we live in. Know what I do? Take care of the fucking creeps. No one else gives a fuck. We only live once. Let's keep us alive!'

Wifeless, childless, careerless, 'good old Matt' listened to 'good old Gerry' extolling 'good old Charley's' progress through the ranks of the 'born again', wondering when, or if, his second birth might be forthcoming, something close to dementia, so far, the only sign of change – other, that is, than the arrival of Simone, the ultimately, to him, unknowable presence who dominated his life to the exclusion, virtually, of everything else. His wife – his former wife – luxuriated, meanwhile, in the provisions of her new existence: severely 'pruned' by the previous exigencies of domestic life, she was blossoming in her maturity: in *his* maturity: hadn't he, after all, done some of the pruning: wasn't he, over and beyond Gerry's acknowledgement, responsible for some of the late fruition? Plus, of course, the impression she and Gerry created of a couple who had been endearingly, successfully, unmorbidly married to one another throughout their adult lives, apophthegms, 'what's life for if not to be lived?' thrust magnanimously in Maddox's direction – in much the same fashion, he recalled, that Simone had been suggested as a 'suitable helper'.

He, Maddox, Mad Ox, Oxey, whatever appellation he went under, was 'finished' – 'completed', had come to the end of the track. It didn't need Devonshire, juvenility again, to remind him, nor Charley, to suggest, to the contrary, he was going through a 'potentially positive' phase. The finished article was before him now: his morning (flinching) gaze into the mirror revealed, after almost seventy years, the features of a stranger: the eyes that looked out were, from within, the eyes of his youth, the eyes that gazed back were those of a wizened creature: whose the terror, who the witness to an otherwise unnameable horror? whose the look of confusion, disbelief, incredulity: doubt? As Charley acquired increasing faith in her destiny, her former husband was, deservedly, it seemed, losing sight of his: behind everything, he concluded, a reservoir of fear, restrained by what he could only describe as a wall of distraction (art as serviceable in this respect as any). The wall, or part of it, in his case, had collapsed: all who failed to recognise 'life' as a distraction were forever on the point of being engulfed. He could feel the 'force' building up behind his back (towering above him, about to descend), resistant to examination, resistant to scrutiny, except at its own discretion: resistant, even, in his case, until recently, to acknowledgement. How could Simone, at

132

that point, step away and, instead of consultation, exploration, explanation, suggest an involvement which abandoned, if not precluded analysis in favour of demonstration? In the presence of a force he couldn't pretend to understand, except as a denial of life as he knew it, another reality was about to impose itself, greater if not infinitely greater than that perceived by the senses, a reality inclined to erupt – predisposed to erupt – out of 'nowhere', a mystical empire invoked tokenly by some, the majority of whom, as far as he was aware, were either insane or dead.

He was intrigued by small things (willingly distracted: a learner, in this field, anxious to begin): in the house, without his jacket, he invariably wore a track-suit top, a present from one of his sons, a reference to a sporting past, if only at school, and the inference he might take exercise. Occasionally he would find himself with one sleeve pulled up, the other down, always, he noticed, the left sleeve up, as if about to undertake a physical if not a menial task; yet, he reminded himself, he was right-handed: his left hand, he recalled, was the one more frequently in use in his love-making with Simone. Was this what, vocationally – unconsciously, empirically, even – he was now about: structuring his life to an activity which had preoccupied him in his youth, and which, if only with difficulty, absorbed him at present? Was this one further absurdity of old age, on the threshold of which he stood (lingering, understandably hesitant, reluctant to go in)?

He was still 'young': Simone frequently reminded him – encouraged him – not indisposed to discovering evidence of 'youthfulness' in herself. What, otherwise, was the purpose of her make-up, her choice of clothes, the 'difficult' problem she had, professionally, of 'what to do with her legs': short skirts, medium skirts, long skirts, or trousers? The drawn-up sleeve, as a consequence, troubled him, as did his recent habit of talking aloud, invariably, he assumed, to consolidate a thought, or feeling, reassuring himself that 'it' and 'he' were there, identifying his behaviour, however, as a further measure of decline: 'Thus, and no further: I must put a stop to this,' only to discover his self-admonition had been spoken aloud.

He thought he might ring Simone, less to speak to her directly (she'd be busy) but merely, if Mrs Beaumont weren't in for the day, to hear the sound of her recorded voice: its authority, its formality, its composure, its self-possession, a quality which, even now, rarely failed to ignite him. He could tell her he'd been fired, by a juvenile. Other than Devonshire and Donaldson knowing, he felt obliged to tell someone, dismissal, to this degree, brought under his own control: ignominy, defeat. On the other hand, no more contentious reviews, the contentiousness of which invariably continued in subsequent weeks' correspondence columns, Maddox's latest offering echoing down the pages, connecting him less with a world he understood than with something he was now consciously fleeing from. Why be 'real'? Hadn't he done enough to be something else entirely? Let it slip away. Let everything slip away. He was speaking aloud. 'I've moved on to, I *am* moving on to, other (higher) things – otherwise, uppermost in your (and Devonshire's) mind today the lining of a budgerigar's cage tomorrow.'

Yet what were these 'higher things'? Something responded to, presumably, through the senses, they themselves, however, comprising an increasingly moribund system, yet sufficiently alert to register its own decline: nature's analgesic, a step-by-step submission to extinction, relief achieved, ironically, by an awareness of the deterioration it was increasingly less able to observe. Here he was, not unlike an athlete turning up, in old age, for a race he might have run in his twenties (*did* run in his twenties, thirties, ever onwards), primed to expectancy, to achievement, confident of the outcome despite his rivals' youth: Devonshire, Donaldson, the latter someone he had taught, for God's sake (almost everything he knew), at the Drayburgh, ambitious (like Taylor) but (unlike Taylor) garrulous to the point of inanity, accommodating his lack of talent by transferring his garrulity to the printed page, he, Maddox, ironically, the first, if not the only one, to point him in this direction. Images of supersession in both an ascending and descending scale had dominated his mind since Devonshire's call. If he were to be tortured in this way had he acquired, or re-acquired, sufficient resilience to absorb the perversities involved?

A Roman sense of abnegation, devoid of religiosity, he couldn't subscribe to (it would have to come upon him, like everything else at present, unawares). Understanding which came from knowledge and, conversely, knowledge which came from understanding, had, presumably, passed him by. Ever since the incident on the tube station platform he had reverted to a view of reality governed by two diametrically opposing forces, one that presumably went on for ever, and that could be perceived as such in a transcendental form – first glimpsed in services experienced as a child and a youth, following his parents' instruction, in St Albans Cathedral and the Quinians school chapel, but most potently – overwhelmingly – in the Arena Chapel murals ('like witnessing a birth') a sensual, galvanic, protean force – and a corresponding protean presence implicit in the impulse, hitherto unregarded, to take his own life, its scenario writ large in a universe where species devoured species, galaxies galaxies, in an aimless appetite to survive.

Rhetoric had always been his strongest suit: a desire to dispel absurdity, invariably by abuse. He was, to this extent, making progress, if the field for opportunity had been suddenly reduced. Divesting himself of previous assumptions – assumptions which, on the whole, had stood him in good stead over the previous sixty-odd years – he was clearing the ground for further progress – presumably on the lines less proposed than insisted on by Simone. New formulations, if they were formulations, were falling into place on either side, a sense of purpose, chiefly, pointing in the one direction (up the hills – Haverstock, Rosslyn, Holly Bush) to her house. The indignity (the humiliation) of the geriatric support group, arguing each other into a less negative frame of mind, had, in itself, inclined him to assume that little by little he was ridding himself of earlier pretensions, earlier perceptions. Having fallen so far, in his own eyes, there was little if any scope to fall further: disencumbered of wife, family and job, he could set about – set in motion – his own revival. He could, to this extent, re-formulate his life, disencumber himself of structures – or have them disencumbered for him – which had supported him until now but which, post-tube train experience, could support him no longer. Bereft of his past there was no knowing what he might achieve.

With reviewing, he'd been on the point of pulling down the temple, the one place which was still, if tenuously, offering him shelter: first his near contemporaries, then those preceding, Cézanne's demise to be followed, presumably, by others: the parodic Picasso's, the decorative Braque's (Matisse and Chagall in a category he had, cautiously, set aside), anticipating, prognosticating that which would last, that which would not, in the same fashion as he was identifying the same within his own nature: what was Maddox now was not what Maddox had been a few weeks ago.

The exclusivity of declining powers, the inclusivity of those ascending: he had a picture devoid of illusions, something pristine, if not prestigious, a resolution to take little of anything for granted: a corresponding willingness to abandon everything – in favour of what?

He had to make clear: he had to define, even if, as yet, he couldn't identify, except for one thing, what he was moving towards: an absence of awareness was one thing, an awareness of the increasing absence of awareness another. Absolutes were beyond him, yet absolutes were what he had previously lived by: love, marriage, paternity, fidelity (not much progress with that), vocation – perceived, all of them, as ideals, anxiously subscribed to.

The anxiety remained, growing stronger, more insistent, that anxiety regressing into terror, terror, in turn, informing his determination (a fresh anxiety) to stay alive. The premium he had put – was putting – on his decline as a necessary precedent to his survival was growing clearer all the while; conversely, his pretensions to a personal life were growing increasingly obscure, his insistence on something outside, and beyond it, all the more marked. The vehicle which, recently, had carried him so far, via the day-hospital, the life-class, was, he concluded, in the process of being dismantled, if not abandoned, broken up, he determined to construct an alternative of his own.

Almost idly, he picked up from the floor the review of the British Millennium Exhibition which Devonshire had rejected and, retrieving a pen, a ball-point, from several scattered on the floor, began to amend the text: Freud's predilection for rendering human flesh as butcher's meat a necessary re-assertion of a Berliner tradition (Bosch, Grünewald, Dürer, Grosz, Auerbach), a redressing of an otherwise British aversion to rendering flesh as anything other than an agreeable transposition of the reflexive angle of the picture plane, Bacon's a not disconnected insistence, Celticly acquired, on the perversity of flesh being flesh at all. The knighted Hodgkin's infectious appetite for colour as much as form – transference of sunlight into a chromatic purity – a Sufistic transposition, sensually extended, resonant of the tiled domes and arches of Isfahan.

As for Moore's Carrara marbles, what more could he say about the nature of stone and its mesmeric identification with the human spirit, a resonance echoing back, as far as he could tell, to the beginning of life itself? Plus, Cézanne's visionary elevation of paint in his final, unfinished pictures to the plasticity not to be rediscovered until half a century later in the textural evocations of American expressionism.

Not convincing, but there it was: thinking, to this degree, had come to a halt, something almost consciously brought about, as if, unbeknown to him, he had been slipping free of everything, nothing left amongst his mental acquisitions but Simone; as if the very act of leaving go had ensured his taking hold of her – a tug, as it were, to tow him back to the ocean. Once free, he surmised, he would float on his own, drawn, once again, into reflecting on the significance of this perplexing woman who, in her own way, if not as comprehensively as himself, was leaving go of something: professional propriety, perhaps – something, he concluded, as simple and, presumably, as damaging as that – moments later lying back on the bed, the amended sheet falling to the floor, the pen still in his hand, the police helicopter, once more, returning, chuntering overhead, conscious only of the approach of that which he had, he concluded, desired the most, next to the embrace of Simone: oblivion.

5

It was as if, in sleep, particularly during the day, he was subjecting everything to clarification, subsequently recalling the contents of his dreams in the hope that something so subjectively arrived at would point him more decisively in the direction he was going (death alone on the skyline). Certainly, on waking, he looked for amendments, if not radical changes to everything which he had been disagreeably aware of, afflicted by, before he had fallen asleep. No such clarity, however, had emerged. More firmly in place than ever, his uncertainties and doubts engaged one another in an increasingly familiar manner. Yet somewhere, somehow, resolution (revelation, even) would arrive, he waking, on this occasion, from his afternoon sleep – no lunch having been taken, a Marks & Spencer prepared food item in his microwave oven (another 'gift' from Charlotte and Gerry, intended, as the others, to do him an unspecified 'good') – aware that the change, or the 'charge', he'd been warned to look out for was still some distance off. Temperament inclined him to expect its arrival at any moment, its speed of approach, unfortunately, as unpredictable as the change or 'charge' itself – this curious conjunction of imminence and discomposure, of expectancy and inertia, sufficient, finally, to get him out of the house.

He resumed his walk of barely a few hours before, turning northwards, however, instead of south and, proceeding, past Chalk Farm, up Haverstock Hill, emerging, as if from a polluted lake, into the fresher air before the less steep ascent to Belsize Park, the restaurant tables partially occupied on the forecourts either side, the level interval beyond leading to the climb of Rosslyn Hill.

A reminder now, in his heart, his lungs, in his knees, his hips, he was getting older, entering the area of boutiques, cafés and restaurants of the High Street until, beyond the tube station, stooped, bent almost double, he set off up the worn stone steps which, rising fifty or sixty feet above his head, took him finally to Simone's door.

Her voice was audible as he entered the hall and, assuming from her tone, its evenness and persistence, she was dictating a letter for Mrs Beaumont, he went upstairs to the kitchen.

Aware of his approach, the cat was already waiting, stretching its hind legs, extending its claws, crossing to the fridge, in front of the door of which it sulkily paraded.

Removing an already opened tin, Maddox measured a spoonful into the bowl by the sink, dropped in several pellets from a container kept beneath the sink, and re-examined the interior of the fridge for what he and Simone might eat.

At moments like this he was aware again of how much he welcomed distractions, however slight, his attention drawn to anything of a familiar nature, preferably undemanding: walking to the house, for instance, the evening rush-hour underway on the tube underneath, the road convoyed with northbound traffic, feeding the cat, examining the possibility of preparing a meal from the contents of the fridge – which, on this occasion, he hadn't supplemented or refurbished – even hoping, in this instant, that Simone would be further delayed (voices on the answering machine, heard every few minutes) so that he could enjoy the indulgence of being in her house alone. Here he was released from those preoccupations which came spontaneously to mind when he was at home, reflecting, on this occasion, in hers, on the propriety of writing (e-mailing or faxing, using Simone's machines) to Donaldson as his former tutor and more recent colleague: 'someone has to throw discretion to the wind. With little left to lose it might as well be me . . .

'. . . as a child brought up during the Second World War my elucidation of what, at the time, was referred to as post-war art is probably more tendentious (more generous, more open-minded) than yours. This drift into trivialisation . . .'

had dominated his consciousness for a considerable number of years, no Third World War having occurred to distract it

'. . . to the point that trivialisation has acquired a dynamic of its own. This transposition of everything into accessibility. Devonshire, by the way, has put me out to grass. I got my head knocked off, as you were probably aware, a year ago – shortly before my recent illness – by suggesting that women, as a whole, had trivialised art and literature throughout the century, this in itself part of an overall process . . .

'. . . a doomsday text which adequately ensured I'd never work – at least, in the field of commentary – again.'

He paused, reminded he'd intended writing to Devonshire to amend (reverse) his previous assessment (flexibility, resilience, adaptability, subservience to the fore), not to his loquacious, prematurely balding former pupil: eyes like marbles, glistening – a peculiar phenomenon – in the dark, due, allegedly, to a congenital eye condition, if not, in Donaldson's own account, a visionary conceit.

Skin like marble, luminescent, too, in certain lights, flecked with acne, a languid, languorous, skeletal figure, suited in blue corduroy as a student, affecting a cravat and a loosely displayed top pocket handkerchief, a conspicuous oddity in a world characterised exclusively at that time by denim, perpetually on the move from one student bar to another, his inimitable nasal drawl now frequently heard on radio and late-night television (occasionally, recently, on news items), someone convinced of his destiny, of one sort or another, from the age of eighteen, his first appearance at the Drayburgh, his paintings – 'expressionist' – suggesting a sensibility, modishly perceived, struggling into existence – to deteriorate, finally, with indecision, into the chaos from which they had presumably emerged, his immoderate commentary on his efforts transposed effortlessly, vocationally, almost, certainly with relief, to the work of others, entertainment ('enchantment') taking over, 'the singing stamen', Pemberton

141

had once described him (his last retrospective having been neglected in Donaldson's column).

No wonder Devonshire, who hadn't witnessed this transformation of slug to butterfly, of weed to orchid, had signed him up at once, an 'intermediary' (as he saw himself) of the same generation, 'conceptualism' (intellect, reason, accessibility) in common, an antagonist of Maddox's New Philistine Agenda, its progenitor ploughing an increasingly solitary furrow (Taylor, a rural heritage behind him, might, in his own time, have been a suitable recruit).

'On the other hand, although we differ on the cyclical nature of creativity, art one moment moving precociously ahead of public perception, the next judiciously behind, the latter phase currently in operation, the regressive element involved is, in my view, full of potential. Namely, in deciphering in the downward surge those elements which may well comprise the next inevitable upward drive. "Progress" has a perverse, self-generating momentum (its only credential), something, as you once gratuitously suggested, "springing from the heart" – in this case, of course, of Judas, worn conspicuously on the sleeve, along with everything else (so many badges! so many designations!). More sobering times, however, I am predicting ahead, not annihilation, exactly, but something appropriate, let's say, to the fate of Ozymandias, the decay of an empire endowed with everything destined, at one time, seemingly, to last for ever. In my view . . .'

In his view?

But then, he hadn't a view: who, in any case, was listening? He was running out of steam. Devonshire's intrusive telephone call had, once again (unwelcome, this time), distracted him. Here was a mind full of Ruths, Annas, Ailsas, Judiths – Alexes and others: the debris of a 'cultural exercise', the like of which had never previously been recorded, bringing him to the daily reality of a life bereft of common sense – and here was art, in its most meretricious and, he now realised, resented form, once again imposing itself. He had, he'd concluded, taken on 'humility' in order to redress a situation in which something like the opposite had operated for the previous sixty-odd years. He had looked to the exalted companionship of the saints in the past, those quattro- and cinquecento giants, Giotto, Donatello, Masaccio, della Francesca, together with their heirs: now, however, he was looking to the companionship of his crazed and largely suicidal fellow sufferers. 'Something's eating out my brain,' he had confessed to Charlotte at the onset of his illness, she, post-illness, offering him Simone to mark, as she described it, his 'recuperative phase'. Continuity, of a sort, he reflected – one which, with hindsight, might develop into something more significant than that, but, he'd confided to Charlotte, this 'eating out' was as tangible as a caterpillar eating a cabbage, its daily consumption removing the possibility of any further source of sustenance ('my brain's disappearing'), day by day, more glaringly, night by night, removing the certainty which came, he'd always assumed, with experience . . .

'. . . judgement increaseth as talent decays an axiom – not Simone's – that scarcely needs confirming . . .'

yet here he was, day by day, almost hour by hour, proposing, if not confirming, something significantly different.

Wasn't this why he resented Devonshire's intrusion? Didn't Donaldson signal an ascendancy he no longer recognised or cared about, the vestigial spasms of a hack still in his system but, like everything else, being gradually, through exhaustion, sifted out?

And there was Simone, a woman he scarcely knew or recognised, coming into the kitchen where, absently, distracted, he'd laid out the cartons to be processed in due order in the microwave (what other devices, he wondered, had she hidden about the house?), he looking up at her lovely face, fatigue lending it sensual charm, taking her face between his hands as if, without this reassurance, it might disappear, securing his lips on hers, aware that she, at some point – conceivably on her way up – had refreshed her make-up, the brown-irised eyes framed beneath the dark-lashed lids, the lids lowered as, out of focus, their faces blended into one another, as if, he reflected, she and he were one.

143

There was something here he would have to construct: the enigma of his death-in-life predicament, the unforeseen attempt to kill himself: wipe the page or the canvas clean, the opportunity here, at least, to start again, to create, compose – to bring her, for instance, steelily alive, page after page, picture after picture, as if she, after her corresponding number of years, was only now becoming recognisable, something mercurial (he'd recognised before: her varied moods, inquisitor, one day, enthraller, the next), something transitional, confining itself to one form, only to precede its re-formation as something else.

His own powers, he further reflected, were consistent with this, recalling sitting beside her in the dark, ensconced in the armchair comfort of a cinema in Belsize Park, turning to gaze at her (the mesmerised look of everyone around, focused on the screen), awareness fluctuating in response to a beam of light, emerging later into the machine-driven street: the fumes, the traffic, an oppressive awareness of too many people, proliferating, or so it seemed, before their eyes, a 'spetial' enterprise, a genetic conundrum, an outrageous extrapolation of 'a reason to live', the highest form, he concluded, of animal life canvassing extinction by means of a machine of its own device.

'It's ready when you are.' He indicated the row of boxes, adding, 'Expediency,' the telephone ringing, she depositing a file on the kitchen table, declaring, 'Give me a minute. I must take a call,' disengaging from his hold, his hands having drifted down to enclose her back, her waist, her hips, her voice, moments later, coming from the sitting-room. He feeding in the boxes, one by one, the pinging of the machine as each one was finished: his laying-out the food and taking it to the table by the window which, with foresight, earlier in the day, she'd prepared: plates, glasses, cutlery, napkins. A glass vase containing flowers, taken that morning from her roof, occupied the centre of the table: beyond that, the window looked out to the studio window opposite, invariably dark, its inner surface strewn with climbing plants.

And she: poised on one foot, one knee resting on a chair: the shape of her calf, her hips, her waist, her breasts delineated

144

within the folds of an almost formal, anonymous black dress which she occasionally wore for clients of 'distinction'. Who today?

Her voice animated, she laughing, evidently female the other end: an arrangement to meet in town one evening.

One less for him, he ungenerously reflected.

A bird (Gerry came censoriously to mind): as elegant as a heron: one leg, a body devoid of post-menopausal flesh, a demonstration of something which her early life – photographs she'd shown him of an urchin-like creature with a more than androgynous look – had scarcely suggested, if not actively denied. Out of that uncertain, unfocused, if not neutered child – dark-haired, dark-eyed, soulful – had emerged this elegant, assertive, straight-backed, celebratory figure, with its unconsciously requesting if not solicitous look – which suggested (insisted) you should tell it all: everything! *everything!* a receptor, a provider, a provisioner of goodwill, a wholly charitable intention contained in that unchangeable, delicately proportioned head.

In regarding her as he set out the food he was aware of what an incredible choice both of them had made.

On more than one occasion she had remarked that she worked from 'instinct' not 'theory, or even common sense': something, for reasons of which he wasn't totally aware, that had not characterised her previous choice of husbands, men who, in their separate photographs, looked curiously alike, balding, each one, at the front of the head (one wearing a moustache, which, she confessed, she hadn't 'liked, though it played no part in our separation'): knowledgeable if not vulnerable eyes (perhaps, he reflected, they had that in common), assertive, determined, thin-lipped mouths, a suggestion they saw her as only one stage in their own advancement: prominent (dominant) noses ('men *of* the world, not apart from it,' she'd observed, he wondering if, in this respect, she were making him an exception). Not brothers, exactly, he'd remarked to himself, but an affinity of a sort, identifying their natural habitat as that of the schoolroom, conceivably a church: priests

145

of an uncommon denomination, she either the object or the subject of their faith.

Markers, she saw them, for her part, of the progress of her emancipation, she affectionately viewing the three of them, in retrospect, as instructors, appropriate, each of them, to each stage of her development, the first persuading her in the direction of medicine, finally analysis (a further need implied of enlightenment of a disingenuous, if not seductive nature, esoteric, mythic, unnervingly secure).

Her study, overhead, adjacent to her bedroom, was lined with books which, other than her, at one time, omnivorous appetite for reading, had no recognisable theme in common. 'I intended to be a biologist,' she'd once explained, 'but gave it up for people, mind more interesting, in that respect, than matter,' going on to announce, 'I always felt I was born for a life different to the one I lived and could only approach it in stages. Hence the marriages, I guess,' concluding, 'Even now, when I'm convinced I've arrived at where I intended to be, I have a strong feeling I should be somewhere else,' looking at him intently, he, at the ferocity of the look, glancing reflectively away.

Now he merely admired the curve of her leg, the sturdiness of its support belying the slimness of the ankle, the tantalising line where the calf disappeared beneath the hem of the dress, the sway of her body as she responded to something reported at the other end, the half-twist of her waist as, still speaking, she turned to smile at him, indicating she would soon be finished, the dying finality of her voice, chilling in its severity, as she disengaged from her caller.

Moments later she was sitting at the table, the image of expectancy as, childlike, she waited to be served.

Having told her of his sacking (dismissal or suspension) by Devonshire – largely to pre-empt what, on other occasions, he welcomed and encouraged, her edited account of her day in the consulting-room below – she immediately responded, 'It'll leave you free,' a curious reaction: he felt free, if not too free, already, 'to do what you want. Look at the way you sweated over your

146

article the last few times,' to the point, she might have said, where syntactical errors crept glaringly in, he blind to most of them until, showing her the copy (a rare occurrence: he seldom took her to the galleries either, anxious to preserve the singularity of his view), she blithely, at times incredulously, pointed them out: a sure sign, she'd concluded, of the artificiality of his position (one he'd used as an indicator of his returning health). 'Isn't it prostitution to have a historian resorting to these tricks?'

'Tricks?'

'Conceits. A requirement to write something which, if informative, is there to entertain. Not normally something you'd go in for.'

He'd waited, surprised, if not distressed by her response.

'After all, you were taken on by his predecessor, who'd been there long before you, who was as old as you and who shared many of your sentiments.'

'They're not sentiments,' he responded.

'Weren't you driven into opposition by a need to come up with something?'

'No.'

'You're not, after all,' she went on, 'his generation. He had to get rid of you sometime.'

He watched her arrange her food in separate piles: an unconscious exercise, signalling what?

'However much you dislike it,' she said, having waited for his further response, 'Devonshire was bound to fire you in the end. The reviews had got so negative. Okay for you. You thought what you were reviewing was negative, too. More than negative, cynical, gratuitous. Fine. But not for him. He won't change his perceptions any more than he can change his age. However ephemeral, without something positive he can't, presumably, sell his paper. That, we can assume, is supposed to be his job.'

'It's not his paper. Even if he likes to think so,' he said.

Again she reassembled her food: the delicate fingers, the delicate hands, the knife and fork manoeuvred like surgeons' instruments, probing, exploring: opening up.

147

'Who cares if culture goes one way and you go another? Your integrity is intact without having to advertise it every other week.'

'Like Donaldson.'

'A performer. An entertainer,' she said. 'You're not.'

It – life, everything: she – could go on without him; that, after all, was what filled him with despair, pain not so much at inertia, or even profusion, but irrelevance. True for everyone, he reflected, so why should he be different? Irrelevance had its own agenda, fortuity a doctrine much exercised in his youth (the world an oyster: seize your chance). Alternately, he didn't wish to diminish what had, at the time, appeared as a miracle, watching Charlie emerge from between Charlotte's legs, an experience he'd never subsequently come to terms with, a mystery which neither time nor later births had in any way reduced.

'You're right,' he said, dismissing it. 'That and Viklund in one day. I'm not altogether sure what *he* was after, either. Everyone I know appears keen I abandon everything. Or, at least, are anxious to discourage me.'

'That's not true, either,' she said. 'You mustn't take one setback as final,' she added.

Resourcefulness, he reflected, was her principal tool: she wasn't a fool: the presumption inferred must be he was. 'Wife, children, job,' he said. 'All I've got left is you.'

'That's not true, either,' she said again.

The food reassembled on her plate: the delicate disposition, he assumed, of her thoughts and feelings: voiced and unvoiced thoughts blended seamlessly, he unsure, in his own case, which was which. Had he told her about Donaldson or not?

'You can still write. Devonshire's proscription, or, indeed, anyone else's, needn't stop you. You could put it, for instance, into a book.'

Her food having been sorted to her satisfaction, she began to eat, thoughtfully, her mind, he concluded, on other things.

There was, he reflected, something tenuous in their relationship, not least the hold he'd imagined he'd had on it. Confident of his own reactions, he was, nevertheless, persuaded by her views not to deny so much as to amend them, something, with Charlotte, he'd rarely done. The inference was that she knew more and better, something, in his present state, he was inclined to go along with (the superstition surrounding psychoanalytical theory giving her an indisputable edge), he persuaded, if not seduced by her accounts not only of others' feelings but, more seductively still, of her own: her need for a constant commentary on what was, or was not – the two mellifluously divided for examination – going on. 'I like your smile,' she'd told him on one occasion. 'I've never seen anyone smile so *thoughtfully*. There's a great deal behind it, not merely melancholy, that intrigues me. As if you're inviting me into a space you're anxious, for my sake, I might fill. I feel I'm being hauled in,' she'd expanded, 'at the end of a line. I know it's going on, but, as you see, I'm not inclined to call a halt,' smiling to confuse him.

He felt, in any case, disinclined to talk: he wanted time to think (an inclination to withdraw, not necessarily of a pathological origin), such conclusions he might come to, not to be separated – impossible to separate – from his being with her. With her beside him – more nearly, with her holding his hand, or holding him elsewhere, he felt free to think, or do, anything, a childlike imperative he was more than reluctant to oppose: hedonism, if of a depleted nature, dominated every aspiration.

'Now you have an opportunity,' she suddenly intruded, 'to clear the ground, move on, see what might come up when everything you've previously been familiar with has been discounted.'

'Therapy,' he said, 'in another form. Down here,' he added, indicating the table, 'and up there,' indicating the ceiling, its inference of her bedroom.

'Where therapy ends is clearly defined,' she said, briskly. 'On the other hand, you could say we're constantly renegotiating where the boundaries might be . . .'

He heard her continue, or thought he did, his own reflections distracted, as they had been increasingly over the previous weeks by the studio window opposite. It represented, he concluded, something of his own condition, the function of the window to admit indirect light – for clarification, examination, expression – encumbered on the inside, its purpose thwarted, by vegetation, specifically climbing plants, placed there, deliberately, he assumed, along its lower edge.

The relevance he was attaching to the window echoed a state of mind he associated with himself: the problems he was confronting were ones which, by definition, warranted no solution: relevance, as opposed to indifference, was one, the evidence of the soul, as distinct from the spirit, another; the purpose of his suffering, a third; the requirement (logical, feasible, extremely practical) to do away with himself an immediate and compelling fourth. He had instinctively (without thought) given himself another chance, stymied by his failure to recognise what 'him' and 'self', combined, might, in the best of all possible worlds, add up to (the inference of self-division), otherwise disassociated partners contentiously opposed within a single frame. He was, he realised, looking to her to identify, if not what he was, what he was becoming, an ongoing process, he assumed, which had no end. All he came up with, however, was her charismatic, impenetrable, mysterious gaze, like the light reflected from a pool, obscuring rather than revealing.

Absit omen.

Was this the source of her fascination, not her appearance nor her manner, though they were seductive enough, but the fact that he had invested in her the means of deciphering what he could no longer decipher for himself? asking her, in effect, to gaze in through the window, ignore, if not remove the encumbrance – the self-propagating accumulation of a lifetime of neglect – and describe to him (God help him) what she saw.

Such an analysis, if true, was unacceptable: he had his own resources (DV): it was up to him, the allegorical significance of the window opposite a distraction. No good looking to someone else to reverse a process, much of which, spontaneously or otherwise, he'd conjured up himself, not even her: addle-brained Maddox, aka Mad Ox, who had endeavoured to re-shape the sensibility of his time, disfiguring his own in the process – he now venturing to discover where the source of such an authority, if not within himself, might be, its voice, its imperative, still echoing in his brain: *'all you have done, all you represent, all you think you are, is fit only to be discarded.'*

A sensibility founded on his earliest experience of a motor-car, isolating its beauty from its function (an instinctive exercise), returning the machine, therein, to its rightful owners, his father, his uncle, in whose recalled appearance, the latter, he recognised a foreshadowing, curiously, of both Donaldson and Viklund.

They were sitting by the fire, the meal finished, watching the news, his arm around her, he focused not on the screen but the sheen of her stocking where it protruded from the hem of her skirt, such aesthetico-sexual sensations, associated with their relationship, something, too, he had failed to analyse, an excitation which never failed to distract him: the curve of her breast beneath the buttoned front of her dress, the shape of her hand as it enclosed his own, the two resting on his trousered knee: a conjunction of desire and reflectiveness which he had come to identify as the dominant feature of their relationship. Meanwhile, spectacularly before them, aircraft bombed, buildings (people, too, presumably) disappeared, explosions illuminated the night sky above a silhouetted city: skeletal figures passed silently before them. Finally, a dog was rescued from a hole (a reckless pursuit of a rabbit).

Transitory events foreshadowing a transitory future.

Later, in bed, he watched the moon through the muslin drape on her window, a three-quarter shape illuminating a patchwork of cloud passing across its surface, a lamp, a light, a governance of some sort, he listening to her breathing, nasal, then oral, then nasal again. Soon she would be snoring (so would he), a struggled, snarling, self-possessive sound (how remote they were from one another) which he scarcely associated with her at all, turning on his side to watch her strange, anonymous, unknown face, illuminated by the filtered light from the window, that of another creature drawn into the

151

bed beside him, transposed by sleep into something oblivious, distant, disowning.

It had been his relationship with his mother she had focused on – been focused on – in the last appointments before her declaration, the date of which they commemorated each month, anxious for the monthly count to add up to a year. Yet his mother was a non-participatory figure, as far as he recalled, in his background, no significant emotions associated with her at all ('perhaps that was the problem'). Overall, he had liked her, her most intimate relationship in the family inevitably with her daughter, his sister Sarah, she precociously, something of a 'mother' herself, solicitous of her younger brothers ('practising', they'd described it, for when she was older; '*I* shan't have children,' had been her reply, 'you two have worn me out *entirely*'). He'd admired his mother: her self-possession, her composure, her ability to get things done (a prefiguring of Simone, he suspected, in his respect): the tweed suits and pork pie hat she invariably wore in public, the briskness, the compactness, the absence of extremes either in her apperance or her manner, her accounts of school life, viewed from her position as secretary, attracted him, in retrospect, immensely, not least his memories of mealtimes, particularly the ritualistic evening affair, whenever they were home together (a Mrs Tyndal coming in to clean and cook, before, during and after the war), for him, again, in retrospect, the highlight of the day, his father's account of the day's adventures in the showroom and garage alternating engagingly with her own, he, on these occasions (frequent, questioned interruptions, eager, flush-faced, from his brother Paul, more measured enquiries from Sarah), drawn to the conclusion he was essentially a listener, an observer: a recorder, too, keeping a diary for much of the time, considered, by the others, an affectation, if not subversive.

In which case, with this pacific background to draw on, wherefrom his appetite for art, and a particular art, at that, something so remote from his place and time he could give no adequate account of it? Similarly, from where had he extracted, from where had arisen, a hitherto unsignalled – undiagnosed, unformalised and unsuspected – appetite not to live? in the half-light of Simone's bedroom, holding up his hand to examine it, configurated, in that light, as if a stranger's – not he, he reflected, lying beside Simone, or she lying beside him, but two enigmas (two problems waiting to be 'solved') laid unknowingly side by side.

She stirred, her head turning towards him on the pillow, the eyes still closed, the lips parted: a position of trust, each sleeping, unnerved, beside someone they scarcely knew, someone who, in his case, had conceivably 'lost touch' (with everything, looking to Taylor, he presumed, absurdly, to set him 'right': the privilege, the authoritative task of evil). So much for sleep, and anticipation, his nerves – his hand was shaking – on edge; so much for relaxation; so much for what had taken place only moments after getting into bed, a prolonged, sustained encounter where sensuality rather than sensibility, or reflection, had played its exclusive part.

What he hadn't faced up to was his sectioning (something definitive, overly definitive, in his life at last), something of which he was sensationally ashamed and inclined, at first instant, to deny. Nor had he faced up to his mother's death, an event precipitating the first, though, at the time, he'd considered it to have little, if anything, to do with it. Preceding that, of course, had been the measured decline of his previous powers – measured, that is, in the ascendancy of Charlotte, of his sons, of almost everyone he knew.

He'd been standing on the northbound platform of Camden Town tube station, intending to walk on Hampstead Heath, when, as the train came in, he'd been seized by what, afterwards, he had described, vividly, as a giant hand. Flung towards the line, he had caught the edge of the driver's cab and been hurled backwards across the platform. Moments later a face was gazing down, joined by others: he was raised towards the curved surface of the ceiling, the motion continuing, the ceiling, however, drawing no nearer. He resented, and was alarmed by, terrifyingly, the intrusion of others, his mind, curiously, occupied by the one speculation: *has this been enough?*

153

Moments – days, hours – previous to that, it seemed, he had been with his mother. She was, in this recollection, lying in a bed, her face unrecognisable from the one he knew, the cheeks drawn in, the mouth, devoid of teeth, wide open.

She was sucking at the air, the suction of her lungs producing a gurgling sound inside her throat.

A cylinder had been positioned by her neck, a tube, running from it, disappearing inside the collar of her nightdress.

A shrivelled, cadaverous creature whom he was willing to die.

Paul, his brother, and Sarah had been and gone, they work and other responsibilities to respond to, he sitting there until he could bear the waiting no longer, getting up, crossing the ward from the alcove where she was lying, and descending the stairs to the hospital entrance.

Passing a stall beside the reception desk, he saw a pile of writing pads and a box of pencils. Buying one of the pads and two of the pencils, along with a pencil sharpener, he returned upstairs to the ward.

Earlier, he had distracted himself by making words from the name of the nurse written on a board in the alcove, opposite the bed: Liebermann, regretting he hadn't a pen or a pencil to write them down, recollecting the list as best he could in order to distract himself from the labouring of the figure beside him: the stentorian breathing which, at intervals, faltered, he assuming, at one point, she might be dying, at another, when the breath was suspended for several seconds, amounting, he guessed, to more than a minute, concluding she had died, feeling the relief that the struggle was over, only, with a staggered intake, a resistant gurgle, for the breathing to be resumed.

At intervals the nurse had come in, felt his mother's pulse and, with a nod, departed. Now, however, sitting beside her, he began, laboriously, to draw her face, sketchily at first, page after page until, his confidence growing, despite his lack of skill, the figures, the faces of *The Deposition* in the Capella Scrovegni vividly in mind, he was drawing not only her face but her head, the caverned eyes, the protuberant nose with its flaring nostrils, sucking at the air, the chasm of her mouth, gasping, grasping,

154

almost biting at the air, the gurgling in her throat, her snores increasing.

The disarray of her hair against the pillow, prongs of it projected across her brow, white, brittle, dishevelled, like strands of wire.

At one point her eyes had opened: a bleared examination of the room before her, the drowsy shifting of the pupils in his direction and, having registered his presence in the chair, the eyelids lowered, mechanically, stiffly, tiny apertures remaining, filling at intervals with liquid which, with his handkerchief, leaning forward, he wiped away.

Then, his drawing finished – completed, satiated – feeling he could draw no more, he had left, driving home, St Albans to London, the telephone ringing as he arrived, he lifting it to hear his sister's voice announce that the hospital had rung to tell her that, not long after his departure, their mother had died. 'I'm constantly going, not arriving, when the moment comes,' he said, unable at that instant, at his sister's enquiry, to understand what he had meant.

After the incident on the tube station platform he had come to in an observation room: a bed and a chair were screwed to the floor. A window, high in the wall, its sill level with his chin, was, he discovered, similarly secured.

In the centre of the door was a glass panel: it offered a view of the corridor outside and of the upper two-thirds of any watching or passing figure. He had wept; he had wept a great deal, having little if anything else to do. Several times a day and occasionally, if he were awake, at night someone had unlocked the door and asked him how he was. He had no clothes: one side of his body, his chest and – or so it felt like – his back, were severely bruised. No bones, he'd been assured, were broken.

Much of the time he stared at his legs, at his feet, at his arms, at his abdomen. He was, he'd told himself, complete, an indivisible hole, his hands held before him to measure how far they might reach; nothing was extraneous; his flesh occupied a space he could legitimately call his own: his limbs reached to

155

what was neither him nor his. Otherwise, he'd concluded, the whole of space eluded him.

At intervals he'd been given a bath: he'd noticed from time to time how his smell (he presumed it was his smell) dominated the room: someone stood over him, invariably foreign, male (circumspect, aloof): jeans and trainers; a vaguely athletic figure. He'd been an athlete once himself, hence his awareness of his body, of its potential and excesses: a decent, enquiring ('Are you all right?'), empirically minded sort of chap (much like himself), the kind who, quite reasonably, he might have encountered on the moon, coming out of a crater to shake his hand as, confused and apprehensive, he descended from his rocket, he the representative of another time, another space, one he could legitimately call his own, not the one he had left for – disowning the one he had left behind.

He'd asked for a transplant, a suggestion made to him by a fellow patient. Acceding to his wishes, they'd put him to sleep, he waking to enquire if the process were complete: everything, he'd concluded, was down to him, someone whose face was growing increasingly familiar appearing at the door, glancing in – entering, on occasion, casualness (familiarity) characterising his manner, enquiring, 'How are you, old fellow?' as he might of a child or a dog.

'Have I been transplanted?' he'd asked, adding, 'Is the machinery in place?' convinced, if they had, they would never tell. 'The same old, reliable matter,' they said, touching his arm, his shoulder, his head. 'I prefer absolution,' he told them. 'A question of habit, of custom,' holding on to that which existed at the conjunction of his legs. 'Without a past, the very next instant is with us now,' he'd said.

He'd been moved (invited) to 'Death's Head Valley', so inscribed on a door by an institutionalised hand, most of the day and all of the night subdued by a drug whose name he knew but could never pronounce (endeavouring to do so to Charlotte, several times, and once to Gerry – smiling, cheerful, full of bounce – and, more often, to his sons, to Paul, to Sarah). 'The hole of what I am,' he said, each time, explaining, days passing.

156

From 'Sleepers Only' he'd been moved (no invitation) to 'Sometimes Awake', the night-time grimaces, the groans, the sighs. 'When I recover (when I recover) I shall be restrained. The drugs are speaking,' he often announced, the recollection of his relatively recent past coming to him – lying in Simone's bed, at this point – with unexpected force, wave after wave of excitation, spasm after spasm erupting in the darkness, he on the point of waking her up, the vibration of his body something he couldn't control.

Helplessness, a recurring feature of his recent illness, appeared, paradoxically, to take charge of his system: a chemical outrage (amongst the structures inside his skull), his recollection of Kavanagh's 'No one knows the causes, though many, unfortunately, profess to do so,' something Simone (and others) had taken exception to, her objections, however, never defined, increasing the sensation this was 'something' that had little, if anything, to do with 'him', an internalised storm which otherwise, quite easily, might have been experienced – probably had been – by someone else: spectated, that is, not suffered 'here'.

Instead, convulsions focused around his abdomen, emanating, seemingly, from his stomach, a visceral evacuation which brought him upright in bed, assured that a previous, curled position, foetal in shape, could not subdue or contain it.

He was standing on the roof, looking across and between the moonlit chimneys, the distant phalanx of lights which indicated London a reflected, ochreish glow on the underside of the clouds. The coldness of the air revived him, as did the flagstones against his bare feet, his arms wrapped, vibratingly, around his chest. Inside, convulsions had given way to tremoring, stillness finally returning, a sense of isolation – a solitariness heightened when he raised his head and, looking elsewhere than at the now faded light, recognised the star shapes to the north and west: the Great Bear, the North Star, the navigational incubus of his early life, looking out from the dormitory windows, 'into the past', forgetful of how far back in time he was.

Then, like a ghost, she drifted out of the door leading onto the roof, bare-footed, too, wraith-like, her face re-formulated, yet again, by shadow, extending her arms, taking him to her, he aware of the warmth of her body, and of how cold, in his nightclothes, he was.

'Are you all right?'

'Sure.'

'I felt you get up.'

'I'm sorry to have disturbed you,' he said, adding, 'Shakey,' as she took his hand, held it to the light, watched it vibrating, her fingers gripping his wrist: the release of his hand, the tightening of her embrace, drawing him once more against her.

And fear, a residual dread which, despite his distractions, despite her, rarely left him: a trajectory of himself, out into the stars: yet here, flushed, the insinuating benevolence of her voice, its intention to reassure him: despite the darkness, despite something intolerable going on for ever, she, he, it, they were here, there, somewhere, he absorbed at that instant by the fragrance of her skin.

6

HE DIDN'T understand what his children did, the ebb and flow of their affairs, the emergence (divergence) of *their* children moving them ever further on, the names and dates of births confusing him as he had seen the names of his own children confuse his father, the oppressive gaze of his clouded-irised eyes as he, engulfed by Charlie, Joseph, Steven, searched their faces, gauging their reactions, with little, at that stage, to guide him: 'am I responsible for all this?' posterity itemised in flesh and blood, corroborated by a legacy of cars, built-in obsolescence, remodelling.

Yet Maddox had been 'fortunate': 'a fortunate life' was, to some degree, how he'd diagnosed his illness: 'it could have been worse' (he might have not recovered, even, previously, he might have died), 'an anomaly that I should have been afflicted', indicating his condition less by gesture than the haunted look in his eyes.

Haunted by what? fortuity, chance, obliquity: another nature could, quite easily, have been formulated by his parents: something in the way of Paul's, a good-natured fellow – or Sarah's (much the same): his parents' – and Paul's and Sarah's – appetite for service, his father a JP, his accounts of cases, at mealtimes, taking over, on certain days, from activities in the showroom: the pavonine figure of his uncle Joseph standing, poised, on the sidelines, cheering life, and specifically his family, on, an embarrassingly garish spectator, particularly in Maddox's life, coming up on one occasion, in a Wolseley, of course, after Maddox had got his First Team colours, to Quinians, startling

159

the boys and the masters by his cries, allegedly of encouragement, the players curious as to which of them he was attached,
his affectations, of dress and manner, his enthusiasm (genuine),
a foil to the Quakerian sobriety of the school and the industrial
environment at the foot of the hill, his uncle, later, the principal
promoter of his career ('can't you interest yourself in work of a
later generation?') inspecting paintings and sculptures at Maddox's invitation with a curious inattention, amounting to
blindness ('they don't speak'), not what Maddox did but what he
was, the focus of his concern.

In his uncle's, and in his parents' incredulity, he recognised
his own incredulity at the progress of his children, inspecting,
occasionally, by invitation, the offices or premises where they
worked, listening to their accounts of their activities, the
complexity and significance of which eluded him. 'The fact is, I
feel a child in our children's eyes, as they, at one time, were in
mine,' he had explained to Charlotte when she enquired, over
the phone, how these occasions had gone, 'their worlds as
confusing to me as mine must have been to them, as children,'
observing, finally, 'It's curious there's no word in the English
language that denotes one's children once they're adults, older
than we were, for instance, when we had them, other than
"offspring", which sounds more technical than human,' confounded as much by this as by their variegated roles, as if,
wordless, they had less departed than simply parted from him.

Was he falling into the trap which, unwittingly, he'd been
preparing throughout his life: a mechanism which would
remove uncertainty (the bait) and, once reassured, the lid would
close?

Rhetoric, he was reminded, his strongest suit, 'enquiry
without resolution' his current theme.

Fulviam ego ut futuam?

Entrapped: lying once more, with Simone, her head on his
shoulder, her hand between his legs, attaching him more
securely to her and the bed: the delicacy of her fingers, the
hollow of her palm, the comfort of her breasts, he reflecting on
his progeny, his route to posterity or extinction still secure, the

moon invisible now beyond the frame of the window, its light, however, still shadowing the muslin, the shape of the roof-tops opposite recalling his and Simone's gaze from the garden, embracing one another, enclosed by the plants, the cat, aroused by their disturbance, beside them (lying now on Simone's side of the bed).

The reflection of London on the underside of the clouds, he awake as she slept on his shoulder, energy, he reflected, in repose, as if he, too, existed simply – eloquently, even, potentially – to be restored to something like, if not more than, his former self, the fortitude, the measure, the strength and coherence of a family behind him: lying beside her, seemingly redundant, and yet enthralled, cohabiting a place he didn't know. He had come too far, his children, once following, now scarcely discernible ahead – he quietening his voice, his perceptions, his views, diminishing his gestures, moving from, if not into, once again, something he neither knew nor understood, resisting his falling-back, as he waved them on, they caught in a momentum exclusively their own.

A limited perspective, the view from the window to the darkened roofs, the steadying assurance of her breath, the submission of her body to something more exclusive than itself, the absence in her being asleep at all, her removal to somewhere neither he nor she, on waking, might discern, the abandonment of what, moments before, she had been on the roof. Once more, internally, he was reaching for a line, an escape, in this instance, from the cavalier object in his head, pursuing his identity before destroying it, a prescription for release, paradise, or confinement, hell.

He was preparing a document: no longer letters to Devonshire and Donaldson, or the mythical figures he had, for some time, been calling to account, or even to himself. A document to whom? A presence whose significance he had once taken for granted, invisible, obscure, as if addressing a wasteland, a horizonless sea, nature no longer an impediment, no longer of account.

There was something in his and Simone's relationship which

161

echoed that between a celibate priest and a favoured parish-
ioner, something – contractually – which shouldn't have been
allowed, uncertainty – anxiety, even – evident in Simone herself
which, initially, she'd denied, and then dismissed. Sleeplessness,
at this point, gave his suspicion edge, he turning again to regard
her, the strange abandonment so close to death, an abandonment to something other than nature: absolution, submission,
he anxious for the same himself, the relegation of consciousness
to an unspeaking process, he fingering the encounter of the
coming day as if he, not Taylor, were imprisoned, guilt of an
abstract, exclusive nature transferred perversely to himself.

Already, mentally, he was pleading on his own behalf, the
prospectus – *a* prospectus – of his past recited: his filial, marital,
paternal credentials, fidelity as son, as husband, as father, a
residue of virtue extracted from each one, free for anyone,
Taylor in particular, to examine. As if, in reality, it were his own
wife and children he had killed, the potential always present, to
destroy everything he had created, everything he was responsible for: those nights, those similar nights, when he'd lain awake,
not Simone but Charlotte given to the same abandonment
beside him, the thought, I am responsible for creating all this:
their pain (his children's), as well as their joy, the inclusivity of
their lives devolved exclusively on him: a feeling he was
transferring to Taylor – his accountability to someone, to
something, charged as he was, or so it felt, with an absolute
crime, the occasion and the nature of which he couldn't
otherwise imagine: a will to destroy everything that had
anything to do with himself, a corresponding volition to escape
abandoned – even here, beside her, security of a kind he had
rarely known, loved separately, for himself alone, not for the
associations he brought with him, absolved of parents, children,
wife, now job, absolved of Devonshire, Donaldson, absolved of
everything, he reflected, except himself, the most savage, the
most unpredictable, the most wearisome burden of all.

7

He'd visited the prison on several occasions, a peculiar situation when he'd been written to by a former Quinians schoolfriend: the Bastillian severity of its walls looming over the streets in north-east London, the gate within a gate designed, perversely, it seemed, to oblige the visitor to lower their head: the crossing from the gatehouse to a taller building, within which, along with the other visitors, he was shown to a room divided by what looked like cattle stalls, his friend coming in from one side, he shown to a seat in a cubicle on the other.

The introductory declaration by his friend he hadn't forgotten, his rage on discovering Maddox had brought no cigarettes, the sole purpose, it was explained, of his visit, he at the time preoccupied by thoughts of loyalty, allegiance, confederacy: the past.

Disengaged, he had listened to his friend's account of being 'fitted up', this unbelievable appeal followed by a request that Maddox find a psychiatrist who would plead on his friend's behalf. 'Another month in here and I'll be completely off my head,' the baleful and wholly credible glare through the grille in the wooden panel: someone, this, whom he had liked at school, one of four brothers varyingly described as Major, Major-Minor, Minor, Mini-Minor (Minor-Minimus for a fifth brother due later) to the amusement of their peers, he, Major-Minor, an enthusiast at sport, something dislodged, however – evidently still dislodgeable – in his nature, inclined aimlessly to ignore convention, rules, enclosure or discipline of any kind, a burly, precociously muscled youth for whom Mad Ox had seemed a suitable partner. Failing to reappear at the end of school holidays – accounts of a voyage as a deckhand on a tanker bound for the Persian Gulf – he had finally been removed by his parents and sent to a naval college, their parting, for Maddox, at least, a memorable event, he bound for orthodoxy, his friend for something, imaginably, more rumbustious (a mark of failure, on his own behalf, in Maddox's mind at the time).

Then, later, came the letter, followed, when he responded, by a warrant licensing one visit, their peculiar confrontation in something not unlike a cattle stall, his friend's familiar features coarsened, as if, internally, the mind behind them had been torn apart, a leering, savage, reproachful stare, that of an animal pinioned in a cage, replacing the helpless, hapless, engaging fecklessness of the former Quinians youth, the cigarettes, the absence of, a seemingly considered provocation. Everyone, evidently, was a criminal, living, one way or another, off others, he, his friend, more honest than most: 'You haven't painted the fucking pictures, you just make money from writing about the fuckers who have,' Major-Minor minor no longer, having written to him via the newspaper in which his first reviews had appeared, he, Maddox, surprised that such a publication should have been available in prison. 'I steal from the insurers, not individuals,' Maddox's incredulous, 'But who do the insurers charge for the thefts? Me and the rest of the community,' adding, 'You cunt,' to reinforce his declaration.

He'd felt sorry for, finally pained by, his friend's delinquency, unable, he decided, to challenge it further on a subsequent visit ('No one else wants to come. My wife's sold our flat and all my possessions and pissed off to Spain'), he handing over a permissible carton of cigarettes, listening, grieved, to further justifications of his friend's decline ('more honest than most'), his friend's anger reignited when Maddox announced the name of the psychiatrist he had, after a great deal of enquiry, discovered: 'He's bent, for fuck's sake. Every court in the fucking country knows him. He'll get me years on not off,' adding, to reciprocate Maddox's previous reproach, 'you cunt.'

By request, he had met his friend at the prison gates on the day, years later, of his release, a considerably reduced figure dressed in a dishevelled suit on a winter morning. Rain was falling. He'd bought him a meal and, on request, had given him money, finally a cheque: 'I could change this easily to make it a hundred.' 'Why don't you?' he'd responded, 'there's less than fifty in the account.' He had had two further, summary encounters with his former chum before he had once again disappeared, only the memory, of something uncompleted, unresolved, removed, remaining, a legacy which, subliminally, he suspected, he carried over into his meeting with Taylor.

Perhaps because of the severity of the sentence, and the conditions under which Taylor was now held, he was shown, after a great deal of scrutiny – electronic and otherwise – into a featureless room furnished with two canvas-seated chairs on either side of a plastic table, a uniformed figure remaining inside the door. Taylor, whom he didn't recognise, had entered in his shirtsleeves, his collar open, a pale, curiously bloated figure with prematurely greying hair, taking his seat on one side of the table without glancing at Maddox at all.

It was as if he were waiting to be assessed, a vestige here of the Taylor he'd known, but so recessive that he, too, sat in silence, his defences, his prospective defences, disarmed.

His former student had been of a stocky, broad, almost round-shouldered build, exuding a sense of physical strength (stoicism, even), an archetypal, to Maddox's then tutorial mind, farm-labourer (he gave evidence of having worked as such), a rural mechanic of some sort: a figure resonant of an assured, two-footed emplacement on the earth (conspicuous amongst the aesthetes who dominated the Drayburgh at that time, Donald-son later to be included), stolid, truculent, fresh-faced, his cheeks shiny, his full lips red, the eyes filled with a stark, unquestioning fervour: something provincial, if not parochial, evoking the sense of an enclosed community, belligerently indisposed, if for good reason, to the world outside, unmannered, reluctant to be approached directly, brusque, suspicious, recalcitrant – other than in a response to painting, an elemental, if not devotional exercise (the one window opening, Maddox had reflected at the time, on an otherwise dark enclosure): passionate, injured, curiously modest, warm.

Maddox, distracted by the morose figure by whom he was confronted, glanced up at the uniformed figure inside the door, he, too, without a jacket, his shirted arms folded across his chest, a protuberant gut – and was conscious of the similarity to Taylor's own appearance, dark trousers, white shirt, as if one were a parody of the other, each involved in an overt if conspiratorial alliance. His immediate response, if unexpressed, had been to suggest he'd been brought the wrong prisoner, Taylor, a relatively common name: how many were there in the prison: how long would it take to sift the right one out?

The silence, which he wasn't disinclined to let continue, was broken by a door clanging in the corridor outside, followed by the sound of voices. 'That one's occupied': the retreating sound of footsteps on a stone-flagged floor.

'I didn't know if you smoked,' Maddox said, reminded of his previous experience of a first-time visit. 'I brought some cigarettes which I've been asked to leave outside.'

Taylor raised his head, his eyes, dark-rimmed, flickering in Maddox's direction, taking him in, swiftly, then glancing away.

'Are we allowed to shake hands?'

Taylor didn't answer: neither did the warder respond, his gaze, abstracted yet nevertheless alert, fixed on the cream-painted brick wall behind Maddox's back.

Drawing up his chair, Maddox placed his arms companionably on the table, Taylor, for his part, sitting with his chair pushed back. His hair, previously dark and thick, was now thinning, with flashes of white at the temples. The sensitised, almost parochial look had vanished, something pained, hesitant, unreflective taking its place. The previously sturdy, ingenuous features, too, had gone, the nose alone, curiously, retaining the sensitivity of the student of fifteen years before: the experience of wife, children, job – disillusionment and terror, too, Maddox assumed – had produced a thickening of the brow, the cheeks, the chin, a dark, vertical line, like an incision, dividing the shifty, hesitant, averted eyes. It was as if Taylor were signalling he

166

wished he hadn't come. As it was, he'd been prepared not only for a more confrontational encounter but a more explicit one, something of a more spirited nature, a vestige of what had passed contentiously between them as student and tutor. Rather than diminished by what had happened, Taylor appeared to be enlarged, if not enhanced, almost, Maddox reflected, complacently so, as though the recent past had returned him to the way things were, or ought to have been, he back with the people, and in the place, where he truly belonged, and from which the Drayburgh had unfortunately divided him. A childlike submissiveness pinned him to the chair, his hands, fisted, thrust in his armpits, an image of resistance and self-enclosure. At any moment Maddox expected him to enquire of his wife and children, specifically of Rebecca, as though she and he, Maddox, were the cause of his current discomfort, Maddox increasingly aware of his own actions, splaying his fingers, unaccountably, on the table before him, as if to indicate to Taylor he had nothing to hide. What curious behaviour for both of us, he thought, concluding at the same time it was up to him to break the pattern (a residual tutor's role). The enormity of what had happened, placing Taylor beyond humanity, or so it seemed, stood between them like an invisible wall. What am I feeling? he asked himself. What sensation do I associate with this unusual encounter? Is it me he wished to see or someone else? conscious of the warranty that had brought him here: his own attempt to kill himself. In no time at all, he reflected, the meeting would be over and nothing would have been said.

'Is there anything I can do for you?' he said, recalling a similar (disastrous) offer made to his Quinians friend.

Taylor shook his head, the first direct acknowledgement he'd given, the gesture not unlike that of someone flicking hair or water out of their eyes, a degree of containment, exasperation, irritation. Feelings of a more dynamic nature were being entertained behind that dark, recessive gaze, inflaming, discomforting, vengeful.

'Have you kept any other contact with the Drayburgh?' he enquired, prompting Taylor, reminding him that the invitation

167

for the visit had come from him. They'd sat in a not dissimilar room – smaller but almost equally spartan – on many occasions in the past: the tutor room next to the sculpture studios in the basement of the Drayburgh – discussing, he recalled, Taylor's essays on his then favoured theme, the return to naturalism – 'poetic naturalism' – from the iconographic formalities of the earlier half of the century, likening it to the emergence of the same in Florentine trecento painting: something of a precocious analogy but curiously – dismayingly – dated now. Yet something echoed, if in reverse, in Taylor's own emergence from provincial life into the vitality of London. Life was first lived, and then endured, had been implicit in much of Taylor's attitude at that time, allied to a voracious appetite to survive. So much of his past, if revoked ('I don't want it'), was only to be introduced at his discretion: marriage, children – the Drayburgh: his enquiry was met by the same dismissive flick of the head.

'Would you like me to stay?' Maddox concluding he'd leave the cigarettes and go, a relief to both of them, he imagined.

The warder's eyes came down to scrutinise, with interest, the back of Taylor's head, and then, momentarily, examined Maddox's enquiring expression.

'Is there anything I can get you?' he asked again. 'A book. Paints. Pencils. Paper. Ink,' and then, more forcefully, 'Is there anything you'd like to talk about?' the Florentine revolution compromised by recent Roman discoveries passing briefly through his mind.

'Rebecca talked about you,' Taylor said, turning his head to meet Maddox's gaze as if he, Maddox, were the prisoner – a peculiar, penetrative insight – and he the visitor.

'They were formative times for us all,' Maddox said.

Removing his hands from his armpits, Taylor lowered them to the table: cupped, they lay there like offerings, or potential containers, a curious sense of displacement, of removal, almost of disowning (there they are, here I am: they have nothing to do with me), Maddox recalling, with a shock, they were the instruments of something which might no longer be mentioned.

The nails, he observed, were black, as if he had been digging, scraping, excavating earth: a subterranean sensation caused the hair at the back of his neck to stiffen.

'It's true. You had a great influence on all of us,' Taylor said, lightly, derisively, disowning the claim as swiftly as he presented it.

'And you on me,' Maddox said, unwilling to let the challenge pass.

'How was that?' The recessed, dark-rimmed eyes were starkly alert. He should be pleased I'm even speaking to him, Maddox thought, withdrawing the speculation the instant he was aware of it.

'Invariably you learn as much, if not more, from your students as they do, ideally,' he said, 'from you. No doubt you found that, too, as a teacher.'

'To take advantage of it, though, is reprehensible,' Taylor swiftly responded.

'So it is.'

It was as if he were seeing Taylor from a distance; or, as if the once familiar but now foreign figure were retreating across the room, beyond the wall, beyond the prison, to a place he, Maddox, didn't know, a curious displacement of the present occurring, as if neither of them were confined by or in the room at all.

Yet there it was: a presence of colossal, almost superhuman proportions, Maddox aware of the likeness of this sensation to that which he associated with the tube station platform: fear, of a similar nature, gripped the centre of his body, as if once again he were enclosed by the fingers of a gigantic hand, aware of a surge of anger, even triumph – ascendancy of some sort – in Taylor's eyes as he examined him more keenly, threateningly, across the table.

'If there's something you'd specifically like to say I'd prefer you to come out with it,' Maddox said, sinking under the look, returning, bleakly, he assumed, to his role of tutor – adviser, outside agent, a representative of an authority that exceeded himself, holding Taylor's gaze, his own hands, he noticed,

169

spread-eagled more firmly across the surface of the table, bracing himself for an assault, of a physical nature, from the other side.

'I'm in the medical wing,' Taylor said, inconsequentially, withdrawing. 'Somewhat better than a cell. Particularly if you have to share.'

'Is there anything you need?' he asked again. 'Anything,' he went on, 'you'd like to tell me?'

'I don't smoke,' Taylor said, capitulation, of some sort, taking place. 'I could swap them. Screws allowing.' Turning his head, half smiling, he indicated the figure at the door: if anything, its attention had grown more acute. Conceivably, Maddox reflected, Taylor was feinting before he struck again: a not unexpected sense of desolation appeared to grip them both. 'Probably,' he suddenly went on, 'it was not a good idea asking you to come.'

'You must have had something in mind,' he said.

'*Persona non grata*, I should think, wondering if the *persona* and the *grata* were still in place.'

'Evidently so,' Maddox said, relieved at the invitation.

'I gave up painting years ago.' Taylor paused. 'I followed your writing. Rebecca didn't. Follow it.

'Why not?'

'She didn't like you.'

'I'm not surprised,' he said.

He waited, too.

'Could have cost you your job.'

'It could.'

'Screwing students.' Taylor smiled, eerily: his teeth, conspicuously white at one time, were discoloured. The whites of the eyes, too, were reddened: no doubt against his wishes he'd been sedated. His smile, moments later, turned into a grimace. 'You old enough to be her father.'

'That's true.'

'Nowadays of no account.'

'That's true also,' he responded.

'You went on, of course, all right.'

170

'I did.' He was about to add, 'and so did she,' but swiftly amended, 'She was capable of making her own decision.'

It was, he realised, a bold intrusion: looking up at the warder he recognised someone vividly, antagonistically alert: someone, he assumed, indisposed to both of them. He regretted Taylor, his back to him, couldn't see the reaction.

'Capable, but not necessarily in a position to do so,' Taylor said, calm suddenly, articulate.

'And,' Maddox went on, recklessly, 'you didn't have to marry her.'

Taylor considered this: 'marry' and 'murder', phonetically, were not that far apart: at any moment, alarmed by his stillness, the sudden evenness of expression, Maddox imagined him leaning across the table, dislodging it, grasping his throat: no reason to hold back. I am not responsible for this situation, he reflected.

'She married me. I didn't marry her,' Taylor finally responded, the evenness of tone remaining.

'She asked you to?' he said, the heat at the back of his neck increasing. Was Taylor implying she was pregnant? That the first of her children was his? The absurdity of this caused him to tighten his pressure on the table, endeavouring, or so it felt, to force its surface down.

The dates of the child, he recalled, didn't match.

'It was her decision,' Taylor said. 'I went along with it. We didn't have to, but she thought we should. As you probably remember, she was determined if not impetuous by nature.'

'Yes.' He waited, Taylor still examining him, aloofly, across the table.

'In reality,' Taylor went on, 'I'm not really here.'

Maddox waited again.

'What you see here I call P.G.'

'P.G.?'

'Putative Ghost.' A coarsened expression crossed Taylor's face, calculated, Maddox reflected, consciously presented. 'I'm watched continuously.' He indicated, without turning, the warder behind his back.

171

For his part, the warder stirred, shifting the weight on his feet: the whiteness of his shirt, the darkness of the tie, the neat line of the sleeve above the elbow: a young, dispassionate, bony face, the forehead and the cheeks prominent, the eyes alert, the previously abstract look displaced by one of enquiry, the mouth, thin-lipped, arrested in a grimace.

'Giotto I pray to each night. God. Something along those lines. Two G's. A freakshow here, otherwise. One I have to attend to. Inattention not allowed. There's a lot I'd like to ask.'

The request came suddenly and, rather than responding, Maddox waited. He was reflecting much himself, not on Taylor, his current or his previous relationship with him, but on the peculiar way he himself had abandoned his life, or endeavoured to do so, here as good a place as any to discover how far, to this extent, he had succeeded, not so much Taylor as the place itself a marker. A feeling of disillusionment, pronounced on his arrival, had strengthened: it only needed a signal from the warder for his own confinement to be confirmed: so much had he done to deserve it, so much was he doing to add to that conviction. No longer could he see any reason why he shouldn't be locked up as well.

'She focused much of her life on you. A prescient signal, I told her.' Taylor's calmness of voice remained: he was invoking something of the mood, the tone, of their tutorials and might well have been reading notes he'd already made. 'He has his wife, his sons. He has his acclaim. I did much, at that time, to defend you. There was much of value, I told her, to preserve. He has done much for me as well, I said. Those eyes. Have you ever seen such eyes? The eyes of Saint Peter betraying Jesus.'

The warder was examining the back of Taylor's head: raising his arm, he glanced at his watch: some, if not much of this, his manner suggested, he had heard before.

'The living dead,' Taylor went on. 'Which is where we are at present.' His cupped hands now he held together, the grimy nails conspicuous. 'For which offence, you might say, to make redress, he was crucified upside down. One up on Christ! If his crucifixion was one to write home about, what about poor Pete?

172

See how far we've come! One up, too, you might say, on Jehovah.'

Maddox, recalling his own past, was contrasting the youth he had known with the figure he was confronting now: the bright provincial with his unlikely passion for something that had happened in Florence, in Padua, in Assisi six hundred or more years before: the sagacity, the weight, the density – the probity, the anguish – the intensity of those muralled figures, gazing out, their horizontally configurated, shadowed eyes, as if, Taylor had suggested at the time, from Plato's cave.

Reality at last! they cried.

'Executing murals for a living comes very close,' Taylor intruded on his thoughts, 'to executing something, or even someone else. What do you think, Herr Professor?'

It was, he concluded, as if indeed they were back in the tutor room: the same confinement, the same bleakness (functional at the Drayburgh, something other here), the same scuffling feet outside the door. Only different was the emanation summoned by the place and the two of them together, Taylor unaware, presumably, of the nature of the effect he was having, Maddox considering whether he might tell him of his recent difficulties, not least of the event precipitating his sectioning, and the nature of the experience associated with that.

'I'm inclined to see us as equals, rather than as tutor and student,' he said, aimlessly, unable to penetrate or decipher Taylor's increasingly hostile expression. Even that, he reflected, was aimless, as if, having prepared one text for their encounter, Taylor was substituting another: retribution, of a sort, had been displaced by a memory of something else: an allegiance, even a confederacy, surviving over all these years, as if both were embarked on a common cause.

'I intended, at some point, to take up painting again,' Taylor said, leaning back, the chair creaking beneath his weight, his hands, still clasped, falling into his lap. 'It's been suggested. An atmosphere not unlike the Drayburgh, wouldn't you say? Apart from the dances, the dinners, the parties. The Drayburgh hostel. Self-portraits, I thought, might be my line. Not who you paint, or how, but what. Necessary, of course, to have an agent. On the outside. I thought of you. Do a favour. Remember the advice you gave me, from time to time? "Don't make your essays too personal." Struck me hard. Viklund as well. Those lectures. Questions he avoided, I thought, at the time. In reality, questions to which there aren't any answers. Absurd, when we're born with the facility to enquire, to be met, at the end of the day, by nothing but silence. A dysfunction built into the system, I'd say. "This is not autobiography", another of your remarks. Personality all the go, now, of course. Before my time.'

The skin had lightened on Taylor's forehead, the furrow deepening between his eyes, expectation and resignation flickering, alternately, in his expression, a shadowed, angered, beaten look, Maddox's feelings of remorse, and identification, increasing. Helplessness of a new sort at Taylor's helplessness intensified. Gratuitous involvement, he reminded himself, not required: keep the horror of what's happened in mind.

A dominant and domineering expression, as a result, appeared to take possession of Taylor's features, he leaning further back from the table, surveying Maddox down the length of his nose: a guarded look, withdrawn, circumspect, less inviting judgement than providing it.

'Though I recall, too, you discouraging me from painting, suggesting I apply for the Courtauld. Encouraging me,' he went on, 'to follow your example. Even invoked Pemberton, on your behalf, the two of you together. *Methuselah*, for Christ's sake. On the other hand, you'll not know what it's like, painting yourself to death. An exercise I've resisted all these years. The monumentality, for instance, of all those figures . . .'

The whiteness of Taylor's forehead gave way to a redness which extended upwards from his collar, across his neck, his cheeks, reaching the fringes of his thinning, brushed-back hair: Maddox was confronting not the grown man but a sullen, swollen replica of the student, the virginal, agrarian look, distorted and malformed.

'There was a surgical element involved I didn't appreciate at the time,' Taylor went on. 'Di Bardone had a problem, wouldn't you say, in the way he incised those ocular expressions? When I pointed it out you said you rather liked it. The reference, I mean. Weren't you called Mad Ox at school? That, too, I recall. A tutorial confidence, a tutorial confession. Confession and confidence being much to the fore. In both of us.' He paused, before adding, 'Mr Tutor,' paused again, and went on, watching Maddox intensely, 'Those cars, for instance. How you drew a distinction between aesthetics and function. I thought *that* aesthetical, too. Preciously so. "Art has no purpose", one of your maxims. Though it might reasonably be described, I would have thought, as useful. Impressed me, however, at the time, no end. What else has no purpose? I mentally enquired. Almost everything, I concluded. Mythology, on my part. Evidently not on yours. The New Philistine Agenda. Quite a thing. Read up on it, of course, every week you wrote. The whole of the second half of the century given over to the very thing! Art up its own arsehole, so to speak. Wonderful! Somebody who can sum it up. The omnipotent eye. God praise to that fellow from – where was it? – St Albans! You and Viklund, who, the latter, wanted no part of it. Confined himself to history. Wily old man! How is he? Still around?' not waiting for Maddox to respond before concluding, 'Maddox, I thought, at least the *real thing*!'

Maddox leant back, exchanging glances once more with the warder; perhaps he too stood in awe of Taylor's situation: Taylor who, once his antagonism had been expressed, was inclined to talk of, if not transpose it to other things. Something Maddox could recognise in the light of his recent experience: a suspension of grace, of forgiveness, looking to Taylor to inform him of how things were on the other side (is hell as bad as they make out? he could guarantee that, of course, himself). Yet, the other side of what? Lunacy, he reflected, unlike his own, of a permanent nature, beyond hope, beyond forgiveness, beyond atonement, Taylor a correspondent from a kingdom that parodied his own. Or was it, he reflected, the other way around? a state of mind, certainly, into which, helplessly, despite advice and medication, despite even love ('love is not enough') he felt

175

he was being drawn, Taylor an emissary, too, beyond – far beyond (his ultimate horror) the reach of anyone.

No difference, in that case, between them, he examining yet again the changes in his former pupil's face, a Faustian regression summoned up, he concluded, from his fevered imagination.

'Who else has been to see you?' he asked, the collateral of the past, he was suggesting, available to both of them, the most significant event of all, the greatest divide between them, the crime itself.

Taylor had shaken his head: intrusion of this sort, at least, he could no longer complain about.

'Is this your only visit?'

'Naturally.' He waved his hand. 'My parents, fortunately, are dead. My brother and my sister have both been once. Even an uncle. Other than that, no one. You were the last I could think of. Pemberton wouldn't want to include me in his c.v. I thought you, on the other hand, might feel an obligation. Knowing both of us,' he added. 'Intimately, in one case.' A moment later, he added, 'I've been told I'll be killed by the other cons. Murdering peers okay. Murdering minors, not.' He shrugged, bringing his body back to the table.

'I thought I'd make an experiment. As relevant, *pace* experiments, as any other. An experimental age, you could say. A unique, artistic enterprise involving not mineral and vegetational elements, but human flesh and blood. How to live the unliveable, surely of interest, at the very least, to succeeding generations, as the race as a whole plunges off, vocationally, into, if not the unknown, extinction. An enterprise on a scale unprecedented in our time. A paradigm, I thought, out-paradigming every other. Something unique, at least, in that. Something you alone might appreciate. Record it in a book. How you like. A series in your paper. Television. Film. Any manner of forms, though the content, as with all art, remains the same. In this instance, you could say, the subject is the human condition, but expressed in an unprecedented manner. At least, something rarely, if ever, done. Certainly not with this

176

degree of deliberation. Such consciousness involved. Someone trained, by masters, you might say, in observation and expression. An art consistent with the times. Surely, with this degree of awareness, never considered, let alone done before.'

The warder, once more, had glanced at his watch: shifting his weight from one foot to the other, and back again, he examined, stolidly, frankly, blankly, Maddox's reaction: curiosity, finally, as much as anything, as if to enquire, 'What do you make of that?'

'I gave up painting some time ago. A belated acknowledgement of your suggestion. Teaching scarcely left me any time for it. The headmaster wrote to me the other day asking if there was anything I wanted. What he would describe as a humanitarian gesture. One of the teachers, an art teacher, a woman, might come. A colleague, and humanist, too. Sent me messages before and after the trial. I never replied to them. In no mind to. Out of it, at the time, and afterwards . . .' He waved one arm, in a gesture reminiscent of Viklund. 'With you I thought there'd be an incentive. In at the beginning, since you knew us both. As if, having been your student, I'm looking to you for an explanation. Something as imbecilic as that. Otherwise, as I say, a twenty-first-century version of a hitherto unconceived twenty-first-century art. Vasari's Vasari, ahead of your time.'

He smiled, to expose once again his seemingly neglected teeth: a sudden warmth went out to him from Maddox, unpremeditated, unexpected, unconsidered, as much to do with grief as guilt, a warmth for someone beyond the reach of consolation, beyond the reach of anything that might possibly be imagined: 'the end of everything': the phrase came to mind, something coincidental with the feelings he associated with his recent past – relevant now to someone he'd known, someone he'd admired, someone who had promised much (someone he'd taught), someone he'd been partly instrumental in destroying, in putting where he was.

'I don't think this adds up to much. To you, I mean,' Taylor said, watching him intensely.

'It adds up to a great deal,' he said. 'Though I couldn't put a word, or words, to it.'

177

'All that count are facts. Isn't that what you used to say?' A moment later, as Maddox shook his head, he added, 'At least, it's someone to speak to. Here I can't describe it.'

'I'll come again,' he said, 'if you like.'

'Let me think about it,' Taylor said. 'It may do more harm than good. Raising expectation,' he added. 'Though of what I've no idea.'

It was, Maddox felt, as if he were divesting himself of a child, one without protection of any kind, both the expression and victim of an otherwise inexpressible force, a feeling which bled into his own experience of the previous months, particularly that experience which medication was endeavouring to appease.

Taylor got up from the table, the warder, startled, stepping forward.

His wrists, curiously, held together, Taylor turned to the door; perhaps, for an instant, he had thought of adding something else but, without glancing back, he waited for the door to be opened, then preceded the warder out.

Some moments later a second uniformed figure appeared, glancing in enquiringly at Maddox who, having risen, was still standing by the table. Getting no response from him, the warder enquired, 'Shall I show you out?' indicating the corridor, waiting for Maddox to step before him.

Outside the main gate he paused: the traffic flowed by beyond a parapet: an aircraft lumbered overhead. Rain was falling: it hissed on the cobbled precinct leading to the gate. He pulled his raincoat on, recalled the inquisitive faces of the warders stationed inside and glanced back at the walls. Something implacable, conveyed by the height and texture of the stone, echoed something similarly featured within himself, something uncherished, unlovable, merciless, antipathetic to everything he might otherwise, before his visit, have cared about. Fear, which had preceded his arrival, and which had been revived during his visit, was vividly reignited.

Thrusting his hands in his pockets he walked away, his head bowed, enduring the curious sensation not that he was leaving the building behind but that he was taking a vital part of it with him, reluctant to look behind him to dissuade himself, breaking, finally, into a run, deciding not to travel back on the tube but to take a bus, anything to avoid going, once more, beneath the ground, anything to avoid reliving what had been, and, he presumed, still was, an ungovernable desire to do away with himself.

The rain had lightened as he reached the house, his fatigue, however, increasing. He no longer knew what to make of Taylor. He recollected how he himself had splayed his fingers on the surface of the plastic table, wondering at the gesture, as if signalling he might leave at any moment, the preliminary movement to departure, or, conversely, a sign he was growing increasingly attached to being where he was.

What he couldn't recall was at what point he had removed his hands, for towards the end he had been sitting, obliviously at the time and only now remembered, with them in his lap. It was as if the unimaginable in their lives had gone by default, life, as he'd experienced it at that moment, a process of extinction, in his case by his own hand – in the case of Taylor, also by his own hand; signalling, however, at the end of the interview, as Maddox had understood it, that what he had done he'd done on behalf of others, an inexorable and unavoidable exercise.

'Mad.' He'd spoken aloud, shrugged, and endeavoured to dismiss the thought. 'Not knowing what I think,' he'd gone on, still aloud, 'until I hear it, or write it down,' sitting in the kitchen, desperate for the company, the presence, the comment of Simone, picking up a pen from the table, extracting an already written-on sheet of paper from one of several piles scattered on the table top, and writing, 'Taylor', crossing it out, substituting 'Eric', pausing before continuing, 'are you invoking amnesia? A desire to eradicate what can't be faced is, I have to tell you, common to us both, if, in my case, at a singularly lesser level ...'

He'd put the pen down: they were both attempting, if disinclined, to talk about something which could scarcely be spoken about: no language, no image: not simply a handing-back of life, but of death, an improbable if irrepressible enterprise: an unalterable good expunged not by an unalterable evil but by the same unalterable good: 'I did this,' he spoke aloud, 'in order to start again.'

He wrote quickly, obscurely, scarcely aware of what he was writing and, having written it, tore it up. So much for that: inverting goodness into vice, vice into virtue. He wondered if he hadn't expected too much of Taylor, his precocious and at one time respected student; whether, should he send his message, as Taylor's elected amanuensis, it might confuse, if not provoke, him further, confound the suicide watch of the warders, subvert their best, more likely ambivalent intentions – he who had expunged his family, they disinclined to expunge themselves. Was not Taylor, in short, commandeering him as a witness, the archivist of his perverse adventure, to exhume what he'd done, to define it retrospectively, the one who, in certain circumstances, knew him better than most, who had witnessed him in formation, the incubus before the revelation? Was Taylor giving him as good a reason to live as any, turning dross into something which, however perversely, offered illumination, presenting his own survival, after initial doubt, as a revelatory gesture? Observe and closely mark (this may not, need not happen again: the human involvement in a seemingly inhuman exercise, the nature, the unique nature of the individual involved), hauling Giotto, as he did so, into the picture.

He was hesitating, curiously, from writing anything further, the pen, however, still in his hand. The conclusion he had come to was that Taylor had, after all, proved to be his ultimate pupil, the Baptismal precursor to his revelatory scheme: the conventional oil or gouache paintings, the pencil, ink and conté drawings he'd done at the Drayburgh the afterglow of a tradition that had been expunged by art-as-action, not as contemplation, refinement, encapsulation – transposition – but simply, and gratuitously, nakedly art-as-life: no longer synthesis by paint and brush, hammer and chisel, clay and spatula, but by kitchen knife, a rudimentary, practical, domestic tool, as close to life, in this case – in this definitive case – as death, Giotto's giant

180

step, in the process, remeasured – to be found longer, broader (more encompassing) than first pronounced. Taylor had come good – unasked: all he had learnt, all he had been taught at the Drayburgh, not in the life-room, the sculpture-room, the antique-room, but in his tutorial encounters with Maddox put to explicit, demonstrable, definitive use: he had gone over the edge in the process – the process of validating Maddox, the process of proving him right. Mad Ox had given him his line: his wife, his progeny, his origins subsumed by a desire to be 'real', conceptualism taken to a demonstrably absurd and comprehensively destructive end – as effortlessly as Mad Ox had opened the world of Florentine trecento art, the principle, the premise, the solution the same: out of the blandness of Norfolk had emerged the shape, had he known it, of things to come.

His immediate reaction was to return to his earlier impulse, to write to Devonshire, not so much a revision or amendment as a re-visioning, in the boldest terms, of his review of the British Millennial Exhibition, his original contribution a preamble to what would now be a comprehensive clearing – atomisation – of the ground: Lucretius – *Lucretius!* all over again! All those parodists painting pictures, plus conceptualism posing as an avant-garde – while Taylor, effortlessly, perversely, in its final context, blew away the dust, drew the record straight, offered the sum total in tendering the final account. 'Over the edge', 'beyond providence': he wrote the phrases down: the provisional titles came to mind, conceptual art turned on its head, the Christian ethic, after two thousand years, definitively endorsed, if not transcended, divinity and inhumanity indivisibly one: Taylor's event presented as Maddox's final statement, Ruskin outRuskined – by perversity – at last.

Conversely, he reflected, the pen still in his hand, he could ask Simone to e-mail it (give Devonshire a shock), standing by her shoulder as the sensational message came up on the screen, pre-empting Donaldson, he hadn't a doubt, Donaldson the self-extolled and self-extolling, the self-realised self-promoter, the precursor precursed by Maddox at last.

181

8

He could hear her talking as he entered. Having waited, vainly, for a taxi (the first time he'd thought of taking one to her house), he'd finally come up on the tube, descending the escalator to where he had had his 'Demon' experience, with scarcely a second thought, the feeling that something not negligible had taken place: a perversity, he reflected, behind which he felt peculiarly secure.

He paused before ascending the stairs, not sure whether she was on the telephone or speaking to an unusually silent client, Mrs Beaumont not in her office. Nor was the cat visible, it invariably scampering down to be let out when it heard the front door, or, if it were out, waiting on a nearby window sill to be let in.

She, however, must have heard the door, for a moment later she appeared from her consulting-room, the door of which, unusually when she was in session, had been ajar.

They both spoke at once, mutually confused, she agitated, he alarmed at the strangeness of her expression, she coming forward to be embraced, more impetuously, he realised, than he had moved towards her. 'Have you seen Taylor?'

'I've just got back.'

'I've cancelled my appointments for the rest of the day,' she drawing away, suddenly composed. 'Come upstairs.'

He followed her up, noticing the creases in her skirt, her jacket, the fact that she was wearing flat-heeled shoes, and concluding she'd been in the house alone for some time – failing

182

to take in the scent which, he following her, would familiarly have been flowing in his direction.

Before reaching the sitting-room she turned to the bathroom, called, 'Make yourself some tea. I've had some,' and was gone, he stepping into the kitchen, putting on the kettle, his anxiety, obviated on his journey up, vividly returning. Wave after wave rose, paroxysmally, from the region of his stomach: had she, he reflected, found, or was she prospecting finding someone else (younger, more attractive, more stirringly engaged)?

A need for air, for somewhere less confining than the minimal proportions of the kitchen, took him to the roof, stepping out, breathing deeply, slowly, retaining his breath, exhaling: the view to the south, the distant smear across the horizon, examining the intervening distance for familiar buildings, then, his agitation scarcely reduced, examining the plants, the burgeoning flowers, the declining ones, sitting down, finally, on one of the two garden chairs drawn up at the outside table.

Moments later, restless, wondering on the desirability of returning downstairs, he got up again, the adjoining roofs and chimneys, the overlooking windows, the sky itself, suddenly oppressive: from alarm to something little short of terror, as if everything he were looking at evoked an unmistakable feeling of aggression, antipathy, dislike, rage. Fear absorbed everything around him, a paroxysmal interlude once again, sourced from outside but endured in the region of his stomach, a visceral exclamation. His heart pounded. Sweat came into his eyes.

Then, still flushed, high-coloured, she came through the door, her voice calling, 'Matt?' a sound which calmed him. 'Are you all right?' holding him, he aware of her scent, the softness of her face, her voice, a look of alarm, however, reflecting his own.

'I came up to rewrite the article,' he said, adding, 'Devonshire's. I thought we might e-mail it, if you have the time,' she drawing back, looking at his face, his arms trembling as he held her.

'I thought you'd given it up.'

'I had.' He waited. 'I thought I might refocus it. On Taylor. A perception of his perception of what he thinks he's done. He practically requested it. I feel I have no choice. I feel,' he paused, 'I owe him it. That, without being aware, discrediting his painting, I left him little choice. The Courtauld, for instance, something which, with hindsight, I should have seen he could only reject. He was, above all, an activist, not a pen or a brush he must have to hand but a tool. Specifically a weapon.'

He was aware, speaking too quickly, of something monstrous in his voice and manner, a look of incredulity replacing the one of confusion on Simone's face. 'Focus,' he went on, more slowly, carefully, 'the operative word. I get the feeling he's moved into another world, not parallel or adjacent to but divergent from our own. One he's anxious, desperate, even vocationally inclined to report on before he disappears for good, murder the last thing left for art to do.'

He was sweating profusely, pausing, first, to wipe his eyes, then to breathe in deeply.

Released, she was sitting down, watching his expression. 'What did he say?' she said, indicating – he having stood up to embrace her – he sit at the table too.

'He suggested I played a significant part in disillusioning him. That, of course, I have to take on board. It was only when I got back, however, that I realised why he'd invited me. He wanted what he had done to be understood. Something seen and expressed from an otherwise unacceptable position. Extreme taken to extreme. Who better than me? Someone who, unknowingly, had pointed him in that direction. Who's better placed to do it? I even knew his wife.'

She waited, examining him intently, her own high colour undiminished.

'He sees his actions, and their implications, as consistent with the circumstances in which he found himself. A moral consideration, a moral awareness. To that degree, consistent with the way things have gone and are going. He's broken through what he sees as a definitively destructive culture into something unprecedented on the other side. My role, as a sceptic, is to report it as it happened, authenticity, on my part, assured by my scepticism, and finally, because he sees his actions as the deployment of a truth – truth to circumstance – transcending it, murder, in his case, a definitive form of self-expression, in my eyes the definitive form of malignancy.'

He was sweating profusely, leaning on the table as if manually to extend his words across it, presenting this to her in an almost physical form. He *was* what he was saying.

'He wishes a great evil to be put to the service of identifying a universal good. *Before it is too late.* The execution of everything which we, in our day-to-day conjugations with and in the literal world, patently overlook if not deny.'

He'd been speaking, he thought, for some time, articulating something not on his own but someone else's behalf, articulating what could, to himself as well as others, only give offence. 'He wants his experience to become available. An artistic, not a pathological event which he is deriding as he does it. Judas's prerogative, without which nothing can be real.'

'All you have in common is that you attempted to kill yourself and so did he.' Her voice was calm, her look increasingly composed. 'You haven't killed anyone. Nor are you likely to. Apart from the fact he was your student, you have no obligation to do anything. Certainly nothing as absurd as authenticating his dementia, a specious form of artistic licence, to say the least.'

'Don't you think his actions had any connection with the circumstances in which he lived, and is living now?'

'Why not take any madman, in that case, and say he's doing the same?'

'Because he isn't Taylor. With his sensibility, his intelligence, his background. He's been through the schools. He's studied the process. Presumably he's even taught it. Look at your clients. Aren't they telling you the same? Life is unliveable, yet they're obliged to go on. Isn't Taylor *giving us the message*, an unliveable existence, for the benefit, or so it now seems, of us all? Isn't it legitimate to record it? Isn't it *real*? Didn't it happen?'

The argument, he realised, was already fading: his own agenda, so crudely expressed, was to recognise Taylor as an examplar, a self-presented one, of all that had gone wrong in the art of his time: all that had gone wrong, in short, in his time, the

185

gratuitous displacing feeling, intellect displacing sense. She wanted him free of such morbidity, equating it, no doubt, with his illness. But then, wasn't that 'true' as well?

She'd crossed her legs, her hands clasped, resting on her knee, the light in her eyes – of concern, even distress – suffused by something more elusive: a darkness, extruding, it seemed, from far inside, a malignancy almost, as if someone he didn't recognise and who only wished him harm were gazing out from within a much loved face.

'Why have you cancelled your appointments?' he asked.

'I've been reported to the NMC.'

'For what?'

'This.' She gestured round, then, more specifically, at the two of them. 'I'm a doctor as well as an analyst. Someone has complained.'

'Who?'

'The client you called Doctor Death. His real name is *Norman*. I've made, he complains, indecent proposals. To him. Allegedly, to you. Also, allegedly, to someone else. Oddly, I thought, with him, I'd been making progress. In some respects, I suppose I had. He's acting on his own behalf, showing initiative. His chief complaint in the past has been that his life has been dominated by other people.'

'What credence will they give it?'

'Some time ago, a little time ago, it would have been ignored. Complaints from cranks are ten a penny. With accountability, and litigation, increasing as they are, rightly or wrongly, they'll feel obliged to look into it.'

'Every time I passed him he gave the same averted look. I'm surprised,' he said, 'you went on with him. He clearly took exception to me, and now, evidently, to both of us.' He waited. 'It doesn't stop you practising.'

'If the complaint is upheld I'd be deregistered as a doctor and my accreditation with the British Psychoanalytical Association would come to an end. I could still practise as a therapist.' She shrugged.

'When were you notified?'

186

'I was told of *a* complaint some time ago. No name was given. I even saw him several times afterwards, not knowing it was him. Peculiar, in the circumstances, why he went on coming. I suppose, like a pyromaniac, he wanted to watch the blaze.'

She gazed at him for a while without speaking.

'Tricky stuff. He not knowing if I knew. Me not knowing it was him. This morning, however, I received a letter. Registered. No e-mail or fax, you'll be pleased to note. *If* they go ahead, after getting my response, I have to appear in front of the Preliminary Proceedings Committee. I've been talking to a lawyer recommended by a colleague. *He* was impressed both by them and the allegation. More business, I presume. A growing market. The Medical Council is a subdivision of the Privy Council, and not to be taken lightly. Ambition, on his part, may not be entirely to my advantage. The ultimate threat to remove me from the Register I have to take seriously as well. As for what credit they give to this complaint, I guess as much as you give, or want to give, to Taylor.'

Something jarred – ricocheted, even – inside his skull, a curious physical sensation. 'Taylor's separate,' he immediately responded.

'I wonder if he is.' She was still watching him. 'If you want to champion him as an artist who kills his family as a definitive form of self-expression, I've a feeling you'll be leaving me, if not a lot of others, a long, long way behind.'

'Let's not argue about it,' he said.

He paused, no longer sure what 'it' might be: a vulgar involvement in a delusional world which, he couldn't help feeling, bordered on his own. He had known the man: he had known one of his victims: what he had done was unimaginable. Yet somehow, somewhere – its sole legacy, other than Taylor's own death, something he was now assuming to be a formality – it had to be explained. Or, in the current fashion, he recalled (cf. Donaldson), 'decoded'. Was this the connection Simone had made with his own involvement, a disturbance which might, quite easily, reactivate his own?

'What happens once you've seen this committee?'

187

'If they conclude there is a case they'll hand it to someone called the Preliminary Screener. He or she examines it and if there is a case to be answered the Registrar invites me to an examination conducted, as the lawyer felicitously described it, by my peers. Alternatively, at this or a later stage, I could offer to resign, without a hearing, and I'd have the opportunity to reapply at an unspecified time in the future. Meanwhile I could function as, what you might term, a quack. With, presumably, a declining list of clients. The Preliminary Screener could, however, refer me back to the Preliminary Proceedings Committee and they, in turn, could refer me back to the Licensing Committee. As you can see, plenty of leeway to shuffle the pack and, for the lawyers, the wonderful opportunity for endless proceedings. I don't, necessarily, have to have a lawyer, of course. But in the present climate anything could happen. I might, for instance, get off with a warning. I might even be commended for taking on an idiot beyond the call of duty. On the other hand, Norman could be a plausible liar. Looking back, I'm inclined to believe he is. On top of which there's the other client, identity unknown.' She paused, measuring his reaction. 'It's not uncommon, particularly in psychiatry, to get a patient, or several, complaining about the way they've been treated. Like art, I assume, at one level, everything goes.'

She had uncrossed her legs and, leaning forward, stretching across the table, she took one of his hands.

'They also, of course, have you. An undoubted corroboration of my lack of judgement, of unprofessional practice, of abuse of my position.'

'Do you want to pack it in?' The thought came to him in the instant he expressed it, he enclosing her hand in both of his. 'Us,' he added, 'not your job.'

'I don't.' She shook her head. 'What would that look like? Confirmation!' She laughed, glancing up, an aircraft whining overhead on its ascent from Heathrow, the vibration of its engines passing through the house. 'I'm worried about you and Taylor,' she added. 'Another phenomenological exercise. Art as

188

life. It's time you moved on. Particularly,' she concluded, 'from that.'

'Art's always close to delinquency,' he said. 'Also to voyeurism. There's not much changed in that. And I can't deny there's a subjective element involved, because I know him, and also knew his wife. Nevertheless, he invited me, even if he does or doesn't succeed in killing himself. Or one of the prisoners does it for him. In addition to which,' he paused. 'I was even more involved with his wife.'

'How?'

'Like we are.' He added, 'She was a first-year student, I was a lecturer. I knew her before she knew Taylor. He took her on the rebound.'

About to respond, she paused, then shook her head. 'Scarcely like us,' she said. 'I would have thought.'

'I'd have to go back and talk to him, in any case. There's no guarantee,' he said, 'he'll see me. The whole thing,' he raised one hand, releasing hers, 'could go on for ever. Even now, on reflection, he won't know precisely why he asked me.'

He was, he realised, in the face of her problem, withdrawing. 'Should there be a hearing is the lawyer you spoke to able to represent you?'

'He's drafting a letter asking for clarification. More details of Norman's allegations. Who the second person is. Expressing my willingness to cooperate.'

'I'll come with you if you have to go.'

'I'll have to ask him whether that's a good idea or not. They might see it as a provocation. But,' she smiled, 'I very much appreciate the offer. As for Taylor,' her smile had faded, 'I'd let it settle before you get in touch with him or Devonshire. Perhaps I should come and see him, too.'

'That,' he said, 'would make it something else. It's far too personal,' he added, 'at present.'

'That's the trouble.' Still she retained his hand in hers. 'Are you aware of your reaction being unusual?'

'It's an unusual situation,' he said.

'Maybe writing about it is a way of exonerating yourself,' she

189

said. 'Getting rid of his accusation of your involvement in what he did.'

They sat in silence, their hands still held across the table, caught in a process, he thought, which could sweep either or both of them away.

'You feel challenged by your situation, I feel challenged by mine,' he finally responded. 'I'll support you in whatever way you like. If the worst comes to the worst we could sell our houses and move separately or jointly into something more modest. We can both of us, in one way or another, go on working. Separately or together, we can both survive.' He waited for her response and, getting none, went on, 'How serious is it with the Medical Council? I can hardly see our arrangement, on its own, jeopardising your career. Otherwise, all they have is the accusations of two presumably nutty clients.'

'I'll have to rely,' she said, 'on their discretion and on how well I put my case. There'll be an inclination, in the present climate, to give the accusations a run. On the other hand, I'm confident I could give a robust response. With us, I stopped the therapy the moment there was an involvement. If every doctor was deregistered because of a relationship with a former patient or client there wouldn't, I assume, be many of us around. After all,' she smiled, 'it's a sure way of meeting a lot of interesting people. You could say that's why some of us take it up. Not, of course, in my case. I already felt *socially* fulfilled. Otherwise, however, there's an *absolute* discretion involved, an absolute commitment. Like you with Taylor. What he has done. The nature, the cause and the purpose of your involvement. We've both, in one sense, breached, if at different times, a professional ethic. On the other hand, if evil is the seat of goodness, as you suggest, what price goodness? What price evil? What price anything? *Who says?*'

He thought for a moment she might go on speaking, but, turning to look at him directly, she smiled again, nodding.

'Taylor,' he said, 'was responding, or thought he was – still thinks he's responding – to something inclusive, not exclusive, as

190

you suggest. All he's asking is for what he did to be seen in the widest possible context, something he thinks I can do for him.'

'Have you told him you've been ill?'

'No.'

'Does he know?'

'I doubt it. I was absent from reviewing for a while, but he wouldn't know the reason. Devonshire only took me back because of it. Didn't wish to be seen regressive, and has regretted it ever since. His present resolve is to treat me as normal in order to show going nuts for him is no different from having measles, or flu, or a broken leg.'

'In a sense, he's right.'

'I wonder.'

'In your case, I mean.'

'I doubt it.'

She was looking at him strangely – not unlike the expression he associated with their first encounters, an aloofness of a clinical nature, mentally stepping back in order, paradoxically, to examine something more closely.

'Insanity,' she said, '*is* exclusive. To assume otherwise is to misunderstand it completely. I think something perverse, on your side, is creeping in. I'm frightened for you.' She added, 'I think, as with Norman, Taylor can still do a lot of damage. The enlightenment that you and your friend Viklund go on about is not, in my view, enlightenment at all. More nearly it's the arrest of a particular kind of perception which galvanises, or appears to, *because* it's arrested. I feel, I felt, I was freeing you from all that.'

'Immaturity,' he suggested.

'Innocence. Viklund, despite his appearances, and manner, is guilelessness writ large.'

He watched an insect, a bumble-bee, move from flower to flower: at each it paused, probed, flew on. Overhead, another aircraft whined up from Heathrow, a frill of condensation flickering from its tailplane and wings. Distracted by the sound, she glanced up, too, the horizontal lines at the base of her neck accentuating her look of concern, bordering, he felt, on disaffection.

'That was your philosophy, which, at the time, you were keen for me to know about.' Having lowered her head, she smiled. 'We are here to destroy and to be destroyed. A dispassionate view of history confirms it. Wars, pogroms, disease, personal as well as communal disasters. The annihilating experience of marriage, motherhood, paternity. It's because the pain of destructiveness is too much that we come to understandings. If I don't hurt you you won't hurt me. Self-interest moves on to an interest in others. Pain, in its mental and physical forms, persuades us, finally, to compromise. Interest in others turns to affection, affection to love, a species of self-love externally confirmed. We love ourselves for loving others. Finally we reach the stage of, "I'll love you if you'll love me", which, of its nature, evolves into "I'll love you even if you don't love me", our exegesis, as you remarked, of the tyranny of nature, of, you concluded, our unrequested end.'

He smiled, listening to her encapsulation of what he had – tendentiously, for the most part, certainly defensively – explained: his own 'governance', he'd described it, pleased – rejoicing – that she recalled it, and, having recalled it, was now discounting.

He was reminded, once again, of his instinctual response to Taylor: someone so far outside his experience – their experience (they were in this together) – must count as something – he realising, too, in that instant, how much he loved her, how completely she over-reached his life, securing him to something he couldn't live without: loving her, in effect, at that moment, for her attempt to dress herself in his (metaphysical) clothes in order to show how absurd he looked.

'What did you think when you heard it?'

'I thought it,' she said, 'an unusual defence.'

'Against what?'

'I never found out. I wondered, nevertheless, if I could bring you back to earth.'

She was smiling once again.

192

'And now?'

Colour, once more, had risen to her cheeks.

'Self-interest is an indeterminate term,' she said. 'I'm always inclined to oppose it. Cynicism,' she added, 'given a plausible face, "we are our relationships" a partial truth, like,' she went on, 'so much else you put my way. The volition towards pleasure is as much a natural volition as a desire to destroy. You mustn't, to that degree, take Taylor as confirmation of your thesis.'

Birds swooped across the roof: swifts, their high-pitched squeaking echoing between the houses. Higher up, house-martins traced more jagged loops, fluttering and falling, diving and climbing, pursuing, he assumed, an invisible, from this distance, cloud of midges.

'What other conclusions did you come to?'

'Not a lot.' She re-crossed her legs, composure of some sort returning: they had long ago released one another's hands. 'I was more interested in you describing art as something useless which, the moment it has a use, becomes something else, utility combined with aesthetics a craft, aesthetics combined with nothing, art. Plus, your evocation of an environment in which the machine had passed the point of service, we obliged to service it. And how, generally, what couldn't be pronounced until the moment it was expressed, creating precedent in the process, was fastened in with what you described as "mechanics". That we *are* mechanics, without choice, art currently, as a result, a mechanism too. The impression, for instance, you create, that you and Viklund, and now Taylor, are the last of the cultural Mohicans.'

She was laughing, leaning back, he following her gaze to the nearby roofs: the attic windows, the variegatedly angled chimney-pots, her own neat enclosure of plants and flowers – more than ever, he reflected, a refuge.

Below, at intervals, the telephone rang: the swift cutting-off as it recorded a message: the inaudible muttering of a voice.

'Your view of art as history, of *anything* as history, come to that. Your admiration for a tradition, a humanist tradition, which is now extinct and which, helplessly, it seems, you feel obliged to revive. I suspect the perversity of Taylor's return to your life is the seal on the verdict you've been looking for. Comes, as it were, at an opportune time, philistinism ending not in suicide but murder, *then* suicide. An explanation of your impulse to self-destruction. He killing others *as* himself, the two, to him, unlike you, indistinguishable. "We are our relationships", his final message.'

He didn't wish Taylor to be 'wrong'; that, too, she could see: his requirement that murder (of 'himself') should be seen as the inevitable outcome of the way things were, the absolution he was seeking without hope of achieving.

'Maybe we should lie down,' she said. 'Recover from all this. I'll bolt the front door. Mrs Beaumont isn't due today, and I've fed the cat.'

Things were more real than they seemed, he reflected, following her down, the slimness of her figure, the texture of her hair, her vulnerability and her determination suddenly apparent, conformity, compliance with everything, or most things, perversely or otherwise, not on her agenda: an ability, he further reflected, to cast herself off, independent, self-reliant (to an extraordinary degree) – a self-reliance which she was inviting him to share, changing its nature, its form, its purpose.

And later, in bed – abandonment of a sort, since it was mid-afternoon – he endured the curious sensation they'd been cast off together, invisibly suspended, surveying the angle of the tiles outside, the sagging line of the older houses, the confirmatory lines of those that had been restored, his feeling, increasingly engendered on each of his visits, once in her bedroom, that they were indeed afloat: the wood-panelling, the reflective figure beside him, her eyes, too, turned to the window – until, finally, lulled by a rhythm which came from them both, she placing her arm around him, he turned on his side, the shape of her body impressed against his back.

His old terror had been that he might survive, his new one that he wouldn't, he, recently, noticing the vagaries of his mind

194

much more, wondering if they were vagaries at all and not the evidence of a parallel existence. Particularly clear were his experiences of 'another place', full of warmth and familiarity (a feeling induced by being in her bed). The moment these sensations were recognised, however, they vanished, as if consciousness alone had dispelled them.

An involitional drama, an involutional exercise: not to be alone, not to be suspended (not to be out of a job) and then, quite simply, not to be afflicted, 'nuts' the condition that looked over the edge, saw what was there, helped solely by familiarity to claw its way back: a neural conflagration with no physical manifestation other than a knitting of the brows, the rocking forward and backward over the axis of the arms, the second-by-second confrontation with what he assumed were the principal questions of existence: why? who? how? where? a mutatory device engaged, seemingly, on its own destruction.

All his decisions, he'd concluded, at the onset of his illness, had been wrong: wrong in space, in time, in sequence: not the right action for the wrong reason, nor the right reason for the wrong action: instead, an accumulation of defects, a litany of excuses (excesses, confessions) – less regret, remorse, contrition, than statement of fact.

One of those mornings, early in their relationship, for instance, he had found himself walking up the hill from his backstreet dwelling by Camden Lock to that welcome enclosure of Georgian, pre-Georgian, Queen Anne dwellings where Simone had her consulting-room as well as her domestic quarters and, for the first time, as he approached her door, saw emerging from it the skeletal, dark-haired, pale-featured, black-suited individual, a briefcase in one hand, a portable telephone in the other, whom he had immediately personified, to Simone's displeasure, moments later, meeting her in the hall, as Doctor Death. 'Aids?' he'd enquired (searing eyes gazing portentously from a skull-like head), to which she'd responded, 'Far from it,' disinclined, at that point, to discuss it. She: her dark hair, on that occasion, lustred to perfection: the delicacy, in the morning light, of her porcelain features, the refinement of nose and brow, dark eyes, thick-lashed, extended laterally with eye-shadow, a hint of blue across the lids, each eye opaque but for its reflection – of the one he was disinclined to see, at that stage: himself – nothing visible of what lay beneath: cheeks subtended to a percipient chin, incised above a percipient mouth, the whole of her face – its asperity, its bird-like gaze – pointing to enquiry: why? her figure, in its fifties, drawn forward to all-consuming, engaging breasts, moving before her, sensual, sensuous, inform-ing: grand. And legs, high-heeled, even in her domestic quarters, the persuasive endorsers of a quisitive nature, the preternatural 'what is it all about?' implicit in the frankness of her look: the framing cheeks, the framing brow: creator, expeller, adviser, judge, her house an arbour on the pilgrim route to St Albans, the Romano-British Christian martyr, he, Maddox, approaching his seventieth year . . .

No wonder Doctor Death had responded in the way he had, much scope, in Simone's appearance, to be misconstrued, not least by someone persuaded (determined) it could be. Perhaps, he concluded, she should dress for work in a less celebratory fashion, her clothes, he recalled, mannered to Paris rather than Rome, less line involved than substance (lascivious, for instance, his own response, illicit, warm): the agate ring she twisted on the third finger of her left hand, the stone she gazed into as if into herself: what stars! what moon! what future – he waking some time later to find her still compressed against his back, he turning over to embrace her, his still to hold, he still hers to do likewise.

He had taken to writing when all else had failed, he, sleepily inspired, reclining in bed, she, restless, having got up, preparing their supper: the sound of crockery and cutlery and cooking utensils coming up the stairs from the kitchen. Earlier, she had been pottering with her plants on the roof above his head: she was 'into' everything, he reflected, he checking her past, his own, for errors, mind subsumed by drugs: dothiepin, thiorida-zine, the side-effects, previously, of seroxat too extreme, in his case, to bear: irregular heartbeat, sensational headaches, convulsive jaw movements, nausea, anxiety increased, not so much wrestling, as Aurelius might have had it, as dancing (to death), wheeling and gliding – pots crashing more vigorously in the kitchen, determination and concentration two of Simone's more obvious traits, even sleeping a convulsionary sound.

He was reading Lucretius (again: a Viklund recommendation): a copy of *De Rerum Natura* by his bed, another by Simone's. Waiting for supper, he'd just put it down: everything was chance, he not so much a god's, or the gods' or even 'the Father's' invention as an asymmetrical, unprogrammed, irrelevant aside, a disencumbrance disencumbered. And Plutarch, Epicurus, Seneca, Cicero, Pliny, practitioners whose practitioning embraced a curious disposition: what was inexplicable abandoned to the divine, an ineradicable omission – life, his life, his and Simone's life, an omission – crime, brutality, passion, efficaciously slotted into position, an irrefragable part of an indissoluble whole. 'You deal with the best in human nature, I the worst,' Simone had written in one of her cryptic notes, posted whenever she was away, with protestations of 'I love you', arriving invariably after she was back ('that's all right: it's what I felt'), 'What's the diff, Professor?' A sophist (she!), he not so much a philosopher (or professor) in response, as a pillager, as Major-Minor, his former schoolfriend, had once remarked, irreality his saviour, what was redeemable, in Simone's life, an ethic, a passion – a vocation, even (*pace* Taylor), passed to him. What was owed, in his case, exceeded what was given, duty seceding to rights.

Building a dossier on himself, he reflected, as others might be building one on her: turning over in the bed to see the photograph of himself she kept beside it, a tiny original of him seated on her roof, wondering, as he did so, on her preparations in the kitchen. Wondering on her.

'Let's face it,' he spoke aloud, savouring the words, finally the meaning, 'I've failed': marriage, paternity, posterity, vocation, job: the imprimatur he'd franked on Simone's life, even if it were a joint decision. Plus, the curious sensation that immobilised him each morning, that he was about to be taken into the street and shot: that he had informed on his neighbours (the worst of his dreams), dealers in crack, plus prostitution, extortion, theft, fencing: Berenice's minder who spent his days in bed, the nights marshalling her punters: black, close-cropped, bulbous, a buttress, he, of the narcotics trade, Maddox, by comparison, a 'clerc', an observer, reporter, redundanteur, spectator: Plato's cavern, he standing at the mouth, avoiding the shadows, identifying the objects stranded outside.

He'd been drawn to Laycock's theories of supra-indifferentiation (and supra-disregard) in his youth: unfashionable in the forties when they'd first appeared (the effect of war on the 'cerebral imagination'), the individual a synthesis of external 'charges', pressures reflecting subliminal as well as overt forces – theories Simone had favoured herself but which he, carelessly at first, then vigorously, had abandoned, genes and epigenetics his current principal 'charges', specifically the influence of methyl groups of chemicals on gene formation, the methylation as much, if not more, an influence than the determinology of the genes themselves: new species formed (misbehaving chromosomes misbehaving on the part of something else: aneuploidy) seeing himself, seeing Taylor, as the precursors of an otherwise unpredictable event – the 'punctuated equilibrium' of mutatory research – he determined to e-mail or fax, or simply post to Devonshire his revised exegesis on post-twentieth-century art, phenomenology taken, in the instance of Taylor, to its logical, amoral, definitive end.

Already she was on the stairs, he with the Lucretius (affinity with nature: affinity with circumstance) still in his hand, she calling, 'Supper's ready,' passing by the bedroom door with a wave, on the way to the roof to collect herbs, a pair of scissors in her hand: the sound of her feet on the flagstones: the creaking of the ceiling, the telephone ringing, the sound of a voice recording a message: everything normal (the atmosphere so unlike that of his own house, where the telephone scarcely rang at all).

'The despair,' he said to her over supper, 'that humanity is succeeding,' they eating at the table beside the familiar window, she, anxious for distraction, perpetually on the move, 'whereas, with you, it's the horrible feeling that it might easily lose. What a combination. The ball, however, in your court. Your turn,' he told her, 'to knock it back.'

She remained distracted (had been since waking), glancing about her, not least towards the window as if, from there, she expected otherwise unseen support.

'Maybe I should go ahead with Taylor, without involving you,' he continued. 'I can get the copy faxed in the High Street. That alone should startle Devonshire. Even then,' he paused, 'I ought to see Taylor again. The idea of handing something in before Donaldson, of course, is out of the question. I must have been ranting when I first came in,' pausing again before enquiring, 'Is this mania, do you think?'

'That's for you,' she said, 'to decide,' turning her gaze to him, a moon-like expression, calm, abstracted, reproaching him, it seemed – or removing him, or about to, from her life. 'Maybe you should pursue it, to see where it leads.'

'Shall I stay the night?' he asked.

'I need time to myself. You, too,' she said. 'I'll see you tomorrow,' moving her food about her plate, examining it, as if undecided whether to eat it or not. 'I'd *like* to see you tomorrow,' she added.

'Should I see your letter?' he said. 'The one from the Council.'

'Later,' she said. 'I'll deal with it now,' dismissing the suggestion with a wave of her hand. 'Let's keep the two things separate. You with Taylor, I with this,' her gaze returning to the window, the steps of someone passing below them, in the street. 'It's odd, but since we've talked about it, I have the feeling we're being watched. That the place is being watched. Obsessional behaviour, of course, is infectious, provoking a similar response in the victim.'

Maddox, too, looked out to the street, little more than a cul-de-sac, centrally approached by the flight of stone steps leading up from Heath Street: whoever had been passing had gone.

199

'I feel quite capable of handling it,' she added.

'All I need is for you to tell me the best way I can help,' he said.

'Sure,' she said, 'I shall,' turning to her food, finally, and beginning to eat.

Later, when he left, she said, 'I don't like you going home alone. You hear of so much trouble nowadays, particularly around your place,' he, embracing her, responding, 'It's only as dangerous as it always was. Neither of us should get uneasy,' wondering, however, as he descended the steps to Heath Street, whether he was being watched, glancing at the figures descending with him from the neighbouring public house, as well as those coming up from below, dismissing the thought once he'd reached the tube station entrance and, the evening being fine, deciding to walk.

The reality was, if Taylor were 'consistent', à la Laycock, with his circumstances, then so was he: an imperative of self-destruction in both their cases, unless the anomalies thrown up by science – those lately discovered chemical accretions which had as much effect on function as the genes themselves – were nevertheless consistent with their environment in which a universal mutatory process was underway, of which few – or even any, other than Taylor and himself – were aware.

The cafés and restaurants were full in the High Street, chairs and tables spilling out on the pavements; similarly, in Belsize Park. Further down the hill, however, the streets were comparatively empty. Where the road dipped down to Chalk Farm he glimpsed the floodlit dome of St Paul's in the distance: it could all, conversely, this scenario, be part of his dilemma: he and Taylor were nuts, his illness no different from that characterising several, if not all, of those members of his 'support' group: poor Beth, and Judith, Ida, Anna, Alex, Sally, geriatricity in action, age alone engulfing what rational qualities he had left, nervous exhaustion inseparable from physical decline.

Once he was in the house he rang her to say he was back: the darkness of the streets, the last walk along a level stretch of pavement, past the lit windows of cafés and pubs, his mind, he

200

realised, no longer calm, if anything, in something of a fever, reactions (in his case) identified with causes, causes misinterpreted as effects, a paradoxically ordered sense of disorder, he inclined to ring her back, to talk over again what might be happening, what had happened, what might well happen (his imagination on the loose again), Laycock's theories of indifferentiation – separating effects, in effect, from causes (the 'Viennese Syndrome' wherein effects were diagnosed as causes) – notwithstanding, a subliminal absorption by (invisible) adjacent forces mirrored in – paralleled by – a mutatory activity in the brain, Taylor and Laycock, in this context, a concatenation of thought and feeling – a conclusion which took him, confusedly, to bed, he missing her, he now realised, acutely (could she trust him, at this moment, not to regress?), the events of the day, he further reflected, coming to a head: the darkening room, the view of the houses opposite, the windows alight beyond his own uncurtained one – absorbed by a sensation corresponding to that which had gripped him earlier that day in the presence of Taylor, a negative element projected by each of them, indistinguishable from the physical sensation experienced on the tube station platform (not three hundred yards from where he was lying), a hand, its individual fingers configured around his body, projecting him, without warning, towards the line.

9

DOCTOR KAVANAGH was a small, muscular, broadly built man, perhaps in his early forties, with blond, receding, short-cropped hair, and – surprisingly, considering his patients – an incredulous, accessible, ingenuous smile: 'now that's a strange thing to say/do', his expression conveyed in response to the complaints, the terror, the resignation, the appetite for death, he encountered amongst the majority of his 'clients', as he preferred to call them, the accounts of decay, decline, disablement, senility an increasing, or so it seemed, mystery to him, the strange foreshortening of everything, for instance, connected with the senses, the awareness of mortality which preoccupied everyone who came to see him, his office a bare, fastidiously undecorated interior, echoing a not dissimilar disinclination to face nature's, and specifically humanity's inevitable end: a suggestion that life, once begun, could be reasonably expected to go on for ever, certainly with the doctor's advice and assistance, Maddox, on this occasion, summoned in at lunchtime from his group, one of those whom the good doctor was more than anxious to turn in this promising direction.

He had, in his youth, he had told Maddox, been a boxer ('a facility for getting hit more frequently than I was hitting others') at medical school ('a dying sport, in more ways than one'), and gymnast ('never any great standard in this country, either'), and had collected paintings ('mainly, if not exclusively, artists you've never heard of, nor are likely to'), an enthusiast, at heart, for obscure pursuits, lunacy amongst the elderly undoubtedly the most significant.

Maddox liked him: in one sense, he believed he must have loved him: faith, devotion, an indefatigable belief in the prolongation of human excitation had, in Maddox's view, to be met by an equivalent, unambiguous response.

Wearing a cardigan and corduroy trousers, an open-necked shirt (an informality of dress he shared with the charge-nurse, Richard), seated only inches away from Maddox, he exuded an air of fraternal, almost physical companionability: if death were in the room he would only have to be informed and, in a matter of seconds, he would have thrown it out (no boxer and gymnast for nothing: even obscure paintings would play their part): 'Tell me,' his look implored. 'I'm here to do whatever you ask,' Maddox aware of the apologetic tone with which he described his symptoms – dragging them behind him, deferentially, through the door – not least the more alarming ones. Kavanagh, he knew from previous encounters, held out the possibility of his getting younger by the hour: come in feeling sixty-nine, go out feeling forty-five, eyes brighter, limbs lighter, spirits higher, brain alert, mortality in abeyance, if not dispensed with – as quickly, as swiftly, with Kavanagh's assistance, as he might have removed his coat. What, previously, might have been measured in terms of regression, were, in reality, indications of progress: the delaying hand in the air, the quizzical look, the smile which greeted any mention of decline ('surely,' the look inferred, 'you must have been mistaken').

'I've a feeling,' Maddox said, coming directly to the point, indicating he would brook no dissension, 'I'm getting nuttier. I'm concocting a rationale which includes both the best and the worst in human nature with the intention of showing that perversity and altruism are not involved, that action and thought are consistent with context, context defined in terms of the circumstances in which each individual finds him- or herself. To this end, chance has led me to a man I knew several years ago who has committed an unpardonable crime. With him, too, I am looking for the same consistency,' pausing to watch Kavanagh's perplexed (confounded) expression, wondering – having no experience of such an event – if this was what

203

happened to someone like the good doctor when, in a boxing-match, his opponent threw a left – a vigorous, idiosyncratic, explosive left – instead of an expected – a singularly signalled – right.

'Laycock's theory,' Kavanagh said, suddenly. 'I read up on him as a student. We don't exist except in terms of, or as a projection of, the specifics and generalities by which we are surrounded. Laycock, if I remember, having a job with geniuses, the explanation thereof. If one could be produced, in Moscow, say – he was very fond of Tolstoy, a Laycockian to the core – "kings are history's slaves" – why aren't all Muscovites geniuses too? A problem he got round with his theory of exception. I liked it. "*Exclusivity of circumstance*". Einstein, of course, another problem. Along with Freud, or, as he referred to him, Fraud. "*Nature's own*". Anticipating, in the process, much of subsequent genetic theory. A bit like a tag of wool, I always thought, hanging from a jumper. Attempt to pull it out and the whole of the garment comes apart.'

He was smiling: optimistic, alert, incorrigibly charming: another shadow dispelled (another chimera disposed of).

All the time, however, he, Maddox, was thinking of Simone: should he mention her (and her present predicament)? And Taylor: should he expand on that? the two of them, he and Simone, not least in his dreams, hopelessly combined, an androgynous couple. Something of a more reassuring response was that he, Maddox, Mad Ox, was taking leave of his senses, or, more pertinently, accurately, they were taking leave of him (going elsewhere, destination to be announced), the 'he' in this equation an entity which had been evolving, surreptitiously, behind his back, throughout his life, an insidious, indescribable, demonic creation, there all the time, now sensationally, frighten-ingly, wickedly revealed, Maddox, in all his absurdity – his cruelties, his perversions, his distortions, above all, his affecta-tions – exposed like a rock by an outgoing tide.

'I can't work out whether it's a rationale based on evidence, or pathology,' he said, 'in another form,' Kavanagh no longer examining him with a smile but a frown. The sound of the physiotherapist came from the hall outside where the day's group were being lightly loosened up after lunch: 'Don't let digestion turn to fat. Bend forward, and back. To your left, to your right. Keep the shoulders straight, Anna,' they seated in a circle in the upholstered, wooden-armed chairs, digestion undoubtedly the least of their problems (the wool unravelling in his mind, destroying his own original design).

Continually he was putting himself in a corner, pinned in, on this occasion, with Simone, who, he suspected, he had wilfully manoeuvred beside him. What part had he played in her seduction of him? consciously, demurely, helplessly, even, she drawn in by his 'circumstance' (open to advances, propositions, suggestions), Doctor Death, the physiognomy as well as figure, becoming indistinguishable from the otherwise sharply contrasted figure of Taylor (death, in both instances, though no similarity, in reality, at all): the last glimpse of his former student hesitating at the interview-room door – Maddox glancing up, at this point, at Kavanagh, looking for a lead, the corduroys, the open-necked khaki shirt (a military association somewhere), the sleeves of the cardigan drawn up, his wrists and forearms bare (a physical engagement with his perpetual opponent): the strange things his patients, his declining patients, came up with, their mental and physical deterioration, unavoidable in any other circumstance, encouragingly ignored. 'A preoccupation with ideas is inevitable,' Kavanagh said, 'considering your background. I should,' he continued, 'let them run. You can always invalidate them,' he added, 'if they don't stand up,' pausing before enquiring, 'Do you find them disturbing or constructive?'

'They appear to have their own momentum,' he said. 'As if the last gesture anyone can make is to find a reason for having done what they have done. If not,' he went on, 'for everything,' gazing at Kavanagh's eager, open face as if there he might find an answer. 'Maybe I should draw back. Be more reluctant to go with it. It can't,' he went on, 'be the medication. I never had this reaction to dothiepin earlier. I take it I'm on the maximum dose?' Kavanagh watching him acutely. Am I, or am I not, he reflected, going mad? Why had Simone been so prompt in allowing him to go the previous evening?

What did madness consist of? a reasonable expectation abandoned, a predisposition to take neither yes nor no for an answer. He was, he reflected, overturning his life (in order to see, for the first time, what lay underneath: the analogy with a car immediately apparent): hoisted up on a ramp, a hallucinatory experience in the context of a room devoid of decoration, its functional chairs, its functional table, their two chairs confronting one another, a room, curiously, if more compact and of more recent construction, not unlike the one in which he'd visited Taylor, and, before that, in which he'd taken tutorials at the Drayburgh.

'Loss is gain', 'Man cometh by death', two songs he might have sung, the freedom Laycock approved of (exercised, promoted), the 'freedom' of being 'in relation' (any number of sources), a romantic extrapolation of a freedom he could, otherwise, have only dreamt about – and one which Laycock more thoroughly examined: a Christianic affiliation with something, someone, he had, previously, only heard rumours about, beyond neighbourliness, beyond a stranger's Samaritanic identification (with the lost, the dying, the inept, the ruined, the hopelessly depraved): here was Maddox, as Simone had suggested, with an answer (to everything, parenthesis included).

No wonder Kavanagh was looking surprised: not many metaphysically inclined geriatrics in Holm House to distract him from his much-admired day clinic, Maddox, as on previous occasions, at school, at college, now here, a much-laboured exception, Mad Ox, of the genus Bos, not named as such for nothing – munching his way into the formalised masses, from there chewing his way back out again, in the hope of returning to a previously abandoned central role: art as murder, or some such thing, killing, a final conceptual marker (the end of contemporary art as we know it): truth-to-nature-Taylor, TTNT, for short.

'Since it appears to have sprung up spontaneously I feel obliged to pursue it,' he said. 'It may even be a sign of recovery,' the look of relief on Kavanagh's face, 'life' convened in all its positive phases. 'To your left, Alex,' from the hall outside. 'To your right, Judith.' 'Libido, too, is very low, if not, at most times, absent. I wonder if I should have a pill.'

'Later, probably,' Kavanagh said. 'It could be the dothiepin's side-effects. Once you're stabilised I can forward you to an appropriate clinic,' glancing up from the file on his knee in which, suddenly, he'd started to write, to enquire, the first overt sign of curiosity he'd shown, 'Is it a problem at present?'

'I get an erection and occasionally can't sustain it,' Maddox said, wondering how relevant this might be.

'It's certainly not ageing,' Kavanagh said, disinclined to concede deterioration in anything. 'There's no reason why you shouldn't have a normal sex life, no reason why you shouldn't return to what you might call your normal state of abnormality,' smiling, instructions, outside the room, continuing, 'You're not trying, Beth. You'll have to put more into it. These soporific afternoons we won't allow,' Kavanagh, unaware, seemingly, of the relevance of the commentary, writing once more in his file.

Maddox turned his gaze to the window: a flower-bed in a lawn, beyond which rose the trees in the back gardens of the houses opposite: Edwardian and post-Edwardian structures – his own sense of confusion increased by what he could only interpret as Kavanagh's disinclination to acknowledge defeat (a doughty boxer, in his youth, he assumed), or further discuss Laycock's relevance to his current situation: nothing as bad as it seemed, the approach of death coinciding with nature's euthanasia (a decrease of facility in perceiving what, precisely, was going on) not something Kavanagh, for the life of him, and others, would endorse, inimical to his vocational way of thinking.

It was, after all, a century of unprecedented disaster, progress from equated, confusingly, with progress to, regression to with regression from, itemised, the confusion, in two global wars and an unprecedented number of smaller ones, tuned, the whole of them, to a Tayloresque conclusion.

From the particular to the universal, in this instance, and

207

back again, in scrupulously recorded stages, philosophy as action – recording two children lying in their beds (nine and eleven), doped before he killed them, and one wife, half doped in the bedroom where she'd struggled with him before being knifed repeatedly in the chest (the back, the sides, the head, the neck, the flailing arms and legs), Taylor, a blood-streaked figure, making an attempt to hang himself (of this will I dispose: it has all gone wrong: it is all revoked: I alone can see it, I alone am *it*), the banister rail to which he had attached the rope breaking, the bursting-in of the police summoned by a neighbour (the wife's screams shattering the silence of the crescent: no one quite the same after that: Taylor's rock in the pool projecting further than he might have assumed). All this a paraphrase, not thought about, prematurely dismissed, in Maddox's mind, as so much else: Laycock's precept of 'civility' (that which thou dost to me I do to thee); that which engineered cohesion, responsiveness, the relationship between 'concept' and 'perception', between the individual and the congruities he or she collated, consciously or otherwise, to make up what s/he knew as 'themselves': the 'motor-mode' of civil existence (another analogy Maddox had been responsive to), life, in short, as only a lunatic would know it, a rationalist, a voyeur (Laycock 'explaining' Hitler at the time: *Thesis and Antithesis* his seminal work of 1940).

Now he was talking Kavanagh's language: that things were improving: libido, even, might soon be on the way: Simone didn't mind: there were more than two ways, he was about to tell Kavanagh, to pluck a goose, to cook a gander, to fuck a femme fatale, which, in Simone's case, left little to be desired: tongue, mouth, finger: a return to his earliest sexual achievements: dexterity (imagination, exercise): he was on the threshold – the edge – of fulfilling a dream (Laycock's, too) containing (constraining) the diversity of human experience within a single rationale, empiricism deployed to a previously undetermined end: his personal experience – his knowledge, in this instance, of the development within and without of a particular man, seeing Taylor as a 'construct': an extrapolation extended to include the whole of his experience – the whole of what, in reality, Maddox considered to be a parallel existence, namely, himself.

'You can call me any time,' Kavanagh said. 'No need to keep to your one day a week,' Maddox reassured that, should the line to which he was attached drag him under – or, conversely, snapping, plunge him, alive, to the foot of the stairs – there was someone here he could talk to, who understood – the phrase came to him at that moment – the language of the dead.

10

IT WAS Viklund who woke him, ringing in the middle of the afternoon (that morning his monthly appointment with Kavanagh), he roused by the telephone and, for a moment, not sure where he was – initially assuming he was at Simone's, reminded of her threatened situation, conceivably the end of her professional life, the instrument of destruction, in this instance, no one but himself.

Picking up the receiver from beside the bed – he'd been sleeping on his back, fully clothed, as he invariably did in the afternoons, on the double bed in the front room – he listened to Viklund's courteous, nevertheless insinuatory voice as if it were an element of a dream itself: the surge of confusion which increased rather than dissipated itself on waking, he recoiling from answering so that, after Viklund's, 'How did you get on with Taylor?' he remained silent, 'Did your visit go ahead?'

'It went very well,' his opinion going out without reflection. 'He'd rationalised, or was attempting to, the experience along the lines of an artistic event convened less by him, he merely being its instrument, than others.'

'Who?'

'Me. You. All of us,' gesturing around the otherwise empty room. 'Laycock's "reductive imperative", if you've ever heard of it. We subsume what we don't like as a matter of form. Truth to his materials, another way of putting it, his materials, in this particular demonstration, being his family and himself, *A Family Group*, as it were, the title of his composition, a long-established, indeed, honourable theme.'

210

Was that right; or was he transposing Taylor's experience into something constructed facetiously by himself?

'Expressing what is there without his necessarily being aware of it,' he added.

'Deranged.' The dog was barking in the background: concurrence or disagreement, hard to tell. On odd occasions, more in rebuke than with affection, Viklund would remark, 'That dog knows *everything*,' examining it with apprehensive eyes. 'Not a term, I realise, you'd prefer to use,' he added, sketching his distance not from him but Taylor.

'I'd thought of writing about him along those lines,' Maddox said, 'he practically inviting me. Certainly it would get up Devonshire's nose. Being an opportunist, he'd feel obliged to use it.'

'Pulling down the temple as long as you aren't in it,' Viklund said. 'Wouldn't opportunism,' he went on, 'be levelled at you? Not to mention trivialisation,' he concluded, 'if done in haste.'

So Daniel thought he was mad as well, shovelling him out of his life along with Taylor.

'It has an authenticity of its own,' he said. 'Both the event and Taylor's perception of it,' he dancing, he was convinced, at the end of a rope – in the same way he had danced when he was a student and Viklund a professor: so much was known by the older man, so much was revealed, and so much held in reserve, either as a challenge, genially extended, to be discovered, or, more obscurely, to be divulged at a strategically chosen moment.

Processes – convolutions of thought and feeling – pursued in eradicating his illness, a biochemical digression, fomented by ageing, from the norm, preoccupied him exclusively at that moment: a strategy of defence, a disintegration of his personality accompanied by, until that moment, a subliminal appetite not to live, formed and re-formed itself, graphically, strenuously, in Maddox's brain – the thought coming to him at that moment that Taylor must have concluded, been actively recalling at the time of their meeting, that he, Taylor, might well have followed Maddox into the Raybourne Professorship of Art History at the

211

Drayburgh in much the same way as Maddox had followed Viklund into the same post. A luminary he might have been at the Courtauld, a junior curator at the Tate, early papers followed by the equivalent of Viklund's early and pre-Renaissance series on television (the charm of youth challenging Viklund's persona of wartime engagé) and his subsequently celebrated books: a life of attainment, his precocious, fevered, inventive mind springing up all over the place: a glorious reputation, no wife and children dead at all.

Instead, obscurity in a comprehensive school, somewhere in the north-east of London, a light extinguished beneath a bushel, a misconceived determination to be the 'real thing'.

He had, he recalled, written Taylor a testimonial, to whom it may concern, on his leaving the Drayburgh, and a second, specific one, several years later, at Taylor's request (coming out of the blue) when he'd applied for a post in the Department of Fine Art at Reading University ('an hour from London,' Taylor had written in his requesting letter, 'just the right distance from where I live now, I'm sure I'll be all right'), presumably a last attempt by Taylor to retrieve himself.

Had he, in that second reference, voiced his misgivings: someone intent on one course when they'd have been better off, years before, pursuing another: someone addicted, mesmerically, to giving subjective reactions a convincing air of objectivity?

Weren't they all, on the other hand, doing that all the while?

He'd assumed his application had been rejected: he'd heard no more about it, neither thanks for the receipt of, nor a report of what had happened. Had he – even – been called for an interview? His wife, too, had been 'invalidated' by not dissimilar circumstances, 'visited' not by Gabriel but Maddox before he, Taylor, had met her. Even she, even the prospect of a post that would have elevated him above the rank of schoolteacher, even that which had been most precious, had gone the wrong way. And now his (Laycockian) brush with the nature of time, of 'civilisation': with several wild blows, with a multitude of wild blows, he'd got rid of the lot.

212

All that remained was an analysis of what had happened.

'Was he vengeful?'

The voice casual, deferential.

'Not more than I'd expected.'

'Did he respond to your interpretation?'

'He offered it himself. Or, rather,' he paused, 'much of what I'd concluded came after I'd left.' After pausing again, he suddenly went on, 'It reminded me of reviewing the galleries on a regular basis, not knowing on the day I went round what I'd write. Invariably, at night, I'd go to sleep my mind a blank. The following morning I'd get up and write a review without a second thought. I became subject to a process, and a product, I could neither understand nor control. Odd, don't you think?' his final enquiry a Viklundian rejoinder.

'Familiar.' Viklund's voice faded, as if he'd turned his head to confront someone coming into the room.

'Morbidity, finally, of course, got hold. That and exhaustion. It's just as well I gave it up. Now I just have the Devonshire pieces, though I'm afraid I've been fired from that. He was always uneasy after my sectioning. Not surprising. *I* felt uneasy after the same. He finds the pieces too abusive. Morbidity, too, of course. Possibly exhaustion. If not lunacy. Am I still recovering, with something new to offer, or am I going mad? Am I, do you think, regressing?'

'I get the feeling,' Viklund said, 'you've been revivified by Taylor. I imagine you see that as morbidity as well.'

'Not really.' Mischief, of a familiar nature, was being passed along the line. He wondered if, bored by his current situation, and by a so far unmentioned source of ill-health, Viklund wasn't looking for something more than entertainment. 'I've a feeling,' he went on, playing along with his friend, 'particularly after visiting Taylor, that this is primarily an age of deceit, the self, as we describe it, on the one hand, asking to be saved, on the other, suppressing to the point of denial the realisation that there's little if anything worth saving. That all those disasters which become the meat of our reported lives estrange us. A suggestion that the worst goes on *over there*, and that the *over there*

213

is always *over there*, not least,' he hurried on, 'when it's *over here* and we don't wish to acknowledge it. Except, of course, when it's *over there*. Isn't that what Taylor's suggesting?'

Without waiting for Viklund's response, he added, 'Displacing *everything*, obsolescence the principal obsession.'

A heavier breathing at the end of the line, alternating with no breathing at all, Viklund conceivably turning his head to engage, visually, someone else in the room, suggested to Maddox that his friend and he had arrived at a significant point of disagreement: a perception, he suspected, had been arrived at, of his (Maddox's) own situation, which was too disagreeable to be acknowledged, let alone condoned.

Or was this his illness speaking?

Was there something significantly different still to be revealed?

Was this what Simone had stepped back from, or decided to approach from an alternative direction: more intimate, more sensual, more loving: more complete – a healing gesture, intrinsic to her nature, perhaps, not to Viklund's?

Or was she, like Viklund, resisting an abhorrent view of him, her commitment only partial – demonstrably so? Was he focusing on something irredeemable in his nature which, inexorably, was coming to the surface, beyond hope, beyond meaning, beyond any reasonable explanation? Was Taylor, whatever he represented, claiming him at last, a revenge he'd always anticipated (it had been lurking out there somewhere) but had hoped had gone away?

'I recall your reaction to Taylor's use of the phrase – I believe it was his,' Viklund said, his voice still restrained, 'in describing the excesses of Giotto's fateful expressions – "mascaraed excesses" – which you referred to as the bewilderment of their emergent roles, the antecedents of Masaccio's Adam and Eve, the same resonance, if more weathered, you traced to Rembrandt's self-portraits and which you thought had been diversified into the body, or the embodiment, of the paint in Picasso and Matisse. A bewilderment, you suggested, amounting to terror, which we – presumably you – had not yet come to grips

214

with. Had "subsumed", the word you used, to the point where distraction would finally consume us all. And I recall his *stare* as you answered. Intense. Obsessive. Other-worldly. And I wondered, what do these two get up to together? But after all, or so you tell me, it was a *woman* you had in common. What do you think?'

The final enquiry came abruptly – a sudden alacrity and alertness – contrasting vividly with the tone which had preceded it, a harshness returning to his voice.

Viklund wasn't, he concluded, glancing away to address someone else in the room, but was speaking with a lowered head, consulting something lying on his desk – his elongated, lectern-like desk – in his study, he seated on the bench before it.

He had often sat there himself, the room, at the top of the house, with its two square windows looking directly onto the park. Facing the windows, and immediately below them, was the desk, itself of sufficient length, with its sloping surface, to accommodate any number of books laid side by side, the bench before it, not unlike a pew, similarly sufficient to accommodate several people sitting side by side.

The two of them, frequently, had sat there together, examining texts and reproductions, or simply gazing out of the windows, they facing, in the evening, the setting sun, as well as the trees which had replaced the diseased elms in the park. The ecclesiastical, almost monastic atmosphere of the room, with its white-painted walls, unlike any other room in the house, otherwise rich with wallpaper, possessed – he imagining his friend at the end of the line – an atmosphere not unlike that of the Danish Church a few hundred yards along the road, which he had only recently discovered Viklund and Ilse attended each week, occasionally several times, Ilse not reluctant to go on her own but invariably capable, evidently, of persuading Viklund to go with her.

Devotional, his nature, he reflected, all this while, and all this while, absorbed in aesthetics, he had never noticed, Viklund leaving this inference to speak for itself: an ecclesiastical saboteur, licensing faith in an age of disassociation, God an

215

aetiological exercise, the significance of which he'd left each artist guilelessly to dissemble: not 'humanity' emerging for the first time, a phenomenological exercise, in Maddox's interpretation, but God, discarding the prospect of no return, opening his arms to redemption: not the disassociative catastrophe Maddox himself had been entertaining (going on about) all these years under the illusion he and Viklund were engaged on the same thing.

All these years, his mentor, friend and colleague had been drawn to him as a protagonist: saw his illness, no doubt, as the inevitable conclusion not so much of his lack as loss of faith – a faith which, unknown to him, Viklund had been preserving, witnessing Maddox's illness, as well as his humiliation (sectioning: peer-group support: what peers!), above all, perhaps, his identification, guilt-ridden, with Taylor (Taylor committing what Maddox had commissioned) – witnessing all this as a definitive form of retribution, forgiveness for which lay, exclusively, now, in Viklund's prayerful hands (and not in those, framed, in Simone's consulting-room).

He was, he concluded, revisualising his founder (imagining him in that upper room), confident of what would finally happen, if he, Viklund, had anything to do with it: the action of a friend, on the one hand, of a salvationist, on the other. Here, too, was a reference to his past which Viklund, presumably, was playing on, a suggestion that retrieval lay not in the direction of the Danish Church but in his own formative experience involving his home town's cathedral, St Albans, the interior – too large, too remote: too grand – he had absorbed and finally fled from as a child: Viklund the diplomat, consistent with the training and manners absorbed in his youth before art – or *as* art, the interpretation of (another diplomatic exercise) – took over.

'I merely wanted to be sure you hadn't been bowled over by Taylor.'

He might, he thought, have said 'evil'.

'Hardly,' Maddox said.

'You are, as you yourself have observed, in a highly impressionable state.'

'The conclusion I came away with,' he said, 'was to do with prodigality. Too many people doing too little and much the same thing. Prodigality the source, paradoxically, of the species' destruction. Taylor's vision of the same. Of he, him, himself, overwhelming everything.'

Not necessarily true, if only abstracted from the confusing impression of his visit: a point to start from, something to play back into Viklund's court.

And, inevitably, an indication he wished Viklund to keep talking (challenging, prompting): that he still cherished this sensitive, elegant provocateur, his demeanour, now he considered it, less that of a diplomat than a sage, inference his method rather than statement, implication if followed through, rather than fact. Taste, sensitivity, fidelity: art politicised in favour of belief: an ideological interpretation, after all (the thought no sooner realised than he wondered if it were true).

He was moving onto treacherous ground: his own treachery, his own ground (occupied now by Taylor): the delusion of 'explanation' was not only his but shared with someone he admired, even deferred to, excusing Viklund as the representative of an older, if largely defunct generation, an observer of war, of exclusion, betrayal, extermination, explaining, again, as an observer, the effect of a disaster greater than anything imagined when the century had begun: the age of means subduing ends, everything, it must have seemed to Viklund, as with Taylor, as with himself, coming to an end.

And yet what was Viklund, in his discreet, self-effacing yet nevertheless – because of that – authoritative role intending to defend – hoping, even at the last moment, the nightmare of his aberrated behaviour concluded, to be handing on to Maddox? a tradition of doubt, of rejection, of repulsion countered by one of acceptance, forgiveness, atonement, a suggestion not that everything was coming to an end but, renewed, was once more beginning (faith as art moving to its summation in the Sistine

217

Chapel roof), he, Viklund, preparing the way which Maddox would more thoroughly establish.

No wonder, he reflected, Viklund had stayed clear of the High Renaissance – God becoming man – the beginning of the slope (man becoming 'other': Laycock), down which the species was descending at an ever-increasing rate, drawn on, mesmerically, by the prospect, the vanity, of its own destruction.

This man was both for and against him, art as graven image, as spiritual exposition: the salvationary imperative (Laycock again: the 'individual' a romantic conception, 'Christ revealed' its template): the moral nature of 'progress', progress confused with expansion, man made 'real', the 'individual' made real, by his figurative advances.

Here was Maddox, on the other hand, with his notion of self-preservation – substituting for a previous notion of self-assertion – taking himself off to a weekly life-class as he took himself off to the geriatric clinic, a fallen angel in Viklund's imperium, *imperium in imperio*, falling, Viklund was hoping (inferring, suggesting), no more.

'I don't want you to be swept away,' his friend was saying, as he might to a child, adding, more firmly, 'by Taylor's anomic disposition. Or would you refer to it as anoetic, consciousness without awareness?'

'Awareness devoid of consciousness,' Maddox responded. 'Displacement no longer a correlative of art.' He paused. 'Maybe I should come round. Or you come here. Better than talking over the phone. This thing, to me, has become important.'

'I don't mind coming,' Viklund said, eagerness evident in his voice, an unexpected development. 'It's time I saw where you live. I've been anxious,' he went on, 'about you living on your own. I don't believe Charlotte and her new husband like it either.'

'How do you know that?'

He waited.

'She's rung me on several occasions to ask how you are.'

218

Concern: love – magnanimity in his wife, so lacking in himself, he was always anxious to discern.

'She could easily have rung Simone.'

'She has.'

'Odd she never told me.'

'It's good to be surrounded,' he paused, 'by people who care.'

Back to that: Taylor, presumably, had cared: 'Love,' he had evidently written in a note read out in court at the time, '*is not enough.*'

'I'll see you soon,' Viklund said, putting the receiver down at the other end.

Scarcely a quarter of an hour later his friend, supported by a walking-stick, appeared at the door, stooping as he came in, as if to indicate the diminutive proportions of the building, pausing, once inside, before the door was closed, to gaze at the houses opposite, the symmetry of doors and windows in the low, one-storeyed façades. 'As both of us have remarked in the past, my place, really Ilse's place, is far too grand,' stepping from the narrow hall into the ground-floor through-room as if he were climbing a ladder, allowing Maddox to take his coat, to lay it over a chair, accepting not the offer of a drink but tea, Maddox talking to him from the kitchen, coming through, finally, and sitting down opposite the spot where the fireplace might have been, in its place, the cavity sealed off, a television set.

'Time we talked,' his visitor said, the mug of tea untouched on the low table Maddox had placed beside him. 'Quite soon,' he added, 'it'll be too late.'

There was, after all, a confederacy between them: the legacy of pictures, sculptures.

'Back to iconography, for instance,' Viklund said. 'I felt drawn at the beginning not to life but art, and was immediately impressed when you drew my attention to motor-cars. Flesh into metal, and back again,' facetiousness in his tone as well as glance.

His friend was dressed in the familiar dark grey suit, a filament of a lighter, vertical line passing through it: light-

219

coloured socks, the slim, sharply pointed, thin-leathered, hand-made shoes, the handkerchief pointing up from the lip of the breast pocket, a lighter-coloured waistcoat visible between the lapels of the jacket, the white shirt and diagonally patterned tie, pink and grey: a uniformity of appearance which Viklund had affected since the moment Maddox had first known him. As far as he could recall he'd been dressed in a similar, if not an identical manner at the first lecture Maddox had attended at the Courtauld, and consistently so, later, at the Drayburgh: a uniform, saddening, almost childish, Viklund had thought congruous with his calling as a gentleman, if more pertinently, a diplomat: serenity, composure, exactness: something entranc-ingly 'away' from life, Pemberton, too, he recalled, inclined to suits, dark and, minus patterning, even more anonymous.

'We've both been pulling on the same rope, but,' Viklund said, 'in divergent directions, not maximising our effort, only convinced of the one thing, the nature of the opposition at the other end, identified by both of us as aggressive, redundant, obscene.'

A moral disposition in both of them, he wondering if the familiarity of his own home, and Viklund's agreement to be in it, licensed a renewed examination of his life-long friend (and, he was beginning to recognise, rival).

He took in the particularities of the face, the sharpness, now the flesh had left it, of the projecting forehead, the darkening cavities, as if moulded by a finger, from within which the eyes gazed out – a look characterised by an unusual candour, one he associated with Viklund's early years: an unblinking, unwittingly oppressive stare (the misleading impression of boyish expecta-tion).

And the mouth, thin-lipped, flexed between bracketed incisions, a self-deprecating grimace creeping in with age, braced to pain, or the prospect of, above it the assertive, autocratic, avian nose: all this, and sensibility, too, from an amalgam, Maddox reflected, of reptilian, apean, human resour-ces, a million million years from spark igniting gas to God's aesthete – bent, or so it appeared, on a final evangelical mission.

Through the walls, as ever, came Berenice's frenetic, expostulating, self-exonerating voice: the intimacy of her domestic regime: 'I've just tidied the fucking room and you're fucking it up already,' followed by the inevitable, '*Right?*'

Or, rather, '*Roight?*'

'*You cunt!*'

Viklund's head went up to acknowledge the sound, pausing before enquiring, 'Would you say we're divergent, or on the same line?'

'The same line. Though we might dispose of the rope,' he added.

The tiny, yellowing teeth appeared: something circumspect in his manner evident at once, a probity which came from values, from a predilection not necessarily his own. He, too, he might have been saying, had had a father – an uncle, even – who had played a determining role in his earliest life, putting in place a refinement he might otherwise never have had: fortuity, on the one hand, predestiny, on the other. 'What's the diff, Professor?' he was mentally enquiring, recalling Simone's observation on the contrary nature of their careers.

And she, what was her place in Viklund's imperium? Would news of her predicament confirm what Viklund had suspected all long – a professional misjudgement on her part?

On both their parts.

'It's odd,' he said, 'when we've been so close, that what was there in you, so significantly, was never recognised by me until now,' the strangeness of Viklund sitting in a place where he had never sat before striking him at that moment with renewed force. This is a reductive experience, he warned himself, he's here on a missionary expedition. 'Faith on one side,' he added, 'something considerably less on mine.'

'Not less,' Viklund said, 'different,' the tone light, inconsequential, the suggestion thrown away.

'What I've been, and am going through, might be seen as a consequence of what I rejected, consciously, in you,' he said.

'Not, as you supposed, that I'm seeking a deathbed conversion.'

221

Maddox shook his head. 'I assume you held such beliefs all along and chose, rightly, not to impose them on me. At this point of our lives, however, they're scarcely important. Certainly Lucretius wouldn't approve. *Nil igitur mors est ad nos*, extinction or life continuing in another, or even similar form, irrelevant.'

'I'm not here to convert,' Viklund said, still smiling. 'I'm not asking you to share anything at all. The antidote to despair isn't further rejection. There's a great deal of resistance to art being about anything at all. That, I scarcely need to add, is still very strong.'

'The best of both worlds,' Maddox said.

'Aestheticism, as an end in itself, however, has never been my line. I merely suggest, it doesn't have to be yours. I believe you've discovered that for yourself.' He lifted his head: once more through the party-wall came Berenice's cry: 'Why don't you do what I fucking ask? All the time I'm talking here and you're taking no fucking notice! *ROIGHT?*' Viklund concluding, 'Belief has its own momentum. It does or it doesn't claim us as its own.'

There was a sudden bleakness in this confession which Maddox hadn't been prepared for: it was as if Viklund were confiding: don't you see, we're both fucked up?

As it was, he was watching Maddox without turning his head, his pupils lodged in the corners of his eyes, a suddenly antagonistic, fierce, unsmiling look: all his reserve appeared to have vanished.

'Without the anguish, farewell to God and hello to perdition, there'd be nothing there at all. Style bereft of content. At the heart of it, otherwise, would be a liking for decoration, something to distract us from an otherwise blank wall.'

He could see – felt aggrieved – that Viklund was speaking – pleading, almost – from exhaustion, someone, foreseeing his end, determined to attract an audience (a congregation, it was turning out), appealing beyond the 'aesthetic provenance', as he invariably described it, to something altogether more demanding and, at the same time, conscious of its irrelevance, he was suggesting, the one sign of its authenticity: a religionist's not an aesthete's, or even a humanist's passion.

'Would all this go down well, I wonder, next door?' Maddox gestured at the wall.

The facetiousness Viklund dismissed with a wave of his hand, the strange, inelegant hand with its small, immaculately cared-for fingers.

'Aesthetes don't illuminate anything. The struggle goes on elsewhere.'

Maddox was, he realised, endeavouring to suppress a feeling of hostility, one which had been there from the moment Viklund had taken up his offer to visit him at home: he, out of deference, had always gone to him, a normal expression of their friendship which neither of them had queried until now.

Viklund, he suspected, had never liked children: something which might have inclined him to stay away in the past. Out of that had evolved a pattern neither had disturbed. Yet even then, the hostility, he realised, was defensive: ever since leaving Simone's house the previous evening he'd been in a state of shock, of not knowing from which direction the next attack might come: the Medical Council, Taylor, Devonshire, Doctor Death himself. The tension, of a paroxysmal nature, one anxiety attack succeeding another, the residual level of anxiety scarcely receding, was causing him not only to sweat but to breathe in a peculiarly irregular manner, he disguising his discomfort by repeatedly moving in his chair, keeping his hands and his arms occupied, breathing deeply and slowly as far as the irregular pattern would allow, willing, almost, the expelled carbon dioxide to remain inside his lungs.

Here was Viklund, speaking to him as if he were a normal human being and all the while he was struggling to contain a disturbance which had little if anything to do with Viklund at all, or with the room, or the house, or with anything he could identify. His body – its reactions – had a life of its own, the brain, sitting on top of this disaster – his stomach contracting as he endeavoured to control the expansion and dilation of his lungs – surveying the catastrophe with a helplessness he recognised as not exclusively his. In rooms up and down the surrounding streets, let alone around the town – at the geriatric day-care centre, at the North London Royal – others would be enduring a not dissimilar sensation: a feeling of being manipulated by a presence other than their own, a feeling that their lives were coming to a halt. He was doing his best not to get to his feet and walk about the room, his arms folded across his chest to constrain the involuntary movements of his body: he was doing his best not to provide Viklund with the evidence – to be communicated presumably to Charlotte, to Simone – that would confirm his worst misgivings, his illness the consequence of a faithless existence, his insistence that the hedonistic principle was the only one that counts.

All this time and energy wasted, he reflected, in being ill; all this time wasted either confessing or denying it: all this time driven by feelings over which, other than by chemicals, he had no control: the irresponsibility of his relationship with Simone: somehow that, and aesthetics and Taylor, even Laycock, Doctor Death, Donaldson and Devonshire were connected. He was in a situation from which he couldn't withdraw – other than by way of the tube station platform. Why, subconsciously, had he chosen that, handing on his affliction, in its most tormented form, to those whom he loved and was loved by, as well as to those who were not otherwise involved? The evidence of his failure (to do something) was vividly before him, Viklund suggesting that the seeds of it lay in his abandonment of the faith of the Florentine masters by whom, otherwise, his life had been consumed: the failure to make a coherent statement of his life now that it was, so plainly, even if not pre-empted by him, coming to an end.

An image of 'Death' came to him in a spectral form, not all that different from the emaciated figure he had seen coming out of and going into Simone's consulting-room; nor, now he came to take more regard of it, from the figure sitting in the chair before him. He was even aware of Berenice's recriminations coming, renewed, through the party-wall: 'What will that cunt next door think? He says I'm fucking nuts. *Right?*' he wondering

224

if she were referring to him or her equally submissive neighbours on her other side.

He was withdrawing into a position from which Viklund would no longer be able to retrieve him (the purpose, he concluded, of his unprecedented visit). Lunacy had no other source than his denial of the divine nature of the origins of life (if it was good enough for Giotto, Fra Angelico, Alberti, it should be good enough for him), to him an electro-chemical event, to Viklund something beyond definition, beyond understanding, beyond the scope of the imagination.

'I'm not sure I'm waiting to be saved, other than in a medical sense,' he said. 'And that, as far as I can tell, is underway. As for Taylor, he fits into a pattern which was there before I ever felt like this,' something helpless in his tone of voice as well as his gestures, his hand flailing before him as if in dismissal, in reality to suggest to Viklund he listen to the voice coming through the wall.

'You're wanting to hit me, *roight!*'

'No.'

'You want to fucking hit me!'

'I don't.'

'You're wanting to fucking kill me. *Roight?*'

'No.'

'You're wanting to fucking kill me because I don't want you in my fucking house!'

'No.'

'*You're wanting to fucking kill me!*' something of a scream.

'I'll fucking kill you, you cunt!'

'You want to fucking kill me! I told you!' screaming. '*Roight?*'

'I'll kill you, you *cunt!*' a door slamming, the sounds continuing, the words inaudible.

A second door slammed. The walls shook. The glass vibrated in the windows. Debris rattled down the chimney and crumbled in the sealed-off fireplace. An impediment of some sort was lodged inside Maddox's throat: what he had hoped might once more be under his control appeared to be so no longer.

'Are you all right?'

225

Viklund had risen, with difficulty, from his chair, pushing himself up against the arms, coming to stand by Maddox's chair while Maddox, suddenly aware of how frail Viklund was, went through all the sensations of being choked – strangled, even, by an invisible hand, something which enclosed his neck. His hand went to his chest, Viklund, if feebly, striking his back. His eyes filled with tears: he indicated the kitchen, managed to exclaim, 'Water!' and waited, alternately doubling over and straightening, while Viklund went to the kitchen and returned moments later with a beaker.

He spluttered, swallowed, endeavoured to speak, swallowed again, and then, with an effort, stood.

Taking deep breaths he walked to the window, almost as if he intended walking through it and into the street (anywhere to get away from here), turned, breathed more deeply, and walked back across the room.

'I don't know what it is. Tension.' His throat, as he spoke, began to clear: the distinct impression that something was trapped there began to fade. He swallowed, swallowed again, exhaled, vigorously, and added, 'I'll be all right. I'm better already. A demon departing, so to speak,' smiling at Viklund's shaking his head.

'Let's hope,' Viklund said, and added, 'What's the tension about?'

'It comes from nowhere,' he said. 'Hormonal. Inside the head. Missing letters in the DNA,' knowing he was playing into Viklund's hands, the older man's alarm nevertheless subsiding, he appearing about to fall, holding onto the back of Maddox's chair. Shadows Maddox had rarely seen fell across Viklund's face, deepening the hollows around the eyes, within the cheeks, below his jaw: a mask, an almost diabolical expression, confused – confounded: a fearful look which intensified as he, in turn, examined Maddox's face. He came to my rescue without a second thought, he reflected. His faith is authentic, something about which he has no choice, as natural as breathing, aware of the opportunity for choice in me, perhaps, even, at this point, envying it.

'I'm all right,' he said again. 'Perhaps I should walk you back, or call you a cab. How did you get here? You arrived so quickly. I forgot to ask.'

'I have the car,' Viklund said.

'Have you parked it?'

'The driver's with it.'

'Outside?'

'Better than leaving it on a meter, don't you think?' the suggestion of a smile: something disagreeable and yet disarming had passed between them, Maddox wasn't sure what: the intrusion of wealth, the suggestion it isolated Viklund more decisively than anything else: his house, his paintings, a chauffeured car – and faith, of an indiscernible but significant nature.

Division was suddenly more apparent than anything which, previously, might have united them: no wonder Viklund had left belief implicit in a relationship which could well have foundered on it.

'I'll walk you to the car,' he said, adding, 'Where is it?' looking round for Viklund's coat.

'He'll see me come out. I wondered if we might talk more.'

Viklund had turned, crossing to his chair, stooping over it, indicating decisively his intention of sitting down, the car, the notion of someone waiting in it (surely not Ilse?) of little or no concern. What a curious impression, Maddox reflected, Viklund must have of service; it was, after all, a cardinal's temperament, a worldly accountability subsumed by a spiritual one, or, more readily, he assumed, the other way around.

Maddox drank again: it had been a mistake to accede to his friend's suggestion he come to the house – the residue of a family home from which anything connected with familial intimacy had been removed; or, more nearly, in reality, had flowed away. It was desertion, he realised, that lay at the heart of his illness – looking round at the anonymous room, previously two rooms, the connecting arch a square-shaped structure, the opening into the equally anonymous kitchen. No wonder Simone rarely wished to stay: no wonder he was glad to escape to her house, its walls covered with mementoes from one stage of her life or another (a consciously recorded advancement): photographs, drawings, paintings, prints, artefacts, maps, testimonials, even framed pages of manuscript (hers and others' from the several books to which she'd contributed essays or introductions), the furniture, too, an accumulation from the past, the house too small to contain all she would have wished to put in it: an interior expressing richness, as opposed to wealth, intimacy, knowledge, diversity, appreciation, even rapacity, conviviality, warmth: *health*.

His ambition – recent, faltering, indecisive, inconclusive – had been to pull the rug from under Donaldson, he as significant a proponent, if not manufacturer, if not manipulator of the New Philistinism as any, certainly the one, in his experience, closest to hand. As it was (right now, too) he was suffering – badly: subject to sudden, involuntary sensations – like killing himself precisely at the moment when it might have been the last thought in his head; subject in general, to a tyranny of effects, many identified deceptively as causes, as if retribution, the form of, had been quietly amassing throughout his life, itself bereft of trauma or retributory desires. A life consumed by a desire to do/be good, guilt otherwise swiftly arising – to illuminate, expand, enhance (ideas, interpretations, people). For this he was being presented with an incomprehensible bill: a pauper (of sorts), he had consumed modestly throughout his life – to be presented with the evidence he had consumed an inordinate amount (enough for several people, if not more: who? when? where were they?). Nothing, so the bill suggested, had he chosen but the best.

And here was Viklund – yet again – the one on whom he had most relied, for guidance, for encouragement, sceptical of Maddox's revolutionary mission but admiring (supportive, in itself) of the way he'd gone about it: someone whose own revolutionary pretensions had been artfully concealed, art, as propaganda, of a more elusive, subtle, intransigent nature, that 'thing' he had never spoken about, that 'thing' on the behalf of which he prayed, presumably, each week at the Danish Church.

228

No point in defending himself, or proposing, even, a different basis on which they might meet. His own misfortunes were grieved over, genuinely, by (he could see) his still-loving friend, but their causes were, to Viklund, painfully apparent: his father's death, for instance, long before his mother's, Taylor's trial, much in the media at the time, and to which he had expected to be called as a witness, his sectioning, the causes of and the recovery, if incomplete, from that, his emergence, Simone vividly in mind, from what he had been slow to realise was a secular version of hell: anomalies in the brain's DNA which triggered off hormonal defects amounting to disarray: genetics, epigenetics, chromosone deficiences, a constitutional disorder, an epidemiology of frightening proportions: the dreaded 'Hox' genes with their 'punctuated equilibrium' – the mutatory engine-room of deviant behaviour – finally, however, the absence of Christ or the equivalence thereof: he had been walking down the road – a road – or so he had thought, to salvation, and Viklund, unbeknown to him, had been walking down another, in a contrary direction, to the same (not least, as he had lately discovered, on Sundays: a particular time, a particular place, where universality could be recognised), less to enlightenment, or so it had seemed, than to something singularly more overwhelming.

All these years, assuming he had been doing one thing and he had, in reality, been doing another. And Viklund, his hands extended behind him to the arms of the chair, having waited for Maddox's acquiescence, had slowly, stiffly sat down and was now waiting, having, evidently, more to say which he wasn't inclined to do from a standing position.

'Shouldn't we invite your driver in?' he asked.

'It's not me he normally hangs around for, but Ilse. I make a change. He has a computer which amuses him for hours.'

'Computer?' Maddox said, dissuaded from sitting.

'A device he carries in his pocket. It's scarcely out of his hand, even when he's driving.' More relaxed still, he leant back in the chair, his arms stretched out beside him. 'If he dislikes the job he can always leave. I've heard no complaints. Ilse, for instance,

229

doesn't like me going out unaccompanied, terrified of something happening if no one is around.'

If Viklund were indicating a sharing of afflictions, Maddox thought, he wasn't inclined to go along with it, demonstrating his changing mood as well as his recovery by walking up and down, such discourtesy, he further reflected, complemented by something he wouldn't previously have considered: a determination to emancipate himself from Viklund's charm: behind it, glaringly, lay the ritualistic cannibalism of the sacred feast, the consumption of God's son in response to an atavistic appetite: the action of primitives, if anything was.

Nevertheless, breathing more freely, oppressed by Viklund's presence but disinclined to carry discourtesy further by asking him to leave, he looked down on his friend, reminded – obscurely – of how he had never gone in for purchasing the objects he had discerningly admired, either on his own or others' behalf – approaches from Sotheby's and Christie's consistently (at the time, seemingly, perversely) dismissed. Something climactic now, however, was about to happen, he suspected, Viklund's own discomfort set aside, as if they were both, in his friend's estimation, about to die – not a one-sided approach to death but a mutually convened arrival, Maddox as close to it, in Viklund's eyes, as himself, he no longer Viklund's successor but his spiritual accomplice.

Further evidence, he reflected, of declining powers which any good-natured doctor would not be disinclined to point out. 'The Socratic suggestion we should spend no time reflecting on death a singularly wise one, endorsed by Epicurus and your favoured Lucretius, in contrast, let's say, to Aurelius, who thought of little else – all positivists, however, in this regard, for even by not-thinking we offer it a significant place, the *only* thing not to contemplate, the one deferring to the unimaginable by resignation, the other by acceptance, both, in my view, producing commendable results.'

He was speaking to ease his throat, repeating much of what he had said before, anxious, at the same time, to reassure

230

Viklund he was, relatively, back to normal as well as to prepare himself for, if not pre-empt, what he imagined might come next.

'Montaigne appears to overlook that the decline of sensory perception is distressing in itself, the method as painful as the final result.'

His voice had developed a drawl, as if, perversely, he were suggesting that lucidity was merely another symptom of the condition he was endeavouring to hide: that *everything* was a symptom of what he was endeavouring to hide, not least his pacing to and fro, an agitation as indicative of his discomfort as if he'd started stuttering – a childhood complaint, ironically, eased, if not disappearing, whenever he was driven in a car – or, as previously, as if he'd started choking, or had been unable to get out of his chair. Now he was simply stating he was unable to get into it.

A childish disinclination to respond to Viklund in anything other than a defensive way was forcing him to avoid looking in his direction, aware merely of a wraith-like figure which came and went in the corner of his eye. He was concentrating on the window as he progressed towards it, and the street outside, then on the opening to the kitchen as he paced the room in the opposite direction. Surely it was plain to Viklund he wished his friend to go? What's this? What's happening to me? he mentally enquired: why am I disturbed by someone I've known for almost the whole of my adult life, and to whom I feel as close as I do to anyone, outside my family, and Simone?

'I've only a matter of weeks to live,' Viklund said, the tone restrained and, because of that, defiant. 'Six might be a reasonable guess. Inevitably, I'm driven to think of other things. Whether, for instance, I should come by car. Or walk. Or where Kellaway would park it. I've to decide whether to end it in the way I've previously suggested or whether I should allow it to take its natural course. "Natural" being a word I'm currently having problems with. It doesn't *feel* natural, for instance, to feel like I do at present.'

He'd paused; Maddox, too: something along these lines he'd been expecting – definitive, inescapable, final – rejecting the thought in much the same way, he reflected, as he had rejected much in his own life, setting it aside, with restraint, in the hope that, having done so, it would do the only decent thing and go away.

A fresh agitation coincided with this realisation: an awareness that Viklund was imposing on him at a time when even he would have conceded he didn't wish to be imposed upon at all, certainly not by something as overwhelming as this.

At the same time he was conscious of a curiously revivifying thought: not an article, for Devonshire, on Taylor – an arts page leader – but a book, encapsulating the art of the previous fifty years, its title immediately apparent, in lower case, to indicate the inconsequentiality he had so often gone on about: *as it happened.*

'How certain are they?' he enquired.

'I'm playing stoppage-time, I believe they call it,' Viklund said. 'Injury time,' he added.

He was smiling, as if he had considered what he was about to say before confiding it.

'Does Ilse know?'

'Why upset her now when she'll be upset enough when it happens? In the end I've concluded I have to tell someone. I hope you'll forgive me.' The look came up, plaintive, something little short of supplication: this I don't have to go on about, the look suggested. What is friendship for, if not, at the very least, this sort of confession? 'The whole of Ilse's life, despite my discouragement, my *frequent* discouragement, has been focused on me. Not a warrantable sacrifice, by any means. But one I've been sufficiently lax to take advantage of. She went off once, for instance, with a fellow she still sees. Affection, I should say, rather than love, or, God forbid it, passion. Otherwise,' he continued, 'there's only been me. Plus, of course, the times we've lived in.'

Watching Maddox's expression, he smiled: the thin lips parted to the diminutive, yellow teeth: something of a dandy's gesture in the way he flicked his arm to one side, Maddox immediately reminded of his uncle, the parodied engagement

232

he'd had with everything, in itself concealing, he'd assumed, something imperturbable yet possibly alarming.

'Those geniuses we've spent our life examining. Justification, in your case, for claiming we're in decline.' He paused again. 'I wouldn't, for my part, concede it's the end of everything. In regard of the species you're convinced is heading for extinction.' Raising one shoulder, he dipped his hand in the side pocket of his jacket, holding up a phial. 'I need this, at the moment, to keep me going. Could you get me some water? My tea's gone cold.'

Maddox went through to the kitchen, found a glass, half filled it from a bottle in the fridge and took it back, standing by Viklund after he'd taken it. Whatever he'd been holding in his hand he'd swallowed and, drinking from the glass, he handed it back. 'I've been intending to tell you for a while. Not least when walking the other day. As time's shortened, my resistance to burdening you has weakened. And now, today, I thought, I'd better take a chance. How curious, I'd been thinking, we should both cave in together. Then I was aware, in more buoyant mood, you have a significant length of time to go and I might therefore hand on everything which is positive on my side to use at your discretion.'

'Is there anything specifically,' Maddox said, 'you'd like me to do? Is there anything,' he went on, his tone despairing, 'you'd like to tell me?'

He moved backwards, as if physically to accommodate whatever Viklund had to say, sitting on the arm of his chair, suggesting, by his posture, a readiness to spring up again.

'My only concern is that whatever impetus my death may give you you use discreetly. I don't care,' he waved his arm again, 'what you do, as long as you do it with conviction. Conviction, should it occur, lies at the heart of it. The approach to *your* conviction is what I most rely on. The approach, as far as I'm concerned, is all that counts. The result I leave to you.' He smiled, a roguish expression. 'The house, of course, I've left to Ilse. Not that you'd want it, in any case. My papers, to which you have exclusive access, I've left to the college archive.'

233

He was on his feet before Maddox had risen, turning to the door. 'Kellaway will be glad to see me. I told him I wouldn't be long.'

Maddox followed him to the hall where, having confirmed his decision to leave, Viklund waited for him to retrieve his coat and stick.

Holding the coat to the other man, he realised how skeletal Viklund's arms were as he slid them in the sleeves; how childlike, even, were the shoulders, how thin the neck and, alarmingly, how vulnerable the hair receding from the scalp, and was conscious of his intimacy with the man, something he'd scarcely been aware of over all these years: the texture of the skin, the colour of the hair, the way it had been rounded at the back of the head, even his odour: something of his father, the fastidiousness, the confederacy, which passed between them, implicit, unhurried, self-declared – the delicacy, even, in Viklund's case – a sensitivity which, having found its outlet, was, almost deliberately, being withdrawn, at the same time declaring, 'I've given you a reason for going on. My case may be worse than yours. Use it to measure how much there's still to do.' All he said, however, as, turning at the door, he embraced Maddox, instead of shaking his hand, was, 'As we've always known, fortuity plays its engaging part, thank God,' turning to the street, towards which he waved his arm.

A car, parked amongst others, pulled out into the road. As it came forward Maddox could see the peaked cap of the driver. 'His idea,' Viklund said, anxious to identify elements of his life with which he was not in accord.

The car pulled up. The man, dressed in a grey uniform, got out. Viklund, registering Maddox's expression, 'Ilse's idea, which Kellaway was keen to endorse. They hatched it up together,' taking Maddox's hand and shaking it, a sign their farewell had been said in the house. 'Let's have another walk before it's too late. Or perhaps you can wheel me round by then. Kellaway sometimes comes when there's no one else. I hate to be alone when Ilse's out. Odd, don't you think, after all these years? As if everything material is being *unconsciously*

234

dispensed with,' turning the final remark to the surprisingly youthful figure of the driver, the eyes almost buried beneath the peak of the cap, the mouth, more broadly visible, smiling. 'The car we hire by the year. It evidently saves on tax. Kellaway by the month. He's taking a year out. Before university. He looks twelve but he's really nineteen. He's to study medicine. Or is it French?'

'Neither,' the youth responded, familiar, evidently, with Viklund's rejuvenated mood, adding to Maddox, 'Law. Mr Viklund's aware of it, but cynical, too. The political nexus of the future. He's loath to agree. He thinks I should do something useful.'

'Law displacing politics,' Viklund said, winking at Maddox. 'He has the right if not the *true* idea, youth ahead without our even knowing. Any fool can do it.'

'Like art,' the young man responded. 'Anyone can, and most of them have.'

'Most of them *do*,' Viklund said, ducking to the rear door as the young man held it open. 'Though I never get in the last word,' he added. 'Art, of course, I wouldn't recommend. It's either on you, or it isn't. Most of those afflicted, however, can easily brush it off,' the door closing, his face plaintively visible behind the glass, his figure shrunken in the interior of the car, he waving, the youthful chauffeur nodding, smiling, as it drew away.

Returning inside Maddox washed up the three mugs and the glass, staring into the tiny yard outside the kitchen window, not sure, even now, what had been the purpose of Viklund's visit: fear, a desire to tell someone to whom the news would be significant: assigning to him a task he couldn't himself complete: promoting the virtues, however reduced, of staying alive: the handing-over of a tradition he hoped he would sustain.

And, returning to fear: the abandonment of something he had taken delight in in favour of something unimaginable: the enquiry that lay at the back of his announcement: is self-death acceptable as grace? Wasn't Christ's knowledge of the context within which he was acting another form of self-submission?

235

The quandary, too, of the Apostles' Creed – the text, in his own case, learnt by heart in company with his mother, his father, his brother, his sister, though never his uncle, and in the chapel, too, at Quinians – the confession of belief in a Christ who prior to his resurrection descended for three days into hell having previously assured the thief (to his right, his left?) that he would that day be with him in paradise – a paradise which Viklund, now it had come to the crunch, was finding elusive. *Eloi, Eloi, lama sabachthani*? no apostasy, exactly, but something of a secular nature he wished to confide, obvious in his proposal they return to the park to walk again. Finally, farewell.

Meanwhile, all this alongside his sudden conviction – his 'vision', even – away from all that, though tangentially, in some way, connected to it: he should 'programme' Taylor into the contents of a book, art in society transposed into art as society, the bleeding heart of 'consciousness' abandoned in favour of a heart more clinically defined.

11

THAT NIGHT, having agreed to spend it apart, he said, involuntarily, without being aware he was about to say it, on the phone to Simone, 'I've a feeling this unipolar illness is turning into a bipolar affair. I'm not sure it's not mania determining things at present, or something, if not more obscure, no less extreme. I wonder if I'm on the wrong drug. Lithium, for instance, instead of dothiepin, or one of the post-prozac derivatives.'

'You could have lithium now,' she said, 'as a booster. You don't have to stabilise before you take it, although it's preferable,' she added, the doctor speaking in the immediacy of her response: distant, circumspect: exact.

'Yet I don't want to be on a drug at all,' he said. 'If I go back to Kavanagh and ask to be reassessed I've a feeling he'll do what he's suggested before. Bring me in for observation, with a heavier dose of everything. Prognoses, as you know, in mental health, aren't always to be relied on. The doctor's often as much in the hands of the patient as the patient is in the hands of the doctor. What do you think?' this final enquiry reminding him once again, inconsequentially, of Viklund.

The urgency of his appeal silenced her at the other end. 'Since Viklund came to see me I've had this urge to crack on with Taylor. Which I know you won't approve of. However, since I'm nuts, I'm no longer sure what I ought to do.'

'You'd better come up this evening,' she said, he sensing – a chill around his heart – her disinclination he should do so: she had a more urgent problem than his own.

She had, he was vividly reminded, a curious confidence both in his recuperative powers, now fully engaged, and in his underlying strength. It was as if his official designation – Emeritus Professor – placed him, cerebrally as well as emotionally, in an impregnable position. He had, on this occasion, scarcely referred to her anxieties at all. 'How are you making out with Death?' he enquired.

'His name is Norman,' she said.

'Norman.'

'I thought you were being affectionate.'

'His given name is Brian.'

He had his own recollections of sitting opposite Simone in her consulting-room: the seductiveness, for one thing, once he was familiar with the routine, of her dress: the relatively short skirts, the occasional long ones: her androgynous suit of trousers and jacket; her attempts to obviate her breasts; the high heels alternating with low ones, he placing himself, on each occasion when variations in her appearance significantly characterised their encounters, in a representative position. What would most men feel? What do I feel? Is she signalling I shouldn't take note of her efforts, or that I should? Norman, he assumed, could have been no different.

Her response to his initial enquiry came with a lowering of her voice. 'I've spoken to two more colleagues whom I trust. They recommend Symonds, the lawyer I mentioned. He's evidently seen several cases through the Medical Council. Only one of his clients had to appear before the vetting committee and the charges against him were dropped. The same, he thinks, will happen on this occasion, though the worrying thing is the climate has changed. He suggests I conscientiously reject the allegations and show willingness to cooperate.'

'Has Norman been to see you again?' he said.

'No.'

'A lunatic. Nobody will believe a word he says. One look at him and they'll know it's ridiculous.'

'That you can't rely on. There is, of course, the other complainant. And,' she went on, 'there's also you.'

'I'm not complaining.'

'Exactly.' Her laughter came from the other end, a lightening of her voice as she continued, 'I thought, with him, I was making progress. I thought, in some respects, he was coming good.'

'What was his problem?'

'A not uncommon one with men.' He waited (she waited): did he fit, had he fitted into this category himself? 'Their wives, after having had children, no longer want sex. Their clitorises are desensitised, often, after childbirth, though they're unaware of the cause. They even suggest to their husbands that they "relieve" themselves elsewhere, disowning any involvement, reducing sex, inadvertently, to a lavatorial function. To men who are dependent on their wives this is often distressing if not abhorrent. If they do have sex with someone else their wives invariably leave them, or they themselves feel obliged to leave. Inevitably this provokes even deeper anxieties. Norman was different in this respect. Having been deserted by his wife and children, whom he still loved, he was suffering not merely from impotence and frustration but a defensive hatred of women. A not unusual outcome.'

It was the most she had ever confided in him about one of her patients, a curious form of discretion, he had always thought, considering the intimacy of their relationship. Conceivably, until now, she had considered him, to some degree, still to be a patient: hence the potency of the charge against her. Consequently, there had been, perhaps, a desire to keep him away from her work, or her work away from him, a difficult thing to do, certainly a challenge, in a house arranged the way it was. Involvement, if only peripherally, with her clients was unavoidable: he and they came and went through the same front door. It might even have been this that had provoked Death into making his charge. Additionally, she might, perversely, have anticipated the situation and, disarmed by its inevitability, have found it difficult to confront: to some degree, at least in his case, it was true, he, too, perversely, an arbiter of her fate.

What, he wondered, had she seen in the three previous men

239

she had married (something, presumably, on each occasion, 'permanent')? As far as he could tell it had been, primarily, an educative function, her own origins, in as much as she was prepared to talk about them, frustratingly obscure: from one she had learnt 'a great deal about science', from another about the Stock Exchange (he was a broker), and from the first, the doctor, 'a great deal about people': a comprehensive, if not definitive list. Perhaps his sobriquet would be 'culture'. Yet she gave little, if any sign of it, the Dürer prints in the consulting-room misleading and, like all her pictures, of sentimental value only (a gift from a previous admirer which had remained in place by default rather than intent: 'they provide suitable subjects for comment, all else failing'), a suggestion, here, of a Nordic sensibility, which she clearly didn't possess, and behind which, he presumed, she could safely hide: she 'liked' them, she confessed, but, unlike some of her other, largely, to him, inconsequential pictures, wasn't 'fond' of them. With this response, curiously, he had always felt relieved.

Several of her clients were endowed with what she approvingly described as 'artistic natures', though none of them were practitioners: producers, directors, actors ('interpreters' – rather than 'originators', painters ('messy: their work, in any case, gives them access to other things') or sculptors ('dirty and, quite rightly, physically rather than psychically engaged'), the 'creative process', nevertheless, 'of interest' to her, yet only so far as it was commented upon by someone else. She read reviews, knew what was on at the cinema and in the theatre, as well as the whereabouts of 'interesting-sounding' exhibitions (to which she rarely went, unless he or someone else accompanied her, in each instance, thereby, a social rather than what she would have described as an 'internal' event).

He, too, as a commentator, was divorced from immediate involvement with the 'creative process' (something so accessible, at least in ascription, it might easily have been purchased in a shop), his belated approach to direct participation, involving the life-class, had left him more bemused by his fellow aspirants, the majority of them women, the majority of those Jewish, than he was by the results he aspired to and had patently failed to achieve. 'It' – creativity – belonged to an area of experience – of knowledge – which he had, so far, only superficially examined, drifting into psychoanalysis, or psychotherapy, on the way and instinctively withdrawing; or, rather, from which he had been withdrawn by someone else.

The mystery of his attraction to her had deepened (was deepening all the while), no resolution or illumination forthcoming. Examining his features in the mirror as he shaved he occasionally saw a younger, more recognisable, altogether more familiar and reassuring face gazing out. It was a shock to pass a shop window and see reflected there a figure he had to glance at twice, sometimes more, to recognise: white-haired, hunched, unconsciously stiff-necked, an incredulous, startled, even frightened expression gazing out: that additional spasm of alarm as he mentally confirmed it was himself. On one occasion he had been walking with Charlie, his eldest son, and as they crossed the road (they were on their way to introduce Charlie to Simone, an event which, despite his misgivings, though not hers – 'I'm sure we'll like one another: we have you in common' – had gone off remarkably well) his attention had been drawn to two men approaching them from the other side, only to realise, concentrating deeply on what he was saying (apprehension uppermost at the forthcoming encounter), that the elderly figure whom he had dismissingly assumed to be in his eighties, if not older – stiffened movements, a shock of white hair – and the vibrantly younger, bigger, bolder figure beside him were, in fact, a reflection of himself and his son in the window of a shop directly opposite.

'Mind', whatever it was, was absorbing him more and more: a feeling of his being subject to it rather than it being subject to something he might, otherwise, reasonably have called 'himself', the evidence that such a thing existed merely his acknowledgement of a bubble-like effusion inside his skull (he, like everyone else, had got 'it'), with more cells than stars in the universe (who, he wondered, had counted?), he looking to Simone to elucidate it further, something which, perversely, so it seemed to him, she refused to do. It was as if, at times, she were disowning not only her own knowledge but her accreditations: as if, more pertinently, she were disembarrassing herself of the material of a lifetime, going back to – wishing to go back to – a period of her life, more pertinently, to another person, she had known intimately, devotedly, before 'all this' began. At times he would find her gazing at him as if he weren't there or were a different person entirely, an abstracted look inspired by a recognition of something deeply familiar, which he could not associate with or identify. Behind – beyond – her lay an area of experience she was unwilling, perhaps unable, to disclose, while other areas – her lives with her husbands – she would refer to without rancour, recalling her involvement like she might have recalled the contents of a favoured book or film – 'we can pick up on that' she might easily have told him, 'when it comes round again' – anxious for him to share what, clearly, had been a 'positive experience'.

Apart from being born and brought up and having gone to school in a Midlands town, he knew little about her: she had a brother who had gone abroad, with whom she was rarely in touch, and a sister, likewise, who still lived in a Midlands town and, apart from having had children, 'had no career', she expressing surprise that he should be astonished she'd married a butcher. 'Why?' she had said.

'It doesn't seem like you,' he said.

'It's not me, it's her,' she responded.

'Or your family, or background,' he told her.

'I don't see why not,' she said, dismissing it.

His own early life, apart from that recounted in her consulting-room, appeared similarly to be of little interest to her: her eyes glazed over whenever he described incidents from his childhood in St Albans and his teenage years at Quinians ('was it *fee*-paying?' was all she had asked: some sort of opprobrium there), he assuming she'd heard much the same before, from a variety of sources, and that now their relationship was on a more intimate footing it was of no relevance any longer, material which, domestically, could be discounted.

242

A mystery, she, as was her science, if it was a science. 'I'll try anything once,' he'd told Charlotte on her suggestion he see a psychoanalyst outside, or apart from, the National Health treatment he was receiving: on the basis of 'empiricism' – a discipline he'd always responded to throughout his relatively unvariegated life – he'd taken up what, as posed by Charlotte, and, if more irritatingly, by Gerry, he'd concluded was a reasonable, if not colourful challenge.

As it was, Simone was less inclined to discuss her 'subject' than he was his, his resumed intermittent stints reviewing the galleries holding out to her little if any interest, she accompanying him on one occasion, at his suggestion, only for him to discover, surprisingly (he'd been looking forward to it), she was a distraction, precipitating his reactions and devitalising his final comments.

The reviews she did read, again at his prompting, she did so with an air of enclosure, the newspaper held up as if to the light but, in reality, to conceal her face, he, excluded from judging her reaction, obliged to observe the reverse side of the paper and her extended arms and hands, and specifically the delicacy – the endearing delicacy – of her fingers and nails, the extraordinary slenderness of her wrists, an infuriating mixture of infatuation and irritation which not even repetition in any way appeased.

Having read his piece – an even more peculiar as well as irritating habit – she would lower the paper and invariably remark on an item adjacent to it ('Have you seen this photograph? Have you read what's written here?') so that finally, when he enquired, 'What do you think?' she'd reply, as if reminded (so memorable the effect), 'You have a gift for this sort of thing. It seems to come so easily,' or, worse, 'I wonder what the artist thinks.'

'It doesn't necessarily come easily,' he'd suggest, and enquire, 'What about the content?'

'Oh, the content,' she'd respond, 'is very good,' as if this were the least of the piece's merits.

The situation now in place whereby he would no longer be

writing at all, unless he could summon up another opening – relatively impossible at his age – she'd welcomed. 'Isn't it, when it comes down to it, trivialisation?' she enquired when he insisted loss, of some sort, might be involved. 'The sort you despise. I'm glad to see you out of it. You're not a hack, and never could be. Certainly,' she went on, 'never *should* be,' adding, when Devonshire came up in their conversation, 'Why don't you tell him to fuck himself? He undoubtedly does, in any case,' a lowering of her guard – a descent into colloquialism – which he was both startled by (what did it reveal which she'd previously kept hidden?) and welcomed. Was this the otherwise unmentioned heritage of the Midlands town excitingly re-emerging? Was it the same – he'd had little experience of anything similar himself – she was hoping to unearth in him?

The latter he doubted: he had no such instincts, nor the equivalent experience to offer in response to opposition, from wherever it might come. Rules had governed his life, sporting or otherwise, at Quinians, and had continued to do so throughout his career: even the dissolution of his marriage had followed a code of practice determined by solicitors and accountants. His relationship with Simone alone had taken him into an area where previously he had never ventured, involving him exclusively in an event the outcome of which could in no way be predetermined. He'd even, earlier, gone mad by rules: the climactic event itself, a selfish, unilateral action, had followed a familiar method – predictable, callous, involving blameless other people. He'd been subsequently treated by rules (prescribed medication, formal confinement) and was, to a large degree, pursuing the same. Simone alone was a sign – as he suspected he was for her – of the breaking-up of a structure which had dominated his life. Even Taylor, he reflected, was bound up in this: he, too, had recoiled from what amounted to a gift as a theoretician in a hopeless attempt to function as a practitioner, an exponent, someone governed by intuition – he had responded exclusively to that – something which, if infinitely more modestly, certainly not definitively, Maddox was doing himself, at little or no cost, with his life-class.

Taylor, in the end, had sacrificed his reason ('getting in touch with his feelings'): he, Maddox, had done the same, with singularly, searingly, lesser results. This, he reflected, was what they had in common, parity of unreason, if nothing else.

Nothing stood still, everything moved, he and Simone no exception.

Where he, or they, were moving to, however, he had no idea. What in him was changed, was changing still, by being observed? Was he in the process of being *evolved*? And she? Was she, in a similar way, evolving too, en route to somewhere where, not unlikely, so unpredictable the process, neither of them would meet, or be able to meet again?

So men with problems often had the same one (how close to a whore did she have to be?) as far as the clinician was concerned: their wives no longer wanted to fuck: did not welcome (further) physical intrusion (their biological function, to this degree, complete): all those men he passed in the street, 'Brian', or Norman, amongst them, dying before their partners, sexuality suspended: the psychological equivalent of turning over a stone, insects scattering in every direction. No wonder, he reflected, dealing repetitively with this, she wanted out (running for cover, in her way, too): no more analysis, no more complaint, no more toleration, no more patience: no more inclination to listen: no longer origins, hers, his, or anyone else's. Only *now*: that which would not come again: imperative: a blessing.

She'd never had children, something which, seemingly, was becoming her principal virtue, enlightenment, on the other hand, of some sort, still her goal, fucking, she must have concluded, a way of being, not of (needlessly) spreading herself around.

She was still talking, much of it, he was alarmed to discover, having gone unheard: a recapitulation of male desire, female unreceptivity. 'What about women?' he heard himself enquire.

'Unable to form adequate relationships with men. Frigidity. Displacement.'

'But then everything,' he said, despairingly, 'is a symptom. Infinity,' he went on, 'which can't be imagined, causes disappearing into the same, their sources speculated on but never disclosed.'

He was endeavouring to bring the subject back to himself, but courteously, without imposing on, or interrupting, what she evidently wished to say. There was something other than what she had mentioned so far – or he had missed while, an increasingly uncontrollable habit, he was 'thinking'.

'And Norman's name is Brian?'

'Usually I think of them by their given names. His was an exception, his surname so like a given name itself. "Brian" seems foreign as a result.' As if another subject had come to mind, she added, 'It's one of the reasons I've gone off the work. Or could.'

'What?' he said.

'Its predictability. The mixture of intimacy and objectivity is highly seductive. Particularly to women. They get in on things in a way that would otherwise be proscribed. Men, on the other hand, see it as a surrogate form of seduction. Not being a man, of course, I can't be sure. It's merely my experience.'

He felt liberated by her statement; and, prompted by the thought, liberated too, bizarrely – disgracefully – by the prospect of Viklund's death: *that* obstacle out of the way, he was thinking, along with *that* involvement out of her way, too: the sadness, the loss, in the case of Viklund, the gain, in the case of Simone.

'The male clients, I suppose, always want to fuck. I did,' he said, adding, 'It's not unlike a cerebral form of prostitution. That must appeal to women, too. A visceral reward substantiated by financial remuneration.'

'I've never had a problem with that,' she said, adding, 'until now. Though I wouldn't wish to agree. At some point a relatively objective recognition of what is involved is arrived at, and that, for me, is the bait, as you'd say, at the end of the line.'

It was as if speaking on the phone, and not face to face, had liberated her – liberated both of them – the threat of suspension having focused her thoughts and feelings in a way which, much to her surprise, she found she welcomed.

246

'Dan,' he said, thinking he had chosen the moment well, 'has told me that he has only a few weeks to live.'

'When did he tell you that?' The immediacy of her response, his invocation of 'Dan' in place of the familiar 'Viklund', suggested her interest was immediately aroused.

'He came today. He hasn't told anyone else. In fact, knowing him, I suspect he finds it difficult to do so.'

'Not his wife?'

'He saw no point. Distressing her, he said, before the event. In that I believe he's mistaken. Having told me he may well tell her. Having rehearsed it, so to speak. He was evidently trying to tell me the other day, in Regent's Park. He has two pills which he's been saving. Given him during the war. Maybe, after all this time, they won't be effective. That, too, he's uncertain about. No Senecan aloofness. As for Rothko, de Staël, Van Gogh, Haydon. The list is endless. All go against his lifelong hidden religious belief. I don't suppose, with that, he wanted it to interfere with what he would call the iconography. The aesthetics. The dating.'

His thoughts ran on, he no longer aware if he were speaking or merely reflecting. Had he mentioned Haydon? Who else? Were these his own preoccupations, in place since, if not before, his own 'incident', as he now described it?

'He still has a choice.' Her voice came clearly in his ear: she was, he assumed, speaking not about Viklund but, more compellingly, about himself: if he should think of it again. 'He can let the illness run its course.'

'He can.'

'Do religious scruples count? Isn't he more sophisticated than that? All the precedents you mention. He must have thought of them, too. Telling you,' she went on, slowly, 'is probably his decision. He *will* go ahead at the time, and wants you to know.'

'His background,' he said, 'was diplomacy. Even after all this time I have difficulty determining what he thinks. Or, more, what he feels. During the war he got up to any number of things he's reluctant to talk about. Was he a double agent, reporting to the Germans as well as the Allies? He certainly seems to have

247

been in with both. Or something even more elusive. He's lived, no doubt as he'll die, an enigma. *God*'s diplomat. With what end in view? Disassociation. God's abrogation of the turgid deal.'

For a while, reflecting on this, neither of them spoke.

'Is that,' she said suddenly, 'what's given you a high?' adding, 'The mania you mentioned at the beginning of your call.'

She was, conceivably, reversing her suggestion he might come up: talking had calmed him down.

'I thought if I rang you,' he said, but added nothing further. The silence resumed.

'I feel less manic than elevated,' he went on.

'It's a decisive moment for both of us,' she said, abruptly, wishing, he concluded, to cut him off. 'We must pull through this together,' much warmth, however, returning to her voice, much camaraderie, he thought, expressed.

Yet the impracticality of what she was saying was evident to them both, his own problem a mystery, hers in the hands, he assumed, of a lunatic. Or, assuming the information was correct, two lunatics. A moment later he amended this to three, he more tangible as evidence than anything suggested by the other two.

There was her resilience, however, a quality, he had come to the conclusion, he was singularly without. Her enthusiasm for whatever she was doing, whether on the roof, or in the kitchen, or 'enfranchising', as she called it, a client, was infectious, heart-warming, something he was incapable of doing without. On several occasions he had seen her come in from the successful delivery of a lecture, from a seminar, a conference, her latest paper having been read (papers they'd pored over together, examining the syntax, the spelling, the construction, before having Mrs Beaumont print them out), and had been aware – poignantly aware – of the value she placed on approval, on appreciation by both her peers and her students, she candid as to the value she gave it, yet needing it as a measure of where she stood. The prospect of being summoned before the Preliminary Proceedings Committee, after a lifetime of struggling to get where she was, had affected her, and him, more deeply than either of them, he suspected, was prepared to acknowledge. He, for his part, at this stage, merely wished to enquire how she could hope to deal with people who were nuts and not be drawn into their obsessions: how, furthermore, could she hope, or believe, she could deal with them on her own, Mrs Beaumont apart, and not be turned aside, be unaffected by – be absorbed by – what they brought in through her own front door?

He'd rarely thought of her, until recently, as helpless; vulnerable, certainly, but with an impressive strength – one more than sufficient to cope with what her vulnerability, her openness, might expose her to. He had always looked up to her, been intimidated by her, afraid both of and for her, something inviolable about her appearance and manner, a sense of self-sufficiency, of authority, the most obvious thing about her. He loved her yet, to a large extent, didn't know where he was with her, discovering her, for the most part, as he went along – a stumbling, erratic enterprise – aware at every moment he, not she, might have misjudged the situation: the suspicion, there all the time, that he had overlooked – was still overlooking – a significant part of their relationship, something obvious, viewed from a distance, but not from where, more intimately, both of them were now standing.

But for his preoccupation with Taylor, he'd almost given up on identifying in art, if not in people, least of all in himself, cause and effect: in letting go of himself he had, at one point, assumed he was letting go of everything, only to realise, almost too late, he'd been letting go of a relic, something from which life had silently departed.

Having abandoned himself to her he was increasingly sensitive to her accounts of her (male) colleagues at the Tavistock, the ubiquitous Analytical Forum, the North London Royal (what embarrassment there, he wondered, when it was discovered he was her partner?), as well as in and around Harley Street, looking for a sign, any sign, of a commitment, an attraction, an affiliation of any sort, elsewhere. Why did she, had she, looked to him? Why was it him who had found his way, if at her prompting, upstairs when there were so many, bonded in a common interest, who might, more easily, have preceded him?

Had preceded him: there were, and had been, other men in her life apart from her husbands: her progress had been almost uniquely marked out by her relationships with men (none of whom, in retrospect, did she view with disfavour: a wholesome, generous, open-ended perception of what he could only assume was a communal venture). Viklund's end, for instance, was, as far as he understood it, characterised by mysticism, less to do with art than his peripatetic childhood and youth: the streets of the European capitals where he'd been brought up, the Swiss and French schools he'd allegedly attended. Simone's goal, on the other hand, was to do with enlightenment – of some kind – achieved, not least, through the intimacy of three consecutive marriages (each one a demonstrable step forward: progress of a sharply definable if idiosyncratic nature), one which, in some way, atoned for a childhood she rarely mentioned, an insecurity which the eclectic nature of the contents of her home bizarrely confirmed: too meticulously ordered, too much under her control: the machinery of communication – e-mail, internet, faxes, radio, television (the cable channels, though she rarely watched them, fed into the house from beneath the pavement outside, he alone, when bored, inclined to flick through them – desolation of some sort – reluctant to have them in his own home: her 'antennae', she called them). If he could manage without, why couldn't she?

Why should she? he would have heard her reply.

At which she would have laughed: she saw him as something of a recluse, growing more reclusive all the while. She didn't question it or complain, for it meant whenever she was inclined to invite him up he was free to respond. Only occasionally, when she enquired, largely out of curiosity rather than reproach, where was it all going? was he unable to give a convincing reply: he was retired, for one thing (he had a bus pass to prove it, an unnecessary piece of council indulgence, in his case); for another, he was mad – or had been, sufficiently so, to make no difference. Something ineluctable in his nature, he'd

250

concluded, had captured both of their imaginations, something disturbing yet mesmerically, if not charmingly unresolved, he narcissistically enquiring of its nature, she unable, or reluctant to give it a name. There it was: there *he* was: somehow caught up in a desire not to live, an impulse which, consciously presented, he would have wholeheartedly denied. Was it this, however obscurely defined and experienced, he had to own up to (bring into the open)? Was it this Viklund was inviting him to deliver – he showing the way, if not by advice, by example? Was it this Simone was tinkering with herself, the final problem (disowned by Plato, Epicurus, Lucretius): death itself?

He had had an agenda: he had wanted to rewrite the present in the way, when younger, he (and Viklund) had attempted to rewrite the past. His reflections on the pre- and early Renaissance had echoed down from that time to the present – and been displaced (were being displaced) and abandoned, Rome, not Florence, moved to the centre. The 'retrieval', as he'd called it, of the post-war years had attempted to revive an ethic which technology had destroyed – other than for him and one or two other crazy creatures who still banged on, for instance, about 'humanism' – a humanism, in effect, which had died before he'd been born, certainly before he'd been recognised as a 'critic': victims of a 'fall-out', it had been argued, of an even more insidious nature. There'd been hope but now, in these later years, unless he were mistaken, it had been extinguished ('noise', for one thing, had taken its place: almost anything, almost anywhere). His latest comment on the scene, his laboured attempt, post-sectioning, had been intended to delay if not reverse the same, to turn the race (the species) back, to look to the past, a coherent, systemised past, in order to bring it into the present (revivifying the ghosts still wandering there).

Here he was, throwing in his hand (one moment), the next on the equivalent of a (delapidated) soap-box, that same hand held by someone else; someone, for one thing, who spoke of 'correlatives', 'parameters', paradigms, who saw behaviour in terms of credible patterns: the universality of human nature, the

251

diversity of custom: primitivism writ large, Simone a deist, he'd concluded, Viklund, for his part, something of the same.

'It doesn't look as though you need to come up.'

She'd been talking for a while, without his being aware, he responding sharply, 'I feel easier having talked it through,' wondering if, in effect, they had, or if, once more, the 'subject' that lay significantly between them had been avoided. 'I wonder if I'm ill at all. The temptation is to jack in the pills and see if I float,' waiting for her response, which didn't come, and adding, 'Let's leave it for tonight. I feel we've covered a lot of ground,' wondering, too, if his support of her had been enough: there was a great deal more she might have wished to hear, not least in response to those self-conscious demands when, almost as a child, she plaintively enquired, 'Do you love me?' he responding, since it was solicited, with, in his view, an unconvincing, 'Yes.'

What was she asking, and what did he need in return? on both sides, he was inclined to think, building up barriers, identifying, in his case, a line of retreat (his life unimaginable without her) – as clearly as she was identifying hers. And at what a price (everything at stake).

Mysterium tremendum: that towards which everything aspired: a ridiculous concept to imagine in her cosy, eighteenth-century house; but on her roof, at night, looking at the stars, the moon, smelling the perfume of the plants around his feet, even with the sound of aircraft overhead, their headlights flaring through the vapour, he was aware of a momentum of which he was an indisputable part: everything moves, and always shall, the microscopic inclusion of himself, of her, his arm around her waist, as if he were retrieving her, she retrieving him, neither, any longer, with anything to lose.

12

GETTING UP in the night, looking out at the narrow street: the narrow houses, the curtained windows, the companionable feeling of people asleep, awake, lying there, thoughts, he assumed, not unlike his own, dreams of a peculiar intensity and nature: descending the stairs, aware that Viklund's visit had left something of his presence in the house, something of his instruction to be responded to. Drifting off, his thoughts, to his former wife, her present husband ('into thy hands'), a feeling of displacement that took him back to Viklund, then his sons, their differing temperaments, careers, Simone, Taylor ('we are our relationships'), his own disassociated presence, the confusion that characterised his current life: a ship (of old) moored in mid-stream, waiting for a favourable wind and tide, true element of nature.

Out there, too, were all those women: the life-class, the support group, the Auschwitz-focused legatees, Berenice's voice audible through the party wall, 'fucking', the only word discernible.

Tat twam asi.

This art thou: his anguish not due to circumstance: miscreant genes.

Something along those lines: 'You are not an epistemologist,' he had written, in red ink, on one of Taylor's essays (the influence of science on the methodology of art, foreshadowing so much of what was to come): those tutor-room encounters recalled, in this instance, in the middle of the night, everything, otherwise, slipping away: separated from something: divided from what? the intelligence and naïvety he associated with Simone; they, the two of them, hand in hand, even at sixty, he nearer seventy, he never sure which aspect of her nature he was engaged with or controlled by, the sophist who sat through accounts of sexual incongruity, failure, incompetence, impotence, finally, loneliness, terror, the fear of being unloved, unpossessed, unknown, unquieted.

The Midlands schoolgirl, socially subdued, familiarly suppressed, riding on a boyfriend's bike, she on the mudguard behind the seat, her arms around his waist, or sitting, sideways, on the crossbar, enclosed by his arms, waiting, if not for a kiss, a further stage in her enlightenment: intelligence, on the one hand, rapacity, on the other: everything inverted in the middle of the night, freedom for one, servility to another.

It was as if, in a curious way, a part of him had 'happened': it had matured, reached satiety, and had then expired, the residue – a witless, shiftless remainder – living on as if expiration had not occurred, the removal of the integral part of him, the organism functioning, deludedly, as normal.

Too late for reflection, yet reflecting all the while, not sure, in the event, where such reflection led: the way *affects* moved through the system: a mind without reference to itself: that organism which existed (looking down) above his legs, his chest, his shoulders, his thoughts competing with Berenice's voice in the next-door room, the contentiously responding voices of her all-night junkies: life! *life!* an impulse to lie down, he, such as he was, resisting, dreams activated while wide awake: the impression, bodily, of being in two places at once, here and here, neither identified, neither familiar: the maelstrom of his present condition, life existing in the region of his head, his stomach, his neck conflagrating, or so it seemed, disengaging him from everything.

That again . . .

He looked through the window from the inside of the restaurant wondering if his brother would come; wondering, even, if he'd remembered. Paul had rung him: they'd arranged to meet for lunch at a place his brother frequented in the City.

He'd travelled there by bus, disinclined to use the tube, comforted by its slow progress (what did speed mean to him any more?), its dreamlike enclosure by the streets: the intermittently shifting traffic, the juxtaposition of stylishly incongruous build-ings: shop windows, plastic surrounds, stone walls, brick, finally glass edifices reflecting one another against a fractious sky, a maze of mirrors and distorted, wavering elevations: the nomen-clature of a vast Caucasian-Semitic-Indo-Asian tribe: the multifarious faces (each with its 'mind', its unholy perceptions), figures, focused elsewhere, processing to and fro.

He had wanted air (security), he had wanted to get out, away, he reflected, from his own reflection; away, for one thing, from thoughts of Simone, his culpability, his sense of receiving displaced by an absence of giving, his negligible contribution to their tenuously joined-up lives. Hercules, Plato reported, felt like this (Plato, Socrates and Lysander), aware of the dull unfolding – Berlioz, Delacroix ... Carlyle, James, Hopkins – of a predictable life where hormones inconsistently manoeuvred, he like no other, yet like them all.

The restaurant was full, the table, he'd been relieved to discover, booked by his brother. He'd arrived early, springing off the bus, reminded, vividly, of the pain in his hips, his ankles, the joints of his toes, surprised how swiftly the City was changing, glass-fronted, metal-fluted, a quaintly domesticated institutional grandeur, personalised brick and stone and plastic façades – the narrow alleyways which the streets had become – the feeling of intimacy impersonally confined: the inadvertent passages, footpaths, the residue of churches, scarred, pale stonework bleached like bone, a skeletal residue between the impassively reflecting towers – he spotting his brother crossing the road, the slender, athletic, prematurely white-haired figure darting between the contending streams of traffic, looking up once to see where, in relation to the buildings opposite, he intended to go – approaching the restaurant, brushing down his hair, briskly, distracted, his thoughts on other things, scarcely,

Maddox reflected, on the prospect ahead, a task – an inconvenience – he'd set himself in the middle of the day, coming in, breathless, the waitress nearest the door recognising him with a smile and, a strange intimacy in the crowded interior, a wave, pointing to the table, his expression lightening as he identified Maddox sitting there.

'Been here long?' stepping round the table, insisting Maddox rise to embrace him, clasping him to him, Maddox a broader, stockier figure, his brother, after breathing heartily beside his ear, sliding into his seat, beside the window, Maddox retaking his own: the attenuated features of his brother's face, sharp, inquisitive, eagerly engaging: a bird of prey, a warning glint as he examined Maddox across the table, the face, Maddox reflected, behind the smile, evoking warmth, camaraderie, affection (disillusionment, too, the way things had gone).

'Not very.'

'I asked them to reserve it. Not always possible.' Paul indicated the privileged space beside the window, signalling, as he did so, to the waitress who had greeted him coming in at the door, another waitress, however, approaching, offering each of them a menu, his brother detaining her, familiarly, with a hand on her arm, until the food was ordered, Paul, once she had gone, reinforcing the impression he hadn't much time to lose. 'How are you feeling?' direct, to the point.

'Nuts. Anxious. Other than that . . .' his brother smiling, the youthful, at-one-time-Church-loving candour, the affectionate tyro (over sixty years of age) with little, if anything, left to lose, learn, control or dismember: the spiritual exorcist turned broker.

'I'm pretty good,' Paul said. 'Rarely better,' suggesting – promoting – an example his brother might follow: the tailored suit, the blue shirt collar, the red tie: a sombre presence behind a genially unaffected one. 'I got your message from Cary' (his wife). 'She assumed it must be money. I told her not. Who's paying for your therapy? Gerry? Charley? I hear good reports of her in the City. Your kids? It can't be cheap.'

'I was paying for it myself,' he said. 'I can afford it. For you,

256

too, if you want in,' his brother smiling, Maddox adding, 'I've dropped it. Charley must have told you. I'm back on the National Health.'

'Any good?' His brother, having ordered a drink by signalling to a waiter across the room – familiarity, once more, in operation – received it, Maddox indicating his own – ordered while he was waiting – was only half consumed.

'How do you measure these things? Every few weeks I see a psychiatrist. One day a week I attend a geriatric clinic. The place is clean. The food like school dinners. The staff kind. The other patients recessive, confused, terrified, incorrigibly defensive. Auschwitz at the back of most of their lives. At the back of mine, in a curious way, too. Don't ask why. Peer support, or so it's described. The reassurance which comes from the knowledge, it's suggested, if not insisted, you're not alone. Not alone,' he carelessly repeated.

His brother was smiling (again): a lean, attentive face, focused, acute, unlike his own: something of their father's asperity, his sensitivity; something of their Uncle Joseph's ability to move enliveningly into and out of any world he chose. And something, too, of their mother's nature: the school secretary (without whom the place couldn't function) and Sunday School leader (at the Cathedral, during and after the war), Paul's own religious curiosity encouraged and promoted by her: his catechism learnt by heart by the age of thirteen, recited in instalments each Sunday afternoon: his (curious) indifference to cars, or anything mechanical: his decision, challengingly announced, at the age of eighteen, to go into the Church ('take up the priesthood, for God's sake!' their uncle's ambiguous cry): an open-minded, free-thinking, apostolically inclined aspirant: an ability to deter (discomfort) evil in all its genially recognised forms. 'What happened to the therapy?'

'I married her.' He smiled. 'Almost. Your kind of thing.' His brother was no longer living with his wife, to whom, however, he remained affectionately connected: his recent address, and telephone number, Maddox had had to get from her, his brother, as in the rest of his life, persistently on the move. 'She's being threatened by complainants to the Medical Council as a result.'

Paul, having taken his glass, drank deeply, put it back on the table – still retaining it, however, in his hand, a strangely disowning gesture. He frowned: presumably, his brother, having gone nuts once, could do so again. 'Get another. There are lots around.'

'And fuck her, too?' this, no doubt, evidence of regression. 'What's she like?'

'Likeable. Enigmatic.' He added, 'I scarcely know her. Probably,' he went on, 'she has the same problem.'

He realised, not for the first time, that his habit of wanting to discompose his brother, interrupting his rhythm, was to do with a familial disappointment that Paul had left the Church – left, that is, in as cavalier a fashion as he'd joined it: somewhere out there, amongst the tall, glass-fronted buildings, each implacably reflecting its neighbours, opaque to its own interiors, was the arena, banked by computers, where his brother 'entertained', the vocational view he took of his operations, work an 'enlivenment' in much the same way as the Church, at one time, had represented an 'enlivenment', too: what his brother had described as 'an appropriate exchange: illusion in place of disillusion: what do you think?'

Paul, to this extent, represented the family, an element and projection of it: its aspirations towards a wider world: his father, his uncle, his mother, his sister – finally, of course, the aspirations of Maddox himself, roamer of the aesthetic seas. Above all, regarding his brother, he recalled their uncle's advocacy of the same, Paul an extemporised version of himself (their uncle had never married, Paul, to this extent, in lieu of a son, his protégé), as disapproving of his ordination as he was exultant at his 'reclamation': 'a winner, from now on, whatever he does.'

Only on his defection (from the Church) to a bank, then the Stock Exchange, finally to a merchant bank, had Maddox's admiration of his younger brother faltered, something of the epicurean in his nature, implicit once, now conspicuously to the

258

fore, as, indeed, there was, and had been, in their uncle's (as there had been, too, in Viklund's). Paul, after all, had 'enjoyed' the Church – in a curious way, had relished it – identifying it less with duty or vocation than good intentions, if not downright pleasure (the pleasure he spoke most frequently of as '*doing* as opposed to *being* good', an antediluvian interpretation, to Maddox's mind). Sermonising had appealed to him, the ritual of service, the giving and the celebration of the host, evidence of a theatrical appetite, one of which, inevitably, he had quickly tired ('the same performance, I realise, every time: do forgive me'): his popularity amongst clergy and congregations alike (his invitations to speak at churches, high and low, across London), a strange fervour associated with such a genial, seemingly spiritual enterprise: the prospect, amounting to promise, of higher office: 'the spiritual credential of our family', in their father's words, transferring its authenticity to the material credibility of a bank: 'First time they've had an ex-pastor in the place, can't fail,' Paul had explained, consistent with his mission, 'to do all of them some good.'

'Money can't be that bad, after all,' their father had suggested, hiding his disappointment more efficaciously than his brother had concealed his jubilation. 'Didn't Doctor Johnson concede its acquisition an innocent amusement?' the same innocence, or so it had seemed – perhaps the same gullibility – which had warranted and sustained, for a while, his brother's ecclesiastical career, informing Paul's conclusion: 'the same mission, Matt, by different means.'

Distracted, Maddox turned his attention to the street, a process of abstraction setting in, Paul, in his turn, diverted by someone grasping his shoulder, looking up, indicating Maddox: 'My art historian brother, Matt. Professor Emeritus by any other name,' the stranger, on his way to an adjoining table, reaching across to shake Maddox's hand, smiling, offering, on his part, 'No mistaking the one with money,' his brother's laughter, effortless, light, infectious, almost singing (liturgical, Maddox concluded), his uncomplicated receptivity to others.

It was, he reflected, that Paul had remained, still was, a

259

credential (an endorsement, of some sort) which he, Maddox, had always cherished (admired: looked up to: he had a weakness for uncomplicated people, seeing them, for one thing, as so unlike himself) – a registration of belief (in something) which, to a degree, he had always envied. Paul was 'healthy', open, accessible, Maddox, his brother (labouring under the epithet Mad Ox), was evidentially not: unhealthy, enclosed. Remote.

Watching Paul acknowledging figures at a nearby table, he realised, not for the first time, that his brother was charismatic. Previously he had assumed him to be merely remarkable: adaptable, resilient, vocationally inclined, much in his nature, since it elicited no problems, taken for granted. Closeness in a family, however, often precluded a broader look: something undoubtedly of their father in his nature, but, more demonstrably, of their uncle, the St Albans macaroon: 'the singing *signore*', as one of his friends had described him, the frequenter of theatres, clubs and bars 'in town', a dropper of names, a provider of vehicles – discounts, to their father's horror, no problem, trade-in prices his 'speciality', many of their customers acquired on his London forays: 'I go into town to work, not to play. Don't let your father mislead you. Most of our custom comes *London way*. Ask Lucy (their mother). She knows what a good team we are,' something of the Josephean efflorescence even more apparent in Paul as he grew older – particularly at that moment as his brother turned back to him, their uncle's excitation evident in his face as well as his manner.

'Quite a crew.' His brother indicated the men he'd been speaking to. 'Arseholes, in reality. You could walk through them in daylight and not know they were there,' a new-found cynicism replacing the charm: was his brother on the point of giving up this 'career', too, the opportunities for doing as opposed to being good unequivocally reduced? 'Money and more money,' his brother was saying, signalling the room.

He wanted Paul to be happy: the protective care he had exercised over his brother at Quinians: Maddox Major, Maddox Minor – a label Paul, understandably, had resented and instinctively fought against, his quicksilver reaction to

260

(almost) everything deriving from a subordinate attribution: to be happy, that is, just as Maddox had wanted their sister – their older sister, who had shared few of their privileges – to be content. Familial responsibility, he assumed, had always resided in him, the eldest son: art, the general consensus, had never been an adequate response: 'engagement' not commentary or analysis had always been their trade.

He was reminded at that moment – his brother now turned to speak to someone else who, confidingly, had crossed the restaurant to speak to him – of a curious incident which had occurred after their father had died.

Having heard the news from the hospital in St Albans, he had driven there the following morning and, before visiting his mother – ill as well, at home in bed – he had asked to see his father's body.

There'd been a delay of a quarter of an hour: he was then directed down corridors to the back of the building where he was met by a man in a khaki overall. Taken into a room with chairs and no window, illuminated solely through plastic panels in the ceiling, he was again requested to wait, aware of movements beyond a further door.

Some moments later the overalled man had reappeared from the corridor outside and, indicating the door opposite, announced, peculiarly, that his father was 'ready'. Half expecting him to be sitting in a chair, or lying on a bed, transparently alive, Maddox opened the door and went inside.

The room was even smaller than the one in which he had waited: illumination, again, came from plastic panels in the ceiling. On a bier in the centre of the room his father lay beneath a shroud, its edge drawn up beneath his chin, his arms and hands laid across his chest. At each corner of the bier a candle burned.

His father's eyes were closed, the features of his face, as the head itself, considerably shrunken, to the proportion, almost, of a child's. The hands – he'd scarcely been aware of them in recent years, other than when he had watched him construct his bench – were curiously gnarled, as if having been engaged over

261

a lifetime in manual labour: suffered, overused, exhausted, the backward curl of the thumb indicating, misleadingly (as with Viklund, he was reminded), someone of an exclusively practical nature.

It was the head, however, which absorbed him, the exaggerated feature of the nose, first in profile, then face on as, helplessly, not sure what he was doing, he circled the body. It was as if – the first impression he'd had on entering the room – his father were posing: at any moment he would rise and, in his usual, unstressed voice, enquire, 'How was that? Was it how it should be? Was I all right? What do you think?' as he might after a demonstration run in the new model of a car. 'Will they be pleased?' followed by an invitation to come home with him.

He hadn't been sure, at that point, what he was thinking or what he should do. Almost mechanically, he had lowered his head and kissed his father's brow: its coldness, its hardness, like a piece of stone, had appalled him: nothing he associated with his father was there at all: something strange, inanimate, something unrecognisable, had, alarmingly, taken his place.

Moments later, unable to decide what he felt, he found himself walking round the bier, wringing his hands and enquiring, 'What shall I do now?' a surprising question, and a surprisingly piteous voice, not his at all, he no more aware of where it, or the question, had come from than he was of what had prompted him to come here in the first place. Tears, conspicuously absent when he'd first arrived, were running into his mouth, his voice, such as it was, repeating the startling question, that part of his mind aware of what was happening standing back appalled.

It was a denatured presence that had come out of the room, wiping its tears on the back of its hand, insufficiently composed even to take out a handkerchief: something more urgent had taken over. He had come to the hospital not to see his father, or even, however pressingly, to say goodbye, but to bring him back (take him home); the finality of what he had seen had severed everything he had previously, however tenuously, considered to be 'himself': a warm and receptive part of him had been

262

wrenched out: whatever it represented, it had been left on the bier, the candle-lit, over-illuminated – artificially illuminated – windowless room a place from which all he had known of life, of affection, all he had known of nature, all he had known of art, had been removed: nothing, he had concluded at that moment, was worth the living.

Now he was looking at a refined version of those features, animated by impatience and displeasure: his brother, his last distraction gone, had turned his attention back to the table.

As the food was eaten he talked about his job, the people he worked with, enquired after his nephews: 'I tried to get Charlie in on the racket. He wouldn't have it. Said he was onto better. "Television is a vacuum," he said, "you can have a hell of a good time filling it." That boy will go far. He's got a lot of Joseph in him. No universals, only *chance*,' his tone not unlike that of their uncle. 'So what is the prognosis?' he asked finally. 'They've taken you off the anti-psychotic medication and put you onto an anti-depressant. Is that progress or regression? Is it doing any good?'

'It takes a while to have effect,' he said. 'On the whole,' he went on, anxious to reassure him, 'I'm very much better. I tried several,' he added, 'before settling on this one. At one point, with one of them, I thought I was dying. Not any longer.' He smiled, in illustration. 'I'm much improved.'

Once again, the image of his father returned, and once again he dispersed it by focusing on his brother.

'You're not short of money.'

'Why do you equate everything with poverty?' he asked.

'It is, for some,' Paul said. 'You couldn't have made much as a teacher, for instance. Even a professor. How much was it worth?'

'Enough,' he said.

'Is the underlying problem *us*?' he suddenly enquired, flinching, visibly, and adding, 'We had a good childhood. Quinians. Lots of people got sent away.'

'Sure.'

'It can't be that.'

263

'Did you have a bad time at Quinians,' Maddox said, 'looking back?'

'You were always there to look after me. After you left,' he waved his hand, 'I floated.'

It was the gesture alone that suggested unease: his brother was eating quickly: he had, presumably, somewhere else to go (something else to do, someone else to see). Already others were leaving the restaurant. He waved to the waiter for another drink. 'You?' he enquired, Maddox shaking his head. 'I'm supposed to be off alcohol with the medication.' He indicated his glass. 'Water,' he said to the waiter. 'Still.'

'If it's not psychological, what do you think it is, assuming psychological means anything?' his brother said.

'Biological. But what's biological? Electrical. Chemical. Hormonal.' He shrugged. 'Nothing unusual. Uncomfortable, perhaps. Difficult to acknowledge. No one likes to admit they're nuts. Not even doctors like to diagnose it. Not least if they're afflicted by it themselves. The stress is on how well you are. Trying to impersonate someone who knows what's going on is a significant part of the battle.'

'Why you?' He examined Maddox intently, coldly, almost ruthlessly, defences of a sort, Maddox concluded, in place. 'Why not me? Or Sarah? Why weren't our parents nuts? What's so special, or so inadequate, it should happen to you?'

He was, Maddox realised, about to mention 'art', unsure of its reception: 'art' had, for Paul, always been an 'excuse', offered gratuitously to cement its intrusion into an otherwise straightforward, practical, 'no problem' life.

'There's art, of course.' Maddox offered it slyly, glancing up as the waiter returned. A bottle was unscrewed, two glasses filled, ice and lemon already in each.

It was Maddox who murmured, 'Thanks.'

'Is that what it is?'

'Like religion. Out of touch.'

'I was always suspicious of Viklund.'

'Why?'

'Much of what he said *was* out of touch. That television series. Another world.'

'I found it inclusive,' Maddox said.

'It's one reason I left the Church.' His brother gazed at him blankly.

'Why?'

'Religion is politics. *Ex*clusivity, not the other way around. Negotiating not with God but with one another. It's why they wear frocks. Cross-dressers. Surrogate lovers. If God is a man then they'll be a woman. Spiritually, in your vernacular, painting pictures by numbers.' He gestured round, startled by his own reaction. Although people had left, others had come in, some acknowledging his brother's presence as they did so, every table crowded. 'The patriarchal society. A self-delusional world, Mammon and God much the same thing.' An unusual complicity had enveloped their encounter, Maddox wondering why, since it was based, very largely, on a denigration of both their worlds. 'Where there's men there's power. Hormonal, in your terms. When women move in as in the Church, you can be sure that the sources, as opposed to the resources of power, have moved elsewhere. Women selling bonds. Okay. Investment managers. Fine. Women bishops. Inevitable. Women *running* anything, other than as surrogates: no chance.' He shook his head, still eating: chewing and thinking appeared to be complementary activities where his brother was concerned, a characteristic of Paul's he had noticed before. 'The real bananas have moved elsewhere.'

'Bananas?'

'Balls. Force of nature. The simulation of power is a turn-on for women.

'So where does that leave us?' Maddox asked.

'Afloat.' His brother laughed, his hand indicating movement again. 'Swimming.' Raising his glass of water he drank: conceivably, Maddox reflected, he needed to dilute the alcohol he'd drunk already.

'You think I'll just get better.'

'Sure.'

'I'll tell the psychiatrist.'

'I should.'

'And the former therapist.'

'I'd leave that well alone.'

'You would?'

'Particularly if, as you say, you're screwing up her career.'

'How are things with you?' he said, diverting Paul's attention.

His brother was looking round. 'I thought she might be here. We usually meet at lunchtimes. I could have introduced you. We book a room and fuck until two o'clock. She's a martinet for time. Martinis, too. That sort of thing.' He turned his gaze to the street outside. 'Where are they all going?' he enquired, indicating the crowds, the traffic.

Maddox, having looked forward to meeting his brother, suddenly felt defeated: an energy here, in Paul, in the restaurant, in the street – on the road, on the pavement – which he couldn't in any way match: life, once engaged in this way, sustained its own momentum: it welcomed no intrusion, probably, he reflected, scarcely even noticed it. He might, to this degree, be invisible, crushed, if not by people, the places they chose to occupy.

He wondered what Simone would make of Paul, or, worse, what he would make of her: her composure, his casualness; her reflectiveness, his restlessness. He assumed Paul saw him as a liability, not least because of his illness: that, if anything, disqualified his past, and authenticated Paul's own.

'What was that about Viklund?' he asked.

'He drew you back,' Paul said, 'to something of no importance. Who gives a fuck who painted what, when, or how? The only relevant thing is you happen to be alive this minute. Don't waste the fucking time. They didn't. The ones who painted the fucking pictures.' He gestured to the street. 'None of this will happen again. What we are will have gone for good.'

His brother had been drinking: had perhaps come to the restaurant from a bar where, briefly, he'd been engaged with people he undoubtedly considered 'real': a phenomenologist in

266

motion (rarely, he concluded, if ever arrested: everything moves, and always will).

'Surely you look to the past to illuminate the present. Isn't that what consciousness,' Maddox said, 'is about? The capacity to look back, as well as forward, as well,' he continued, 'as around.' He, too, waved his arm at the street, then, for reinforcement, at the surrounding tables.

The tendentiousness appeared to irritate his brother: there was, after all, this residual authority in Paul: he was an operator, a functionary, a practitioner. If everything moved, then he moved with it: you couldn't get much more 'authentic' than that. Whereas he himself was always standing still, a denial (if an illusion) of the first imperative of nature.

The vertical lines had hardened between his brother's eyes: something here, he reflected, of their mother: the masters, even the head-teacher of the school where she had worked had been intimidated by her – had been said to be actively afraid of her.

'So which of us goes nuts?' his brother said, drawing a line beneath everything.

'Sure.'

Severity in Paul's face mellowed to something approaching despair.

'Which isn't what I meant to say.'

Having finished eating, Paul pushed his plate away, waving to the waiter to take it, a gesture reminiscent of his behaviour at home when he'd signal Mrs Tyndal, their domestic, to do the same, an arrogance which neither time nor age had improved. Placing his elbows on the table, he picked up his water again, something prohibitive and exclusive about the two-handed gesture, cradling the glass between his palms. 'You might so easily have gone into the Church,' he said. 'You had the temperament. At the time I felt I was doing you a favour. Completing our family's commitment. Providing a stamp of acceptance. Doing it,' he concluded, 'instead of you.'

'I thought,' Maddox said, 'it was the other way around,' surprised by, if not suspicious of this sudden confession.

'Unworldly, for you, wouldn't be quite the word. All those

267

books you bought. You were only fifteen. The next thing, I thought, he'll be a priest. That earnest look that came over you in church, in chapel. As for me.' He put the glass down. 'Some of the mysticism still hangs around. Fucked by God. It taught me a lot. Largely I shouldn't be there. Also, at the time, a great deal about people. After a while they assume you're a cipher. Social work, to the point where you begin to assume you're a rumour put around by someone else.' He gestured to the street. 'Consciousness works in bits and pieces, the whole being inconceivable.'

Maddox had seldom heard his brother in this mood before: he leant to the table to physically as well as mentally encourage him.

'A parasite,' he went on. 'If you were paid pro rata you'd be chasing corpses, pregnancies, divorced couples who want to marry, an unsecularised solicitor-cum-mortician, in a chasuble one day, a cassock the next, jeans and sweater the day after. Take my word,' leaning back. 'The secular *and* the divine. You see which one I've chosen.'

Maddox, in response, drew back too. Paul was suggesting, frustratedly, that he'd gone into the Church in order to forestall his brother, his older brother, doing the same, to relieve him, presumably, of an onerous task, something which, with his occluded nature, could only have done him harm: spontaneously, Paul had pre-empted a disaster, sacrificing himself on behalf of someone who, even at that age, he could see should not be encouraged to be more of what he already was, other-worldly, 'spiritual', 'soul-searching' – when (his brother could authenticate this), he'd 'been there', no 'soul', in his view, to be found.

'Those books.' Paul shook his head. 'Jesus.' He shook his head again. 'Those fucking saints, miracles that never happened. Didn't it ever strike you, none of that was real?'

'Those happened to be books on painting,' he said.

'At *fifteen*?' He resisted shaking his head. 'The fourteenth fucking century!' something jubilant in his brother's response. Though leaning back from the table, he had now extended his arms towards it, holding its edge with the tips of his fingers, a gesture which reminded Maddox, sharply, of a similar gesture, made by himself, when visiting Taylor. Did Paul see him in an equivalent light? Had madness, at least the potential of, been so apparent as a youth, a child?

'I was pre-empted,' he enquired, 'by you?'

'Kind of.'

'Or were you persuaded by my absorption that there was something there worth going into?'

'I might have been.' Already he was losing interest, looking round, anxious, it seemed, not only to be disengaged from the table but from Maddox as well. 'I wanted also,' he said, 'to be different. In this respect, more different than you. If you could absorb yourself in all those fucking books, I thought, I can do it for real. A light-headed gesture at the time, but since I couldn't think of anything else, religiosity being very much a part of Mother's and Father's lives, particularly Mother's, she seeing it as a form of community work before community work had even been invented, I thought I'd chip in as well. If not one chip ahead. Instead of looking at God you'd have first to look at me!' He laughed, lightly, removing one hand from the table and waving it at Maddox. 'That Sunday School crap. The catechism learnt by the age of thirteen. Would anyone believe it?'

He was looking round the room again, maybe still looking for his latest partner, anxious to introduce her, one further illustration of his message. 'Think about it,' he went on, signalling to someone on the way out. 'There's nothing in our background, genetically speaking, or otherwise, which would predispose you to crack up. *That* must have come out of not what you are but what you've done. Spent most of your life, like Viklund, with your head up your fucking arse. I'm speaking candidly, brother. No one else will find the time, or know you as much to tell you. I love you. I want to see you come through. I don't want to feel I spent my time being a fucking saint for nothing. Consciousness doth make cowards of us all, if it doesn't first drive you round the fucking bend. Life is there to be lived, not studied. Studying maketh no man. Nor woman, come to that. Knowledge moveth no one. It only dries you up. You went off into art, I went up the pole with Jesus. One of the two of us changed position. What's all this crap, by the way, about prison?'

He'd released the table and, pushed back from it, folded his arms: self-containment, exclusivity: reproach.

'What prison?'

'This guy you've been to see. The one who murdered his kids.' He paused. 'And wife.'

'Who told you?'

'What does it matter, for fuck's sake, who told me? Charlotte. I rang her to see how you were.' He shook his head, a more than condemnatory gesture. 'Haven't you enough trouble without getting caught up in that?'

'How caught up?'

'For fuck's sake.' His brother was looking round once more, less to identify someone across the room than to measure the distance to the nearest tables, disinclined, suddenly, to be overheard. ' "A former student," she said.'

'He asked me to go and see him.'

'You didn't have to go.'

'I thought I should.'

'There you are! A fucking priest!'

'Charlotte didn't have to tell you. You didn't have to ring. Just as easily you could have rung me.'

'To be told that everything was fucking perfect?' He waved his hand, the gesture restrained. 'You,' he went on, 'didn't have to tell her. She's enough on her plate with Gerry. Or are you anxious to keep her involved? You don't honestly think she's going to come back? She's well out of it. I've never seen so many books in one house.'

'I hardly have one at present.'

His brother examined him in silence: a lateral movement of his head, scarcely discernible, indicated which way his thoughts were moving.

'As for Gerry,' he said, assured that Maddox had nothing further to add, 'bullshit. That's his charm. Can't complain.

270

Plenty of it, I'd say, around. As for Charlotte, she doesn't wish to see you hung out to dry. She wants to see you up and about.'

'She told you about Simone.'

'Some time ago,' he said. 'And now she comes up with this fucking student.'

'Former student.'

'So what?' He shrugged, unfolding his arms. 'For fuck's sake. He killed his fucking family. What's all this to do with you?'

'I used to be his tutor. He wrote asking me to visit him. I knew his wife. As a student. Before they married.'

'Know, biblical? Or social?'

'Both.'

His brother didn't respond: incredulity gave way to bemusement: aspects of Maddox were being revealed which, post-sectioning, post-North London Royal, were still capable of causing surprise.

'He asked you to go and see him because you fucked his wife.'

'Before he knew her.'

His brother shrugged again.

'I admired him as a student. I wrote testimonials for him, both at the time he left and later. I thought, at one time, I might have been called at his trial.'

Paul was delaying what, moments before, might have been his departure: behind his back other figures were leaving, several calling out but receiving no response, his brother turned resolutely away from the rest of the room: over half the tables had emptied. 'What's he want?'

'What did the thief want on the cross?'

Maddox turned to the window: the grid-locked traffic, the crowd, denser than before, passing on the pavement: suddenly he had a measure of how far he was separated from what he was inclined to call his brother's world. 'I had the feeling he wanted me to write him up. In something other than a journalistic fashion. See him, as you might describe him, focused on the present, as a phenomenon. See him, in his terms, along conceptual lines.'

'What the fuck does that mean?'

'See what he did in terms of everything around him. Immortality. In a fashion.'

His brother was examining him with increasing concern: his eyes had darkened, his mouth tightened: a grimace – of apprehension – mask-like, characterised his features.

'Does he know you're receiving treatment?'

'No reason why he should.'

'Does he know you were sectioned?'

'I doubt it.'

'You haven't told him?'

'No.'

'Don't you think you should?'

'I don't see why.'

Clearly, Paul was thinking, 'two of them together': would the worse of the two drive the lesser down?

'What does your former therapist think?'

'I should leave well alone.'

'Not advice you're inclined to follow?'

'Evidently not.'

'And she's going to be struck off?'

'That's still some way ahead.'

'Because of you.'

'Two clients have made accusations. That's as far as it goes.'

'Jesus.'

'As you say.'

'And I should know.'

His brother watched him in silence. Finally, he added, 'Do you think the treatment you're getting is effective?'

'As far as I can tell.' He paused. 'Some days I feel worse. Progress is not in an even line.'

His brother moved closer to the table. 'I could put you in touch with someone I believe could help.'

'Who?'

'Someone who wouldn't fuck around. It wouldn't interfere with your present treatment. It'd be complementary. He might even find out why you're so pissed off.'

'I'm not pissed off.'

'Suicidal.'

Maddox waited.

'He wouldn't put up with all this crap.'

'Yours?' Maddox said.

'Yours.'

Now his brother waited, intense: a reminiscence of a childhood encounter: any moment one of them would call out for a parent or their uncle to adjudicate.

'This would be free,' his brother went on. 'He comes expensive but I want to pay. It's something,' he added, earnestly, 'I want to do.' The table creaked beneath his weight: urgency, and something more intangible, characterised his manner. He glanced at his watch. 'I've asked around. He's highly recommended. You won't lose anything by going. He's already agreed to see you once.'

'Agreed with you?'

'A colleague of mine who recommended him.'

'I'm being put out to tender?' he said.

'Oh, fuck you.' His brother drew back.

'I probably don't need to see anyone,' Maddox said. 'Apart from those I see already. I appreciate what you've done,' he added.

'Sure.'

His brother's head turned to survey the tables, most of them now deserted. A moment later he took Maddox's arm. 'See him once. No obligation. Do me a favour. If he tells you to piss off, nothing lost. One great man to another. He knows your writing. Collects pictures.' Pausing, he concluded, 'I do, too.'

A final, unexpected endorsement.

'Since when?'

'Since recent.'

'What kind?'

'Picture fucking pictures. What kind are there? Paintings. Definitely not religious.' He laughed, his hand retained on Maddox's arm: no escape, his tightening grip suggested. 'What d'you say?'

'Okay.'

273

'To see him?'

'Right.'

'I'll ring you and give you the time. The rest,' he released his arm, 'is up to you.'

'So you came with this already set?'

'Why not? I want to see you better. That's another thing,' leaning back, at ease, his purpose accomplished, anxiety, animosity, even, no longer evident in his face or figure. 'You need an interest. Something other than art. Are you still reviewing?'

'I've been fired.'

'There you are.' His brother spread out his hands. 'I thought we'd never see it.' He waved his hand. 'All that *crap*. How could you go on so long?' waving for the bill, the waiter coming across the now deserted restaurant.

'I'll walk back with you,' Maddox said.

'Fuck that,' his brother said. 'Let's walk. I don't want to go back indoors after this.'

'Where?' he said when, the bill paid, he'd followed Paul out.

'The river. It's years,' his brother said, 'since we've been down there,' linking his arm in his in much the same manner Viklund had done, walking in the park. 'Moments like this you realise how far we've come from St Albans.'

'Or how little.'

'Or how little. What would Mother and Father say if they could see us now? Going the same way, would you say, at last?'

They were moving south, lost, Maddox reflected, in the energy of the crowd, he no longer sure how much more of his brother's charm, his disingenuousness, he could take: inertia, of a peculiar sort, absorbed him. At odd moments he had the impression he was walking with his uncle, the same companionable arm in his, the same monologue (work, colleagues, women): a similar attraction along with a similar longing to escape. From what? An irrelevance which, nevertheless, captivated his senses: this, and only this, was what life, as he should have known it, was 'about': plus, an unquestioning curiosity, in prolonging the event, to see where it might lead.

274

A feeling, too, whenever he had been with his uncle, and now with his brother, that something significant had been purposely left unsaid, an element of their lives, common to all three, which only his uncle, now Paul, knew anything about: 'what shall I do now?' his strange enquiry while walking aimlessly around his father's corpse, unnerved, beyond his understanding, weeping, as if his father, had possessed the answer, one, perversely, all these years, held from him and which now, he presumed, he would never know.

Were his own attachments deeper than he had previously imagined, more concrete, more specific, formulated in another time, another place? Had he, throughout his life, been focused on events which were tangential to them, while 'reality' (that word again) went on elsewhere, he oblivious, unknowing?

His brother was laughing, animated, stimulated by what he must have considered his 'success'. 'As for the paintings, nothing much you'd like. Of course, none of this futuristic fucking stuff. I thought of asking you but then thought he's never asked me about investing. Fuck him, I'll buy this shit myself. Though I have advised your kids, by the way. And Charley and Gerry. And Sarah, though she hasn't much and refuses hand-outs. A bit like you in that respect. Who gives a fuck, after all, about money?' his final enquiry suggesting, surprisingly, he had problems in this area himself.

'Other than that,' he continued, 'I find I'm going against earlier convictions. Put a black hole in front of you and ask where the fuck are we in all that? Then I ask, why have I bought all these fucking paintings? I look at them for an hour or so. About "about", is all I come up with. The point of a point is a circle. The snake, consuming its own tail, comes finally to its head. "Eat that," the fucker tells itself. That's more or less where I am at present. Whereas you, unlike me, take all that crap to heart. Cary, by the way, has got a lover. What does a woman do at fifty? Fifty-five, in her case, come to that. "Don't think," I tell her, "it has to last for ever." What I told her when we divorced. They go away at weekends and screw the fuck out of one another. A different place each week. Sandra, on the other

275

hand, the one to whom I would have introduced you, wants five kids. Intends to retire at thirty and pump them out over the next ten years. Private schools. Nannies. "God Christ, do you think I'm made of money?" I tell her. "Bonds will be over and out before you finish." She says, "Sweetheart, not before *I'm* done." At her age, and my age, I have to watch my back. Eighty, I'll be, with teenage children. At her age she'll get laid by someone else. That's why, I guess, I'm looking at pictures. Maybe, after all, there's something in it. Maybe, after all, I've been missing out. Maybe eternity is all we have, endlessness, our kid, going on for ever.'

They were threading through the sidestreets past Petticoat Lane, the old churches, the cemeteries, the occasional oasis of original Georgian houses, the residue of a Regency city which, Maddox realised, he knew little about, pausing at plaques to read the inscriptions, the extended booms of stalk-like cranes manoeuvring high above their heads.

'We used to walk round here in the old days,' his brother said.

'I don't remember,' Maddox said.

'Or was it with Joe? The old bugger. Though he was more West End. Or was it when we came to town with Father to view a new model and he brought us here as a matter of course? Didn't we go on the river to Hampton Court, and another time to Greenwich? Must have been,' he concluded.

It was the river they gazed at, finally, leaning over the rails by the Tower, the bridge to their left, the *Belfast* moored on the opposite bank, the crowds threading their way into the Tower behind, another queue onto the boats at the pier, his brother's attention, however, focused on the river, flowing eastwards, to their left, the tide going out.

'You'll give this chap a go?'

'Sure.'

'Don't have to hang in if it doesn't work out.'

'That's right.'

'This is on me, a retirement present. You think that might be at the heart of it?'

276

'No,' Maddox said. He shook his head.

He had leant like this on a metal rail, overlooking, on that occasion, a beach, with his brother, Paul having announced his intention of going into the Church. He couldn't remember, of the several resorts the family had visited over those years, which one it was – the sea, on that occasion, relatively calm: the boats, the sails, the recollection of a harbour to his right, houses rising up a slope behind: the smell of seaweed, the salty tang, figures reclining or running to and fro on the beach, a paradisiacal sensation, associated with his brother's decision and the place itself, and which, in his early teens, he had come to associate with art, specifically, magically, with Florentine names, with Siena, Padua, a humanising fervour which, unlike his reaction to his brother's 'calling', he had wished to expand and sustain.

Later, Paul had summoned a taxi, his hand on Maddox's back as he stooped inside, saying, 'I won't come with you. I need to think. Not about you. My pissed-up life. I haven't been down here for a very long time. I think I'll walk,' Maddox wondering if he hadn't an afternoon appointment at the nearby hotel, cynical about Paul, he reflected, as he was about himself. 'I feel *charged*,' his brother went on, grasping his chest. 'Glad that we met, and hoping we'll do it again before long. Let me know, by the way, how you get on with this chap. His name is Isaacs. You may have heard of him.'

'No,' he said.

'If it doesn't work out I might try him myself,' waving his arm, laughing, as the taxi drew away.

Even then, perhaps more obviously than before, something significant, if not crucial, had been left unsaid: it was as if, he reflected, there were no language in which to express it, no action or sign to convey it, no gesture, no name, merely, startled by the conclusion, the language of omission. At one point, walking through the narrowing streets towards the river, avoiding the main road, coming out at Pepys's house above Tower Hill, his brother had enquired, 'It's not to do with ageing? Something as incontrovertible as that? I'm old enough, more than old enough, to pack it in. I don't think, despite suggesting otherwise, I'll hold Sandra for very long. On the other hand,' he'd paused, 'do you think it's to do with something in us? The three of us, if you count Sarah? What do you think?' Maddox declining – unable – to give an answer, wondering at his reluctance to do so and at the curiously unquestioning look on his brother's face, as if he himself were assured of the answer, something he knew and, at Maddox's lack of response, felt it still necessary, if not his duty, to keep to himself.

A familiar desire to return to St Albans sprang to mind – to revisit the park, the tiny, grass-banked Roman theatre, but not the Cathedral, the one place which, apart from their vanished home, had meant most to him at the time – and with which, in his youth, he had had the strongest connections: drunks had been sprawled around the gate the last occasion he'd gone there.

Now, seated in the taxi, lulled by its slow progress through the congested streets (lurching its way towards the Exchange and then, beyond, turning north from Holborn), the familiarity of the buildings induced a feeling that, whatever he felt about his home near Camden Lock, its modest proportions, its meagre possessions, its disreputable neighbours, it was something to which he now belonged (but of which he could easily divest himself: a skin to shed, like any other). Yet he felt exhausted rather than exhilarated by the conversation with Paul, wondering if, despite appearances, he had done more for his brother than Paul had done for him. In one sense, he'd been written off (as something little short of a disaster), his brother reluctant to admit it, at least until he had offered him one more chance: art had fucked him up: the new man, Isaacs, would reverse it.

Despite his exhaustion, he endured a curious feeling of exclusion – displacement, even: he would have liked, for instance, to have seen his brother's pictures (something in common at last), aware, too, that Paul's pursuit of eternal vigour had become something of an affectation, offered more by way of provocation, of intent or challenge.

At which point his preoccupation with Taylor returned: grief for his wife and children overwhelmed him, flinging him back, stunned, against the taxi's seat, conscious of the rear of the driver, of the traffic in the road beyond – as if he were once more in his uncle's car, being driven in it on that first occasion, the hallucinatory smell he associated with it, and the galvanising juxtaposition of the bonnet against the irregularities of the view ahead.

Set down in the street, he discovered his brother had paid the driver, disturbed that he hadn't noticed, disturbed at being patronised, his reaction deflected by a further thought: a recognition of the care his brother had shown him, his avuncular if no longer convincing charm, mannered and self-conscious, concealing a doubt as significant as his own, as if Paul, too, had been flung back on resources which, if previously much talked about, he suspected might not be there.

13

I⟶ WASN'T Simone ringing, but his sister; for a moment, since –
characteristically – she didn't give her name, he was uncertain
who it was, the almost formal, 'How are you, Matthew?'
followed by enquiries about his sons. Then he recognised the
ebullient tone which, if constrained, had characterised their
encounters in the past – increasingly rare in recent years: she it
was who invariably called, or wrote, he rarely calling her, her
tone on this occasion cautious, anxious to point out her
appreciation of the distance he'd insisted, if largely by default,
on maintaining between them. Paul, he assumed, had rung her,
conceivably Charlotte. 'I'm in the district. I wondered if you
were in.'

'Sure.'

Submission of this sort was comparatively new: it had been
with him now for over a year, pre-dating the incident on the
tube station platform. He couldn't recall a moment, throughout
this time, when he'd decided anything significant for himself:
he was adrift – 'hanging in', as Paul would have it, largely, he
assumed, to see what might happen. He would, at that point, he
concluded, have a choice – a feeling of fear, amounting to
terror, visiting him at predictable intervals throughout the day,
strongest in the morning, fading towards evening, an unliveable
life to a bearable life within the span of every twenty-four hours.

Listening to his sister's voice he realised all he had generated
in his brother had been a feeling of concern – one, evidently,
he'd transmitted to their sister, but one which, curiously, he
didn't share himself. Describing to her the route to the house,

280

he was reminded she'd never, previously, been invited, driven now to invite herself, something in her manner, not least its note of restraint, which recalled his former wife: the 'woman role' she'd adopted for herself – had mandated, almost – in their early family life (their mother's absorption in other things), the eldest sibling foraging ahead, prospecting for the first time what things were 'like', coming up, finally, with laughter, the ebullience, much of which rubbed off on Paul, little, Maddox reflected, on himself: a domineering, matriarchal urge which had swept her swiftly into marriage, children, a career, and, in her sixties, back out again, she, self-proclaimed, a 'human being again'.

He met her at the door, having watched for her at the upstairs window, strangely excited, almost unnerved – not sure, despite their long relationship, what, on this occasion, he might expect from her. That she'd made a specific journey to see him he had no doubt. Moments before, between her telephone call and her arrival, he'd rung Simone, leaving a message in the hope, if within hearing distance, she might have responded, anxious, increasingly anxious, for her to return the call as he stood waiting for Sarah, glimpsing her, finally, in the street below, startled by her appearance.

Considerably stouter than before and, he reflected, looking proportionately older, but for her raised head, examining the numbers, he might not have recognised her, an anonymous figure in a characterless coat, a scarf tucked into its collar: a homely, practical, no-nonsense figure, the head turned stiffly towards each door, no evidence of the animation he associated with her, or of the Josephean vivacity of his brother which had characterised the afternoon.

Having hurried down he'd called her from the door, she having passed the gate, an iron grille construction opening onto the shallow forecourt of the house, immediately below the ground-floor window: all he had there, as in the backyard, were several plantless, weedful pots left by the previous owner.

He saw her face ignite, spontaneously, warmly, relieved: the Maddox face, a stubborn, if ageing facsimile of much of what he

281

had seen in their father, a singular combination of sensitivity, reticence, foreboding – little of the quixotic, the enigmatic, the epigrammatic, certainly the didactic he associated with their uncle, he stepping forward to release the gate, she looking up at the house, startled, then at him, before thrusting out her arms and – more her wish, as with his brother, than his – embracing him.

The force of her arms around his shoulders reminded him of the expansiveness, the openness and generosity which had characterised her as a child and a mother: it was, on this occasion, a maternal presence, a consciously presented one, he was submitting to, the strange sensation of calling her name, 'Sarah!', a possessive tone, summoning her from a distance, the involuntary movement backwards at the sound of his voice before she turned towards him.

At her insistence he showed her the house, taking her coat, laying it on a chair in the through-room, stepping into the kitchen where he'd already boiled the kettle, opening the door to the yard, taking her out to look at the pots he had scattered there, she lamenting the lack of flowers, the yard itself paved, the soil enclosed in a narrow border circuiting the edge.

She looked up at the rear of the building: the landing window, the back bedroom window, then at the houses opposite and on either side: the symmetry, the butterfly roofs with their central gutter, a concertina-like effect against the fading light of the sky. 'Reminds me of our home. Much smaller, of course.'

'Of course.'

She laughing, taking his arm as companionably as Paul had done. He was suffering (he was oppressed), he was to be relieved, he was there to be rescued: adversity of some sort had overwhelmed him. No one knew why. Everyone guessed. Charlotte leaving him, for instance – his retirement, the sequence of their father's and their mother's deaths. And now the former student: death in its most macabre form. No doubt she'd heard about that (bound, he reflected, to impress everyone).

She was wearing a jacket beneath her coat, square-cut, oddly fashionable: she bought all her clothes from Oxfam, she had told him on a previous occasion: 'cheap, good quality, a very wide choice'. Underneath the jacket was a jumper, around her neck a string of beads, red, vivid, like drops of blood, intended, he suspected, to amuse, the clothes, otherwise, sombre. Her skirt, long, ended at her ankles, full, capacious, her feet shod unobtrusively in flat-heeled shoes: a mixture of practicality and second-hand fashion, vaguely facetious, carelessly conjoined.

Without her coat, her face flushed – with urgency, curiosity, goodwill – her hair flung up and backwards in a characteristic Maddox fashion, like a stilled impression of someone moving at speed (an effect which reminded him of Viklund), he was aware of another woman, a comparative stranger, someone who had little to do with him, someone in conflict with the one who had appeared in the street, stepping towards him, suddenly uncertain, she now a vitalising figure, taking his arm securely, turning him towards the rear door of the house, saying, 'What have you got upstairs?' Berenice's voice audible from an adjoining window, 'Will you keep quiet, you cunt? I'm talking on the fucking telephone,' Sarah, startled, unable to locate the sound, looking across the low dividing-wall up which, in the past, the previous tenant had vainly trained several climbing plants.

'My neighbour.'

'Good God,' glancing at the adjoining window, Berenice's remonstrating figure inside.

'I'm the cunt who lives next door. Not the one she's presently addressing. He's inside.'

'What does she do?'

'Definitely not art history. The police look in from time to time. They even observed her from a neighbour's room across the street. Otherwise a stream of brutalised figures pass swiftly in and out.'

'How does she afford to live here?'

'The house is owned by the council. So are half the properties in the street. A post-war decision to knock most of them down to build tower blocks was belatedly rescinded. These are the vestiges of the properties they bought before the decision was reversed. The result is what they call a mixed community. More mixed than community, I'm afraid,' he added.

They'd returned inside the house, he reminded that he liked his sister, over and beyond her being his sister: her late-life stoutness gave her substance (scale, strength, sobriety, judgement): solid, stoical, self-amused, femininity without the affectation, her image of herself, he imagined, corresponding to the way she dressed. Or, alternately, the other way around. Her almost proprietorial inspection of the two rooms upstairs – the papers, books and folders, scattered on the floor, the desk, the bed, the chair in the bedroom at the rear, the comparative bareness of the one at the front, prompting her to enquire, 'Who sleeps in here?'

'We do, when Simone comes,' he said. 'Though we usually sleep at her place.'

'How is she?'

Primed, he suspected, by Charlotte and Paul.

'Well. I, I can't help feeling, a current liability.'

She had always been inclined, contrary to her own experience of marriage – a middle-aged husband leaving for a significantly younger woman – to a view that Charlotte shouldn't have left him, at least not for the husband she ended up with. Yet for Maddox it had always seemed a positive move, he laying no great claims to his role either as a husband or a father, much though the effort he'd put into both. No one was complaining, other than Sarah. On the whole, he concluded his wife – his ex-wife – had made a bold choice, Gerry a refreshing change from anyone previously she might have known, most of all an academic who, relatively late in life, was, surreptitiously, without informing anyone, searching for a connection between himself and a disinterested universe, species devouring species in order to survive, galaxies similarly confronting galaxies. Someone looking for common sense in the face of such brutalisation was not someone an ageing wife could, with much expectation, time running out, be overly entertained or cheered by. A declining belief in virtue being able to sustain itself characterised, profoundly, the latter years of their pre-Gerry existence.

Simone, too, was looking for something – scarcely aware a search was in progress. This alone, he suspected, was the thing that had drawn them together: a presentiment that something significant was about to occur, in which Doctor Death, aka Norman, aka Brian, and Taylor, played, comparatively, little part. Simone, during her mandatory analysis (seven years, she'd told him), must have examined to the point of extinction the past which she was presently averse to describing. With her he experienced the feeling that she knew – was aware of – everything before it happened, singularly so, with the possible exception of Death, though he, too, she might well have suspected (had already suggested something along these lines), was not all he claimed to be – a not infrequent analytical experience, he imagined, on both sides of the analyst's room: not only ahead of her patients, clients, engagés, analysands, but in many respects, perhaps to her own consternation, ahead of herself – so far ahead, in his case, that for much of the time she was out of sight, waiting patiently, occasionally impatiently, for him to catch her up.

'We nevertheless get on well,' he said, speaking directly from his thoughts. Indicating the way downstairs, he added, 'Would you like tea, or something stronger?'

'What's stronger?'

'Wine.'

'No gin?'

That's her fuel, he reflected.

'Afraid not. I'm fortunate to have wine. Alcohol is advised against with my medication.'

'Is it doing any good?'

Scepticism in her enquiry: all, he reflected further, to the good. On the other hand, what had Paul or Charlotte told her?

'On the whole,' he said carefully, 'I'm better than I was. Pathology at an end. No longer susceptible to psychotic phases. Though I'm never quite sure what they are, the brain adjusting in its own sweet way, "clinical" a word, in mental health, lacking, I would say, definition.'

Having reached the room downstairs she'd turned, facing

285

him in much the same manner she might have done fifty years before, determined to say something but not sure what it was, or, if she were sure, how precisely to go about it.

'I tried several pills before finally settling on this one. One or two of them almost killed me. Though, on reflection, that might have been the idea.'

She'd turned away, selecting a chair – curiously, the one Viklund had chosen, adjacent to the television set and the fireplace.

'Could you get that replaced?' She indicated the walled-up opening.

'The house is exactly as it was when I first moved in. I don't feel inclined to change a thing.'

'A house without a fireplace isn't really a home. It needs a focus. Otherwise,' she gestured at the television.

'I'm sure it does.'

Relieved to have expressed something, she smiled and said, 'Tea. Have you a biscuit to go with it?'

He talked through from the kitchen, describing his encounter with Paul, presuming that earlier she had heard Paul's own description of it.

'Still something of the cavalier?' she asked.

'Like Joseph,' he said, 'without the affectation.'

She laughed, the sound filling the house: it even silenced Berenice's voice audible through the party-wall.

'To some degree,' he went on, 'he's something like me.'

'How like you?'

Having given her the tea and arranged a low table to put it on – a duplication of the arrangement he'd made with Viklund – he said, 'Reorientating himself in a way he's suspicious of.'

'Aren't we all?' she said, less enquiry than proclamation. 'Manoeuvring himself to die. At least, trying not to.' She'd spoken condemningly, a tone, he calculated, of self-reproach.

A compact figure, seated, she pulled down her jacket and loosened the beads which had slipped above the lapel.

'You think so?'

286

'He was always much influenced by you. As we all were, of course,' she added.

'I wasn't aware of that.'

'That cultural high-flying? The equivalent, *your* equivalent, of Joseph's flamboyance. I think Paul went into the Church because of you. A cultural hauteur he couldn't otherwise match. At least, you couldn't in those days. Now that science has shown the primacy of matter, the scene, as Paul was the first to acknowledge, has changed. I felt when I married poor Arthur, who was only a mathematics teacher, I was crawling away from a house where my expectations, as defined by you, were so pathetic they hadn't even been noticed. That school you and Paul went to whose name sounded like a medicine.'

'Quinians.'

'Where did that come from?'

'Quinian Hall. The original house around which the school was built. Originally Quinians' Proprietary School, set up by nineteenth-century philanthropists disillusioned by the education provided for their sons.'

She wasn't much interested in this and wondered why, suddenly, he was: perhaps that, too, he had misjudged: more had gone on there than he had realised.

'They didn't send me away because of the bombing,' his sister said. 'They assumed I was expendable. Odd,' she went on, 'because at first I thought it was because they loved me more and couldn't bear to do without me.'

'Perhaps they couldn't,' he said, anxious to prompt her, curious to see, at this late stage of their lives, what she might come up with: something relevant to his own dilemma, or something, even, to hers. 'You were certainly indispensable,' he added.

'Domestically!' She laughed: a clattering sound, not unlike hands clapping.

'Paul rang you up,' he prompted again.

'He's worried about you. We all are. Those symptoms you describe. What are they about? Manoeuvring to die is maybe

287

what all of us are up to. In the process, of course, discovering how to live.'

She, too, she was suggesting, had had her problems: *still* had her problems: his suffering, if it were such, was not exclusive.

She was looking up, her head lowered, her eyes shadowed. She wore little if any make-up. Simone, by comparison, though deploying it discreetly, probably used a lot. Certainly before she went down on a morning she spent a long time in the bathroom, one wall of which was given over almost entirely to a mirror: a frank, uncompromising image it offered to anyone, particularly at that hour, gazing into it. She, too, he reflected, was much preoccupied with ageing, though resolutely not with 'age': age, she was inclined to suggest, rather like Kavanagh, didn't count. What did was something arrived at or acquired by application, to do exclusively with her job. Negativity, day after day, had to be confronted by something; if not by something positive, at least by something distracting.

Like make-up.

'Paul's arranged for me to see someone a colleague has recommended. I assume it's a colleague. A materialistic crew normally, the ones he hangs around with. Like all Paul's enthusiasms, not to be taken at face value, he today telling me he's buying pictures.'

'Only to sell on. They're scarcely in his house ten minutes.'

'So all that "change of life" is bullshit?'

'Paul does lots of things on impulse.' His sister smiled, raising the cup of tea, saluting. 'This woman he has at the moment is the silliest he's come up with. Scarcely thirty and intends to retire at thirty-five and have five children. Paul, foolishly, thinks by him. Eighty years old with teenage children!'

'Has he told you that?'

'She did. He brought her round. He thinks I'm a fount of familial wisdom. Charlotte had rung him asking if he'd see you.'

'To do what?'

'See how you are.'

'It's reassuring,' he said, 'so many want to help. An

embarrassment of riches. I'm fortunate, very fortunate,' he added.

'We feel you're moving away from us. Even further away,' she went on, 'than you were before. We feel, in a way, you're not coming back.'

Once more Berenice's voice came through the wall, the only audible words, as usual, 'fucking' and '*roight?*'

'I haven't come back. I've departed. Where to,' he said, 'I've no idea.'

'I re-read your article, by the way. The one you wrote at the time of Daddy's death. "We are here to kill and be killed." '

'We are here to destroy and be destroyed.'

'It's so evidently not the case.'

'You think so.'

It was odd, he thought, that Paul hadn't mentioned this: not a few had remarked on it at the time. But then, ideology was, along with the Church, a thing he had abandoned long ago.

'I know so!' His sister was triumphant. 'Nicholas,' she added, mentioning one of her sons-in-law, 'follows your reviews. Over the past few years, he says, they've become increasingly negative. Not surprising. What's happening, what has happened, in your private life must have played a significant part. Paul told me today, for instance, you've been fired. It was always absurd, an academic involving himself in contemporary events. You're no wiser, in that respect, than anyone else. History, to a large degree, is fiction. So are retrospective views of art.'

He didn't respond, looking into the space behind her, the opening to the kitchen. To one side was a window facing the yard, a round table and four chairs placed before it. Moments ago, they'd been standing there, somewhere, he strangely concluded, where neither of them belonged.

'It's not a negative view,' he finally announced, 'considering the scale and extent of male destructiveness. Nor the reverse of it,' he went on, 'when the same destructiveness is deployed in disassembling the past and recreating it in the light of the present. Destruction is the basis of love. I won't hurt you if you won't hurt me. Out of that emerges the inevitable need for succour and protection, first from the consequences of our destructiveness, then out of a requirement to distract the destructiveness of others. From this collusion of interests grows mutual regard. Out of mutual regard grows affiliation. Out of affiliation grows affection. Out of affection grows love. If I love you will you love me? Out of that emerges the final, sanctifying ethic, I'll love you even if you don't love me, our exegesis of a life we were never free to choose.'

She had heard all this before. Her gaze turned to follow his, then, disillusioned, was turned back again.

'This killer you've befriended.'

Maddox shrugged: incomprehension, even horror, was evident in her look – something familiar from their earliest encounters: his unworldliness had always alarmed if not enraged her: he lived – had spent most of his life – not in the present century but one, as she'd been inclined in the past to point out, 'six of them ago'.

What had happened then that appeared to be relevant now? He was no longer sure: Savonarola, the inspirer of Michelangelo, had been burnt alive, the crowd throwing stones to dislodge the flesh still hanging from the bones, the remains ground down and thrown into the Arno: everything, at an alarming rate, was, in his life, moving backwards. Something inexplicable was happening, specifically to him, something he could look on only, paradoxically, with the same concern as his brother and sister – but not the concern, he realised, with a shock, of Simone: whatever she saw did not discourage her.

Something he hadn't acknowledged: he might, at this moment, quite easily, have been dead, this posthumous existence a ghost-like phenomenon. Sectioning, too, had been a death: what had emerged, by way of chemicals, was not something he knew, any longer, how to recognise, or even, he was beginning to suspect, respond to: a spectral presence bordering on what Simone, undoubtedly – and Neil, the t'ai-chi-addicted life-class instructor – would have described as 'essence', the 'substance' of which, presumably, he represented – and was living – now.

'He used to be my student. I had an affair with his wife, before he met her, for which, at the time, had it been discovered, I might have been fired. Why he wanted to see me I'm not sure. He isn't either. Although he's unaware of it, we have attempted-suicide in common, his consciously determined, mine not. The fact that he's unaware of it affects the way I see him.' He paused, unsure if any of this had registered: she was, after all, he reflected, like his brother, like their uncle, or even perhaps their father: weren't cars, at the time, a distraction, rather than a requirement: wasn't *pleasure* the principle involved?

The structure on which he was basing – had based – everything was beginning to shake. *He* was beginning to shake: he could feel the tremor pass through his body, into his arms, his hands, down to his legs, his feet: familiar convulsions were taking place in the region of his heart. His voice thickened, an odd, inarticulate sound emerging from his mouth, he turning his head aside, thankfully, as the telephone rang.

At first he was inclined to let it ring: the instrument stood on a bookshelf within reach of where his sister was sitting. She, startled by the sound, had also turned.

He rose, lifted the receiver, and heard Simone's voice.

'I got your message.'

'I'm with my sister,' he said. How swiftly she could put him at his ease, just as on other occasions how swiftly she could alarm him. 'I'll come up later,' he added.

'Whenever you like. I'll be in bed. I've had a tiring day. Probably like you.'

The phone was replaced the other end: one of her list of calls, he assumed, she had to make, seeing her clearly, at that moment, standing, stooped to the names, to see who else remained.

'I'm not keeping you?' Sarah said.

'I'm glad of a chance to talk,' he said.

'That was her.'

'Simone.'

291

'Is she English?'

'As far as I'm aware.'

She waited: she might, the next instant, enquire if he had a photograph.

'I feel, with Taylor, my former student, I have something in common. He was the brightest, if not the best, of those I dealt with. Precocious, but not aware of it. I thought, at the time, he might have done anything. Anything other than painting. Politics. Religion. Business. Even the Chair at the Drayburgh when I left. Unfortunately, he only wanted to paint. Unlike his wife he hadn't the talent.'

'Paul doesn't think it'll do much good. Seeing him,' she said.

'He got in touch with me. Not I with him.'

'You didn't have to respond.'

'I'd have felt much worse not,' he told her. 'I'm perhaps the one person left he can talk to.' He waited. 'One way forward,' he added, 'is to do the things I would have done if I hadn't been ill. Certainly, in those conditions, I'd have gone and seen him. A residual duty, curiosity, self-help, illumination, what you will.'

He turned to the window, looking out to the yard. Another thought struck him.

'I was watching a blackbird out there the other day. Pulling up a worm. A cat came over the wall. The blackbird didn't see it. The cat crept up. When, finally, quivering on its haunches, it was about to spring, I tapped the window. The bird flew up, the cat shot off. The worm, presumably, returned to its hole. A chain of destruction ending with a species with the unique capacity to destroy itself. I'm inclined to think the destruction will go on unimpeded, licensed, after all, by nature. What stronger endorsement could it have than that?'

'You'll go on seeing him?' statement, rather than enquiry.

'Not without his permission. If he's transferred to a unit outside London they may decide it's better he sees no one. Least of all someone who, from past association, might disturb him.'

She appeared to be gazing at him as if from a distance. He, too, seemed to see her from a long way off, an increasingly diminishing figure who, at that instant, he wanted to call back:

soon, he reflected, she would disappear entirely, beyond his reach, beyond his touch.

'Is an appetite for such a life as the one I've described a sign, not of morbidity, but of the cold-heartedness of others? Am I the only one to recognise reality, that an existence based on species devouring species, galaxies annihilating galaxies, is not only unacceptable but wrong? Free will doesn't operate amongst birds and beasts, least of all original sin. In which case, morality is a fiction and not an explanation of, or even an excuse for, a universe based on force. It's why,' he went on, 'I responded to Giotto. No more Gods to fuck around. No more to atone to. No more Gods, thank God, for anything.'

'I thought all his paintings were religious,' she said. 'The ones you and Viklund authenticated, dismissing most of the rest.'

How often in the past had she looked over his shoulder, provoked, as the whole family were, by an enthusiasm on his part he couldn't, other than by his absorption, communicate. Now he merely shook his head. 'Were religious,' he said. 'In reality were, and are, increasingly, something else.'

Berenice's voice had faded, possibly to another room: invariably his speculation, on the rare occasions she fell silent, was that one of her customers, her clients, her participatory addicts, who bore the brunt of her reproaches, her self-exonerating speeches, had struck her down (cut her up, disposed of her – a frequent thought – in black bin-liners – so many, normally, taken from her house), he listening, hopefully, for confirmatory signals: banging, cries, the sound of a saw, a hammer, the thump of weights being dragged across the floor. Inevitably, fantasies, wishes, scarcely mobilised, the recriminatory expletives would confirm that immortality, in her case, was assured.

'Even when you were younger I always thought you too intense.' His sister sank back in her chair, in much the same fashion Viklund had – in his case, to indicate, despite signals to the contrary, he felt at home. With Sarah, the gesture was one of resignation. 'Do you remember the times I tried to josh you out of it?'

'Often.'

'And Paul.'

'All of you. Such biblical names, too,' he added. 'Sarah. Matthew. I wonder what they intended? Paul was telling me he went into the Church to pre-empt my doing the same. Either that,' he went on, 'or to placate Mother. The masters at Quinians thought the same. Going by the reproductions I used to pin up in my locker. To end up with what? A visitation on a tube station platform that even now I can't explain. Condoning, or otherwise, a different matter.'

'Did Paul say that?' she said. 'Pre-empting?'

'He sought to divert me from what, even at that age, like you, he recognised as morbidity. As for the Cathedral. There it was. Down the road. Our weekly attendance. No avoiding. Religiosity built into the house, built into the business, "straight as an arrow" in lower-case gold lettering across the showroom window, the Roman examplar immediately outside. On top of that, the war. Nothing quite so socially cohesive could have been invented to bring God and Mammon side by side. The notion of divine participation, an absolute evil prompting, on our side, an absolute good. I don't think anyone who experienced it, as a child, of a certain age, ever quite got over it. On formative years it had an indescribable and largely unexplored effect. Goodness exemplified in flesh and blood, in coal and steel. At Quinians, away from the bombing, though we could see the glow from Sheffield burning beyond the skyline, the constant thread of conversation amongst the younger boys was the number of aircraft, on the other side, shot down, guns captured, ships sunk, miles retaken. The blackout gave a strange homogeneity to everything. Plus, at Quinians, the sound of anti-aircraft guns from a nearby battery, its searchlights, ethereally, at night, probing at the sky, the throbbing of aircraft overhead. Everything compounded a sense of destiny, where we were, what we were, above all else, who we were. The sense of a highly visible force dominating everything on behalf of a common good. Not a mile from the school, in the valley bottom, between us and the town, was a factory given over to the manufacture of tanks. We'd run down the hill to watch them go by, Valentines, Churchills, their tracks leaving white weals on the tarmac, they rattling off to their testing-ground outside the town where they'd bounce around at speed in half-wooded countryside before they were shipped off, tarpaulined, on goods trains to the south.'

Breathless, one anxiety attack coalescing with another, prompted, no doubt, by what he had described: the absence, in the present, of any equivalent.

'All the time,' he went on, holding his chest, 'a natural force relocating itself. Implacable. Irresistible. God help us, never ending.'

It was as if he were outside the room, suspended above it, endeavouring to get back. Little of what he had intended to say, what his sister, no doubt, had intended to say, had been expressed.

'How are you?' he concluded.

Enough here to reassure her, he reflected, he was completely off his head, she resting her elbows on the arms of the chair, her hands, lightly held together, pressed against her mouth, gazing at him over the top of them.

'I've rarely been better. Which is why I'd very much like you to be the same.'

'Still teaching.'

'Long retired. Though I help in a local school.'

'Sounds like Mother.'

'It does.' She paused. 'I take art lessons, too, like you. A foundation course. On top of which,' she paused again, her hands lowered, still clenched together. 'The children. The grandchildren. There doesn't seem time enough. Women,' she released one hand, 'are better at that sort of thing.'

'What sort of thing?' his thoughts dominated at that moment by the reflection that he and she and Paul came from a common stock, the father he'd walked around, weeping, the morning after his death, a helplessness that had increased rather than decreased with time. What had been removed from him that hadn't, evidently, been removed from Paul and his sister? she, for instance, increasingly absorbed in life, absorbed in pleasure, a simple, unadulterated hedonistic drive: acceptance instead of resignation, openness instead of reserve, sympathy in place of disillusionment.

'Friendship. Companionship. The social instinct is more pronounced in women than men. At least, is expressed in a different way. Maybe because of subjugation, a sense of sharing a common situation. Like the war. But permanent, and women only. Men's feelings are expressed, where not in work, in sport. In addition, women talk about their feelings, men invariably, because of the reasons given, not.'

'I talk,' he said, belligerently, 'about little else. And have been given much encouragement to do so. After all, who are the great talkers, in this respect, philosophers apart? Freud. Jung. Adler.' He paused, waiting for her response. Getting none, he added, 'However, there is not much left to say.'

'I'm sure there's a lot,' she said, 'but we don't know how to say it. What can't be communicated,' she went on, 'is what our parents used to call "God's pasture".'

'What can't be communicated,' he said, 'doesn't appear to be my problem. As for "God's pasture". Clearly something we can't imagine needn't necessarily dispose us to assume it isn't there. Infinity, for instance.'

'Or a new colour.'

'Or me in a better mood.'

Evenings at home when the two, or the three of them had competed in banter: the shadowed living-room at the sunless back of the house, the never altogether absent smell of leather, fumes, polish, fuel; that odour that came in on their father's clothes never entirely overcome by the smell of cooking, or of the pipe tobacco he smoked.

Competed, too, in attracting the attention of their uncle, the genial guardian of the place, whose flamboyancy both bemused and intimidated them as children, and distracted, if not openly amused them later on: the glazed stare with which Sarah would listen to accounts of the plays he'd seen, her eyes moving from detail to detail of her uncle's coat, his cravat, his collar, his cuffs, his tie-pin, his cuff-links, his turn-ups, his shoes, his words adjuncts of his appearance. Finally, after this examination, her eyes would turn to his face: his moustache, his full-blooded, full-lipped mouth, his conspicuous nose, his neatly trimmed brows, his suavely cut hair – his twinkling, galvanising, dark-brown eyes: something here which gave the impression of a mask, just as, with his clothes, came the impression of a costume, one which might just as well have been worn by, or borrowed from, someone else.

To some extent she had modelled her behaviour on what she had seen and heard: a temperamental, loquacious, opinionated performer who took over the living-room whenever her brothers were home from school, determined, on each of these occasions, to re-assert her ascendancy. Something of her histrionics Paul had taken on himself, a 'longing to wear a dress' a later facetious excuse for his entering the Church, and a 'disillusionment with wearing frocks' an even later excuse for leaving it.

'Paul has suggested someone you could speak to,' Sarah said, entering his thoughts.

'He sees it as complementary to what I'm up to at present.'

Recapitulation, he assumed, while she assessed where their conversation might be going: she looked to the window, the darkening street, in much the same fashion as Viklund had looked out, equating what was in the room with what might be outside it, he struck by the insistence with which Viklund remained in and constantly revivified his thoughts.

As if prompted by the silence, once more, through the party-wall, came the sound of Berenice's voice.

'That woman certainly comes across. Don't you ever complain?'

'We have an understanding.'

'Of what?'

'Sorts.'

'I see.'

'How much each other can stand.'

Perversity – obscurity, even – was something Sarah instinctively responded to: her legs crossed, her hands splayed on her knee, she said, 'You're sure there's nothing more we can do?'

'It was Paul's idea to suggest this other man. I'm determined, as far as I can, to manage on my own. All this, as I've said, is new to me. Ten years ago, five years ago, even less, I wouldn't have believed any of this could have happened. Looking back, you could say it fits into a pattern, but not necessarily one I recognise.'

She looked across intensely. 'What pattern?'

'Weren't we supposed to have come from merchants? Artisans. Tailors. *Cobblers.* Ending up as the first car salesmen in St Albans? Joseph, nowadays, I imagine, would be a hustler, somewhat on the lines of Paul. Do you remember how he used to talk of built-in obsolescence as if it were a feature for which there'd be a charge?'

Amity, of a sort, had been restored; Sarah having extended her sympathy – her understanding, her involvement – as far as they could reach. Her own life, she was suggesting, had been extended, too, if in the opposite direction, to expectancy, anticipation, not to anxiety and doubt.

Yet, he too, he reflected, was expectant: he was looking to something – looking for something – something to which, finally, he might attach himself – like Simone, for instance. He and his sister and his brother might, from time to time, still call to one another, as now, but – bleak, impassable, intransigent – they were aware of the increasing distance between themselves: something sad and absolute about all that.

'Weren't our family Jews? Didn't father convert at a significant moment of his youth, in order to further his chances? Weren't we enclosed in a system we were intended to endorse? Wasn't Paul the imprimatur placed, finally, on all of us? One he dismissed when he realised it didn't count?'

'So what?'

'Doesn't it have an effect?' Maddox said.

His sister shrugged. 'Sectarianism of any sort I despise. Tradition kills. It doesn't augment. It diminishes. Embraces.

Stifles. I hate the thought of our being *anything* other than ourselves. Who gives a fuck,' she smiled, 'who or what we were in the past?'

'I do.'

'Why?'

He shook his head.

'It's like dragging a corpse around,' she said. 'Catholic. Muslim. Hindu. *Protestant.* Haven't we, as a family, outgrown these things? Whatever Mother and Father deployed in the past, we don't have to oblige them any longer.'

So that was it: it didn't count – hadn't counted: an imperative, not a choice.

'More tea?'

The irony didn't elude her.

'You have your partner to see,' she said.

'Not quite a partnership yet.'

'Do you like her?'

'I do.'

'Does she like you?'

'I believe she must.' A moment later, he added, 'She's all I have at present.'

'Barring me. And Paul. And Charlotte. Your children. Even Viklund, I gather, is still around. I never knew whether you were his amanuensis or he was yours. Is he well?'

'Not very.'

'Paul says you may have compromised Simone's position with the Medical Council.'

'I'm corroborative evidence. Her complainants are two of her clients. One look at her principal accuser there'll be no case to answer. I'm sure of that.'

'But for you.'

'If every doctor, particularly in her field, were suspended because of a relationship with a client there wouldn't be many around.

'Really?'

'Exaggerating.'

'Naturally. Otherwise, it wouldn't be you.'

She was showing signs of leaving, looking round for her coat. A moment later she was rising, putting out her arms. 'You always were the prodigal child,' she added, he rising, too, she holding him against her. 'Paul,' she went on, releasing him, 'told me you'd been fired.'

'A good week, on the whole. I'm expecting the ground to open and swallow me tomorrow.'

A certain bleakness, and lack of conviction here, he thought, yet, laughing, she was picking up her coat with one hand, still retaining him, however, with the other. 'You might take Paul as an example. He has a fine sense of the irrelevance of running when all you need to do is walk. It hasn't done him badly.'

She was smiling, he now holding the coat while she slipped her arms inside.

At the door she added, 'You don't have to end up losing instead of fearing God,' turning, as if to mystify him further. 'The thing that's lost is still around,' stepping into the street, closing the gate behind her. 'Joseph, alone, remained true to his faith. What did he become? A peacock!' moving away, not glancing back, he waiting at the door until she'd reached the corner where, sensing he was still watching, she turned and waved.

14

SHE WAS in bed and had been asleep, turning to him, releasing the cat which, sensing his intrusion, fled to the door and out. 'Do you want to give it some food?' she said, adding, 'In compensation,' he returning to the kitchen, opening the fridge, getting out the tin, scooping a spoonful into the bowl, wondering why she slept with the cat at all, and then, unsure whether he'd bolted the front door, going back down to discover he had.

By the time he'd returned to the bedroom she was snoring and, breathless, he was panting: crawling in beside her, he pressed himself against her back, cupped his hand around her breast, pleased that she was naked, and felt her back ease into his groin. In no time at all he was asleep himself.

She was up before him, the breakfast cereals set out on a tray on the roof. They sat at the garden table, he half awake, aware that by now, normally, she might well have been working, hesitating to ask her why not, he giving her an account of the previous day, the conversations with his brother, his sister, not withholding, however, the latter's final observations. He felt refreshed (unintruded-upon, surprisingly so: untransgressed): on waking, in the middle of the night, they'd swiftly joined and, just as swiftly, fallen asleep again.

Without make-up, her hair brushed, a housecoat buttoned beneath her chin, he in a dressing-gown, they might have been any normal couple, companionable, relaxed, at ease with one another.

'Aren't you working?' he finally asked.

'I need time to think.' The paleness of her skin without make-up, the unaccustomed lightness, as a result, around her eyes, drama of any sort missing from her expression: instead, a sleepy acquiescence, he, too, inclined to assume, if only for a while, that nothing unusual was happening.

'Let's get married,' he said.

'Sure.' Leaning back, she laughed, one finger extended to the table, her breakfast finished, indicating the cat could lick her bowl. Finally, she set it on the flagstones, the cat lowering its head, its metal identity cylinder clinking against the bowl's side, they watching it together. 'Afraid I might run off?'

'That's it.'

'Some place to run to.' She gestured round. 'Is this what you get from your family? Marriage.'

'Leave,' he said, 'while the going's good.'

'I'd better meet them.'

'You better had.'

She was in a good mood but, though he thought he knew the reason, and was reluctant to disturb it, he wasn't convinced. Overhead, swifts swooped, squeaking, above and between the roofs. Higher up, house-martins fluttered, ducked and dived in slower patterns. A feeling of contentment absorbed him at that moment, she watching him, smiling.

'Does it need a warranty?' she asked.

'To match the one,' he said, 'I had before.'

'Plus three of mine.'

'Would you,' he enquired, 'get married again?'

'And go against your family?' her smile extended. Moments later she raised her head to watch the birds fluttering into the cavities beneath the eaves, turning then to watch the cat. Finally, she stooped to a nearby plant to pull off several dying petals. He watched her fingers extend to each stalk, the sifting sound as the petals came away, she screwing them in her palm and dropping them into a basket beneath the table. Her gardening tools and gloves were laid on a bench behind her: a picture of control, sufficiency: no need of marriage, the gesture

302

implied, I'm on my own, he wondering if he evoked a similar image (I'm nuts, he reflected, in any case). How much time would she take off work? How much, for instance, could she afford? the speculation sufficient for him to conclude she'd already worked out what she intended to do, 'with everything,' he said, involuntarily, aloud, glancing at her as she looked across.

' "With everything" what?'

'Some thought.' He waved his hand.

'Sounded like an order in a restaurant.'

'I was wondering,' he gestured round, 'where we go from here.'

'We needn't go anywhere,' she said. 'Unless there's something today you want to do.'

'I'd like to spend it with you.'

'I have people coming this afternoon. Other than that I'm okay.'

'How about this evening?'

'Sure.'

All the time he was testing the ground, unsure of her intentions; unsure, even, who she was, blind to his own appeal. If he hung in long enough, he reminded himself, it wasn't unlikely he might find out, and then, distracted, 'as long as she will have me,' speaking aloud.

She was glancing across again: he was, he reflected, concerned himself, something stirring at a moment when there was no immediate need of it. Here they were, on her roof, in the early sunlight, birds and insects overhead, flowers, a morning breeze: 'We're going on,' she said, reaching across to take his hand.

'Why?'

'We have no alternative, Matt.'

Her strength – at least, his awareness of it – flowed down her arm and into his hand.

'I believe your family haven't done you much good. What's the analyst you say your brother has found?'

'Someone,' he said, 'a colleague recommended.'

303

'Whom you're inclined to go along with?'

'Wouldn't that be your advice?' They had discussed his continuing therapy several times, both at the point they had themselves discontinued it and at regular intervals since.

'I'm not really in a position to judge,' she said. 'It depends who it is. I'd say if you felt you needed it you should go ahead. On the other hand,' she continued, 'what is "need"? I'm beginning to suspect the word myself.'

He was, increasingly, coming across elements in her he didn't understand: elements he perceived but didn't recognise. To a large extent she was a woman in the process of being created – by him; alternately, she had, to this degree, been created by three previous husbands, and probably by several other unnamed men. It was as if her own perception of herself had started at zero, a tabula rasa, an idealised opacity, the purpose of each relationship to raise herself up, man by man, step by step, to an ascendancy, a self-realisation, about which she would have no doubts: an assessment of herself placed vividly in a far from hypothetical world: the route of all her relationships pointed in the same direction.

Where he was in this progress he had no idea: finality in her discovery of herself had no doubt arrived some time before he had appeared. Perhaps this was the key to the relationship, less a continuing process of self-awareness than a celebration – of her having arrived at her goal, he the created or resurrected one.

Yet it was as if that part of his own life which had, evidently, gone on without him would continue its passage without her, he, engaged by her, moving in one direction while, in reality, this unknown element was moving in another – the consequence of which would be announced, as on the previous occasion, in a catastrophic manner.

Looking across at her, his hand more firmly clenched in hers, he suspected much of his appeal was realised in his helplessness, a curiously unfounded and unfounding nature, something, conceivably, not unlike her own.

'I don't think, on reflection, it's analysis you need,' she said.

'Why not?'

'I came to that conclusion once we'd started. Process and habit, for instance, are already in place. It's how you administrate rather than how you change them that's relevant at our age. Of that,' she continued, 'I'm convinced.' Her other hand came over, enclosing his. 'What you want,' she concluded, 'is *us*.'

Her directness made him laugh: it reminded him of his sister: behind every sophisticate was something of the reverse, having to struggle not unduly to get out.

Delighted to have amused him, she watched him with a smile, humour, he reflected, not her strongest suit. 'Fun, after all,' she said, 'is what we're after. That,' she went on, 'and keeping up with our chums.'

So they sat across the table from one another, the flowers around them, the birds above them, sweeping low, in squeaking flocks, in the morning light, their hands held, each secure in the knowledge, he presumed, of what the other wasn't rather than what the other was.

The house was in Ladbroke Road, at the back of Notting Hill Gate, tall, stuccoed, cream-painted, one of a terrace. A single bell beside the yellow door indicated that, unlike the houses adjoining, the place wasn't divided into flats.

A considerable time elapsed before, having rung the bell a second time, the door was finally opened. An elderly woman, small, stooped, with unruly hair, her face deeply faceted with vertical lines, from within which a pair of indifferent, exhausted eyes gazed out, enquired, 'Yes?' closing the door to little more than an aperture.

He gave her his name.

Stepping behind the door, she opened it wider.

A hallway stretched down to a flight of stairs up which a large dog was slowly climbing, its massive rear haunches, overhung by a drooping tail, swinging ponderously, painfully, even, from side to side.

Having closed the door the woman indicated a door to his

305

left. 'He's in there if he's come down,' she said. 'If he hasn't you'll have to wait. He's in a pretty foul temper, I can tell you.'

She disappeared at the rear of the hall, a door closing: moments later came the fluctuating sound of popular music: an announcer's voice, terminated abruptly, was followed once again by music, presumably from another station.

Pushing open the door she'd indicated he entered what was evidently the front room of the house. Its ceiling was cavernous and cracked: a piece of moulding in one corner was missing. A desk was arranged with its back to the tall, curtained, bay window, its surface, apart from an uncovered manual type-writer, strewn with books, magazines and papers. Recesses on either side of a marble fireplace, caryatids supporting the mantelpiece, were occupied by shelves, their irregular spaces, horizontally and vertically, crammed with books. Similarly, the wall opposite, above a large cabinet, several drawers and the cupboard of which were open, as if subjected to a recent search, was also occupied with shelves, the books, as if long abandoned, stacked in disorderly rows. At the back of the room, facing the desk and adjacent to the door, a low bookcase, glass fronted, was overhung by numerous ill-assorted paintings in a variety of singularly inappropriate frames. No common denominator, at first glance, was discernible, other than they were naturalistic – figures and landscapes, still lifes and interiors – no skill of any sort evident in their representation or design.

The centre of the room was dominated by a buttoned leather couch on which were strewn a number of rugs, several of them frayed. An armchair, also leather-covered, was arranged diago-nally to the fireplace which the couch itself was directly facing. The low suspension of the chair suggested that the springs were broken, the seat resting on the floor. Piles of books in the hearth further suggested that the fireplace itself was rarely if ever used. A second chair, half-upholstered, with wooden arms, stood at the back of the room, adjacent to the rear wall. Cardboard boxes, containing variously coloured files, were strewn around it as if recently discarded. A smell of tobacco, faded cloth and decaying paper, underlain by damp, dominated the room, the

306

tall, heavily curtained windows, tassels at the base of the curtains sweeping the floor, looked out, across a small, railed forecourt, to the street. From below, the sound of bottles being broken indicated there was a basement.

Not sure which area of the room to occupy, he crossed to the window. More substantial stuccoed houses, with front gardens, were visible through a barrier of trees opposite. Glancing at the desk, beside which he was standing, his attention was drawn to a sheet of paper rolled into the typewriter, the projecting half already typed on. Stooping to read it, his eyes screwed up without his glasses, he deciphered, 'Eternity is not a problem, temporality is all the rage. Neither the contents nor the layout of your bill shows, in my view, the slightest improvement and, as I have observed on several previous occasions, they do not in any way warrant a response . . .'

Aware of the creaking of woodwork outside the door, he was examining the paintings at the back of the room when a small, dishevelled man came in.

Older than himself, unshaven, a cardigan arranged around a curiously misshapen body, his uneven shoulders dipping to one side, his expression was one of consternation, fierce, choleric, the cheeks inflamed, the nose also, the eyes, small, dilated, dark, intense. White hair was flung backwards and upwards from a prominent brow: tight, wirely sprung curls rose in successive tiers. His look of surprise at seeing Maddox turned suddenly to one of disappointment. 'Who are you?' Saliva spurted from the corner of his mouth, his lips gleaming. An expression, one of enquiry, revealed several irregularly projecting teeth.

'Maddox,' he said, putting out his hand, and added, lamely, when this appeared to increase the man's displeasure, 'Matthew.'

Ignoring his hand, the man turned back to the door, losing, as he did so, a downtrodden slipper and, returning to the hall, called, 'Somebody's arrived.'

A muffled voice, presumably that of the woman who had shown him in, came from the rear of the hall, the sound of music increasing.

307

'The dog had to fetch me,' he called.

'You make your own arrangements,' the voice came out, quaveringly yet clear, its subsequent remark drowned by the ringing of a telephone, evidently in the hall, the man announcing, 'I'm taking no calls. You answer it. It's always you they're after.' Returning to the room, he closed the door, retrieved his slipper, scuffing his foot inside it several times before securing it and, tapping the pockets of his cardigan, crossed to the desk. Examining its surface for several seconds, moving books and magazines and papers aside, he finally announced, 'I've lost my glasses. Not that it matters. I won't need them,' turning to Maddox to conclude, 'What can I do for you?'

'I had an appointment,' Maddox said. 'Arranged by a colleague of my brother's.'

'Your brother.'

'*Paul* Maddox,' Maddox said.

'Your father, I imagine, must be dead.'

'Yes.'

'Your mother, too.'

He nodded.

'Distressed by their dying?' Saliva spurted from his mouth.

'Yes,' he said.

'Unnatural, otherwise.'

'Yes.'

'How many brothers have you?'

'One.'

'Sisters?'

'One.'

'Older?'

'Yes.'

'Fucked her?'

'No.'

For further confirmation, after a moment, he shook his head.

'Brother?'

'No.'

'Younger?'

'He's younger.'

308

Maddox was standing in front of the desk as he might, fifty-odd years before, have stood before the headmaster at Quinians: not dissimilar feelings passed through his head, not least those associated with subordination, misdemeanour, subterfuge, and dread.

His inquisitor, meanwhile, had picked up several loose sheets of paper from the desk, holding each one, closely, to his eyes before, releasing them, they drifted back to the desk or onto the floor. Finally, sitting in the chair behind the desk, the woodwork of which creaked as it took his weight, his glance turned to the sheet of paper rolled into the typewriter. Examining the print, his head lowered to its surface, the eyes screwed up, he enquired, 'You don't mind if I sit?' waving his hand to add, 'You sit where you like. Or stand. My wife, if you ask her, might bring us a cup of tea. Or coffee. Shout down the hall and ask her. Which do you prefer?'

'Whichever is convenient,' Maddox said.

'Neither,' the man said, 'but it doesn't prevent you from asking. I would ask for tea. Which means she will bring me coffee. Which is the one that I prefer.' Looking up, finally, to glance at him directly, he added, 'Get the picture?'

Maddox returned to the hall, walked down to the door at the rear, from behind which the music still emerged, knocked on it and, receiving no response, pushed it open.

A small, sparsely furnished room overlooked an overgrown garden at the rear: two worn, upholstered chairs were set diagonally facing a tall, sash window. The room was empty, the radio standing on a cabinet behind the door. A carpet, its design faded, and holed in several places, covered much of the otherwise stained wood floor.

Returning to the room at the front he reported, 'No one there,' hesitating to close the door in case he was to be despatched on a further errand, and added, when there was no response from the figure behind the desk, its head stooped once more to the typewriter, 'Should I look elsewhere?'

'To find her?' the figure enquired. 'Or simply to piss off?'

'To find her.'

'No bother.' The figure straightened. 'She'll probably make it. But not until you're leaving. Do you smoke?'

'No,' he said.

'Mind if I do?'

'No,' he said.

'Would you say you're an equable fellow?'

'On the whole,' he said, pausing before he offered his response, 'I am.'

A packet of cigarettes had been produced from the cardigan: a box of matches was raised from the litter of books and papers on the desk. A match was struck and, having been held to the cigarette, was dropped, still burning, on the floor. Leaning back, the figure remarked, 'You look pretty healthy to me.'

'I feel quite well,' he said.

'Any reason why you shouldn't?'

'None.'

'Why don't you sit down?' He gestured with the cigarette. 'After you've closed the door. There's a hell of a draught. Mild, at this time of the year, but inconvenient, at my age.'

Having crossed to the door and closed it the man called, as if Maddox had removed himself a considerable distance, 'Sit on the couch. That's where most of you sit,' Maddox removing several books and a rug from the end furthest away from the desk, turning to the silhouetted figure behind it.

'Your brother Paul's colleague suggested you'd attempted to jump under a train. Not an experience you'd have every day, but not to that extent unusual. Were you prosecuted for the inconvenience?'

'No,' he said, the thought, previously, never having occurred to him.

The springs creaking beneath him, he endeavoured to change his position.

'What do you think to the pictures?'

The man was leaning on the desk, his elbows on either side of the typewriter as if whatever was written there were still his principal concern. His head he cupped in his hands, the cigarette, held in one of them, smoking by his ear.

'Not good,' Maddox said, assuming that anything less than candour would earn his questioner's disfavour.

'Why in front of a train?'

'I wasn't aware I was going to do it until I did. Which is the curious thing about it,' he said.

'Quite common.'

'Really?'

'Premeditation is rarely involved. At,' he went on, 'the critical moment.'

'I see.'

'Sectioned?'

'Yes.'

'How long?'

'Fifty-six days. I was in for about eight weeks. Two months,' he amended.

'Apart from trains, what other methods attracted your attention?'

'Not any. I hadn't,' he continued, 'given it any thought.'

'If you had, what other methods would you recommend?'

'Pills?' Maddox suggested, thinking of Viklund.

'Hard to get hold of. In a hurry. Forethought there, if anything.'

'What would you recommend?' Maddox said, returning, he reflected, the ball to his court.

'It's a question of opportunity,' the man responded. 'Personally, I'd choose pills because I'm a doctor. You, on the other hand, would have to save up. Your anti-depressants, for instance. Little less than a hundred, your size and weight, to make sure. Paracetamol, I'd say, likewise. You might, then again, strike lucky and get away with less. You never know. That's the magic of the thing. As I see it, the problem is, other than having a medical, or a veterinary qualification, you have an infinite number of choices. Lorries, cliffs, bridges. Rivers. Even the humble kitchen knife has proved invaluable on numerous occasions. Also, of course, the bathroom razor. It's the way the world is. Doctors are especially vulnerable. Sitting day after day listening to people with boils on their balls and

311

thinking who'd do this for a living? As for women.' Returning the cigarette to his mouth he blew out a cloud of smoke.

Maddox, for his part, gazing into the light, had moved into an abstracted state, wondering, even, if he'd got the right address, or, if he had, he'd registered with the appropriate occupant inside.

'Married?'

'Divorced.' He spoke as if in a dream.

'Children?'

'Three.'

'What?'

'Sons.'

'Look after you?'

'They're all concerned.'

'Would you say you're delusional?'

'No.'

'How are you fixed for money?'

'I have a pension.'

'Enough?'

'Yes.'

'House okay?'

'Yes.'

'Any worries?'

'Not immediate.'

The head, having been withdrawn from the hands, was now a confused shape against the light: a skein of smoke drifted across the window.

'What are you taking?'

'Dothiepin,' he said.

'Anything else?'

'Thioridazine, whenever things get bad. Less and less, recently,' he added.

'National Health.'

'Yes.'

The man got up, picked up the packet of cigarettes and the box of matches and shuffled to the chair by the empty fire.

312

Sinking into it, he sighed, and, with two hands, sparks flashing from the cigarette, hoisted one thigh over the other.

'Not much of a life,' he said, and added, 'Yours, I imagine, you think is no better.'

Maddox could see, for the first time, the distortion of the man's figure, the ribs pushed out to one side, the shoulder above them lowered. The teeth protruded unevenly, almost fragmented, the eyes, more clearly visible, suggesting a lava-like effusion, dark, reddened. He recalled a not dissimilar quality, if more diffuse, he'd occasionally witnessed in Simone.

'Not that the fees add up to much, compared to what you make selling pictures.'

'I don't sell pictures,' he said.

'Why not?'

'I write about them.'

'Berenson made a fortune.'

'I believe he did.'

'And this latter-day Berenson. Viklund.'

Surprised, even disconcerted, Maddox asked, 'Do you know him?'

'Dan and I go back a long way.'

'I didn't know.'

'No reason why you should.' The cigarette, hanging from the corner of his mouth, trailed out another stream of smoke. 'I followed his series. The re-emergence of the species in when did he say it was? As if.' He paused. '*New* philistinism, in your case. But, then, when did it ever stop?'

The door opened: the woman who had let him in reappeared, one hand retained on the doorknob behind.

'Where's the dog?' she said.

'It's upstairs,' the man told her. 'It had to come up and fetch me.'

The telephone rang once more in the hall outside, the previous ringing having ended abruptly, as if an extension had been lifted in another room. The sound of music was audible again.

'Answer it,' the man said. 'Or ask the dog.'

313

'You answer it,' the woman said. 'I've other things to do.'

'What other things?'

'Other things,' the woman insisted. 'If you don't want me here I'll be outside.'

The door was closed. Moments later the telephone stopped. The woman's voice, faintly, came from the hall.

We could have asked her for your tea,' the figure said by the empty fire. 'And me for my cup of coffee.'

'I'm okay,' Maddox said, reluctant to approach the woman again.

Stubbing the cigarette, half smoked, in the hearth, the man took out and lit another. 'Sure?' he said, holding it up.

'No,' he said.

'I'd hate to leave you worse than when you came in. What do think to the psychiatric profession?'

'I've found them helpful, on the whole,' he said.

'If you're asking me about orthodoxy I haven't got one. Freud a junkie. Adler an idler. Jung a fucker of his women patients. Cunt is very much part of the system. Are you an admirer of the muse of Lichfield? You'll find the whole of it in there. What did you want to see me about?'

'I don't know. You were recommended,' Maddox said, helplessness, he reflected, evident on both their parts.

'By a colleague of your brother's.'

'Yes.'

He surveyed Maddox for several seconds through a cloud of smoke.

'I can't do anything for you, of course.'

'Why not?'

'I can't stop people killing themselves. It's a reasonable thing to do. It's the ones who don't that I normally address. The tube station at Notting Hill, for instance, is just as convenient as the one at Camden Town. Though the one at Camden Town, being a junction, has four lines, the corresponding number of platforms, and a proportionately greater number of trains. In that respect, you're fortunate having it on your doorstep. You weren't fucked by your father?'

314

'No.'

'Amongst men of your age there's an awful lot of that around. Unmentioned over the previous thirty years and suddenly the fashion. The nineteen forties and 'fifties were particularly strong. Possibly the war, soldiers returning, an, at the time, unbroachable postscript. How about your mother?'

'No.'

'Sister?'

'No.'

'That used to be pretty strong. Keep it in the family. Threat of scandal. Neighbours?'

'No.'

'Relatives?'

'No.'

'Vicar?'

He shook his head.

'Rabbi?'

'No.'

'Priest?'

He shook his head again.

'Mullah?'

'No.'

'How about school?'

'None there either.'

'A pretty fuckless childhood.'

'Yes.'

'Where were you brought up?'

'St Albans.'

'St Albans.' He brushed cigarette ash from his cardigan. 'I've had one or two interesting cases from there. Anything I've missed? Or should I say *anyone*?'

He shook his head.

'Doesn't seem much fun if you haven't been fucked by somebody. Other than your wife and what might be described as your female peers.' Lifting his thigh once more with both hands he lowered it to the ground, grasped the other thigh and lifted it over the first. The slipper, suspended from the upraised foot, fell off. The foot was bare. 'You may have been told, my principal subject is incest. Are you aware what the most significant problem is for members of a family who, knowingly or unknowingly, have been separated at birth, or shortly thereafter, and are suddenly reunited?'

Despite an increasing desire not to disappoint his interlocutor, he was obliged to shake his head again.

'G.S.A. Genetic Sexual Attraction. An irresistible desire to fuck one another. The respectable mother attracted to her long-lost son. Son to mother. Father to daughter. Daughter to father. Sister to brother. Brother to sister. Brother to brother. Sister to sister. It suggests the principal underlying element in family life is grievously overlooked at present. Oedipus, who, after all, was never aware he was fucking his mother, doesn't come into it. This is Dionysus, without the alcohol.' Stroking with both hands his upraised knee, he added, 'My name is Isaacson, by the way, not Isaacs. Your intermediary, when he rang, had got it wrong.'

'I'm sorry.'

'It'll have to be overlooked at present. What are your feelings on euthanasia?'

'I feel okay about it,' he said. 'Each case to be taken on its merit.'

'How well do you know Dan Viklund?'

'I succeeded him at the Drayburgh. Before that, long before that, I was his student. At the Courtauld.'

'He got me out of Germany. Before the war. He had quite a line in that sort of thing. My parents, who hesitated, didn't make it. Similarly my sister. Similarly my brother. The Notting Hill tube station, either east or west, doesn't nearly come into it.'

He contemplated Maddox through a cloud of suddenly exhaled smoke.

'I ended up at a Quaker residential school, within a year had passed my exams and seven years later qualified as a doctor in time for the Korean War. Or, rather, out of gratitude to the British nation – and the United Nations – I volunteered. Read Boswell?'

'I have,' he said.

'Biography or diary?'

'Both.'

'A necessary in-filler to what the genius wrote. I thought, at the time, I'd do the same. The equivalent of the *Rambler* essays. *The Adventurer*, *The Idler*. Dilatory titles, but exemplary. I got blown up.'

Smoke, once more, was exhaled between them.

'What by?'

'A bomb. By mistake. American. But you don't want to hear my sordid story.'

'I'd like to,' Maddox said, relieved, to a degree, their roles had been reversed.

'Every few years a piece of shrapnel works its way out. Abdomen. Arm. Leg. I've got them on the mantelpiece, if you'd care to look. If I hadn't been a medic I'd have died. A tourniquet on both my legs and an arm. It fucked me up for quite a while. Could say I never recovered.'

He regarded Maddox through the thickening smoke, an assessment of some sort underway, if not completed.

'What school were you at?'

'St Albans. After that, the north of England. During the war years and after,' he added.

'Religion?'

'No.'

'Agnostic?'

'Yes.'

'Atheist?'

'Still to find out.'

'Not apostate Jewish?'

'My father was.'

'Problem?'

'Not really.'

'But some.'

'I doubt it.'

'Mother?'

'The same.'

317

'I've read your reviews.' He gestured to the wall behind Maddox's back. 'Not, in your view, a wasted talent.'

'No.'

'Most people affect to like them.'

'I'm trying,' he said, 'to keep up with you.'

'I was called Kike at school, Quakers notwithstanding. At one time, a group of twelve men with a charismatic leader might well have been treated with suspicion. St Paul, too, I'm not sure about. Sexual invert?'

'No.'

'Telling people what they know already is how I stay in business. As you're probably aware, knowledge and awareness are different things.'

'You think so.'

'I do.'

Maddox's mood of abstraction had increased, he struggling to keep the figure before him in focus, its features, seemingly, fused together. He had noticed this hallucinatory effect before, either with people whose conversations bored him or with those whose presence was reassuring, a tendency he associated with ageing, if not his medical condition, the seemingly manic mask that represented Isaacson – if he'd got the name correct – acquiring a conspiratorial intensity, the eyes dilated, the hair, as he spoke, darting to and fro at the back of his head as if a second, more sinister presence lurked behind him.

'This philistinism you go on about. A self-degenerating force that can't be controlled. A mannerist age. Most of them are. Irrelevant. Too obvious. What do you think?'

'I wonder,' Maddox said, 'what precisely I'm doing here. Discussing what I know already, or merely having the privilege of paying to listen to you.'

'The paintings,' Isaacson said, 'are by me.'

Turning, Maddox looked at them again. 'Good job you stuck to psychiatry,' he said.

'I did them in my youth, which is a considerable time ago, before the Korean War. I went to Jerusalem on an extended visit, for no accountable reason, and, without warning, psychosis intervened. Voices. People there whom no one else could see. Definitive views on everything. The sort of thing you get with LSD. Things to come. Much of it in the Talmud.'

He waited, smiling, his head on one side.

'Did you recover?'

'That's for you to decide.' He spread out his arms. Cigarette smoke drifted up again.

'What should I do,' Maddox said, 'in a not dissimilar situation?'

'How not dissimilar?'

'Things destabilising,' he said. 'Forces coming from inside, but experienced as coming from the outside, on a scale and with a strength greater than anything I've previously known. Approaching, say,' he added, half smiling, 'the size of an aircraft-carrier to someone paddling in the sea.'

'Were you paddling?'

'I think so.'

'Pathology, in your case, I wouldn't know about. My sort of intervention, nowadays, is unfashionable. Symptoms like yours are primarily seen as functional disorders. Hormones, enzymes, genes. You name it. Cognitive behavioural therapy may be more your thing. Consciousness inserted between awareness and action. Rather along the lines of what we're doing now. You feeling pissed off when you arrive, I in bed, having forgotten about you, the dog coming up to fetch me. It doesn't like visitors and only comes up when they arrive. By pissing around we're both distracted. What you get from me you won't get from anyone else. I won't ask you, for Yahweh's sake, to revert to a Jew.' He laughed, a brief, inconsequential sound, the prominent teeth once more displayed. If anything, Maddox reflected, he felt confident about him because of the irregularity of the teeth, an authenticity, of a sort, engagingly revealed. 'What you want is something to replace what you were doing before you felt inclined to put an end to what you were doing, accidie leading to cachexia a not uncommon complaint amongst – how should I describe it? – people like you. I take it you're still reviewing. Or have you something of interest up your sleeve?'

319

He extended his hand.

'I'm thinking of writing about a former student of mine who I visited recently in prison.'

'What's he do?' Isaacson said.

'Killed his wife and children.'

'Eric Taylor,' Isaacson said.

'You heard about him?'

'I was asked to appear at his trial. After the defence read my curriculum vitae they changed their mind. I don't know why. It was his idea to invite me.'

'Did you meet him?'

'A time and place were appointed, and then cancelled. Your services, they told me, are no longer required. The defence of insanity, you'll remember, was not sustained. Anything else you have in the kitchen?'

'An analyst I went to and with whom I am now half living, therapy abandoned, has been reported to the Medical Council by two of her clients who cite the irregularity of our relationship, along with accounts of being propositioned along similar lines themselves.'

'There you go again,' Isaacson said, stubbing the second cigarette out, half smoked, in the hearth. 'There's no end to these complications. I'll be telling you my problems next, and asking your advice.' Waving his hand again, he signalled Maddox to continue.

'I'm inclined to turn what might be described as pathology into a metaphysical proposition.'

'Why not? Philosophy's in the doldrums. So's psychiatry, come to that. These rituals we once went in for are still of use. Self-validating assertions can be negative, too. "I'm the worst person in the world, doctor. I'm a failure. No one loves me. I'm just about the most incomprehensible shit you'll ever come across." Apart from the facts of age, height, weight, address, occupation, income, marital status, children, the rest is self-appraisal. Validation comes in any form you like, but principally in the shape of the perception, "I see myself in this light." The seeing and the I involved, whatever the substance of the perception, substantiate the self which the analysand assumes is missing. As the two of us are doing now. Screwing your therapist or analyst, for instance, isn't par for the course but I wouldn't exclude it. It appears, from where I'm sitting, to have served you well. She's not still charging you, I take it?'

Maddox's posture on the couch had changed: from one of alertness – square-shouldered, upright, confrontational – he'd relaxed into one not unlike that of Isaacson himself, lying back, his legs crossed, his hands, in his own case, placed beside him to balance himself amongst the protruding springs – which, he'd now discovered, it was the purpose of the rugs, and perhaps the scattered books, to conceal. Maybe it was the analogy between his posture and his situation, described to Isaacson, that prompted him to laugh, a realisation that his inclination to write about Taylor was being reinforced by the other man, a realisation Isaacson had come to, too.

'As for transcendental solutions – an areligious milieu to you; an acultural one, to me – I'd ask you to look at the pictures on the wall. Not much to you, but meaningful to me. A reminder of questions I once asked and answers I'd otherwise have forgotten. Irrelevant, now, of course, for questions and answers, after a certain age, no longer count. As for Taylor, whom I never met, I suspect you'll find the same. The total, whatever it adds up to, rarely matters. Why, I'm inclined to ask, did you pick on him? What's his attitude to you?'

'Vengefulness. See where I've ended up. See where my wife and children the same.'

'Did you buy it?'

'Some I did.'

'Why?'

'It's true.'

'Some of it.'

'Some of it.'

Isaacson waited.

'Maybe you could help me,' he added.

'Blow me away.' Isaacson extended his hand again: an invitation, physically, to place something in it.

'To what degree *is* it cultural, to what degree something else?'

'No dice.' Pointing a finger at his chest, he added, 'Bang!' Pointing the same finger at Maddox, he exclaimed, 'Bingo! Shot you first. You're *dead*! Y.P.'

'Why pee?'

'Your problem.'

The door had opened again.

'Are you wanting tea?' the woman said, not appearing in the door but, her hand presumably on the handle, remaining in the hall outside.

'It's too late for that,' Isaacson said. 'We're into business. If you came round the door you'd see.'

'Mr Cavendish is due in ten minutes.'

'Ask him to come back.'

'You ask him.'

'You ask him.'

'I won't tell him anything. It's up to you.'

The door was closed.

A moment later Isaacson got up, with considerable alacrity – an alacrity not previously shown – and, in crab-like strides, crossed, with one slippered and one bare foot, to the door. Opening it, he called, 'What the fuck do I pay you for if you won't answer the fucking door?'

'What you paid me for you still owe,' came the voice from outside.

Isaacson closed the door and came back to his seat. Lowering himself into it with difficulty, he said, 'Either you piss off or Cavendish does. Do you know him, by the way?'

Maddox shook his head.

'Someone with more good intentions you'd have to crawl a fucking long way, I can tell you, to find.'

'Maybe,' Maddox said, 'I'm the same.'

'Think so?' Isaacson said. 'I haven't noticed,' adding, 'If your friend needs advice, vis-à-vis the Council, she's only got to ring. Don't ask her to come round. I've enough to deal with at present. Remember the Camden Town tube has a definite edge.'

322

'I'm inclined to see it all,' Maddox said, as he got up, his legs and back aching more than he'd been previously aware, 'in the form of contracts. There's a contract for me to live. Taken out without my knowledge, signed on my behalf, not by me. There's an endless stream of contracts that flows from it. To do with family. Friends. Jobs. Education. With everything I think and do and feel. Endlessly we endorse, renege, or renegotiate, or endeavour to. Like, for instance, the contract I have with you. Similarly, the one you have with Cavendish. Unilaterally, we absent ourselves from some, as others do with us. Always at a price. I absented myself from the primary one in attempting to take my life. Taylor's contract, too, with his family, even with himself, he decided was null and void. *Hamlet*,' he went on, perplexed as to why he was suddenly so engaged, 'is composed of nothing else. It's the terms of these contracts that we're preoccupied by throughout our lives. In my case, the initiating one.'

Isaacson was looking up at him with an expression less of surprise than amusement: the trivialisation of something – Maddox wasn't sure what – was now involved, he feeling the compression of the springs against his back and thighs even though he was now standing, crossing to the door with the curious sensation the couch was strapped to his shoulders.

Isaacson, reaching into his cardigan pocket, had produced another cigarette. Lighting it with a match, waving the flame before him, he said, 'The contractual world is your invention. Make an appointment.'

'I'll think about it.'

'Not too long.' He threw the match, still burning, into the hearth. 'I have a secretary, but she's rarely here. My wife, as you can see, is no fucking good.'

Hearing a sound behind him as he opened the door he turned to see Isaacson getting out of his chair. 'Look at this,' he said, crossing to the desk.

Pulling open a drawer he searched in it for several seconds, taking out several sheets of paper from which, finally, he extracted a photograph. Yellowed, folded over at the corner, he straightened it, fiercely, before holding it out. 'What do you think?'

A young man in uniform was standing to attention, the head, close-cropped, thrust up powerfully from the square-set shoulders, the arms thrust down, the hands fisted, the thumbs to the front. 'A contract, too, in its own sort of way.'

'You,' Maddox said.

'Korea. Before I got hit. The thought of it might do some good. After Jerusalem, of course.'

His thumb closed over the photograph, returning it to the drawer. 'See you sometime,' he added, 'if you so decide,' turning back to his chair.

After letting himself out of the front door, Maddox glanced across at the front room window: the shape of the desk and the chair behind it were visible between the tasselled curtains, Isaacson, having returned to the desk, was stooping over the typewriter, attempting to decipher the print on the rolled-in sheet of paper. A moment later, as Maddox turned away, he was surprised to see the figure he identified as Doctor Death approaching from the direction of Notting Hill, he nodding, startled, as the figure passed, receiving a nod of acknowledgement in return – glancing back before he'd gone much further to see the figure mounting the steps to Isaacson's door, the door opening immediately he rang and, with a look in his direction, its head bowing, the figure stepping inside.

15

PAUL HAD rung him the morning of the interview to tell him the time of the appointment, he, Maddox, having been with Simone the previous day, apart from the afternoon which he'd spent wandering on Hampstead Heath. 'Why don't you get an answering machine?' his brother had complained. 'Move into the twenty-first fucking century. Or even the twentieth, come to that. I go to all this trouble with what is evidently a booked-up man and you're not around to speak to or be left a message.' There'd been barely an hour to get to Notting Hill. 'Get a taxi.'

'The tube will be quick enough,' he said.

'Tell him your symptoms. Don't, for fuck's sake, talk about God, metaphysics, or the fucking universe.' After a moment, he added, 'Nor art. Don't fuck it up like you did with Simone.'

'I'm hardly likely to,' he said. 'He's a man.'

'I'm not sure how much I should be reassured by that,' his brother said. 'Tell him you tried to kill yourself and what does he think. Put him in the picture.'

'Maybe I should take you with me,' Maddox said. 'You can slip in the things you think I've missed out.'

'If I had time I would. At least, see you got there. This is not religion. No sins against God, Jesus, or the Holy Ghost.'

'*Am* I becoming religious?' he asked.

'You are,' his brother said. '*Spiritual.* I've been through all that fucking racket. I don't want to see you do the same.'

'I'll do my best,' he said.

'That's all I ask.' His brother had paused. 'The guilt you feel about Taylor. Maybe you could tell him you screwed his wife.

His wife got killed. Maybe that played a part in it. Give him,' he went on, 'the total picture. Don't, for fuck's sake, mention art.'

'Right.'

'Remember how much it costs.'

'How much does it cost?'

'That's my problem. Rather,' he added, it's in my gift. Remember he's strong on cranks. Two fucking minutes and they're out. Get a cab. He's written several books.'

'What on?'

'Psychology, for fuck's sake. How should I know? Remember I love you. Sarah loves you. Everybody loves you. Ask him what's going to stop you pissing around.'

'Right.'

No further remonstration to be queried or required.

Now, returning, he rang Simone: midday, she was on her answering machine. He left a message, cryptic, confused, and decided he'd go and see her between patients. Rarely did he go up, however, without having arranged it beforehand.

He let himself in with his key and heard Mrs Beaumont's voice in the room on the right. The door to Simone's consulting-room was open. Replacing the phone as he came in, she said, 'Simone's out with her lawyer. She has her next appointment in an hour,' looking at a watch pinned to the front of her dress.

'I'll be upstairs,' he said. 'I'll wait.'

The cat had come in with him: it preceded him up the stairs, hesitating at intervals to see if he would follow. In the kitchen he got out its food, spooned some into its bowl, and wondered what else he might do.

Finally, stifling a temptation to flick on her television, he went onto the roof. The sky was clear, streaked with vapour trails: the roof umbrella was open above the table, an extra chair arranged there as if, in his absence, Simone had had visitors. An ashtray, with stubs, suggested it was someone she didn't know: one of the stubs was marked with lipstick. Odd, he reflected, she hadn't cleared it away: normally she was allergic to smoking.

He sat in the shade, the cat emerging after a while, sitting, licking its face with its paw, looking up at him, whenever he stirred, before resuming. He was still confused from his encounter with Isaacson, and, further, by his 'contractual' outburst – and confused, even more, by the appearance of Cavendish, unable to recall whether this was the name he'd used with Simone. Also, the strange connection with Viklund. Was it Dan, after all, who had advised his brother: even made the contact, arranging the appointment, explaining Paul's skittishness on the phone?

The more he reflected on what had taken place the more perplexed he felt, the heat rising at the back of his neck, the same familiar sensation in the region of his stomach, symptoms synonymous with the helplessness he associated with the absence of Simone and the realisation of how much, increasingly, he relied on her. Until he described the encounter to her he wouldn't be sure what his reaction should be – gazing across the roofs, getting up at one point to examine the horizon to the south, noting the smear of the upland, the television mast at Crystal Palace, reassuring himself they were still in place, the planes circling overhead, their engines whining in their descent to Heathrow. Perhaps he could talk to Mrs Beaumont, or go down and sleep before Simone returned, having glanced in the bedroom at the turned-down bed on the way up (what had the visitors made of that?). Regularly, from below, came the telephone ringing: occasionally, he assumed, it was picked up by Mrs Beaumont, the sound terminating abruptly. Other times, presumably, as when he had rung, she'd allowed the machine to record. He was, he was aware, in a state of suspense, a feeling generated by his encounter with Isaacson, and his own peculiar, departing speech, but more certainly by Cavendish appearing as he left.

When, some time later, he heard Simone's steps on the stairs, he stood up, anxiety flooding out in anticipation.

She must have gone to the bathroom; then he heard her voice on the telephone, talking from the living-room, she presumably having come up to make a call out of earshot of

327

Mrs Beaumont, he standing at the roof door, his head craned to catch her tone, his anxiety increasing.

Her voice paused, after an evident farewell to the speaker at the other end, then, in a fresh tone – alert, expectant, startled, even – she spoke to someone else.

He went back to the seat, his attention returning to the sky. Moments later, agitated, perplexed, he crossed to the parapet at the rear of the roof. There, beyond a metal railing, lay a drop of – he estimated – thirty feet into the tiny yard at the back of the house, a lightless well around the perimeter of which grew a desultory bed of flowers. In seconds, should he feel summoned in that direction, whatever he was feeling now – whatever he had ever felt – would be at an end, the sensation of release restoring him in a wave of reassurance: even now, an act of vengeance, ostensibly on himself but, more defencelessly, on those he loved and who loved him in return. Again and again, he had imagined Taylor sedating the children's drinks at bedtime: the look in their eyes: the familiarity of their smell after a bath: talcum, scented soap: the intimacy of their nightclothes: the total dependency on him and his wife: the affectionate embrace before going to bed, he hurrying them along, impatient, before the sedative took hold. And then his wife: she, too, preparing for bed ('let's make it,' he saying, 'an early night'), the children, by this time, fast asleep, drugged, mouths open, snoring.

The affectionate kiss on each forehead as he tucked them in, 'for the last time': everything normal – a natural extension, what he was about to do, of everyday life.

Into the bedroom where his wife was undressing, the realisation, having planned it, he must kill her first, the knife secreted beneath the pillow, taking it out ('look what I'm doing: none of this is real: not only it mustn't but it cannot happen'), she turning at a sound, incredulous as she sees his look (a prank, a game, a simulation), the blade gripped in his hand, realising, terrifyingly, blindly, the unrehearsed intention, the end of everything in their (previously) loving world.

Her resistance, the first blow delivered, the sifting sound as the blade went in: so soft, so easy, her fighting-back, the scream, unexpected, unlike anything he (or she) had previously heard: the withdrawal, the suction: the fear the children had been roused, he looking round, the door empty: unreal, unlike anything (still) he had imagined ('because of that it is not occurring'), her strength expiring, resignation, a weird acceptance (why give up, he reflects, as quickly as that?), her chest, her throat, her head (the end of everything, time itself), the blood determining he mustn't stop (all this will be retrieved, go back to normal), onto his hand, his arm, his face: into her throat, her head, her leg, her hip (into anywhere he liked: will she live like this for ever, will she not, dear Jesus, dear God, dear Beccie, come back to life?), he cutting her throat, her wrists, she not resisting, pretending dead (even now the dream is over: none of this, in fact, occurs). Once more in the chest, deep and central (see how easy, once you try), departing, reassured, for the children's bedroom (beyond where any other being can reach), not to falter, execute his masterpiece, plunging in the blade (in his mind the event completed), the upheaval of the (childish) body at the blade's withdrawal, the stillness (of the girl, the boy), the repetition of the blow in each (this I created, this I destroy), the subsidiary blows, ensuring they won't suffer (more than I, for instance, am suffering now), returning to the bedroom to be quite sure (I shall live like this for ever), the rope, the noose, already prepared, suspended from the banister rail, going back to each bedroom, listening by each mouth for breath (the absurdity of stillness, the absurdity of death), returning to the landing (all is over): all I have to do is drop . . .

The cracking of wood above his head, the searing pain around his neck, the smell of blood inside his nose, the banging at the window, door (all is not over: everything is lost).

Feeling her hand, then her arm on his shoulder: the pressure of her lips against his neck, turning to her, smelling her scent, the fragrance of her hair (the world is redeemable): what, he reflected, had he done to deserve it?

'I didn't know you were coming, Matt,' her face alight, the

329

unexpectedness of his arrival, forewarned by Mrs Beaumont, enlivening her, delighting her, occasioning her to laugh.

'I've been to see this character my brother recommended.'

'Already?'

'I wasn't at home yesterday to receive the message. I had an hour to get there. I'd better give him your e-mail or fax, or get a machine myself.'

'That's what I've told you!' delighted. 'How did it go?'

'Have we time to talk?' she looking at her watch, he bemused, turned over by his imaging of death, prospecting, in the process, he reflected, his own: his mother's, his father's. Odd, her reassurance, her warmth.

'What was his name?'

'Isaacson.'

'Not Michael?'

'I don't know his Christian name.'

'His given name.' She had taken his hand, leading him to the table, absent-mindedly shifting the ashtray, about to tip its contents into the flowers, then, equally abruptly, pushing it across the table.

'Who on earth recommended him?'

'Someone my brother knows. It might even have been Viklund, he reluctant to do it directly. He knew Isaacson, evidently, in the past. Now you mention it, I must have heard of him. *Michael* Isaacson. It's not an area I had much time for . . .'

She waited; when he didn't continue, she said, 'Has he taken you on?'

'He left it to me.'

'He being willing.'

'Since he does most of the talking I assumed that he was.'

'Did you talk about us?'

'Sure.'

'By name?'

'No.' He paused. 'The odd thing was, when I came out, your complainant, Death, was going in.'

For a while he thought she wouldn't respond: he had seen the

330

look before, but never so fiercely presented: something of a child turning on its abuser.

'The other curious thing,' he added. 'They spoke about him before he arrived, Isaacson and his wife. They said his name was Cavendish.'

Still gazing at him, his hand was released: he watched her arm retreat across the table. The cat, delighted by her return, had followed her up: leaping onto her lap, it settled down, purring, her fingers, absently, moving to and fro across its back. 'That's odd.'

'He's a serial analysand,' he said. 'Or, better still, a serial complainant, giving a different name with each.'

'I've had the former, but not the latter,' she said, still withdrawn. 'A first time, I suppose, for everything.'

'If I go back I can mention it to him,' he said.

'Where's he live?' Her gaze returned to him, leaning back, as if to survey him from a distance.

'Notting Hill.'

'Did you get on?'

'He and his wife can't leave each other alone. Particularly when someone else is around, a minimal routine of minimal abuse. He was wounded in Korea, and only mentioned it, I thought, as a play on the word career. Fucked up, was his general view. Therapy, otherwise,' he went on, 'turned on its head, he doing the talking. To a degree, I suspect, he's given up, doing it for amusement. A couple of sessions with me and that'll be that distraction over. You therapise him and, in the process, therapise yourself, appeared to be his message. For some unaccountable reason, when I was leaving, I started off about contracts, *Hamlet* a play mirroring a life comprised of little if nothing else. Since coming back all I can think about is Taylor. I mentioned him. He, Isaacson, had been told to stand by in his defence, but wasn't called after Taylor's counsel had seen his c.v. As for Cavendish,' he paused. 'He said he was full of good intentions.'

A chortling sound inside her throat: pain of an otherwise incommunicable nature.

331

He then realised, astonished, she was laughing.

'Did you tell him about the NMC?'

'I did.'

About to respond, looking down at the cat, examining its fur, she was distracted by the ringing of the doorbell below.

'I'd better go down.'

The cat sprang away as she stood.

'I won't be free until this evening,' she added. 'I was seeing someone, but I can cancel it.'

'I'd like to come up,' he said, disturbed by her departure.

'I'll see you this evening,' she said, and was gone.

For a while he regarded the empty door, the cat having followed her through it; then, rising, he crossed once more to the edge of the roof. There was a ringing in his ears, heat flooding up from his chest, the imagery of the morning returning, the distorted figure of the analyst, the expression on the face in the photograph, surprised he should have thought to show him, the innocence, the alertness, the good intent, the inference of something having been maligned, the contrast with what was Isaacson now. And Taylor: the imaging of that, death in another form. And Cavendish.

Returning downstairs, he paused to listen to the voice audible in her consulting-room, failing to recognise it, male again, taking something of its resonance with him as he walked, a feeling of retreat – of alarm, of obfuscation – persuading him, when he got to the house, to lie on his bed.

Through the back window the afternoon sun was glowing on the houses opposite, shadowing the concertina-like configuration of the terraced roofs. Birds fluttered amongst the shrubs, an aircraft lumbered overhead, its fuselage alternately glinting and shadowed by clouds gathering, unseen, on the other side of the house. High above it, a vapour trail pencilled in a pointed orange beam moving, a pinpoint, to the north.

It was time, he reflected, to go back to St Albans, the Roman apostate turned Christian – to what purpose, he had no idea; and wondered, too, what he might tell Paul, other than not to waste his money; or what, more remotely, he might tell his sister.

He fumbled in the pillboxes by his bed, took out two thioridazine, managed to swallow them without water and, some twenty minutes later, feeling their effect, a haziness he didn't like and which drove his spirits down, turned on his side and, curled in something of a foetal position, went to sleep.

In his dream he was summarising his life to a figure mounted on a platform set on the roof of Simone's house. The feet of the figure came level with his head: one moment it was Taylor, the next someone he didn't recognise, an abstracted version, perhaps, of Isaacson, possibly of a teacher or the headmaster at Quinians – even Pemberton from the Drayburgh – aware, in the dream, of negotiating the identity of this figure as he went along, first one person, then the next, unable, in this respect, to reach a satisfactory conclusion.

His summarising consisted of his listing events which should have taken place but hadn't; when he was reproached by the figure on the platform, the phrase, 'But none of this is true', came floating down, he aware of the falsity of his claims, as well as his incomprehension at having made them. 'Surely all you're trying to assert,' came the voice, 'is something you've no right to,' the tone contemptuous, jeering. 'Ask Simone,' he heard himself responding. 'She lives here,' anxious, looking round, aware, behind him, of a very long drop, the area of the roof contracting, a process which, he realised, had been underway since the dream had begun, the stage, similarly, in the process of floating away, he clinging, finally, to a rail, the roof reduced to a single set of tiles, then to a sliver down the side of which his feet began to slip.

The phone woke him as he fell; by the time he'd got to the other bedroom it had stopped. The street outside was dark, the sun having set beyond the houses: a livid light, pink, deepening to ochre streaked with purple, occupied a clouded sky.

Half awake he went downstairs: an awareness of something abject in his nature, and which, in this mood, he was convinced nothing could reverse, brought him into the kitchen. Unlocking the back door he went out to the yard, looking for something, he wasn't sure what, gazing up at the rear of the house, at the weed-strewn flower-beds on either side, the weeds indistinguishable from the indigenous plants cultivated by the previous owner. The sky was now flooded with red, its source invisible beyond the house: it was as if, in reality, he were still asleep, struggling into consciousness, plagued by doubt and then, more certainly, by fear: a feeling that the whole of his life had been – was in the process of being – rejected.

By whom? a commentator of some sort, presumably a part of himself, authority – significance: order, even – lying somewhere else. Authenticity is what he lacked (what Taylor had inferred he lacked), a commitment to something which, dextrously, he had avoided throughout his life: marriage, children, job.

Against that was opposed a force he recognised in Isaacson, in Simone, particularly during that last moment on her roof: a force that pointed upwards, rather than down, north, rather than south, a force whose inversion had seized him on the tube station platform, a malignancy he recognised in Taylor and now, fatally, blindly, horrifically, within himself.

When he returned to Simone's a note on the stairs told him she'd rung, had got no answer and, unable, after all, to cancel her appointment, had gone out.

He thought of waiting until she returned, found the emptiness of the house without her daunting, the cat, mewing, following him around, waiting, anxious, as always, to be fed.

He put food in its bowl and returned downstairs: finding the door to her consulting-room locked, he began to reflect on the force of her anger, on her independence, that part of her which, in many respects – his own, perverse calculation – appeared menacingly indisposed towards himself.

The door to the room opposite was open, the desk, behind which Mrs Beaumont invariably sat, with its computer terminal and answering machine, visible inside, the house, without Simone's presence, something of a hulk, the significance of what she meant to him defined by her absence, an alternately bemusing and terrifying force, seductive, challenging, oppressive, the emptiness he felt in endeavouring to oppose it equally strong.

Perhaps it was his age – exhaustion, even – which left him feeling like this, then, recalling Kavanagh's insistence that age had little if anything to do with it, he let himself out of the front door.

Lamps were lit along the street, culminating in the glow of the public house at the opposite end: figures were scattered on benches against its façade. The studio window opposite Simone's was also illuminated, a shadow thrown across it of someone moving inside.

Descending the steps to Heath Street, he waited in the High Street for the bus to take him back in the direction of Camden Town.

It was the phone ringing that brought him hurriedly into the house, snatching it up, the front door left open – not Simone's voice, as he had been anticipating, coming back on the bus – but his brother's.

'Do you know how many times I've called? Get a fucking answering machine. What's the matter with you, for Christ's sake?'

'How many times?' he asked.

His brother paused. 'Twice,' pausing again. 'This is the third time. How did you get on?' Conciliatory, the tone: the news better be good.

'Well.'

'Do you think he can help?'

'Probably.'

'Are you going again?'

'I assumed he was willing. Particularly since he saw it as an opportunity to talk exclusively about himself. He should be paying you.'

'He's highly thought of.'

'Who by?'

His brother waited.

'Everybody.'

'Like who?'

'Everyone I've asked.'

'How many?'

'How many does it fucking take? He's supposed to be a genius.'

'You even got his name wrong.'

'Oh, fuck you,' his brother said.

The gap between himself and Paul had widened: prolixity, on his brother's part, had always been a problem: prolixity had taken him into the Church and, just as swiftly, brought him out again – presumably to take him on to where he was at present: talk long enough and anything might happen. Familiarity had taken the edge off that. There was a challenge here, too, to which he had never responded, Paul blaming him for a problem the solution of which only he, Maddox, could supply.

No reciprocal reproach, he concluded, was evident in himself: he owed Paul nothing – the 'gift' of the sessions he might have with Isaacson something he could well afford himself, recognising only the benefit to Paul in his agreeing to receive it.

'I'm really appreciative – *really* appreciative – of what you've done,' he said. 'Even if it goes nowhere it's been a reassuring gesture.'

'Fuck the gesture,' Paul said. 'Make it go somewhere. It's up to you.'

For a while the two of them were silent.

'So what's his name?'

'Isaacson.'

'What did I say?'

'Isaacs.'

'So what's the difference? Maybe I should go and see him.'

'What about?'

'Ask him what he thinks. Maybe the two of us together will make more sense.'

'And Sarah.'

'And Sarah, too, if she wants to.'

Still his brother waited.

'Did he suggest you might get better? That you are better. Not be tempted to try again.'

'It doesn't work that way. He doesn't work that way. Cures are not, I suspect, what he's about.'

'Your brains, his reputation, you ought to be able to produce something,' his brother said.

'My reputation and his brains, too,' he said. 'On the whole, as I understand it, he hands the conclusions back to you.'

'I'd like this thing to work out,' Paul said, something other than the stated, other than the obvious, involved in his response: his sudden, uncharacteristic deference.

'I'm sure it will,' he said. 'One way or another.'

'It's the other I'm concerned about,' Paul said.

'The person who recommended him didn't happen to be Dan?' he said, and added, when his brother didn't respond, 'Viklund.'

'Why should it be Viklund?'

'They know one another. Or did.'

'First I heard of it,' Paul said. 'It was someone I know from work. I thought I'd mentioned that.'

'I'll probably see him again.'

'Good.'

'I'll let you know how it goes.'

'Do,' his brother said. 'I want this to work out right. We deserve it of one another.'

Then he was gone, the phone put down at the other end.

No sooner had he replaced the receiver than the telephone rang again.

'I shouldn't have left you so quickly,' Simone said. 'I was angered you'd spoken to Isaacson about our situation, though there's no reason why you shouldn't.'

'That's okay,' he said. 'I've just been talking to Paul. He's disappointed about the outcome, too. He doesn't, by nature, hang around. If it doesn't happen now it never will, more or less his motto.'

He wondered why he had sought to reassure her so quickly:

there were voices in the background. She wasn't talking from home.

'It was you reporting Norman turning up that threw me,' she said. 'I wonder how long he's been seeing Isaacson. Did it come as news to him that you and I were together?'

'I'd have thought so,' he said. 'Apart from that, he doesn't know your name. Nor did he ask for it, either.'

'If he talks about other clients to you, presumably he talks about you to them.'

'I don't see why.'

'He told you Cavendish, so-called, was full of good intentions. That breaches confidentiality, for a start.'

'I see.'

'I've hired a detective.'

'For what?'

'I'm curious to know what he's up to. Symonds recommended him.'

'Who's Symonds?'

'The lawyer I told you about. He came with a barrister friend to see me this morning.'

'Don't you normally go to see them?'

'He wanted to see what the set-up was.'

'What set-up?'

'How we live. The lay-out.'

Voices drowned out a further remark.

'Where are you calling from?' he asked.

'A restaurant. I'm having supper with a friend. I wanted another view. *She's* been stalked herself and knows precisely what to do.'

'Is this stalking?' he said.

'Obsessive behaviour of this nature, I'd have thought, comes pretty close,' she said.

Voices once again intruded: she must have been phoning in a passage, people, at intervals, passing by.

'I came without my mobile. I'll probably be exhausted by the end of the evening, but my friend will see me home. If you want to go up and wait I'll try and get back sooner.'

'I'll hang around here,' he said. 'And come up tomorrow.'

'When?'

'I presume you're working all day?'

'There's lunchtime.'

'Okay.'

'Then again, there isn't. I'm booked.'

'I'm also booked. I've got the life-class.'

He would have given it up, he reflected, if she'd been free as well.

'How about the evening?'

'Okay.'

'I love you.'

He wanted to respond, but didn't know how, resisting, he discovered, a similar declaration. Why, at that moment, he had no idea.

'I'm not sure what love means,' he said.

'Even now?'

Distress, if only at his silence, was indicated at the other end.

'I believe Isaacson has disturbed you,' she said. 'Which wouldn't be unusual, even if he were normal.'

'How abnormal?' he said.

'He was involved in the anti-psychiatry movement in the sixties. Knew Szasz. Foucault. Illych. Not that any of them agreed. They never do. He was sectioned at one time. In the seventies. I don't suppose he mentioned that.'

'He mentioned a breakdown in Jerusalem, after the war.'

'He was in a locked ward at night and teaching in medical school during the day. Have you heard anything more ridiculous? Have you heard anything more *irresponsible*?'

His heart warmed to Isaacson, suddenly, unequivocally: it had warmed to him, he realised, from the moment he had entered his house, despite Cavendish, aka Death, aka Norman: the home of another soul, he reflected, with nothing left to lose: the home of another soul who, for the fuck of him, didn't know any more what he ought to do.

It also warmed him, he realised, to Simone: her protestations, her concern, her disapproval: her hiring a detective. Her sturdy, determined – to him, unnecessary – effort to stay in control: how abandoned – how unliveable, how unlikeable – how meaningless, his life would be without her: a dependency coming out of nowhere, alarming, dismaying, exhilarating in its intensity.

'He's quite a card,' he told her.

'He practises reverse therapy. He must have told you.'

'He didn't put a word to it,' he said. 'If that's what it was.'

'Something he cooked up in the fifties with Allied prisoners-of-war returned from Korea. Not many, of course, care to use it. It's been much discredited since.'

'I'd better look out when I see him,' he said.

'*If* you see him,' she said.

'I think I will,' he said. 'After your recommendation, it would be hard to refuse.'

'When shall I see you, Matt?' she said.

'Tomorrow evening,' he confirmed.

'I'll have to go. I've already been longer than I said.'

'Don't get back too late,' he said.

'If you'd have been there I'd have got back all the sooner,' she said. 'Goodnight, my love,' the phone put down the other end.

The house was in darkness, Berenice's voice reverberating through the building, coming through the windows, penetrating the walls: 'If somebody grasses on you you have to teach them a fucking lesson. *Right?* If somebody grasses you up you know what you have to do. *Right?*' A pause, the suggestion, presumably, digested by a silent interlocutor. '*Roight?*'

'Right.'

'I'll kill the fucker if he comes again.'

'I'll kill him for you, Benny. Just give the fucking word.'

'Right.'

'Just give the fucking word.'

'Right.'

'Give me the fucking word.'

'Right.'

'I'll kill the fucker.'

'Right.'

'I'll kill the fucking cunt.'

'Right.'

'If somebody grasses on you.'

'Right.'

'I'll kill the fucker.'

'Right.'

'Right.'

A door closed: the building shook. Glass trembled in the windows. The conversation continued, inaudibly, in another room, '*Roight!*' alone vibrating through several successive walls.

Remembering that his own front door was open, Maddox went out to the hall. Closing it, he locked it, putting on the chain. Energy, which had previously drained out of him, had suddenly returned: all as a result, he reminded himself, of her ringing him up: her apology, her confession: her extrapolation: his life. Everything!

Passing through the house, he reassured himself that the back door, too, was locked, securing the bolts at the top and the bottom.

From an open window in the adjoining yard came the sound of Berenice speaking on the telephone: 'Nobody grasses on me and gets away with it. Right? His life isn't worth a piece of shit.' Pause. 'I'm going to cut his fucking balls off and shove them down his fucking throat. Right? *Isaiah* is going to cut his fucking balls off. Right? Just tell him that from me. *Right?*'

Why did he insist on living in this egalitarian nightmare, conceived, executed, supervised by no one who troubled to live in it themselves? He could be living somewhere else. He didn't have to listen to all this crap. But where? With whom? With what? Not up the hill, for instance, with Simone (he couldn't afford it: social conformity, too, prohibited it).

He was lucky – fortunate – on the other hand, to be living at all, saved by forces which, at one time, were no more explainable than the one which, spontaneously, had disposed him to self-murder, he finding his way, with these reflections, to his room upstairs, Berenice's voice echoing across the backs;

341

what of other neighbours tuned in to this decibel-crunching sound, ahuman, splenetic, intransigently enquiring?

Was it those on the other side to whom she was referring, or was it him? Had he given the impression (loaded, as he was, with the evidence) of someone grassing? He had rarely troubled to call at her door: not him at all, he concluded (safe at least), easing himself into the chair beside his bed, picking up the block of wood on which he rested his paper, retrieving a pen from the floor, one of several lying there, his typewriter shrouded on the desk before him, the room providing little space for anything else, something the size, he reflected, of a prison cell, twelve feet by eight – getting up, after a moment, opening the window to the evening air, the reading-lamp clamped to the top of a radiator controlled by a switch in the skirting-board behind the chair, settling his thoughts, noting the pointed style of the pen, thinking what was he thinking? What was he thinking he was thinking he was thinking? A recapitulation of his life: car-showroom to the Drayburgh to a back room in a backstreet close to the market of Camden Lock, an attempt at self-murder intervening: an aircraft hurtling up from Heathrow, the metallic whining roar as it passed above his head, its fuselage suspended between bowed wings, its navigation lights twinkling green and red, Berenice's voice summoning the dead: 'I'll cut his fucking balls off,' he assuming that the noise of someone moving – or so it seemed – in the bedroom at the front was the distortion of a sound from the street beyond, convinced, moments later, that the sound of someone breathing, heavily, could only have come from the room itself, getting up, slowly, going to the door where, on the landing, he saw the access to the roof space, a small trap-door, had been pushed aside, the sound of breathing, more nearly panting, coming from the bedroom – stepping inside to find a man standing there, black, in jeans and a sweatshirt, a knife in his hand, his hair ringleted around a bulbously featured head.

He had seen the man on several occasions, along with others, going in and out of Berenice's house: one arm, he noted (anxious to take in every detail), the hand of which was clenched around the knife, had a thin gold chain suspended from the wrist: the bicep bulged beneath the short sleeve of the sweatshirt. On the other wrist, equally decorous, was a silver-strapped watch. The man gazed fraternally in his direction, the nostrils flared, the teeth, visible as he panted, reminding him of Isaacson's, each projecting at a different angle. He indicated the party-wall behind his back, announcing, companionably, 'I'm trying to get in.'

'Where?' Maddox said.

'Berenice's.' He spoke with a lisp: in his twenties, muscular, the knife, flat-bladed, indicating the wall and then the street. 'The window's locked. I can climb in from there.'

'How did you get in?' Maddox enquired, civility, he concluded, taking the lead from his intruder, his principal concern.

'The front door was open. Berenice owes me money. She won't pay up. I'm going to fucking kill her.'

'Why not try her door?' he said, civility, again, he concluded, to the fore: something of the sort, his tone suggested, happened almost every night. On the other hand, he recalled the poker-work wood panel beside Berenice's bell: the snarling Dobermann head, the five-second warning: impropriety, crime: compassion: love!

'She won't let me in,' something unreasonable in her behaviour suggested by his voice. 'She won't pay up. I'll fucking kill her and that fucking Isaiah,' an inference Maddox might share in his distress.

'You can't get into her house from here,' he said.

'I can reach it from your window.' He indicated it once again.

'It's too far away,' Maddox said: a logistical enterprise in which he might play a vital part. 'You'll never reach across.'

'Have you got the thing that unfastens it?' the man crossing to the window, glancing out, then, reminded, turning back to the room. 'I can get in through the roof as well. I was trying your trap-door when you came upstairs.' He gestured to the landing.

'It only leads into the roof space,' Maddox said.

'There's a trap-door that lets you onto the roof. Berenice has

343

one. I can get in there. Have you a chair or a pair of steps? I'll easily reach up.' Already he was on the landing, leaping up at the dislodged panel.

'I'm sorry. I can't help you,' Maddox said. 'Either you leave or I'll call the police,' he added. 'I can't say fairer than that.'

'Fuck the police,' the man said. 'Just get me a fucking ladder.'

'I'll unlock the front door. I'll leave it open for you to go out,' he said.

'Just get the fucking steps, man,' still leaping, his trainer-shod feet pounding on the landing. 'Nobody knows I'm here,' gasping, the hole fully revealed, the panel thrust aside.

'They'll know you've come over the roof,' he said.

'Just get the fucking steps. She won't let me in at the front. She owes me fucking money.'

'Why not try the back?'

A foolish suggestion: collusion, on his part, evident again.

'Her back window's got a grille. Like the front. Just get the fucking steps,' switching the knife from hand to hand as he leapt up at the space again.

'I could ring her doorbell,' he said.

'No way, man. She knows I'm coming. Get the fucking steps. Or a chair. I'll leave you alone after that.' Already he was going down the stairs, arriving at the bottom, blocking Maddox's way, looking into the room off the hall, failing to see the choice of four appropriate chairs arranged around the table by the rear window. 'Get the fucking ladder,' the knife pointing at him now, companionability no longer a negotiable matter.

'I want you to leave,' Maddox said, 'by the door,' feeling, demonstratively, in his pocket for the key.

'The fucking door was open, man!' reasonableness, if only the vestige of, still to be deployed.

'I want you to leave,' Maddox said, he merely an adjunct, his manner suggested, of the logistics involved. Fear, of a familiar nature, brought the heat up around his neck. This he had felt before, he reflected. 'So what's the diff?' he said, surprisingly, aloud. He had begun to relax. For a moment, confusingly, he thought of Taylor.

344

'I only want to see Berenice for five fucking minutes. It's no shit to you, man. She owes me fucking money.'

'How much?' he enquired.

'A lot.'

'How much?'

'You got it, or something?'

'I wondered how much it was worth to get yourself arrested.'

'I want a fucking chair. I can reach up from a chair. I'll tell her I climbed up a drainpipe.' Moving closer, he blocked the way to the door.

Pausing on the next-to-bottom stair, Maddox saw the veins swelling at the back of the man's hand, the muscle swelling, too, on his lower arm: sweat ran into the man's eyes, and into the top of his shirt. Closer to, he was aware of the discoloration of the man's eyes. Saliva had crusted white at the corners of his mouth. The smell of the man's body came to him as the knife was pressed against his chest. He was increasingly aware, too, of the intimacy which the incident had introduced, a closeness to someone greater than that he had experienced with his brother, with Viklund, with anyone recently he had known, other than Simone and, before her, Charlotte.

'Back up.'

Maddox turned, removing the pressure of the knife from his chest, feeling it raised, lengthways, across the back of his neck. He's not serious, or he would have applied the point, he thought, nevertheless moving upwards.

'Faster. No fucking funny stuff,' the man had added.

'Go ahead,' he said, lamely, not sure what he meant. Turning to him, he added, 'How many years will you get? Fifteen? If you've got any form it could be more.'

The man was breathing through his nose, his lips closed, his head level with his chest.

He's thinking whether to do it or not, he reflected.

'Your fingerprints are all over the place. The window, the trap-door, the banister,' looking into the dilated, reddened eyes.

'Got any money?'

'Sure.'

345

'How much?'

'I've no idea.'

'Where is it?'

'How much do you want?'

'Give me fifty.'

'I haven't that much.'

'Thirty.'

'Twenty.'

'Twenty.'

'Ten.'

'Just give me some fucking money!' The knife pointed at his chest.

Maddox felt in his back pocket: there he had a wallet: he wasn't sure how much was in it, certainly more than ten.

'Don't do anything fucking stupid. Just give me the fucking money.'

'Sure.'

'Don't call the fucking police.'

'Right.'

'If you do I'll be fucking back.'

'Right.'

Getting, he reflected, into Berenice's habit: infectious behaviour on every side.

He drew the wallet out. Concealing its contents, he drew out a ten-pound note.

He wondered why he was doing this: the man, just as easily, could appropriate the wallet. On the other hand, he was negotiating with a malleable witness: something to be gained on either side, as something to be lost. They were coming to an agreement, negotiating a contract (a world of contracts: *caveat emptor*). Weren't all contracts, to some degree, one-sided, expediency the guide?

On the other hand (again), here was an opportunity to bring his own contract, unilaterally, to an end, the instrument rising at his throat: an optimum solution. He held out the note.

'You fuck me up and I'll be fucking back.'

'Sure.' He gestured to the banisters, the overhead trap. 'I'll leave your fingerprints untouched.'

'Give me another.' The man's hand enclosed the note.

'No thanks.'

'Another ten.'

'No deal.'

'Five.'

'I haven't a five-pound note,' looking for the first time directly into the man's eyes, evenly, unblinking: kill me now, he might have said: kill me and take the wallet, his own eyes filling with moisture. He blinked. 'Take the ten and think you're lucky. Don't come back again.'

'I know where you live.'

'Next to Berenice.'

'Fuck me up, I'll be back,' the man moving down the hall, removing the chain from the door, trying the handle. 'It's locked.'

'I've got the key,' following him, the proprieties of the contract they had concluded preoccupying him unduly: even now, even now, not too late to bring it to an end.

Taking out the key, he unlocked the door. The man stepped outside.

The door to Berenice's house opened at precisely the same moment: a black figure came out. The man beside Maddox gave a shout, darted across the forecourt of Maddox's house, vaulted the wall into the forecourt of Berenice's, reaching the door as it was slammed shut from inside. 'Open this fucking door, you cunt! I want that fucking money!' screaming, his intruder, kicking at the door, beating it, kicking it, beating it again. 'I'll come in and fucking kill you, you cunt! Open this fucking door!' a voice responding, inaudibly, from inside.

'I should go while you have the chance,' Maddox said, his calmness increasing, stepping into his forecourt, calling across. He wiped his neck, the sweat pouring into his collar, his hand, as he withdrew it, smeared with blood. He felt the skin beneath his chin: blood, he now saw, was dripping on his chest. In turning to the knife on the stairs the blade must have made an

347

incision. Irritated by his touch it began to sting, a burning sensation.

'Open this fucking door. I just want to talk to you,' a relative lowering of volume. 'I'm here to get my money,' the window opening above his head, Berenice's formidable head protruding: gaunt, the blonde dyed hair dishevelled.

'I've called the police, you cunt. They're coming,' dropping, each word, like rocks, below.

'You owe me fucking money. You and that fucking Isaiah.'

Leaning out of the window further, glimpsing Maddox for the first time, her next remark diverted: 'Call the police,' she said. 'Tell them he's got a knife. This man is threatening to kill us,' no interrogative, '*Right.*'

'Come down, Berenice. I only want to talk,' the voice more conciliatory than ever.

'Go fuck yourself,' Berenice's head withdrawing, her further appeal to Maddox, 'Call the police. Tell them he's got a knife,' the window, having been raised, drawn down.

The figure was leaving: he slammed the gate against its hinges, a contraption already damaged from previous assaults, walking backwards, calling to Maddox, 'I'll kill the cunt, once I fucking get her. And that fucking shit inside,' starting to run, still calling, the words no longer audible, accompanied by the sifting sound of his trainer-shod feet against the pavement.

As Maddox turned back to his door the upstairs window reopened. Berenice's head once more emerged.

'Have you called the police?' more threat than enquiry.

'I haven't,' he said.

Another contract, he prospected, to exchange.

'We haven't called them, either. We will,' she went on, 'if he comes again. Right?'

'Right,' he said.

'So we haven't called them.'

'We haven't,' he said.

The first civil words they had ever exchanged: things looking up, he reflected.

The head was withdrawn: before the window was closed a

348

renewal of complaint, directed, presumably, to Isaiah inside: 'I'm *talking* to the cunt next door,' followed by an inaudible response, and then, definitively, 'The cunt *next* door. All right?'

A vibration of glass indicated the window was now secured.

In the bathroom he washed the cut, examining it in the mirror: a light incision, like a thread of red cotton, drawn unevenly, and several inches long, around the front of his neck. He put on antiseptic, waiting for the blood to congeal, a peripheral event on the edge of a catastrophe but not embracing it, returning downstairs, carrying the step-ladder from behind the kitchen door to the landing, opening it out, climbing up, looking into the roof space, returning to the kitchen to find a torch, returning upstairs, aware of how defeated he felt.

No sign that the outer trap-door leading directly onto the roof had been disturbed, he replaced the landing trap-door and, taking the steps and the torch, went back to the kitchen.

Domestic felicities: wondering on the propriety, should the opportunity occur, of living with Simone, an increasing source of speculation, reassuring himself that the back door was secure, returning upstairs, closing the front bedroom window which the intruder had opened as far as the burglar locks, and went back to his room where, only moments before, it now seemed, he had been peacefully sitting.

He was relieved – glad – he was still alive (a satisfactory piece of negotiating there), his well-being, nevertheless, increasingly, he concluded, in the hands of others. This satisfaction, however, when he finally sat down, had not communicated itself to his body: he picked up the block of wood, the paper, the pen, sitting there, vibrating: a heavier convulsion took place inside his chest: blood – he fingered it lightly – still oozed from his neck. And yet, the strange relief he was experiencing alongside the agitation: the awareness that whatever the distress he was reacting to it was not an otherwise indiscernible encounter taking place inside his head.

Unsure, previously, what he might have been driven to write, he found the words coming easily: a resurrection, of a kind, however tenuous, he thought, and cheap at the price, the

349

consequences, however, not immediately ascertainable. Other visits, for instance, were possible from next door. How would Isaacson have reacted (taken the knife and plunged it in himself?). Did this take him any further into his imaging of Taylor's experience? Was Doctor Death, alias Cavendish, alias Norman, a comparable intruder? Was Taylor? Was everything, in short, nearer its end? How much further, in his own case, did he have to go?

16

THE MODEL was, ironically, black, and insisted on wearing shorts: a muscular, moustached and bearded figure who had entered the room wearing a broad-brimmed, black felt hat, angled sharply to one side, a cloak, also black, and khaki trousers with bulging, buttoned pockets at the calves, his feet shod in boots which reached above his ankles.

Naked, but for his shorts, he appeared aloof, glaring at the women with a cornered, baleful expression, Maddox finding it difficult to disassociate this aura from the figure itself, and difficult, too, to distinguish between the shadows and the colour of the skin, this a rationalisation, he concluded – as was his inability to follow the articulation of the hips inside the shorts – of his longing for the sense of dispossession which had characterised the young Kosovan mother, a sense subtler, however, than the one characterised by humiliation, truculence and pride, before him now. He wished he hadn't come (had mentally given up on the life-class as he had on the support group), fingering the stinging at his neck which had irritated him throughout the night, staining the sheets, the pillow, his pyjama top, wondering where the blade had been, what contact it had had with other blood before penetrating his skin.

His own indignity, too, he'd been assessing: the privileges – his own as well as those he shared with others – which enhanced his life, looking across at Genius as, groaning, scuffing his booted feet, he charcoaled the sheet of paper before him, other, identical sheets, screed with charcoal, his earlier efforts, strewn on the floor beneath his own and adjoining easels: a curious, white-skinned, exclamatory version of the half-naked figure in the centre of the room, Genius, his and the model's eyes, without a trace of mutual recognition, occasionally meeting – the self-preoccupied, occluded gaze of the damned.

His attention – he was drawing very little – drifted to the women – past Duncan in his beret (playing the part), seated disconsolately on his donkey, rarely attempting to mark his paper despite a perplexed, obsessive scrutiny of the model – the stoical, intrepid, fearsome women who drew uncomplainingly, devoutly, devotedly (they might so easily have been in church, in chapel, principally the synagogue), hand-maidens, hand-men, none of them a virgin, the former spoken for by men, the latter, presumably (Duncan alone in doubt), by women, penetrated, the majority, penetrating, presumably, the other two.

Rachel, as usual, he singled out, wondering why, with Simone in the background, he found her so attractive: the activity of her breast as she drew, her arm, her delicate, thinly muscled arm, thrust out to the easel: a hand, darkened by charcoal, which he might, so easily, stretching over, kiss: the shower of dust descending from her drawing, smeared across her overalled front, the streaks of dust across her cheeks as, intermittently, she drew back her hair (too long, and yet enchanting), a figure – the epitome – of application (dedication, domesticity, strength): the ascendancy of ends beyond her means: the shading-in of shadows hopelessly confused with the colour of the skin.

And Ailsa (Mrs Loewenstein), sensitively featured, drawing with her sleeves rolled above her elbows, a jumper beneath her smock: coloured fingers (wrists and arms) as if having plunged her limbs in blood, indecipherable shapes splayed out before her, she drawing successive, repetitive shapes on tinted paper, becalmed in widowhood (fighting in a strange arena, locked into an aperceptive view of herself); Mary (Mrs Sutor) creaking on her donkey as she laboured at her board, eyes levelled, for an instant, above its upper edge, scuffling at the sheet before her, harrying its surface: sensitised Rachel (moving back to her), frail, tensed, braced as though against a storm, he, too, taking in something of the elements – their unpredictability, their

352

intransigence – scouring his drawing, features and figure wrenched out of its carbon-slivered surface, forcing depth into and out of a two-dimensional form.

Rachel once again distracting: the intimacy of their close encounter, she, in the confined, jostled, crowded space, beside him, feet apart, drawing some distance above his head, sturdily, engrossed, enthralled, he seated, his attention returning to Mrs Sutor (Mary), a fastidious dresser, on his other side, her belted skirt, her blouse, equipped for summer – lightness, efflorescence – a restless figure, hair folded back beneath a ribbon, a schoolgirl style, its fringe drawn up above her brow, her thigh potently outlined along her donkey, crouching . . . dysfunctional Sheba (abrupt departures to the crèche to see her child) beyond, waiting, as if for a revelation, before her easel poking at the paper: Susannah (Mrs Samuels) a plain, high-breasted figure with the shoulders of a pugilist, labouring at her easel as she might at cleaning out an oven, hand, arm and shoulder applied from one direction, then the other, Jeanette, the retired, diminutive teacher, consulting her drawing, on a donkey, scoring in a line, looking up with a furrowed, enquiring, self-acclamatory smile, forehead puckered with concentration: the wheezing, groaning, tropically attired, booted, bare-armed, short-trousered figure of Genius, the boots, at intervals, stamping on the wood-block floor, Maddox looking round, perplexed, at his fellow artists wondering why he was here at all.

Something fortuitous in his engagement; something self-enquiring (tortuous): something in common with them all: 'Where are you from?' curiosity aroused at the beginning of the term, the turning-away in disappointment, a signal, a code, not recognised or given: serving a sentence, or so it seemed to him, the attention he paid this peculiar, ostracising class: serving out a sentence, leaving from the start (what Taylor, for instance, had painfully discovered: no talent, no gift, no freedom of expression), starting from scratch (the studios he'd visited, on invitation, as a critic), the distance he maintained to preserve his judgement, Rachel a template for the others – himself, too, if the truth were known: a generality of women, a specificity of

353

men: women of a particular persuasion, suffered, skirting the edge of a previous if scarcely referred-to disaster, phantoms occupying their strips of paper, his, too, for no reason he could account for, attempts to relocate themselves graphically defined.

Invariably he felt exhausted returning from the life-class (no afternoon sleep, for one thing): placing his drawings on the living-room floor, intending, in a different context, and with a more focused concentration, to identify more clearly what he might have done – pinning one, and then several to the wall, to come across them by surprise as, over the next day or two, he entered the room from the stairs or the kitchen, or merely raised his head from something he was reading or from talking on the phone, allowing them, momentarily, to be the centre of his life.

As for what was, in reality, going on in his life in general, he had little or no idea, events overtaking him, not he initiating or supervising them: tubing up the hill that evening to hear, coming in the door, a voice droning on – anonymous, ingratiating, male again – in Simone's room, the door to the office ajar, the light flashing on the answering machine, the telephone ringing moments later, then cutting off as a message was recorded (another voice: male, anonymous, urgent, he not troubling to listen): her allegiance – constant, unwavering – to things outside.

Aching, he climbed upstairs to find the table laid for supper and something cooking in the oven: she had – his heart, warmed, turned over – anticipated his coming! taciturnity (in him) was not the answer. Here, in reality, was the focus of his life: domesticity, a female world to ascend to, after a life of reminiscence, recreating the time he lived in in order to rearrange the past: feeding the cat, its identity cylinder clinking melodiously against the bowl as it ate, watching it licking its lips, once finished, pausing to look up to see if there might be more: licking once again, the rasp of its tongue on its fur in the silence of the house, it raising its head as the doorbell rang and, moments later, a different voice in the hall below, the previous client leaving.

354

From the window overlooking the street he caught a glimpse of a stout, middle-aged, raincoated figure, a centrally balding head uncovered, crossing to the steps leading down to Heath Street, buttoning its raincoat as it went: a client departing, he reflected, as if from a brothel. What had people done before analysis had been invented? drink, drugs, promiscuity, religion, or were they simply obliged to discover resources within themselves? And now? his thoughts distracted by the sound of Simone's feet on the stairs, the soft padding of her soles (flat-heeled shoes) against the carpet, the creaking of the woodwork, he going to the landing to receive her, watching her pause, a few steps down, seeing him, her face flushed, untired, excited. 'I've another appointment. Could you turn off the oven? It'll be overcooked. Are you okay? I'll be an hour. Give it forty minutes. Sorry,' and was gone, returning moments later, scampering up the stairs, pressing her lips against his, squeezing his hand, then, for a second time, was gone, as elusive, as intangible, as mysterious as ever.

He climbed upstairs and opened the roof door, the cat, pinned, he assumed, all day indoors, preceding him. The air was cool, the light fading: to the south, the declivity of the Thames was covered by a mist: lights glimmered from the scattered tower blocks, the skyline invisible. Back there, between the houses, was the pilgrim route to St Albans, the road which, at some point, he would have to take himself; meanwhile, directly below, the thirty-foot drop to the tiny, enclosed yard at the rear.

He hadn't told Simone of the incident with the intruder, anticipating – at least, over the telephone – her concluding it had been his fault: if he'd had an answering machine, like everyone else, he wouldn't have felt obliged to scamper inside, leaving the front door open. Of course, he could have been killed. What was he doing here, sitting amongst her flowers, the evidence, as was the cat, of her overwhelming, more meaningful occupation?

Perhaps she merely wanted a man, there when required, dismissed whenever not, he, for his part, bent on a mission – *here* on a mission – to accomplish something, to achieve something (if he hadn't, as yet, discovered what), drawing pictures one day a week in one location, something little different in another, the purpose of both, one 'release', the other 'expression', still obscure.

Caught, he reflected, in art's mesmeric embrace, he was struggling to release himself from something else entirely: a vengeful, insatiable appetite which not only had he energised but evidently created, the expression, the formulation of a witless, unperceiving, negating nature. Heaven, which had seemed so accessible, if not present, a few hours before, was no longer to be found in this place at all.

Having sat absently at the garden table, he began to wonder where else he might look, the cat, attracted by his immobility, leaping into his lap, he stroking it – unusually, for him – for reassurance, as if the animal might say what its mistress was up to – what *his* mistress was up to – what he himself might be destined for: another night-time visitant who might complete what the previous one had only tentatively started.

Simone was good (positive, outward-going), he self-enclosed, abandoned to vagaries he no longer knew how to analyse or control. No wonder he had gravitated (instinctively) to women – curiously, of a particular kind, not a premeditated choice at all yet circumstantially defined: elderly, artistically inclined if not appropriately gifted, they as precariously placed on the periphery of their lives, he suspected, as he, for different reasons entirely, was placed peripherally on his (and, he reflected, on the edge of theirs). No wonder they had little if any time for him, only listening to his appreciation of their drawings, their paintings with a smile: despite his lack of graphic skill, he would, he reflected, have made a good teacher, the suffering mad ox, a bovine resuscitant, remnant of a herd otherwise extinct (transported, slaughtered, fed to the dogs), he alone surviving, he of the bleeding anxious heart, his aspiration for a better understanding, for self-control, his yearning to transpose fear, terror, premonitions of something even worse, into something acceptable – even revelatory.

What an arsehole, his flaky, black intruder might (must) have thought, the person he had been closest to, other than Simone, for as long as he cared to remember: his killer, his assassin: the details of his eyes, his nose, his strangely – as Isaacson's – divergent teeth: someone – evidently – in poorer shape than he was, the particularities of his odour (the smell of fear – he recognised it – evident, too), the colour of his skin, the aura – the 'essence' (back to that again) of someone else with, demonstrably, nothing left to lose: civility, candour. Condescension – life lived at the apex of what was gradually, as far as he could tell, coming to resemble the outline of a cross: the via dolorosa along which presently he was heading. Was this what he had been planning – what, unknowingly, had been planned for him – all along: self-sacrifice on a previously unmeditated scale: another God-invested recipient of the Order of the Lost?

Returning downstairs, looking for distraction, he was suddenly aware he'd forgotten to turn the oven off, the smell of burning rising up the stairs, he descending briskly to the kitchen, opening the oven door: a rectangular metal container smouldering on the upper shelf: picking it up in a cloth, taking it to the sink, running cold water around it, spooning off the surface of the contents to the level of something other than blackness underneath: placing the scraped-off debris in a newspaper – pastry, of some sort, recognisably a fish and vegetable mixture, spooning it into a separate dish, replacing it in the turned-off oven to keep warm.

Opening the window to let out the smoke, he descended to the backyard – the sound of another male voice interspersed with Simone's, passing her room – placing the newspaper in a black bin-liner, taken from a roll, characteristically, thoughtfully, placed by her behind the back door, securing the bag and placing it in the dustbin (to be taken up twice a week to the street entrance to be emptied, a task frequently performed by himself), looking up at the parapet, reflecting that, up there, he had contemplated leaping down, registering, suddenly, the significance of the fall, the imperative which had taken possession of his life, insistent (not to be ignored). He would, he reflected, look back no more.

When she finally appeared it was with an anguished expression, standing in the living-room door, he absorbed in the television: floods, starvation – preceded by a fanfare announcing the news: showbiz! – unnumbered, if not innumerable dead, dysentery, cholera, skeletal figures, skulls misplaced as heads, unvaryingly black, passing, re-passing, condemningly, reductively, senselessly, ceaselessly, to and fro. 'What happened?'

'Floods.' (Civil war: tribalities: 'So what's the diff?' he wanted to ask.)

'What's happened?' evidently aghast.

'Madagascar.'

'In the kitchen.'

'I forgot the oven.'

'Is it burnt?'

'Some I saved. Decide if you want to throw it out,' still on the screen.

'All you had to do was switch it off.'

Not connected to her mood, not connected to his own reflection, he got up and turned the television off.

'I was feeding the cat. I assumed it was still cooking. I went on the roof.' He paused, aware, for the first time, of how vexed she was. 'I must have been distracted.'

Already, however, she had disappeared to the kitchen.

'It's uneatable,' she said, when he followed her in.

'Let's find something else.' Already he was opening the refrigerator door.

'I made it specially. I went,' she said, peculiarly distressed, 'to all this trouble.'

'I'm sorry,' he said.

She was staring at his neck.

'What's happened to your collar?'

He felt beneath his chin: his fingers, when he withdrew them, were smeared with blood. With stooping, bagging the burnt food, he had, he assumed, reopened the cut.

'A guy came into the house last night.'

358

'What guy?'

'Trying to get in Berenice's next door.'

He'd gone to the sink, turned on the cold water and, running his hand beneath it, dabbed at his neck.

'Have you got some lint?'

She'd gone to a cupboard in the corner: reaching up, she lifted down a biscuit tin. From inside she methodically took out scissors, antiseptic cream, plasters, a roll of lint: cutting off a piece, she handed it to him and watched him dab at his neck.

'That's no good,' she said, insisting, then, on looking.

'A scratch,' he told her.

'A cut.'

'A scratch. The cat would have dug deeper.'

'Did he do it with a knife?'

'By accident. I shouldn't have turned my back. I gave him ten pounds and he left. We made a deal. My mind keeps reverting to contracts. These deals,' he went on, 'we're making all the time without our always being aware. *Contracts!*' he concluded, definitively, even now not knowing why.

'You *paid* him to go?'

'It seemed the best thing. He requested more. We compromised. The relevance of that,' he went on, increasingly confused, 'appeared to dominate everything. On the other hand.' He paused. 'He wasn't quite with it.'

'Was he drugged?'

'That's what I assumed.'

'From next door?'

'He was trying to get in next door. He said they owed him money. He was hoping to get in either through an upstairs window, which appeared unreal – Berenice has grilles and shutters on her downstairs windows – or across the roof. There's a trap-door in mine which would have given him access, he thought, to the one in hers. Though, unlike mine, I'm sure Berenice's is bolted. Her house is a fortress.'

She was watching him with a shadowed expression: impossible to decide what she was thinking.

'Did you call the police?'

'It was part of the deal,' he said, 'that I didn't.'

They were facing one another across the kitchen: the bleeding, as far as he could tell, had stopped: white blotches on her cheeks, a darkening of her eyes. In a curious way, she reminded him of his intruder: perplexity, rage. Incomprehension.

'Let's get something to eat,' he said.

'You ought to report it.'

'He won't come back.'

'Of that you can't be sure.'

She was already looking round, going, finally, into the next room, returning with several sheets of newspaper: her back to him, her elbows flung out demonstratively on either side, she scraped the remnants of the food into the paper and screwed it up.

'I'll take it down. The rest's gone down already,' he said.

When he returned she was heating a pan of soup, the extractor fan whirring above the oven (why hadn't he thought of that?), the window, which he'd opened, closed. There was no end, her gestures inferred, to what he didn't understand, something atrophied in her nature countering something equally magnanimous, she wrenched, seemingly, between the two, continually presenting herself in a confusing, varying light.

'It was done by a knife?' her back still to him.

'He had it at the back of my neck. When I turned, he mustn't have pulled it away. He didn't intend to do it, I'm convinced.'

'So what was it doing at the back of your neck?'

'A precaution.' He paused. 'On his side,' he added.

He had, after all, invited the man to kill him: a gesture which, morally, would have let him, Maddox, off the hook.

'Shouldn't you go to the hospital?' More statement than enquiry.

'A scratch.'

'A cut.' She paused. 'Have you any idea where the knife has been?' Again, he reflected, less enquiry than statement.

Turning to him, she held a spoon with which she'd been

360

stirring the soup. Her eyes, he was surprised to see, were full of tears: not sorrow, however – rage.

He spread out his hands. 'How do I know?'

'Did you put anything on it?'

'Antiseptic.' He added, 'Like yours.'

She turned back to the soup.

A moment later she turned it off: the contents of the pan poured into two bowls.

She took them through to the other room, the table already prepared (earlier in the day, by her).

Neither, as they ate, was inclined to talk: when they had finished, the silence lengthened.

'You realise,' she said, finally, 'you might have been infected.'

'With what?'

'Think.'

A demonstrative gesture with her spoon. Her eyes, once more, were full of tears: powerlessness, in any situation, roused her fury.

Something, in his case undemonstrative, was gripping him inside: a reciprocal anger which brought to mind, absurdly, the image of Taylor, of a particular form of destitution: without her, without this place, without this part of her life, he was – unlike her – finished.

'Anything is possible with those people you have next door. There's no knowing what blood the knife might have been in contact with.'

She was picking up her bowl, having left much of her soup, and was going through to the kitchen: he could hear a cupboard door being slammed: something childlike, he reflected, in her reaction, the finality of which he couldn't bear to think about. Despite the brevity of her absence, the sight of her, he knew, would ease him. Yet he continued sitting there undecided, persuaded – terrified – he might lose her: that she didn't love and, as a moment like this showed, never had.

'The blade might easily have been infected,' she said, behind his back, having, evidently, returned. 'I'm basing that on the

361

kind of people who live next door. The ones I've asked you to move away from, time and time again.'

He waited, no longer sure of his response.

'Don't they take as well as deal in drugs?'

'I hardly know anyone,' he said, 'who doesn't,' adding, 'in that part of town. I'm no authority, and I might be wrong. Even Viklund, when it comes down to it, has a drug he believes – he hopes – can kill him.'

He had turned in his chair to confront her: now he picked up his bowl and took it past her into the kitchen. He placed it, and hers, in the washing-up machine by the sink.

The kettle, which she'd evidently switched on, came to the boil, the extractor fan still whirring above the oven.

'Shall we call it a day?'

His enquiry came with scarcely any preparation: if the relationship were to be terminated, if he were to be executed, let her get it over.

'Call what a day?'

He gestured round: something magnetic in her nature: he felt the force of it drawing him in: first the burnt food, then the scratch (little enquiry about the nature of the assault): when disassembly of anything took place how swiftly it happened.

'All this.' He swung out his arm again. 'Common sense, if it is common sense, appears scarcely to have been involved from the start.'

She was considering carefully – too carefully – what he was saying, an expression on her face he'd only previously seen on the first day of their encounter; engaged, yet distant: objectivity was being measured, recorded, assessed: he wouldn't have been surprised if, at any moment, she had taken out a file – his file – and started making notes: the way she could write while not looking at the page but at her subject (the way, absorbed, some of the women drew at the life-class), an automatic, almost somnolent reaction.

He added, 'I don't know where I am with you. Whereas I feel you know precisely where you are with me. What it is you want. What it is you don't. Everything's so partial. Living,' he went

362

on, 'contrary lives. I reducing mine, you expanding yours. All this,' he gestured round once more, 'proposed by my former wife on the recommendation of her current husband. A man I scarcely know, and what I do know, I invariably object to or dislike. The bullshitting Gerry with his buccaneering.'

He was sweating: much of what he was saying came out of a part of him to which he rarely gave expression: a part which, for much of his life, without his being aware of it, he had elected to keep hidden: unforbearing, confused, obscure – a vacuum: that area which once might have been occupied by what his brother Paul would refer to, contemptuously, as 'religion': spirituality of some sort, if not quite the same thing – something to which, at the best of times, he had felt himself only tenuously attached: the Quinians injunction, facile, well intentioned: blank.

Her own reaction, seeing him pinioned there, or so it must have seemed, had been to come forward, smiling, taking his shoulders, drawing him against her: he could feel her heart – he assumed it was her heart – beating against his chest, matching, seemingly, his agitation.

'All I'm suggesting is what anyone would. It's like scratching you, for instance, with a used needle. The previous user *might* have been okay. With your neighbours there's a possibility not. Don't we need, after all, to look out for one another? Don't we do that – *haven't* we done that all along? Isn't this a difficult passage we have to get through?' She was speaking by his ear, her breath warm against his neck. 'Don't you see what a shock it is? You might have been killed. I've asked you to leave that place before. If he's come in once he could come in again. Why don't you sell the place and come and live up here?'

'With you?' He was holding her at a distance, pulling back.

'Separately. At least I'd know where you were. There's not much time left for either of us. Give us, at the most, twenty years. After that, if we're still here, deterioration will inhibit almost everything.'

'You'd like us to keep going?'

'I'd like to.'

'I realise,' he said, 'we've only just started. That there's a

363

great deal about one another we scarcely know.' He was pausing again, their relationship full of reservations: a list of extenuating circumstances, of carefully, or even carelessly crafted exemptions, underlying everything.

'Why don't we go upstairs?' she said, he aware, suddenly, of a reciprocal desperation: if he was prepared to go to the edge, she, she was suggesting, was prepared to go with him: commitment had gone past the point of no return, he lying back, some time later, in her bed, gazing out at the nearby house with its ivy-covered walls, its curiously leaning chimneys, the image of Isaacson coming to mind, and his intruder, Simone having gone through to the bathroom, the water splashing in the bath and – a unique occurrence – the sound of her singing, a light, almost frivolous, uncharacteristically childish voice, celebratory, he thought, if not triumphant.

He was drawing, as instructed, an animal that he liked and one that he didn't, Beth's figure, a cardigan over her track suit, bowed to her drawing, blocking the light from the window. Her hair was conspicuously thicker, and greyer, at the back (receding over her forehead), a distorted, arthritic silhouette, her groans accompanying her laboured movements – not least her inclination to hide the paper before its necessary pinning-up on the wall or the back of the door.

Alex, as usual, had gone into a corner, his thin, ochre-coloured hair brushed smoothly to the rear of his head, a spectral mask suspended over his sheet of paper, his right arm vigorously employed, forwards and backwards, as he scored in his message for the week, his drawing-board tilted conspiratorially towards him: tight-lipped, an intense, preoccupied if not tormented figure, each violent lateral then vertical stroke of his crayon accompanied by a brief, indecipherable exclamation: evacuee from Dunkirk, dispossessed, inadvertent (unprepared) liberator of Belsen: furious, violent, self-lacerating gestures as if he were responsible for both (contracts abandoned, disengagement impossible), the table creaking to maximise his complaint.

Anna, the crepuscular creature with her winsome, forgiving,

forbearing smile, was, Melissa had announced, back in the geriatric ward at the North London Royal (the base from which most of them had originally emerged), her drawing from the previous week still pinned to the door, a statement of some sort – three carefully tinted flower-beds – of which, because of her absence, Melissa had forbidden discussion, she sitting immediately behind Maddox, writing a letter (perhaps to her: he suspected not) as they painted and drew, Judith, the Jerusalemite ('why not make it the world's first universal city and stop all this killing?' her earlier morning's suggestion), stabbing at her drawing, to one side of Maddox (sharing the same rocking table) – as if ridding it of an infestation, an assortment of pencils, crayons and chalks, cornered as she entered the room, laid before her, not looking up as she substituted one for another. Fragments of chalk had attached themselves to the sleeves of her dress, a voluminous, cape-like creation which enveloped both her and the chair – and from the hem of which her tiny, slippered feet protruded, tapping silently, alternately, on the wood-block floor.

Ida, the cockney housewife, was singing as she drew, a robust, if misleading demonstration of her lightness of spirit, flicking paint at her picture, leaning back, her neatly jumpered and trousered figure, her head, a powerfully configurated feature with large, dark, almost luminous eyes and a prominent, arc-like nose, the mouth generously extended with lipstick (a painstaking grimace, even in repose), held with incongruous delicacy to one side, she screwing the paper up and, raising it above her, holding it there, illustrationally, drawing attention to the gesture, before dropping it on the floor.

'Don't make the room untidy, Ida,' Melissa said, scarcely taking her eyes off the letter. 'Others have to use it,' adding, 'Five more minutes. I'll want to see the screwed-up one, of course, as well as any previous or subsequent effort,' re-reading her correspondence with silently moving lips before signing it with a flourish, pausing, and adding an exclamation mark to the final sentence.

The women formalised the room: gave it strength – he and

Alex, he reflected, singularly apart, a masculine intrusiveness, synonymous, in Alex's case, with violence, a suicidal imperative scarcely constrained – not least, he further reflected, against the background of the work of other day-patients also pinned to the walls: inchoate colours, invariably abstracted: confusion, doubt, remonstration, something struggled-for, if notably not achieved.

A dog, he'd drawn, a blackened hulk against a diagonally rising skyline, and a snake, a coloured spiral, a series, in effect, of interlocking spirals, he, too, inclined, surprisingly, to hum as he drew, crayoned, charcoaled or painted, singing sub voce – the words mentally recalled – texts learnt in the Cathedral at St Albans – Sunday School, Morning Service, Evensong, later, Crusaders – and in the chapel at Quinians – inclined to do the same in the life-class, the movement of his hand and eye prompting a reciprocal activity associated with sound – of a singularly devotional nature. Abstruse, otherwise, the act of drawing or painting; instinctual, unthinking – prompt, precise: the vaguest sensation of distraction, of his mind felicitously engaged.

He was coming to identify his mind with what he would have been inclined to call a mechanical process: a machine serviced by a variety of lubricants and fuels, overlooked by technicians who came on the scene when the mechanism refused to function in an agreeable way: hormones, neurones, synapses: his vocabulary was increasing, the dozen or so transmitters which flashed between neurological extremes, more dextrous, more complex – more unfathomable – than the mechanisms which determined the motion of a car, but an enterprise, nevertheless, which could be identified exclusively in terms of function, perpetuation (self-perpetuation) its principal concern.

Fortuity (again: Lucretius) governing his existence, taking him from one person to another, one circumstance to another, while tenuously – obsessively – finally, good-naturedly, he endeav-oured to identify a pattern (a synchronicity) which, as much was now reminding him, had not been there in the first place. Extraordinary claims made on behalf of extraordinary events would not, in the end, evoke anything other than the nature, not the purpose, of the process he'd recognised – and at the very least acknowledged – he listening, some time later, this in mind, to Melissa encouraging her recalcitrant charges, mortified in more ways than one, to extemporise on their drawings or paintings, Alex's boss-eyed face demonstrating once again the indefatigable fury which drove him, mentally, to the edge of chasms and gorges, a dynamo of distress, the graphic delineation of which appeared more to exacerbate than diminish or assuage.

'Why does he do it?' Maddox enquired of Melissa. 'Alex comes up each week with these wild-eyed charges, men attached to bombs, descending rockets, or being torn apart by uniformed figures, the iconography almost too conformist, and – good old Alex, mild-mannered like the rest of us – after presenting us with his suicide note, turns up the following week to deliver yet another. As it is,' he gestured to the relevant drawing on the wall, 'we were asked – he was asked – to draw an animal he liked and one he disliked, and he comes up, yet again, with a figure in a cage. The analogy's obvious, repetitive, malignant. Life is unliveable. Too much to bear. Yet here we are, apart from Anna, who's back in the nut-house, still living it. What we want to know from him is where do we go *after* the bomb has dropped, the rocket has landed, the victim been abused by the uniformed figures? What the fuck do we do when we've come to the edge, gone over, and dropped? If life is how he describes it, what are all of us doing here?'

The 'fuck', in this context – women, lunatic or otherwise, present – was, he realised, a mistake: silence registered the rebuke before Melissa, measuring it precisely, responded, 'Do you think it is unbearable?' adding, 'Life,' turning the question to the rest of the room, like she might, conversationally, have enquired about the weather, Alex's pinched, drained, post-Dunkirk-Belsenic face, the eyes leeched, or so it seemed, of colour, gazing across at Maddox with a singularly appealing and appreciative expression, a grateful, retributory fervour . . .

'Mine isn't, otherwise I wouldn't be here,' Maddox said. 'But isn't Beth's, or Judith's, or Ida's focused around the unbearable?

After all,' he went on, glancing at the women he'd named, each bemused at being included, 'we hear, when it comes down to it, very little different, week after week.'

'What does Alex think?' Melissa persisted, crossing her legs beneath her patchwork skirt, her arms folding across her bloused front, Alex taking time to respond, the familiar fissures in his face invigorated by his effort to focus on what, on other occasions – reluctant to talk about them – he would refer to as his 'feelings' – intangible 'events' which went on remotely and yet vividly, annihilatingly, somewhere 'inside'. Taking his cue from Melissa, he crossed his legs too, displaying, as he did so, sockless feet, his pullover, home-knitted and too large, hanging around his withered chest in folds.

'I don't know what I think,' he said. 'I only know what I feel. Isn't that what we're supposed to be doing?'

'Whether it's thought or feeling is irrelevant,' Maddox said. 'It's always the same. Week after week. Monotony, I'd say, was our greatest problem. We appear to be sustaining our symptoms, not eradicating them. Suffering, you could say, to the point of self-indulgence. It sits on us like a rock, inhibiting thought and feeling. Life, despite all our advantages, not least the facilities here, lived beyond recognisable limits.' He indicated Beth's drawing of a dog in flames, curling red and yellow patches flickering from its head, its shoulders, along its haunches, down its tail, out of its eyes, its ears, its mouth, its nose, adding, 'I suppose that, too, is a metaphor,' recognising too late the swastika on its flank. 'Here we are telling each other we're nuts and nobody appears to listen.'

'At least we're talking about it,' Melissa said, her cheeks flushed, her eyes alight, her hands tucked tightly beneath her arms.

'In circles,' Maddox said.

'So what are your priorities?' Melissa gestured at his drawings.

'One's a dog, the other's a snake.'

'Which one do you like?'

'The dog.'

368

'A symbol of death.'

'Of devotion, companionship, acceptance, loyalty, service.' He might have gone on, but couldn't think of anything else.

'And the snake?'

'Sinister. Subversive. Scheming.' These epithets, too, ran out.

'Phallic,' Melissa suggested.

'Like Alex, but without being repetitive. I merely drew what came into my head.'

Melissa re-crossed her legs. 'You brightly colour the snake and do the dog in monochrome. Black,' she concluded.

Her arms tightened across her blouse.

'What's phallic?' Ida enquired, her face, constructed from a variety of tints and colours, bright, inquisitive, engaging.

'It relates to a penis,' Melissa said.

'What's a penis?' Ida further enquired. 'Something you pour out?'

'A cock,' Alex said, the half-circle of faces suddenly enthralled.

'A hen cock or a cock cock?' Ida persisted: innocence, ignorance? bemusement, perhaps . . .

'A cock like I've got,' Alex said.

'I didn't know you kept hens, Alex,' Ida said. 'You've never mentioned it before.'

'A cock like I have between my legs,' Alex said, increasingly confused.

'It's symbolic,' Melissa said, to clarify the situation.

'It just looks like a snake to me,' Ida said. 'Comfy, wriggly, friendly,' she expanded.

'And a cock,' Alex insisted, some sort of violation involved: colour had risen to his sunken cheeks, his eyes acquiring a feverish, pinkish tinge.

'I like all animals,' Ida said, straightening her jumper, the outline of her brassière evokingly revealed.

'Cocks, too, Ida,' Alex persisted.

'Hens especially,' Ida confirmed.

'We're all barmy,' the silent until now Judith said. 'Which is why we're here. Isn't that right?' she added, appealing to Melissa.

'It's not a term I would use,' Melissa said, her arms unfolding.

'What would you use, Melissa?' Ida enquired, this her first ever involvement in a discussion, as far as Maddox recalled, she invariably complaining, plaintively, 'everything's above my head'.

'Unwell,' Melissa said. 'Despondent. But determined to understand why and, having discovered that, to anticipate getting better. Better,' she went on, 'through understanding. And by sharing that understanding,' she concluded, 'with others.'

'Not better through distraction?' Maddox said.

'Not distraction for its own sake,' Melissa said. 'But by association. Of knowing in your suffering you're not alone.'

'I feel worse in the morning,' Ida said, carried away, not least by Alex's attention and the controversy she'd provoked. 'When I wake up I don't want to live. I don't want to live for most of the day. My mother was the same. She put on her make-up. Finished her ironing. Hoovered the house. Washed the bath-room. And the toilet. Then went to the bedroom and swallowed her pills. A neighbour was coming to take her out and saw her through the letter-box. Just her feet. As if she'd changed her mind and gone to the door but died in the hall before she reached it.'

'Then, of course,' Melissa said, 'you did the same.'

'My son-in-law called when he wasn't supposed to.' Ida pulled down her jumper: the figure, the gesture implied – correctly, Maddox reflected – of a woman younger than she looked (not seventy-five, let's say, he conjectured, but sixty-seven), her face alone betraying her decline, the heavy lines bracketing the over-painted mouth, the tinted cheeks smeared unevenly with dabbed-in lipstick, the mascaraed cavities around the eyes – pain, he reflected, rarely so graphically defined. 'Though my father treated her badly,' Ida went on, pausing before confirming, 'when he was alive.'

'Whereas Matthew's method was a tube train,' Melissa said,

370

anxious to draw Maddox in, or on, she seeing him as her principal challenge.

'Thoughtless, even to attempt it,' Maddox said. 'Involving others. I'm not sure, even now, how or why it occurred.'

'The intention, nevertheless, was clear,' Melissa said.

'I'd say the intention was obscure,' he said, wondering if this were true: obscurity certainly characterised his subsequent attempts to explain it: far worse circumstances, the geriatric support group suggested, could produce less dramatic results.

'The thoughtlessness, as you describe it, in involving others shows how compelling the gesture was,' Melissa said.

'Are we grading the efficacy of our suicidal intentions,' Maddox said, 'in order to point the way to others? Ida, pills. Me, tube trains. Anna, poor Anna, ever higher windows.'

'We're here to get rid of anger by expressing it, in this case, visually,' Alex said. 'That's the value of our coming. And to see, in doing that, we're not alone.'

It was the most eloquent statement that Alex, in Maddox's experience, had ever made, derived, he assumed, from another authority and possibly learnt by heart. 'I wouldn't want any man to go through what I've been through,' he said. 'I see bodies, in flashback, every night, like strings of meat, still living, hung on hooks. The eyes, the eyes alone, showing what's been done to them.' He waved his arm to encompass the room. 'You've no idea,' he concluded.

'Post-traumatic stress,' Melissa said.

'Fuck what you call it, I call it hell,' Alex said, his anger, like his eloquence, unprecedented on any previous occasion.

'I don't wish to talk about it,' Beth said, her arthritic figure pinioned, so it seemed, to her chair, an attempt to move ending in something of a convulsion. She waved her arm as Melissa turned towards her. 'It's too painful for public discussion. That's my feeling.'

'If we don't talk about it, what's the point in coming?' Alex said.

'I don't like your language, either,' Beth said.

'Soldier's language,' Alex said.

371

'All soldiers don't talk like that,' Beth persisted.

'All soldiers haven't been through what I've been through,' Alex said. 'If you'd seen what I'd seen you wouldn't be so glib.'

'I have seen what you've seen,' Beth said, 'and I don't want to say any more about it.'

'Walking carcases made into carcases by well-fed men, with families and children and dogs,' Alex said, his confidence decreasing.

'I don't wish to hear any more.' Beth covered her ears. 'I'm not well. I shouldn't have to listen to any of this. I've lived through it. He's only witnessed it. I know what it's like from the inside,' she pleaded.

Silence returned, broken by the sound of people passing – voices, feet – in the corridor outside.

'Something as important as this can't be left in the air,' Melissa said. 'What does Judith think?' she added.

'I'd like to go to the toilet,' Judith said. Rising from her chair, she added, 'Is that all right?' moving to the door, on the back of which the drawings and paintings were pinned.

'I prefer no one to leave until the end of the session,' Melissa said.

'I have to go,' Judith said.

The drawings and paintings disappeared as the door was pulled open, reappearing as it closed behind Judith's back.

'She always goes when it's getting difficult,' Alex said. 'All that Jerusalem stuff she goes on about. The Jews and the British. The Arabs. That soldier. I agree with the Universal City. But you'd think she'd lived in a fucking cave. Ten to a room. One toilet for twenty. Do you know what it was like in the Gorbals? Do you think the *Jews* there, like me, didn't have to suffer?'

'On that scale, and with that intensity, probably not,' Maddox said.

'Oh, fuck you!' Alex said, weeping into his hand.

Later, walking back up the hill, he concluded he should finish at the clinic: the discursive nature of the exercise: they had done all that could reasonably be expected. Most who attended did so for two days a week, some, a minority, like him, one day only. Most stayed for several months, occasionally, in one or two instances, for two or three years, he adding up the length of time in his own case (six months?) – entering Simone's front door as he might have entered his own, her voice alternating with a woman's in her consulting-room, his exhaustion suddenly apparent. The whole arrangement – the rearrangement – he had made of his life was leading him no nearer to where, he assumed, he ought to go (enlightenment, of some sort, elusively at hand).

Was he, after all, in terminal decline? Simone had arranged an appointment at a clinic in Westminster: after a period of incubation he would be tested: an agonising seven to ten days before the result was known. Meanwhile they would entertain one another by different means. What would his former wife and his children make of this? Decrepitude, absorption by depravity, by dissolution, by which, living how he did, where he did, he was exclusively surrounded.

Climbing the stairs, feeding the cat, preparing the food he'd brought in for supper: setting the table; while, below, he heard one client leave, another arrive, the interval of silence followed by the closing of a door.

In suspension: sitting in the kitchen, watching, in a glass-fronted oven, the food cooking: the bubbling of the cheese-covered surface of the dish (calculations completed to make sure it wouldn't burn). Quite soon he might be killed: several nights after his confrontation with his intruder he'd answered a ring at the door to find Berenice standing there. The flickering eyelids, the pouching and the shadowing of the skin beneath, the dark-eyed, venomous expression, a dress which revealed the surpris-ingly firm outline of her breasts, the skirt flared out in a schoolgirl fashion, her sturdy, bare, athletic legs, her feet bare, too, he noticed, she immediately enquiring, 'Did you ring the fucking police?' an earth-bound, dissonant, gravelly sound from which he extracted the words – their immediacy, their implication – only after several seconds, meanwhile staring at her with a glazed expression which only fitfully came alive with recognition.

'No,' he said.

'Wayne was taken in last night. He says you fucked him up.'

'Who's Wayne?' increasingly confused.

'The one you were talking to the other night.'

'The one who tried to break in your door?'

'He only wanted to talk. I asked him to come back another time.'

'He said he wanted to kill you. It's a wonder,' he said, 'he doesn't blame you.'

Forces, of an obscure nature, were being assembled: thief indebted to thief, Maddox, in this arrangement, not included.

Yet all he was thinking of were his vacillating moods, how reality – his perception of what, schematically, he took to be reality – shifted from one moment to another – unlike, for instance, his perception of the figure standing before him now: someone habitually he heard rather than saw, nevertheless an intimate (in some respects, the most intimate) part of his domestic life, more consistently and persistently present even than Simone: someone who, judged by the prevalence of her voice through the party-wall, rarely if ever slept, he, at times, imagining her suspended from her ceiling, bat-like, head down, feet attached to the plaster, eyes open – her mouth likewise – a liquid, venomous, accusing stare which, now she was at his door, he refused to acknowledge.

'Maybe you should tell him it wasn't me. There must,' he went on, 'be plenty of alternatives, you amongst them. You told him, after all, you'd called the police. And Isaiah. The one he threatened through the door. All he did with me was walk in the house when I wasn't looking in order to break into yours. Apart from threatening me with a knife and taking ten pounds, that's all that happened.'

'Ten pounds?'

Incredulity gave way to something more reflective: he saw her lips extend, broaden, and realised, apart from the blemished skin, what an attractive mouth she had: a different culture, a

374

different class: what, given the opportunities he'd had, for instance, might she have turned into?

'Presumably,' he shrugged, 'he was taken in for more than that.'

Gazing at him, still transfixed – transported, even – by calculation: how much, he wondered, might she demand?

'There're no sort of things you want?' she asked.

'Like what?'

'Soap. Hair shampoo.' She waited, registering his surprise. 'Make-up.'

'I don't use make-up,' a smile, eerily, crossing her features, her lips parting to surprisingly cared-for teeth: as swiftly presented, however, as retracted: pain galvanised by pain: he got the message. 'Or your girlfriend?' she enquired.

'I'll let you know,' he said, 'if we ever run out,' adding, 'I'd appreciate you putting in a good word with Wayne. I'm sure if he works it out he'll see it couldn't have been me.'

'When Wayne's in trouble we are,' she said, more obscure demands he presumed waiting to be presented. 'You ring the police about us?' she added.

'I haven't,' she glancing off, in response, along the street, retreating to his gate, uncertain what to add, her voice, her manner – her thoughts and speculations – in abeyance, glancing up, after calling, 'I'll see you,' with a wave, he acknowledging it (how friendly) to realise it had been directed upwards, to her house, Isaiah undoubtedly watching from a window.

Death, he was thinking in Simone's kitchen, endeavouring to match the timing of his cooking with her return, might be closer than he'd thought. Since the intrusion he'd got out the step-ladder again and climbed through the ceiling into the roof space, a tiny area confined by diagonally sloping beams. Balancing on the joists, he'd opened the trap-door leading onto the roof itself. Several tiles, he'd observed, required replacing, concluding, otherwise, it would take little effort to climb over the party-wall, by the chimney, to the trap-door on Berenice's side. Having discovered the route, he was surprised, considering what went on next door, and considering, too, its accessibility, that it hadn't been used before. Previously, his own perception, conveyed reassuringly to Simone, had been that foxes rarely killed near their holes: it was in Berenice's interest to keep things as they were. At least, this was what he concluded as he examined the food in the oven and, Simone delayed, switched it off.

He had little left to lose: his best energies had been expended. Taylor alone remained as a subject. With Viklund, he was surprised to discover, he was inclined to keep his distance. He was, nevertheless, tormented by the women to whom, throughout his illness, he had become connected. He recalled allusions to Judaism in his past (discriminatory, swept derisively aside): a relative who had occupied a cobbler's premises in a sidestreet in St Albans; a brother of the same who had occupied the premises of a tailor, Maddox an Anglicised version of an otherwise unpronounceable name. And Paul, who, at the time of his ordination, had gone to considerable trouble first to examine and then disown their past: 'continuity, our present lives,' he'd concluded, 'by a different name.' All he knew, at the moment, was that his connection to these women was visceral, to do with maternity, creativity, an idealisation of some sort, art and sex ineluctably combined – watching, enthralled, as they drew or painted, or, as at the day-centre, refused to examine their pasts – pasts which allegedly had no depths but which nevertheless went down for ever. Why did he feel so at ease with them?

Then she was coming up the stairs, the sound preceded by that of the front door closing. 'I don't make notes immediately after every session,' she said, embracing him, taking in the smell of the food, exclaiming, 'Wonderful! No burning.'

And then an evening of watching the news, phone calls, he, during the latter, lying on the bed upstairs, listening to the radio. When, finally, she came up, she said, 'How do you feel about a night on your own? I'm particularly tired and need to rest,' he responding, 'I won't disturb you. I could sleep on the floor or the settee downstairs.'

'I prefer alone,' she said, so that, once more, he was walking down the hill, heart ringing with rejection while reproachfully he reflected, she needs time on her own, as I do myself, aware of the moon before him, to the south, a skein of cloud passing across its surface, the configuration of the trees beneath which he walked, glancing, for distraction, into the shop windows beyond Chalk Farm before turning into his street, looking up, instinctively, at Berenice's windows, listening, after opening the front door, for any incriminatory sound, securing the door without putting on the light, indifferent to whether there was anyone there or not, moments later sitting in the darkness, in the downstairs room, wondering what it was, since it could be dismissed so easily, he and Simone shared.

17

He'd done overseas lecture tours frequently in the past, invariably when the children were young: a reasonable (well-paid) excuse to escape the rigours and routines, the stultifying predictability of domestic life. The difficulty with most of them had arisen when it had come to parting from the women to whom he had, on many of these occasions, become attached. Everywhere, or so it had seemed, there was someone waiting to be delivered from an aversion to habit, the majority of them, he had been surprised to discover, of Judaic origin, something of which he was unaware at the moment of attraction, and all, without exception, the product of a mixed relationship, nearly always Jewish and Catholic (on two occasions Presbyterian). It was as if instinctively he were drawn less to a race or a culture than to a conflict of a specific, but indefinable, and unresolvable nature: something beyond belief, or idealisation, beyond faith or identification, a hinterland of displacement which echoed something of the same within himself. So della Francesca in the States, Cimabue and Giotto in Canada, the pre- and early Renaissance in a curious three-month tour of Brazil, Argentina, Chile and Peru, the cultural emissaries he had met on the way, the resourceful, flawed, self-determined women, dark-haired, dark-eyed, pale-skinned, waiting, inexplicably, to be 'delivered'. Of what? To whom? a connection which remained obscure from first meeting to departure, a receptivity on both sides instantly perceived and, in almost every instance, painfully ended.

On each occasion he had endured the curious sensation of

leaving an integral part of himself in the hands of someone who, despite the intimacy involved, remained both a stranger and yet more familiar than anyone else he had known. Soon, when new enterprises were suggested, he was aware that there was very little of what he had come to suspect might be 'himself' to take with him, to the extent that the sense of loss – the aching sense of omission – which he had come to associate with travel persuaded him to desist. After all, there was Charlotte (what did she represent but an early, unheeding aspiration? neither of her parents, unlike his, had had any religious affiliation), and their three sons. No wonder, one by one, all four of them had left, he, he finally concluded – prior to Charlotte's leaving – having departed long before them.

Now there was Simone to come home to, as perplexing a union as any he had prospected, let alone encountered, no departure from her (as this evening) without an awareness it might be the last; similarly, too, her departures for lectures, conferences, seminars, 'weekends', she having merely to leave the room for him to become aware of the possibility of removal as opposed to absence, a reminder of that element within himself which singularly, as he had got older, had failed to reassure or even remind him of who or what or even where, let alone why, he was.

Associated with this feeling was the one he had experienced on numerous occasions at airports: the significance, at Simone's, sitting on her roof, of the passing of aircraft overhead, the alignment of the airport with the setting sun, expiration inseparable from a diurnal, observable pattern, subliminal, for the most part, its resonance all the greater and, after so many months, inseparable from those feelings he associated with both her and her house: the echoes of those restrained and restraining looks of women he had left behind – and who, alarmingly, epitomised in Simone, were capable, suddenly, of leaving him: looks of desertion, amounting, almost, to annihilation, associated with the Americas, Eastern Europe, Russia, Israel: letters, telephone calls, clandestine, for the most part, even pursuing visits, the feelings of disruption, disloyalty, fracture, immense. So many disassociated lives coalesced, at this instant, in Simone: when would he ever learn? *what* would he ever learn? the final sensation, with her, he had come to rest: the definitive image of a specific face, evaluated through Giotto, Masaccio, so much else: Bathsheba, Judith, Mary, Martha, elusive in its meaning, if focused, sensationally, in its charms, his susceptibility associated with arrival, a constant re-arrival, with return, a constant re-return, with a final awareness of coming in.

The warrant came from a prison in the north of England; and then, surprised, having 'processed' Taylor to the back of his mind, he realised, coincidentally, from the town to which he had been evacuated during the war, Quinians standing enigmatically on its western skyline (braced, once more, from the viewpoint of the town, against the setting sun).

The grey stone encirclement of the prison walls had been visible from the school's upper (dormitory) windows, its lateral extension breaking up the vertical escarpment of mills and warehouses and, at the summit of the opposing ridge, the soot-encrusted outline of the town's municipal buildings.

Even more conspicuous, at the centre of the prison, stood the structure from which the cell blocks radiated like the spokes of a wheel. From the station, leaving or arriving by train, the barbican-like presence dominated the view, its greyness a foil to the brickwork of industrial, commercial and domestic buildings which enclosed it on every side.

Absorbed so constitutionally within the context of the town, its silence, and air of containment, had reduced its significance to Maddox over the years when, on leaving and arrival, he had gazed at it, either from carriage windows or remotely, from the school playing-field or the school itself. Now, however, arriving in response to the invitation from Taylor, it reasserted its presence in a singularly oppressive way. In a curious sense, it had, after years of benignity, come dramatically alive, the familiar feeling, long ago abandoned, of returning to school, displaced by something remindful, painfully, of abandonment, of deceit and disloyalty, of betrayal, the sensations he associated with the journey overlain by something which, if he had anticipated it more astutely, he would have seen could only do him harm: a visit into the past. The book with which he had begun the journey had long been abandoned by the time the train had passed beyond the southern stretches of the York Plain and into the once colliery-infested hill-land of South Yorkshire, the absence of the pits endorsing the feeling of desolation.

Getting out of his seat as the train approached the town, he crossed the carriage to the opposite window to see the once familiar edifice come into view – inconveniencing the passengers there and finally going to the door to gaze out at the remaining mill shapes bulked in the valley bottom, then, once again, at the serpentine grey stone walls of the prison – in the distance, on the furthest skyline, enclosed by trees, the profile of the school.

It was as if, entering the prison, through a gate which he had walked past many times (the ironically named Love Lane leading directly to it from the station), he were returning to a community he already knew, a further adjunct, an extended dormitory, of the school itself – expecting, even, familiar faces, familiar responses: teachers, youths, the benevolent Head with his Quaker aspirations – smiling at the warder who examined his warrant, smiling at those who searched his clothes, the bag of cigarettes, food and chocolate – and, a last-minute decision, unsure of its perversity, the drawing-block and oil crayons (taken away separately to be looked at).

Cleansed, seemingly, he was led into a recently constructed building adjacent to the central yard. Looking up, and outwards, he was aware only of the overcast sky, no sign of any reassuring external structures. Moments later, he was sitting in a recently decorated room smelling of paint and, possibly, detergent – sitting on a plastic chair at a plastic table, other identical chairs and tables unoccupied around.

The door opened: a figure he failed to recognise entered, the face rotund, the eyes recessive: a heavy jowl overhung the collar of a light blue shirt: dark trousers scarcely restrained a protuberant gut. A warder, having closed the door, stood beside it – an elderly man, white-haired, genially featured, nodding and smiling at Maddox, an extension, seemingly, of his own good intentions, an endorsement of any positive sentiment he might have: white shirt, dark tie, dark trousers, Maddox taking in these details as he would those of a scene he might be obliged, almost formally, later, to account for to someone else.

Taylor extended his hand: 'We're allowed to shake hands,' derisively, adding, 'How are you? Was the journey okay?' retaining his hand, the gesture drawing him to an engagement he would otherwise have tried to avoid.

'I'm fine,' he said. 'And you?' releasing his hand, enquiring, mentally, an engagement with what? something at that point he couldn't name, sitting once more, having stood at Taylor's entrance, Taylor himself rearranging his chair on the other side of the table, repositioning it once more before he finally sat.

'I'm fine, too.' He gestured round. 'It's been repainted. Just for you,' smiling. 'Kidding. They said, "We'll have the interview room repainted, Peter." Did I tell you I've changed my name? By deed poll. "Now someone's agreed to come to see you." Or words to that effect,' Maddox leaning on the table with his elbows, a companionable gesture intended to set both of them at ease, glancing round at the framed reproductions hanging on the cream walls. 'I chose them. Poor Vincent. One lunatic to another. I've really made myself at home up here. What d'you think? They aren't quite up to Piero. As for Tommaso. No dice. Do you realise he must have died by the age of twenty-seven? Like Girtin. Another prodigal talent. Art, wouldn't you say, transcends love? You must have found that out yourself. Being, as you are – your fondest impersonation, and the one I always preferred – a wise old man. Another of your maxims. Choosers can't be losers. Or was it the other way around? What d'you think? Didn't Viklund invariably end a statement with the interrogative? The ball always in your court. Or, rather, ball back in your court. Or for ever hold your tongue. Whether you cared to play or not. I've been thinking about that. You and he together. Me in here. A suspended life. An unreturnable cargo. An unreclaimable deposit.' He gestured again at the room,

382

disinclined, Maddox concluded, to allow him to respond. 'Masaccio the greatest, in my view, not only because of his lost potential. Do you remember the old Medici prints? No longer around, I discovered. Vincents you can get in Woolworths. Johnny went out and bought them. A redecorating fund.' He indicated the warder behind his back. ' "You're an artist, Mr Taylor," they said. "This should be up your street. Pictures for the interview room." ' He smiled, a snarling expression, the teeth discoloured, one of them missing at the front of his mouth. 'John had to be taken into account. Inmates, likewise. Feel at ease with the familiar, even if they don't enjoy it. Attending art classes, I a studio assistant. Cimabue's workshop not, I might tell you, a suitable comparison. Odd, nevertheless, that what is meaningful, if not inevitable to one generation, is inaccessible to another. It suggests that those of us who are one thing at the present are something significantly other later on. What d'you think? Ball in your court,' he concluded, 'so to speak,' waiting for Maddox to respond before continuing, reassured, or so it seemed, by his silence, 'This is my tutor, John,' turning to the warder, the chair creaking beneath his weight. 'Years ago. A lasting influence,' adding directly to Maddox, turning back to the table, 'John's a fan. Believes in redemption. Values life like you and I would value,' pausing to consider. 'What would we value, art aside? Something greater? I doubt it. In terms of flesh and blood what is there to value that hasn't been, how should I put it? fucked up by one or both of us?'

His look remained calm, almost indifferent: it was, Maddox reflected, as if once again he were the prisoner and Taylor his visitor, their roles, in this case, explicitly reversed: the plastic chair creaked as Taylor readjusted his position. Mimicking Maddox, he had leant his arms on the table, Maddox further reflecting that he was here only to be abused, consoling himself with the thought that in an hour or so he'd be on his way, via Love Lane, its cottages and trees, to the station.

'Do you remember Pemberton hanging out for Courbet?' Taylor went on. 'I thought that odd. A Francophile in the middle of the twentieth century plumping for a realism of a particularly pedantic kind. As well as, in Courbet's case, a very mixed kettle of fish. And Degas. That, to some degree, I understood. As a basis, a basis only, mind, for everything. And Giacometti. The fourth dimension. As if three, for God's sake, were not enough. Pre-dating all that, of course, Piero. Your rebirth of man. Preposterous, when you come to think of it. Innocent, too. *Innocence!* As if we could ever have enough. As if anything or anyone ever was,' he turning in his chair to remark to the figure behind him, 'This is a man you should admire. Believes art is in terminal decline,' returning his look to Maddox to add, 'That fifties return to nature is all right for people without a visual imagination but for people like us, it hardly works. I'm back with Soutine. Trees like cauliflowers, faces like squashed tomatoes. Art up its arsehole. Nowhere to go but everyone to go with. This, by the way, should there be any doubt, is the anti-depressant talking. I'm loaded up to the eyeballs with amitriptyline. You do any art?'

Maddox waited, subdued. 'A life-class,' he finally announced.

'That's interesting.' Taylor waited, too, before adding, 'I always thought that odd, a fellow who never drew or painted teaching in an institution devoted to little else. You'd have thought absence of participation would put you off. I have, by the way, you'll be pleased to hear, been revising my essays. I got the police, of all people, to retrieve them from my house. I burnt most of them some time ago, retaining those on which you'd written some of your asperic comments. Rebecca didn't approve, of course. She'd acquired, by the time I came to know her, an aversion to seeing your writing. Perspicacious, some of your stuff. Took the breath away, foresight, I'd say, your strongest suit. Informed of what is to come around the corner and it comes up behind instead.'

He was leaning back, laughing, a staggered, fractured sound, as if he were finding the visit more of an ordeal than his manner suggested.

Intending to distract him, Maddox said, 'I was at school here. I know it well,' adding, 'Quinians,' glancing at the warder to

384

receive a signal of recognition. 'It has some of the feelings of returning home.'

'Home's the last word I would use for this place,' Taylor said. 'Apologies to John, and that,' adding, 'I'm in a special unit. John is one of the screws. We get on well, though didn't when I arrived. I was fucked up with largactil, which he was instrumental, I might add, in getting changed. An archangel in disguise beneath that uniform, is John. I've sent his name to Downing Street as a suggested recipient of a national award. He doesn't agree with it, but, in my view, he deserves it. As it was, before I came here, I was on my way to a medical unit. The psychiatrist who saw me happened to have a daughter at the Drayburgh. By the time I'd finished extolling the place he put me down as stable.' He tapped his head. 'Cognisance. Awareness. Reality of other people. Van Gogh syndrome not allowed. "Are all geniuses mad?" Ergo, I, who am not a genius, must be relatively sane. Put him on the spot. "I believe you are," he said, meeting my gaze. What are your drawings like, I wonder?'

For a moment, unsure he was being addressed directly, Maddox paused. 'Not good.' He indicated Taylor might laugh. 'I go as much for the company as anything else. Though I was always curious to know what it was like. As you say, odd to be at the Drayburgh and not have any practical experience. I always felt deferential to those who had.'

'Were you deferential?'

The enquiry came with a look of surprise.

'I thought I was.'

'On reflection,' Taylor said, 'you probably were.' He turned to one side. 'Why is he deferential to me? I used to ask. I only come from Norfolk. On one of my finer efforts you wrote, "There is nothing more illuminating I can add," I taking it, initially, as an insult. Until I realised, flatteringly, what you meant. I imagine you've forgotten.'

'I was inclined to write at length on all of them,' Maddox said.

'Viklund was more reticent. Epigrammatic. Keen to come

385

down, I heard, on inaccuracies, not, as you were, on generalisations. Wrong church. Wrong chapel. Wrong date. Interpretations treated with reservation. One of your strong points. Looking *in* not always detrimental to looking at. UnViklund-like, if you don't mind my abusing him.' Turning to the warder, he called, 'Professor Maddox is an art historian, John, his involvement with me an infinitesimal part of his overall vocation. Emeritus Professor, I should call him now. Nevertheless, where I'm concerned, a bona fide credential.'

The warder nodded, unsmiling on this occasion, a resistance to being Taylor's foil hardening his expression.

'John and I have discussions. Who is the best painter? He likes Velázquez. Thought, with that, he'd catch me on the hop, knowing my predilection for the Florentines. I got back with Rembrandt. Self-scrutiny. Van Gogh,' he gestured at the walls, 'was a compromise. Woolworths, and all that. The common man. There are lots of common men in here. How common I scarcely need to describe. And women, too, I suppose, out there. The world, as it is, has become a strange place. Stranger even than when I was out.' He held his head a moment, as if recalling. 'John is not a common man, I should add.'

'I think Peter is trying to impress us, Mr Maddox,' the warder said, speaking for the first time, something other than a formal relationship evident both in his voice and the unfolding of his arms: an urgent desire, perhaps to mediate.

'Circumstances unmade me,' Taylor said. 'John and I are endeavouring to fit the pieces together. With the hope we don't come up with the previous whole. We have to keep it quiet. Otherwise,' he tapped his nose, 'everyone will be at it and we'd have no peace at all.' A tightening of the skin was evident around the eyes: a rash was visible inside the collar of his shirt, one reminiscent of a rash he recalled seeing on Berenice's cheek, a connection between his neighbour and Taylor suddenly apparent.

'I never really got on with Rebecca,' Taylor said.

He was leaning on the table more firmly, looking at Maddox

directly: one cheek had been pulled in as if he were biting the skin inside.

'A difficult woman to deal with,' he added.

'I always found her very open. Full of curiosity. Expansive,' Maddox said.

'Naturally.' Taylor watched him with a smile. 'You would.' A moment later, he added, 'She was very much bound up with her family.'

'She rarely referred to them,' he said.

'Oh, yes.' It was as if he were talking, confidingly, about someone else who, the next moment, was scheduled to enter the room. 'A curious case of self-possession. This East End mystique you get in London, and foreign as hell to someone like me. Though hell, retrospectively speaking, is no longer foreign at all. At first, however,' he pointed a finger at Maddox, 'I was very intrigued. Coming from Norfolk. But alienating, claustrophobic. Oppressive. Particularly after we married. I was telling John before you arrived, though he's pretty bored by most of it now. He's strong on family himself. Four grown-up children, one almost as old as me. I had two. They both took after their mother. As if, in her case, Rebecca's, she couldn't live without her family. Not even when, between us, we had a pretty good one of our own.'

Having examined his expression, Taylor had glanced away. His head, a moment later, he propped on his hand, his look, abstracted, drifting to the wall behind Maddox's head. 'You never found that, not knowing her so well. When all's said and done, carnal knowledge is pretty superficial, wouldn't you say? Talked up, of course. But ambivalence always shows. Wanting to escape the East End, in her case, and "do" the West End. Particularly Cork Street. A cultural invasion, not a voyeuristic one. Yet always drawn back. The atavistic imperative, her family. No longer relevant to me. *That* atavism I got rid of. Even when she didn't want it she couldn't, she discovered, *we* discovered, live without it. Boom. There it was. All the time. Ask John. He knows the sort of thing. With the East End, however, it was something else. Not merely familial but *tribal*. The war.

387

The blitz. Class cohesion. The mixture you always get. Russians. Lithuanians. Greeks. Turks. Bulgars. Poles. Chinese. You get the picture?'

Releasing his hand from his head, he rubbed his nose.

'Can get on your wick if you give it a chance. Her father was a dominant man. So were her sisters. Three, but with all the space they filled they might have been seven. Most of the things I had have disappeared. Some of the paintings I did at the Drayburgh. Not many after. Some of the essays. Despite the fact that women aren't good at painting, the best of them derivative, Rebecca did quite well. Found her own line. All those, her family have removed. I'm trying to get their ownership sorted out. They went in the house and took the lot. Furniture. Pictures. Clothes. Everything to do with me they got rid of. Much of what she knew about painting came from me. Apart from a sentimental attachment to art, as a means to an end, until you and I came along she didn't know a Botticelli from a Bonnard. Between the two of us, I'd say we taught her quite a lot.' He smiled, the provocation, Maddox assumed, complete.

'Was she religious?' he said.

'Not really.'

'She never mentioned church. Or God.'

Taylor laughed, surveying Maddox down the length of his nose.

'Synagogue, for Christ's sake.'

He laughed again.

'Not Christ's sake. Abraham's fucking sake.' He shrugged, spreading out his arms. 'Excuse me, John,' he called over his shoulder. 'Another ten p I owe you,' adding, 'Religions, in my book, are political organisations. Primarily, secondarily, finally. Hence the pogroms, the Inquisition, the Holocaust. Religious sentiment, on the other hand, is an intrinsic affair. Institutional-ised, it acts, thinks, proselytises as any self-interested body – faith, pronouncements, edicts the instruments at its disposal. Fear the primary one. Without that the whole thing would disappear. In that respect I blame her family. They were as blindly addicted to their mythology as Marx, for similar reasons, was to his. Poor Beccie, another piece of ideological meat. In the end, I felt I was married to her sisters. And her brother. They were never out of the house. "Why don't you discourage them?" I'd ask her, and, as swiftly as anything, she'd say, "They *are* my family," as if they had precedence, which, indeed, they had, over the one she and I had created.'

Pausing, he invited Maddox to respond, Maddox, for his part, refocusing his look on Taylor who, as he spoke, appeared to be getting larger all the time, an oppressive, weighty presence which was gradually enveloping the room. The warder, caught between restraint and conciliation, gazed bemusedly at the back of Taylor's head.

' "Look at my family," I'd tell her,' Taylor went on. ' "They don't come round seven days of the week." "That's because they live in Norfolk," she said. "That," I said, "is because I wouldn't want them," she dressing the children like facsimiles of her sisters, even though one of them was a boy. Like you, Professor, I'm against cultural identity. The most boring fucking thing in the world. The parochialisation of human nature. The *trivialisation* of human nature. Subservience of the self in deference to the whole. A partial whole, at that. Fuck the family. There's nothing good come out of it. I'm here, after all, to prove it. Irrefutable. Undeniable. Not to be ignored.'

Maddox, contrary to his previous impression, now found himself listening to Taylor as if from a distance, his former pupil's figure receding before him, his voice, too, transposed, as if he were listening to it from inside his head. He wondered if he should mention Simone, the geriatric day group, anything that might turn the conversation back to something less obsessive. What would Taylor make of that – registering it as an endorsement, no doubt, of his present state of mind? In any case, his own reflections were becoming confused with the atmosphere of the room – even with the expression of the warder, a visitor, so it seemed, to the scene, he listening to Taylor with increasing interest, at one point leaning forward to catch precisely what he said.

'I came to London a virgin. And left it,' Taylor went on, 'as

389

something else. I'm taking steps to reconstitute myself in the light of that. *Eric* Taylor is dead. Completed. An aberration. *Peter* is back to where he started. Returning to the virginity with which he began. John will tell you. He has it all worked out.' He turned to glance at the warder, smiling. 'I've plenty of time. I'm waiting to be unearthed. Like your lectures. Inspiriting at the time. A sense of immanence. The inference of a second chance. You see it, otherwise, all around you. Knowledge without understanding. Knowledge which will kill us in the end.'

Maddox found himself gazing at the warder, as if measuring his own attentiveness in the other man's eyes, sharing, he concluded, an unconcealable element of alarm: at any moment he imagined the man stepping forward and announcing the visit at an end.

'Are Rebecca's family still in touch?' he asked, anxious to return Taylor to something real.

'I have a letter from their lawyer. We are, would you believe it, quarrelling over the money. When the mortgage is paid off there'll be quite a lot, the value of the property having gone up. I never had sufficient money when I lived there and now, assuming they can sell the house, I'll have more than I know what to do with. They, of course, are saying I shouldn't have any. Her sisters, her brother. She died intestate. Something of an irony there. Then again,' he pushed his chair back from the table, 'fuck the money. When I leave this place it'll only be to go to another. If you keep coming back, Professor, I can keep tabs on what's going on. Launch a crusade. Phenomenological art no longer the fashion. Join your brigade. Everything no longer confined to expression.'

Having pushed back his chair from the table, he indicated to the warder his intention to leave.

'Last few minutes, Peter,' the warder said, indicating, in turn, there was time in hand.

'Not a holiday camp.' Taylor took out a handkerchief and blew his nose: his eyes had filled with tears. 'Irrelevance another thing I would like to study. Was it you or Viklund who was keen on Lucretius? Chance! *Nil igitur mors est ad nos.* Epicurean, don't

390

you think? I'll send you my conclusions. Might mark them, if you like. Would appreciate your comments. What is suffering? my principal concern. Similarly, when everything counts and nothing adds up what is the bottom line? Plus, what is the significance of murder in the light of biological determinism? Has it got a future? Why aren't animals brought to account? If you'd make your remarks in red ink I'll be able to identify them more quickly. We might publish the results as question and answer. "A Convict's Reply to Questions Raised by a Novel Consensus". Might make a splash. Not least in that paper you write for. I recall you did Greek and Latin at school. Two languages, after all, in which everything has been expressed. We might do the same for English. Have to make an effort, otherwise,' he paused, half turned from the table, 'nothing gets done. This room, for instance, I wouldn't mind turning over to Angelico. "Illumination from a Dark Interior", I the fuel, John, here, for instance, the wick.'

He was on his feet, moving to the door, waving an arm in dismissal.

'Good of you to come. Not a place, otherwise, to recommend, Having been here to school, you'll understand. Good at last, Professor, to have something else in common. Destiny, you might almost say, has driven us together. Remember me to Viklund,' the warder nodding to Maddox as he followed Taylor out. 'I'll send another warrant,' came floating from the corridor outside.

In the train, watching the familiar landscape pass, his thoughts moved on from Taylor to recollections of Taylor's wife, she evidently the first of a subsequent pattern. Of what? Displacement. Disaffection, an instinctual response to something similarly fractured within himself, his notion of writing about Taylor reduced, not least by the brevity of the visit and the length of the journey, to speculations about himself, the fortuitous connections which were linking up disparate elements of his life, Simone alone an unassimilated feature.

For no reason he could account for, once home he rang not

her, to say he was back, but Isaacson, enquiring if he might see him again.

Having taken some time to be brought to the phone, he announced, 'I've nothing available. The next two weeks are solid. So is the third. I already have far too many people demanding to be seen. Next month might be the best option.'

'How about tomorrow?' he enquired, it now being mid-evening.

'Ten-thirty,' Isaacson responded.

'A.m., or p.m.?'

'Yours to decide.'

'A.m.'

'Come early. There's a chance I'll be out.'

Talking to Simone later in the evening he declined her suggestion he might go up, telling her of his encounter with Taylor, responding to her curiosity as to how it had gone by replying, 'Dementia. Simulated or otherwise, I couldn't decide. Perhaps you'd better go up the next time, I believe he's stringing me along,' adding, 'I'm seeing Isaacson tomorrow.'

'I didn't know.' He sensed her apprehension.

'I've only just decided.'

'To see him what about?'

'I'm not sure until I get there. I'm leaving everything to chance.'

'Will you talk about Norman?'

'If that's okay with you.'

'It is,' she said, uncertain.

'What progress have you made yourself?'

'I've received notification from the Council,' she said. 'They've passed the complaints back to the Preliminary Screener. Good thing or bad, I can't decide. I'm waiting their decision. It's more likely the Proceedings Committee will ask to see me. This according to Symonds.'

'How about the detective?'

'I'm having to hurry him on. He's followed him to two appointments. One to Isaacson. One to someone I've never heard of. He thinks there may be others. He knows a goldmine

392

when he sees one. I'm paying him over the odds, though Symonds recommended him.'

'Who recommended Symonds?'

'Colleagues.'

'Who are they?'

'For God's sake, you're not getting suspicious yourself?'

'I wondered. Norman must have followed me here, at some time. I am, I assume, part of the equation.'

'Don't worry.' She sounded relieved. 'I'll get to the bottom of this or sink. As for Isaacson, watch your back.'

'I'm not at all sure he's as tricky as you make out. He *sounds* tricky, but curiously isn't. I'm sure, if he isn't nuts, which must be a possibility, he's harmless.'

'In the sixties, when I first heard of him,' she said, 'he was known affectionately as Mic Isaacson. Psychiatry without the doctorial manner. A companionable, no-nonsense, down-to-earth, no-pill-required agenda. Then, after his seminal *The Sequencing of Sexual Behaviour*, apes back into fashion, collusional patterning, he was more widely known as Micky Isaacson, something of an intimate, endearing diminutive, anti-psychiatry's principal spokesman. Then, after further consolidation with *Incest and Family Rites*, he became more formally celebrated as M. F. Isaacson. I needn't go on. He's simply known as Isaacson now, a throw-away point of reference. Keep your wits about you if he happens to talk about me. God knows what he and Norman, or Cavendish, are up to.'

'I shouldn't think it's anything other than what we already know, or, at least, suspect,' he said.

'When will I see you?'

He registered the plaintive note in her voice.

'I'll ring you as soon as I've seen him,' he said. 'There is absolutely no reason to worry.'

'Are you going on the tube?' she said.

'I'd intended to,' he said.

'Take care of that, too,' she told him, after a relevant pause.

It was Isaacson himself who opened the door: in shirtsleeves and a pullover plainly too small to accommodate his curiously distorted body, the trousers uneasily suspended below the waist, the shirt protruding in the gap between, a cigarette alight, the smoke of which he waved away with the cigarette-holding hand as he preceded Maddox down the hall, calling over his shoulder, 'Good of you to come,' enquiring, as they reached the door into the front room, 'Do you want tea? We'd better get the order in,' Maddox declining, Isaacson closing the door behind them, indicating the couch, 'Sit,' crossing to the collapsed armchair by the fireplace, sinking down, groaning, between its rug-covered arms.

The familiar springs once again indented Maddox's back and thighs: swivelling in the couch, he faced Isaacson to his left.

'I don't normally see anyone as quickly as this,' Isaacson said. 'It had better be something important. Though what's important?' he added, before Maddox could reply. 'Fuck all, at the moment. How about you?'

'I wondered what your conclusions were after my previous visit,' Maddox said.

He shook his head, looking at him, however, with genuine surprise, his strangely contorted features suddenly enlivened. He gestured to the wall behind Maddox's back.

Turning, he saw that the paintings previously hanging there had been removed: stained wall-covering indicated their irregular positions, hooks still protruding from the plaster.

'The Old Philistinism.' Isaacson waved his cigarette, the smoke spiralling above his head.

'Where have they gone?'

'Burnt.'

'Why?'

'Every time I looked at them they reminded me of you. I've been looking for a reasonable excuse to dispose of them for over forty years. Until you came along I didn't have one. I would say I was waiting for the licence. Good?'

'Good.' A definitive response, he assumed, was what Isaacson was after.

'I've hardly slept a wink since I burnt the fucking things.

Pissed all over me, you did. What punishment have you lined up this time?'

'Is this the reverse therapy that people go on about?' he asked.

'What reverse therapy? And who,' Isaacson enquired, 'goes on about it?'

'My partner,' Maddox said.

'You've mentioned her before. Been called before the NMC by one or more of her clients.'

'Maybe.'

'Heard any more?'

'She has.'

'Is that why you rang?'

'No.' A moment later, he added, 'I went to see Taylor, this one-time student of mine.'

'In good shape?'

'Not really.' He paused, readjusting the springs beneath him. 'He's putting on weight. Talks abstractly. Appears to be retreating into dementia. If not already there. Asks for my support.'

'What's your complaint?'

'I've little to offer.'

'He evidently thinks you have.'

The cloud of smoke thickened above Isaacson's head.

'You don't mind if I smoke?' he added.

'No,' he said.

'Cancer. Plus heart condition. Apart from that.' He waved his hand. 'Nicotine works wonders. It's the delivery by inhalation that causes the problem. Once solved there's no reason we shouldn't live a relatively contented life.'

'He's changed his name to Peter.'

'What was it before?'

'Eric.'

Isaacson glanced at the blank wall behind Maddox's back. 'S'hardly worth the effort. You're not called Peter, by any chance?'

'Matthew.'

'Of course.'

'Identification with the saint,' Maddox suggested.

'Why?'

'Cockerel.'

'I see.'

'Betrayal.'

'Quite.'

'As a prelude, I believe, to killing himself. I rather got the impression he invited me in order to be certain. And to put the warders off their guard. Even suggesting I come again. It was, after all, his original intention.'

'Doesn't mean he can't change his mind.'

'Can't live with the thought of what he's done.'

'Can't live without it, either. How about you? Any similar persuasion?'

'No.' He shook his head.

'But, then, like him, you can't be sure.'

Isaacson stubbed out his cigarette, leaning to the hearth to do so, then, reaching into the recesses of the chair beneath him, produced another, together with a box of matches. 'As your re-named collegiate chum no doubt is finding out. Go down with a smile. If not.' Lighting the cigarette, he threw the match towards the hearth.

'He's been moved to a town where I was at school,' he said.

'Has a resonance,' Isaacson suggested.

'It integrates him more closely with my past. It's that, I suspect, I came to see you about.'

'Not much of an excuse,' Isaacson said, and added, 'Taylor is an effect. The cause, we assume, must lie elsewhere.'

'Where?'

'You tell me. It's my time you're wasting, otherwise,' he said. 'I'm only here to listen.' Having waited for Maddox to respond, he added, 'Did you dislike the paintings as much as you said?'

'Yes.'

'I wondered.'

'Ridding yourself of them gives you the opportunity,' Maddox said, 'to start again.'

'Generous of you to say so.' Hoisting one thigh with both hands, Isaacson laid it across the other, massaging the upper knee, then, more clumsily, the one below it. 'As for *Peter*, we're obliged, in the end, to enquire who gives a fuck? A great deal of time and money, and, in your case, distraction, would be saved if he went ahead with what he intended. I'm not here to save life, as I explained on your previous visit. What do you think? As Daniel, our confrère, might have asked.'

'How well did you know him?'

'Hardly at all. At the time. He and his father were patients of my father, along with several diplomats from the Swedish Embassy. He and my father got on well, not least because of a common interest in pictures. My father had a modest collection. It was because of them, I sometimes think, he refused to leave. Along with my mother. A suspicion on my part. Nevertheless, because Dan could provide me with papers, they insisted I should. False documentation, as it turned out, but it got me to Belgium. From there a prearranged passage to Britain. I'd asked to go to America. I wanted to become an actor.'

He studied Maddox through a thickening cloud of smoke, having spoken, at intervals, with the cigarette in his mouth, other times exhaling, thoughtfully, towards the ceiling.

'What else do you think I ought to tell you? Nothing about contracts. I took all that on board without saying a word.'

'I apologise for that,' Maddox said.

'It's probably why you came. Indentured. To whom? To do what? The source, you might say, of all your problems. Doctors often complain that the commonest characteristic of their patients is a tendency not to reveal the purpose of their visit until they are about to leave. As for contracts, you got all that from Laycock.'

'I probably did.'

'Laycock got it from Donne. "No man is an island". Unless you're a woman.'

His strange, misshapen body was readjusted in the chair.

'The individual, per se, does not exist. What you,' he went on, 'are struggling to confound.'

397

'Mistakenly?' Maddox enquired.

'What do you think?'

'You're probably right.'

'I knew Laycock. He died in 1955. In Battersea. Neglected. The sort of genius the English occasionally throw up. Blake. Bunyan. Angels seen in trees. Something so obvious it scarcely needs remarking.

'He influenced you,' Maddox suggested.

'He gave a lecture at the UCL Medical School. Elderly. Inconspicuous. Talked of his encounters with Freud, Jung and Adler. Was the first to point out they worked in threes, consistent with early mythology. Three Graces. Three Sisters. Three Brothers. Three Wise Men. Id, ego, superego. Premiss, antithesis, synthesis. Father, Son and Holy Ghost, three a mystical number. "The Fallacy of the Trinity", his catchy title. Disassembled what was then the whole of psychoanalysis. He'd been doing it for years, no one taking any notice. Couldn't answer some of the questions because of his hearing. Used it, I thought, to avoid the meretricious. As for "corporate presence" and the jargon he invented, long before his time, "we are our relationships" the theme tune of the fifties. As it is,' he blew out a cloud of smoke, 'it was a method of perceiving, whereas invariably he was criticised for it being the perceived itself. I found it useful when I came to write on incest, still the most unmentioned, if not unmentionable element of everyday family life, nuclear or otherwise, maritally sanctioned or not. Fucking,' he continued, 'is a serious *effect*. From it,' he concluded, 'everything else flows.'

'Did you see him again?' Maddox asked.

'I ran what was called "The Lecture Society" amongst the students. Invited him back for another. He declined. Said he was too old to do it more than once. "I've given you a pointer," he said. "It's up to you to see where it goes." But he invited me to visit him. He lived in an apartment block with a wife who was blind. In Battersea. They used to communicate by ringing bells, he ringing one to indicate where he was, she likewise. He played a game with her while I was there, ringing the bell then moving

398

to another room, she ringing hers, following him, evidently familiar with the humour, it ending with an embrace. Quite squalid, the set-up. Not unlike here. My wife has a dislike of housework. The woman who comes in leaves us in a worse state than when she arrived. Feel obliged to use her. Lone parent. Five children. "Why so many, when the fathers leave you every time?" I ask her. "I like the feeling," she said, "of being fucked." '

He waited for Maddox to respond, inhaled, then exhaled, adding, 'Laycock's relevance will eventually be recognised, of course. He delineated the line between what he described as the intrinsic and the extrinsic self, delineated, that is, in order to destroy, no such line, contra almost everyone in his time, existing. A post-Cartesian romance. Most psychiatrists, for instance, have never heard of him. Many, if not most, use his techniques without their being aware of it. His discoveries, if they could be described as such, certainly his insights, have been integrated, if misunderstood, without most practitioners who deploy them being aware of their source. A mythical man, you might describe him.'

He waved his cigarette in Maddox's direction, a linear pattern of smoke rising above his curiously featured head. 'Meet another who likewise has disappeared into the woodwork. Patients still arrive, their problem invariably the same, a suspicion, amounting to a conviction, they don't exist. Evidence of what, at one time, was referred to as 'the Laycock phenomenon'. Corporate man, and woman, incorporated to the point where they've disappeared. When I assure them, à la Laycock, that this is a reasonable assumption, the tide, to some degree, is turned. Of course, once inducted into the system, since many of them happen to be executives, they have an unfair advantage over their colleagues and subordinates. In no time at all more of the same are knocking at the door. The individual, as you've discovered in your case, doesn't exist, a Cartesian fallacy, he or she a rumour put about by someone else, invariably similarly afflicted parents assuming, inductively, that the shape of a nose or a face, or that a language, or even a

399

race, should make a difference. Laycock, if we'd only known it, put a positive stop to that. Maybe, for instance, your former student is right. He didn't commit his murders, per se, but his constituency did it for him. Or, as Laycock would have it, *as* him.'

The unevenly angled teeth were exposed in what Maddox assumed to be an ingratiating smile. The cigarette, little more than half smoked, was stubbed out in the hearth: an accumulation of stubbed-out remains was visible amongst the books and papers scattered there.

'Laycock's greatest problem was pain. Who feels it? Us or I? Cellular differentiation never quite worked. Particularly if you had toothache, or were lined up to be shot. Even then, he transposed perception at what he called the unicellular level into something which, at extremes, could be registered as what he termed universal fusion. Hence his singling out of Christ, an anti-Semitic response from which he and his reputation never quite recovered. "We are all Nazis". Nevertheless his conception of Christ as "collusional disfavour" was, for me, the most convincing of his studies. Similarly, Taylor's response to what, no doubt, he no longer perceives to be himself. As for Laycock, the poor bugger died with his recognition registering zero. If not minus. Not only ignored but buried. I used to see his widow. She asked me to speak at his funeral. He believed in a God, but not one, as he described it, that anyone would wish to put about. In addition, she saw anti-psychiatry as a travesty of what he represented, and reproached me for being involved. I said, "We only disagree on form, not content." That she wouldn't buy. Nevertheless, I spoke at *her* funeral, the only medical person present. Laycock, you see, I couldn't match. For one thing, I'm too lazy. For another, unlike him, I hate being ignored.'

His laughter was answered by a banging at the door, to which, still laughing, he called out, 'Come,' raising his thigh with two hands and setting both slippered feet on the floor.

'Are you finished?' The door remained shut, the voice evidently that of his wife.

400

'Not for a long time. Why don't you listen to the radio?' he responded.

Silence he registered by raising his hand. 'She doesn't want to,' he added. 'What was it you wanted to ask?'

'Who was the patient who followed me in last time?'

'I've no idea.' His laughter having subsided, he examined Maddox with a frown. 'Why?'

'You said his name was Cavendish.'

He felt in the chair beside him, producing the now crumpled packet of cigarettes. 'I can't persuade you to try one?' he asked. 'Prove at least I've done something,' extracting a cigarette as Maddox shook his head, feeling down, once more, for the matches, adding, 'I like matches. Something visceral, is it, in striking up a flame?' doing so as he spoke.

The expended match he threw in the hearth.

'My partner has him as a client,' he said.

'Fuck me.' He examined Maddox through an extending cloud of smoke. 'A serial analysand. I've had them before.'

'A serial complainant,' Maddox said, 'as likely. He might not approve of what he sees in here.'

'He shows no sign of it,' Isaacson said. 'He brought me a bottle of wine the other day. Cigarettes on several previous occasions.'

'Do you smoke when he's here?'

'With his permission.'

'How about cavalier views, and swearing?'

'I don't think I'm responsible for either,' Isaacson said, suddenly severe.

'He's the one who's reported her to the Medical Council.'

'No expletive, you notice.'

'Under a different name.'

'I see. Or, rather,' he said, 'I don't. What would Laycock have made of that? He, too, you know, was taken off the Register. Prescribing drugs in inordinate amounts, some for his wife, often taking them himself. Relatively common, in those days, but frowned upon, rather, since. "If Sigmund got away

401

with it," he complained, "why not I?" Like royalty, in that respect. Never underestimated his own potential.'

He leant back in his chair, the springs creaking, the wooden structure groaning. 'Look here,' he continued, 'I haven't billed your brother, as he requested. Nor you. Mark this one down to a friend of the family. Viklund, and all that. Anything else I can help with? In the sixties I was much criticised for the number of suicides amongst my patients. Frequently I took on cases no one else would touch. I only take stable people at present, stability measured by executive status, or the wife of – quite a lot of those. Self-destruction as a way of life not as a terminal event very much my present line. I don't want someone like you on my hands. Think of the tabloid reaction. Patient of Isaacson dead again. At one time I appeared more frequently at coroners' courts than I did at psychiatric clinics. I was even tempted to buy a house close to the one at St Pancras in order to save on travelling. I've had my dose of what, once, was referred to as the Roman way. Romantic is far more like it. As for Cavendish. Is he citing you in his complaint?'

'Yes.'

'Did he recognise you when you saw him?'

'Yes.'

'You'll look an arsehole appearing for two psychiatrists. "One I fuck, the other I talk to." Can see it all over the national press. You'll be able to sell serialisation, if Cavendish hasn't beaten you to it.'

He coughed: phlegm rattled in his chest; moments later a laugh emerged, a ruminative sound, harsh, derisive.

'What are his motives?'

'You tell me. I only know him to talk to.' He waved his cigarette, smoke moving in a band around his head. 'Some collect stamps. Others, Cavendish, for instance, defamations. I can see the temptation. Rich area to move in. Keeps you busy. Can talk about yourself, a different one each time. Daytime study up symptoms. A lot to choose from. Night-time write up complaints. Background study on Medical Council procedures. Post-traumatic shock is popular at present. Though, in my

experience, is being overtaken by non-traumatic inertia. Accidie, so-called, at one time. Cachexia, by others, anoesis the one
I prefer, consciousness without awareness. An awful lot around.
Pollution, the media, additives, too many people, asteroids,
terrorism.' He waved his hand.

'Would you like my partner to get in touch with you?'

'Sure.'

'She's hired a detective.'

'Good.' Incredulity displaced by amusement.

'Cavendish has at least one other analyst he goes to.'

Some other grievance caused Isaacson to look away: he
hoisted himself up in his chair, grimacing, the structure creaking
once more beneath him.

'Not Jewish?'

'I've no idea.'

'Enlightenment, even where defamation is concerned,
ensures today a broader target. Has anything happened to your
partner?'

'Her lawyer suggests she'll be called before the Preliminary
Proceedings Committee.'

'Anything else?'

'Cavendish calls himself Norman.'

'His given name with me.'

'His surname with her.'

'Any other disasters I might facilitate?' He was hauling
himself forward, stooping, bending, pressing upwards, groaning
with the effort, waving Maddox away, however, as he rose to
help. 'I'm part of the post-pre-post-pre-Raphaelite-post-philis-
tine revival,' crossing to the cupboard behind the door, swinging
round from that, saying, 'She's been in here before me,' turning
to his desk, opening a drawer, taking out a bottle, then a glass,
searching the books and papers on his desk, finally extracting a
cup and saucer, pouring the contents of the former into the
latter, his eyes narrowed against the smoke of the cigarette
which now hung in the corner of his mouth. 'Cognac. All she's
left. Provided by our friend. Another gift. Be registered, I
imagine, as a bribe. Or poisoned. A drunk as well as a

403

psychiatrist. Do you think he sports a hidden camera? How about it?' handing Maddox the glass into which he poured a measure, pouring rather more into the cup, raising it and declaring, 'To Laycock. And his successors. That's both of us. Good health!'

18

'I WAS wondering,' Viklund said, 'how you got on,' Maddox moving the phone to his other ear.

'I should have called you earlier. I'll come over,' Maddox said, setting off a few minutes later: freedom and senility: no accountability to anything: tidy up, adjust, correct: peace that passeth credibility no more in question – Viklund coming to the door when he rang the bell: dark suit, white shirt, his (incongruous) club tie, the pink and grey echoed in the colours of the handkerchief hanging from his breast pocket.

His manner and appearance were improved from when Maddox had last seen him, he thrusting out his hand, shaking Maddox's firmly, with scarcely a tremble, the idiosyncratic grasp that Viklund used on these occasions, gripping the thumb in a gesture suggesting intimacy as well as circumspection, affording him the opportunity either to draw the other person to him or hold them off.

Unlike his previous visit, Ilse came up directly from the kitchen. 'We've guests, this evening. The cook,' Viklund said, indicating her as she appeared in an apron, 'is preparing the roast.'

'Roast, nonsense,' Ilse said, embracing Maddox. 'And I'm not,' she added, 'the cook. I'm supervising.'

The sound of the girl's singing came from below.

'Everything all right, Matt?' she enquired, a concern echoing back over several decades, he, in some respects, an ambivalently cherished surrogate son. 'I was hoping to have finished before

405

you arrived. I'll get you tea or coffee. Which do you prefer? Ignore anything Daniel has to suggest.'

'Oh, we know Matt well enough. Tea,' Viklund said, a lightness in his manner which had not been there, Maddox suspected, before his arrival. 'I'll have tea as well.'

'And how is Simone?' he added, after Ilse had gone, his eyes, unlike his manner, lightless, Maddox's intention to keep his friend distracted, one urged on him by Viklund himself.

'Coping,' he said, and added, 'She relishes a challenge. It brings her into focus in an alarming way,' continuing a moment later, 'Though not exactly true. It undermines her. She's coming and going the whole of the time, like a light switching on and off for no apparent reason. Though in this case, of course,' he paused again, 'there's reason enough,' struck by the conflicting nature of what he was saying as well as by the realisation that much of it had been prompted by Viklund himself, the strengthening conviction of the need to distract him.

'You'll have to bring her,' Viklund said. 'No more excuses. There may not be many opportunities left. I'd like to meet her. See in whose hands you are at present. Ilse is determined to keep me busy. Disinclined to let me think. Reflect. An ambition I share. I'm more than half convinced she is in fact *aware*,' coming to the point abruptly, 'And how are you?'

'Improving.' He waited for Viklund to sit before he sat himself. 'To the extent I've decided to give up the day-hospital. I find it too predictable. It drains me, rather than reassures. I make them uncomfortable. I make myself uncomfortable. I'm too impatient. As for Simone, the process is underway. She's hired a lawyer and a detective. Her principal accuser may turn out to be a fake. A serial analysand if not serial complainant.' Pausing to examine Viklund's look, he finally enquired, 'And you?'

'I alternate between good and bad days,' Viklund said, 'not surprisingly,' sitting, legs crossed, arms propped on those of the chair, his hands clenched, tensely, beneath his chin. 'Today not good. I feel much brighter, however, seeing you. You mustn't mind Ilse appreciating these visits. She sees me with a long face

406

far too often. I endeavour to distract her, as she does me. But, the fact of the matter is, I'm frightened. A difficult thing to describe. Particularly since fear, curiously, has played no part in my life at all. Not of dying, but of the curtailment of the senses. Tell me how your former student is.'

Unsure which of Viklund's entreaties he should respond to, he said, 'I went to see him in the town, as it turned out, where I used to be at school. School-life and prison-life curiously blended, Taylor a product not of the relatively recent but the distant past. Other than geographically, however, they have nothing in common.'

'Other than being insititutions.'

'Other than being embodiments, to my mind, of the industry around. The collieries, for instance, have gone, several of the mills, plus the warehouses by the river. What they appear to have thrown up is Taylor. Residue or product, I've yet to find out.'

Viklund, sitting at an angle to him, by the fireplace, in his usual chair, had turned towards him: his eyes had narrowed, his lips tightened, as if he were preparing to smile but not succeeding.

'I've decided not to write about him,' he added.

'Why?'

'I don't know him. Even less, what he's become. Chasing history, so to speak, no longer seems worthwhile.'

'What will you chase instead?'

'Whatever it is,' he said, 'that's chasing me.'

'Perhaps,' Viklund said, 'I should start you off.'

'With what?'

'Your nihilism. Your millenarianism. Philistinism writ large. Taylor, in your scenario, the final throw. Conceptualism no other place to go.'

Now he was smiling, reminding Maddox, curiously, of Isaacson. The door had opened: the girl came in with a tray: without a glance at either of them she poured the tea, indicating the milk, a plate of biscuits and, finally, with a smile at Maddox, was gone.

407

'You have no alternative.' Viklund's smile had broadened. 'Your *dernier cri*. Unstoppable. Much better than a tube train line.'

'Surely,' he said, 'there's a choice,' crossing to the tray, taking up a cup in its saucer, declining Viklund's invitation to take a biscuit, pouring the milk, returning to his chair. 'How well did you know Isaacson?' he added.

'Michael?' Viklund was surprised, perhaps shocked, certainly distracted. 'In the recent past,' he added, 'scarcely at all. I thought he'd retired.'

'My brother arranged for me to see him. He thought it might do some good. I've seen him twice.'

'Did he mention me?'

'He did.'

'I liked him very much.'

He waited for Maddox's reaction.

'He, too, is visited by the man who has complained to the Council about Simone.'

'Michael's been threatened with being struck off more times than I can count,' Viklund said. 'I appeared at one of his hearings – I even provided him with a lawyer who succeeded in getting him off. Did you find him any good?'

'I did,' he said. 'But don't know why.'

'He was sectioned once, and allowed, for no reason I can understand, to go on teaching. Forty years ago he was perhaps the best-known psychiatrist in the country. He went in for what was referred to contemptuously as reverse therapy. The patient did the questioning, he providing the answers. A disingenuous way of getting the patient to unbend. He belonged to what became known as the anti-psychiatry alliance, a curious band of psychiatrists who disclaimed belonging to anything. Following in the wake of Laycock's theories of indifferentiation whereby we are all expressions of processes indifferent to ourselves in a universe where the self, as a recognisable entity, does not exist. Unicellular cohesion, another of his dictums. He had a maverick influence on younger psychiatrists, most of whom were recoiling from, and endeavouring to rationalise "The Process", as it was called. Laycock was a leading influence. Mickey, as he was then affectionately known, acquired a similar reputation. His study of incest I took to be a search for his own lost family. Presumptuous.' He smiled. 'There was also the number of his patients who committed suicide. I guess your brother wasn't aware of that.'

' "The Process" was what?' Maddox enquired.

'You'll have to ask him. More of a label than anything else. Individuation a Cartesian myth. We live under the illusion of individuality. In effect, corporately, we are the one thing. Laycock, its proposer, was taken for a fascist. Though brain biology, as I understand it, appears to be proving him right. Something, culturally, of an endorsement of your views on what you at one time referred to contemptuously as "Cartesian art". The dying phase of which, in conceptualism, we are seeing now.'

Maddox, for a while, didn't respond, watching Viklund, whose smile, while speaking, had scarcely faded.

'You got him out of Berlin,' he finally said, adding, 'Isaacson.'

'My father did. His parents, foolishly, refused to leave. They were under surveillance and thought they wouldn't make it. With Michael, their youngest child, they thought there'd be a chance. Not least by their appearing to be going about their normal business. His father was, amongst other things, a doctor at the embassy. They tried later, however, and didn't succeed. I was merely a go-between. My father, by that time, had been moved to Rome.'

Viklund held his chest: his smile had faded, his breathing suddenly heavy, his cheeks unnaturally shadowed, almost yellow in the afternoon light.

'There's something I've written,' he added, 'which I'd like you to take. It may start you off. If not in the direction you intended. Who knows? You may come back to it. See what you think.'

He indicated a foolscap envelope lying on the table beside the tea-tray and his chair. 'Two items, not unconnected. Something you might bite on. It may even change your mind on Taylor.

409

Each time we look to the past we inevitably rewrite it. *A Second View*, I thought you might call it. Or, what was that title you once suggested? *As it happened.*'

'Lower case.'

'A half attempt at something. Even if, at one time, you thought it was the whole.'

'Did you know Laycock?' Maddox asked, suspecting this was where Viklund might be leading.

'In there.' He gestured at the envelope. 'I went to him as a patient. He, too, was recommended. By Michael. I don't suppose he mentioned that.'

Maddox shook his head.

'Discreet, surprisingly, in some things. Not, unsurprisingly, in others.'

'How did you find Laycock?'

'He was living in Battersea. Neglected. Short of funds. In a rundown apartment, looked after by his wife who was blind. They communicated, much of the time, with bells. More of a game they'd invented, with an elemental edge. The sound of a bell used frequently has something of a ritual about it. It was shortly after the war. My father had been posted to London. I'd decided already to make it my home. It was one reason why he came. He thought I was disturbed. It was at his suggestion I got in touch with Michael. His family name was Froy, Isaacson his mother's family name, and that of the relative he came to stay with in England. Similarly Michael. His given name was Avram.' He paused. 'That's how I got to Laycock.'

Maddox was silent: the sound of the girl singing somewhere below them, in the kitchen, came faintly to the room.

'To what purpose?' he finally enquired.

'To get what had happened into perspective. One I was lacking at the time. In reality it was a question of faith. Art, as I'd come to see it, particularly the period in which, by that time, I'd absorbed myself, had been ravished by religion. I really went to Laycock to ask about God. In the process about myself. I wish I had him now to refer to. I wonder what he would have made of this? At that time, because of our neutrality, I'd rather

410

viewed the war as a spectator event. Spectatorship, so-called, particularly of an event of that kind, unprecedented, making up its horrendous rules as it went along, carpet-bombing, fire-bombing, the nuclear bomb, the camps, detachment and involvement a schizoid process. I rather used Florentine painting to recover my faith. I rather used Laycock to discover what that faith was about. Until the war started, for instance, I'd not focused on anything. Pleasure apart. My parents bought pictures. Something they had in common with Michael's parents. Sold long ago. I've never been one for possessions, unlike Ilse, who regards them as indivisible from something she calls "home". I've never wanted to belong. Or anything, for that matter, to belong to me. Like children. Even the dog, as you see, I often resist.'

He shrugged. 'I became acquainted, because of my parents, with a lot of artists. And writers. Particularly writers. I also saw a lot of disagreeable and singularly unforgettable sights. Rather like your experience on the tube station platform. Something that, seemingly, came from elsewhere but, in reality, from within oneself. What you might call, in your case, Taylor's nightmare. As it was,' he waved his hand, in a characteristic gesture, 'a revised view, not only of myself but of everyone, I thought was called for. Michael, who at that point was still at medical school, and with whom I'd renewed contact, recom- mended Laycock, who he'd got to know while a student. I found him impressive. Unperturbed. Something of a prophet with an other-worldly voice. That of someone who had witnessed more than might reasonably be accounted for. Been to the summit of the mountain and come back to report. In his own peculiar way, as I withdrew, or so it seemed, from life, aghast, no longer able to make an excuse for it, or offer even the most spurious recommendation, he turned me round and pointed me back. Despite the neglect he'd suffered, he saw life not as a challenge or a gift, not in any moral terms at all, "rather like God, in that respect", he told me, but, blankly, as the only thing there is. "That gives it," he said, "its definition. You never know what it might come up with. In addition to which," he drew his hand

411

across his throat, "you can end it any time you wish. Another admirable property." He had an extremely unfashionable and, at the time, much criticised view of human nature, and this, for my money, and at that time, seemed to run directly counter to it. Of course, it was nothing of the sort. He was offering nostrums to a very young and extremely privileged fellow who had been dismayed to discover that, until then, despite appearances to the contrary, he had been living on the edge of things. It was, I realised afterwards, the providence of suicide that finally persuaded me. That, and his refusal to see existence as anything other than an indivisible whole. All those things from which we instinctively recoil. A curiously religious ethic. "Disassociate at your peril", another of his dictums, after which he would enquire, "What do you associate with 'peril'?" I liked him. I saw him for a year. In the end we chatted, like you and Michael, as if I'd dropped by for tea. Which, in most respects, I had. He needed the money. I needed reassurance. Humanity, as I then saw it, not merely possessed but was the instrument of its own destruction, the process already in place. But for him, I'd never have ended up at the Courtauld. Or the Drayburgh. Or the College. You and I would never have met, nor, let's face it, experienced much of what we have. Your brother, by the way, rang me since we last spoke.'

He waited for Maddox's surprise to express itself, more with a raising of his arm than any other gesture.

'He wanted my view on how you were. I told him, confidently, much improved.'

'Did he make any comment himself?'

Maddox, once more, was examining the room: the Matthew Smith above the fireplace: a misplaced enthusiasm for, if not a northerly misconception of – what? a Mediterranean exuberance, mentally putting it and his brother together, as if Paul had, at that moment, entered the door.

'He said you gave him the impression of someone reading a book on a train who, absorbed for a very long time – a lifetime, in fact – looks up to be confused by what he sees. Where is he? Where is he going? For what purpose? He thinks of you as a

412

"confounded man", meaning, I assume, not of this world, or, if you are, not in agreement with it. "He's accepted nothing," he said, hoping, as a last resort, that Isaacson might set you right.'

'I don't agree with the diagnosis,' Maddox said. 'But he probably has.'

'In what way?'

'Irrelevance,' he said. 'Something to that effect. Disengagement. Charm of his sort leads to connection. Galvanised by example, rather than dictum or direction. Probably the same went for Laycock and you.'

'Probably,' Viklund said. 'Hard to gauge how much influence these encounters have. Ineffective, seemingly, at first. Then something shows on the surface, perceptions and receptivity change, to the point where you suspect magic has intervened. Your magic. Something struggled for and achieved oneself. It has all the appearance of being yours. As for Taylor, I should stay plugged in. Apart from a residual curiosity, you never know where it might lead. As with Laycock, "face the front".'

He had begun to tire: his tea remained untouched, his head laid back against the chair. Finally, his eyes had closed. 'Maybe I should rest,' he said. 'I've talked too long. Let's meet again. Take the essays. Which is what they are,' gesturing at the manila envelope. 'Tell me what you think. I won't get up. Give me your hand,' Maddox standing over him, his thumb seized in that curious grasp, the eyes briefly opening. 'Nothing unusual,' he added. 'I often drop off like this,' Ilse, whom Maddox called out to from the hall, coming up once more from the kitchen to see him to the door. 'Come soon,' she said, embracing him. 'There's so much, Dan thinks, for you to do,' gesturing at the envelope as if she knew its contents.

It was, he reflected, walking away, not unlike his last encounter with his father, even the same question rising spontaneously to his mind, 'What shall I do now?' – the delight which had greeted him on his arrival, the climactic, or so it had seemed, animation, followed abruptly by tiredness and a desire he should leave. He wondered if it would be the same for his children: the unLaycockian sensation of the solitariness, amounting to the abandonment, of each existence, the suggestion that union is illusory, that, as in birth, 'everything separates, distinction is all', a phrase, he recalled, Taylor, much given to statement as well as insight, had underlined in one of his essays and which he had queried at the time. Perhaps, after all, he knows more than I do – more, even, than I ever will know, arriving home to find the envelope a distraction, his thoughts refocused, again to the north.

Sitting in the kitchen, opening the envelope with a knife, he discovered two files of paper, separately secured, reading the introductory paragraphs to each to realise both were sequential accounts of Viklund's early career, not least his years in Berlin, Rome and Paris before and during the Second World War: Camus, Mrs Picabia, Guttuso, Sartre, Malraux, Breton, the encounters alternating with descriptions of journeys to Lisbon, Stockholm, one to London (his first: a piano recital, Myra Hess, at the National Gallery), the mention of packages carried but not the contents – he ringing Viklund to leave a message with Ilse expressing his appreciation, Viklund himself, however, coming on the line.

'I'm awake. Sorry to have dropped off. No reflection on you. I rather wish I'd extended them. They were written at the time I saw Laycock. He, by the way, very much a League of Nations man. The first to suggest, in the thirties, when he saw the way things – inevitably, in his view – were going, that Jerusalem, for instance, should be declared a Universal City. Very much a confirmation of his "indifferentiation", as I understood it. Didn't get far, as we've seen, but you'll get a *disciple*'s feeling for the unity of art and social progress, the latest, if perverse expression of which, I take it, from what you've said, is Taylor. Start off in hope, with Laycock and Viklund – Isaacson, too, if you wish – and end up with your portent of what's to come.'

'I take the hint,' he said, 'but I'm not sure, not having read it, I recognise the agenda.'

'Pragmatism in lieu of ideology. See, when you fit the pieces together, and end up with Taylor, what a faithless enterprise it has become.'

414

'An evangelical mission, after all,' Maddox said, suddenly subdued. 'I'm beginning to lose faith in faithlessness and, partly because of Taylor, more certainly because of Simone, I'm registering something different. Conversion, perhaps,' he added.

'Not to anything prescribed. Find your own *as it happened.* See what I was like as a youth. Measure it with what you feel at present. The train arrives at the station, the preoccupied reader looks up. Immediately come to mind the primary questions.'

Viklund's voice, reanimated, just as quickly faded.

'That's all,' he said, 'I have to say. Can't stick my chin out *too* far, particularly in your direction.'

They were the last words he heard from Viklund: a phone call later that evening from Ilse told him that his friend had been taken into intensive care, at University College Hospital – ironically, where Isaacson had undergone his medical training – and that he was too ill to be visited. 'He collapsed,' she said, 'as he watched the six o'clock news. I think, though he insists on watching it, it gets him down. "I've always been one for a *certain kind* of realism," he says, whenever I complain. What does that mean? Is there a certain kind? I've always believed there was only one.'

'If unknowable,' Maddox said.

'I wouldn't say that,' she said. 'I'm surprised you should come to that conclusion. Someone with your sensibility, Matt. As you're aware, he sees you very much as his successor. He's always hoped, particularly in the later years, when his mind has wandered, you'll be kind to him. He's taken up many of *his* father's attitudes which, throughout his life, have meant so much to him. "Neutrality is mine," he sometimes complains, "by second nature. Even God is neutral in my pantheistic heaven. I rather regret that he isn't." ' She added, swiftly, 'I'm not sure what that means, either. The man I've been married to all these years has remained a mystery to me from the start. And now, I suppose, I shall never know. Other than he was a mystery. "He *divested* himself," he once said, "*in art.*" '

The following morning, lying beside Simone, turning on the radio by the bed, he heard the announcement of Viklund's death, a testament to his national and international reputation. 'Celebrity at last,' he said to Simone. 'I wonder if he used his pill,' the rest of the day, having returned home, taken up with answering the telephone – a piece, dictated, for Devonshire's arts pages ('So you need me, after all. Do you think I'm up to this?'), requests from other papers, a radio and a television interview, the former done over the telephone, the latter in the street (Berenice and Isaiah incredulous at their window), he finally leaving the house, having spoken at length to Ilse, and returning to Simone's. 'No one knows I'm here,' reaching her in the evening, crawling into her bed, pulling the covers over him, dismayed by his reaction. 'Somehow Viklund, Taylor, Isaacson, Laycock, you and I, are all bound up in this together. But I'm not sure why,' his thoughts moving on, once more, to his walking around his father's bier, his curious, unheralded lamentation, 'What shall I do now?'

Yet again, aircraft were lumbering noisily overhead, the guttural, crackling roar of their engines, Simone, the next morning, after he had spoken to Ilse again, bringing up a letter to where he sat on the roof, standing by him as he read it, a summons for her to appear at a yet-to-be-decided date before the Preliminary Proceedings Committee of the Medical Council.

'I've rung Symonds,' she said. 'He's convinced the charges will be dismissed. At the worst I'll get off with a warning. Evidently Norman has gone to a newspaper with the story.'

He was gazing up at her, perplexed by her composure. Smilingly, she added, 'At the worst, we can serve an injunction. Norman's evidently approached them with similar claims before. It appears to be a pastime. What a sinister fellow he is. Is the world made up of people like that?'

'What a curious question for someone like you to ask. You should be telling me,' he added.

The bell had rung in the house below.

'I'll have to go,' she said, retaking the letter. 'Are you staying? We can talk in an hour, if you're prepared to wait.'

'I'll stay,' he said. 'I'll ring Ilse again. She's not inclined to be visited, but at some point I'll have to go down.'

Yet he remained on the roof, watching the aircraft, the birds, swooping between the eaves, the flowers, the insects, getting up at one point to ease his back, his legs, his neck, yawning, stretching, his thoughts moving on from Ilse to Viklund, to his father, his mother, to his devastation by a force which only now was he beginning to understand, and, finally, restoratively, to Simone: the way she had chosen to ring Symonds before showing him the letter, her restraint in keeping him abreast of what was going on, not only her need but her ability to stand alone – another unLaycockian gesture to match a similar impulse of his own.

Viklund dead, his mother, his father, Taylor's wife and children – sometime soon, presumably, Taylor himself: hadn't he been signalling that before he left: or would there be further trips to that northern town? And Viklund: hadn't he offered him an identical engagement, the line between a life worth living and a life worth not, Laycock, Isaacson, an evolving pattern, one which he would have the privilege to complete, a tenuous juxtaposition of meaning with meaning – surprised, at that instant, to see the cat start up by his feet where evidently it had lain (he'd almost trodden on it), he reaching down to lift it, placing it in his lap, sitting there, stroking it – an unusual custom for him – aware, once more, of the flowers, their movement in the breeze, the incongruity of their appearance amongst the roofs, the oddity, too, of his own situation: the chimney-stacks, the aerials, the insects, the birds – the aircraft, forming and re-forming, amidst vapour, above his head, a confirmation of something which, elusively, refused to be identified.

When Simone reappeared, bringing with her, in one hand, a cup of tea for him, in the other a cup of coffee for herself, he was under the impression she had left him only a moment before, looking up, startled, the cat jumping down. 'Been here all the while?' she said, sitting in the chair on the opposite side of the table. 'Did you ring Mrs Viklund?'

'I didn't,' he said. 'But I will again soon,' wondering why he had postponed it. 'Already she's talking of a memorial service. Or others are. I'll probably have to arrange it.'

417

'The newspaper, meanwhile,' she said, 'has rung. You I couldn't deny. The rest I dismissed. Symonds says I should have said nothing. There we are. I don't seem to mind. I feel peculiarly free of everything,' taking the cat as it leapt on her lap, looking over at Maddox with a smile, almost a radiance, the warmth of which, he was aware, enveloped him entirely.

'Is there anything more I can do to help?' he said. 'Other than the damage I've done already?'

'Of course!' She laughed, her exclamation disturbing the cat: it dropped from her lap and, after some hesitation, made for the roof door and disappeared inside. 'Without you, well,' she waved her hand. 'The whole thing would be impossible!'

'It's as if,' he said, 'we're thin-ice skaters, the cracks catching up with us all the while, the whole thing about to break up around us,' he surprised by the conclusion he had come to, looking across at her to deny it.

'Of course!' she said again. 'Don't you think that's fine? Don't you think,' she added, 'that's precisely what we should be doing? Don't we want to be exceptional? Daring! Innovative! Not knowing, for an instant, what might come next? What's your life been about, for God's sake? What's all this, Matt, been *for*?' laughing, gazing across at him, a part of her, he could see, on her own as well as his behalf, triumphant.

'I wouldn't nail us out,' he said, 'as nakedly as that.' 'What do I do now?' had been a question that had tormented him since his father died: now, for the first time, he felt it answered, asked and answered, she in her life, he in his, the force that had gripped him on the tube station platform, Peter's denial.

He was gazing at the sky, aware of the relevance of its bird and insect and aircraft activity: nothing changed, yet everything had: the paradox they would live with, separately and together, 'What do I do now? no longer a question,' surprised to discover he had spoken aloud, she, on this occasion, not answering.

19

THEY WERE drawing the Albanian refugee, the Kosovan mother: she had put on weight, the rotundity of her body more pronounced, a feeling of fecundity, of richness, he wondering what the women in the room made of it, how much they identified with her sensuality, the unconscious movement of her hips, her thighs as, abstractedly, she eased her position, he watching her as intently as he watched the other mysteries in the room – Rachel, Mary, Hannah, Ruth – speculating on their origins, then his own, speculating on the model's origin and his own, disavowing its relevance.

Here they were, in this room, intent on delineation; that, he concluded, as far as it went, no further recognition required: Masaccio's tormented Edenic figures, joined in rejection, joined in awareness, joined in departure, joined in love.

He had been engaged – still was – in giving an account of himself (as graphic as the figure before him now): at the present, in this location, partially there (much yet to be discovered, recovered, examined, laid bare), Simone engaged on an identical venture, stripped of illusion: the peculiar markers they had each laid down, the possibility of professional disgrace in her case, of something as specific, the result of a blood test, in his, the image of Isaacson coming to him: Taylor's pronouncement, murder the signature at the foot of every page – his pencil returning to the sheet of paper, his gaze moving on from its engagement with the model to Rachel . . . And Viklund, whose coffin he had seen glide behind the curtain at the crematorium

419

the previous day, he taking Ilse's arm as they left, the child they'd never had, but now the one appointed.

She hadn't been to St Albans before: they drove there one afternoon in her car, parking by the Cathedral, going in (alcoholics assembled around the gate): the impression of an ark inverted (two of everything notably not inside: two of them, instead, alone): the colour of the fabric, the height of the windows, the sepulchral light: outside, the greenery of the Abbey's former site, the place of Alban's execution – the echo of a belief which, for his part, he assumed he had outlived. Sainthood, for instance, he had taken for granted (as, at one time, he had done the prophets): something separate from existence, not to be absorbed or even followed: suffering where the mind departed from the body, took its leave, going where and for what he had no idea . . . taking her to the place he had once considered home, nothing of the house or the showroom remaining, the latter, fronting the London Road, a parade of shops, the site of the house behind occupied by several others. 'Might just as well never have been there,' he said. 'Except we were. The same sort of visit we can make to your place. And find out,' he added, 'who you really are.'